DUCHESS' CROWN

(Book 1 of the Ashridge Duology)

Kimberly M. Ringer

Kimberly M. Ringer

CONTENTS

Contact Information: www.kimberlymringer.com

ISBN Paperback: 978-1-957447-01-8

ISBN E-Book: 978-1-957447-02-5

First Edition: November 2022

Content Considerations

Graphic violence
Blood
SA, not followed through
Homophobia
(not within main cast)
Abusive Parent
Murder
Coersion
Threats
Parental Death
Suicide (not on page)
BDSM

Note from Author

This book contains spoilers from *The Five Angels* trilogy. If you have not read those three books, there will be content in this story that spoils events and resolutions that occurred in that story. While you can read *Duchess' Crown* and *Duchess' Throne* as its own story, it is based in an "existing world" with characters we already know and love making appearances.

This is
Aiden Mathewson and Jessika Valenti's Story

Thank you to my Hype Girls.

DUCHESS' CROWN

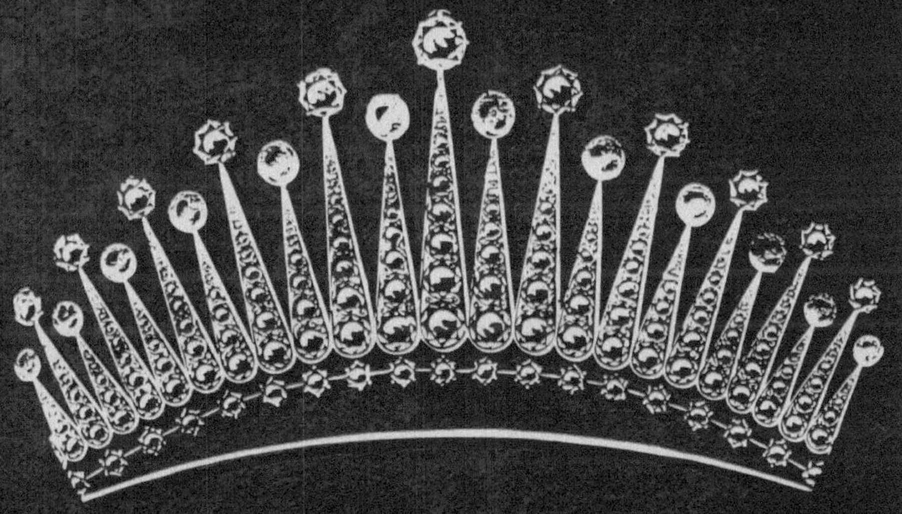

KIMBERLY M. RINGER

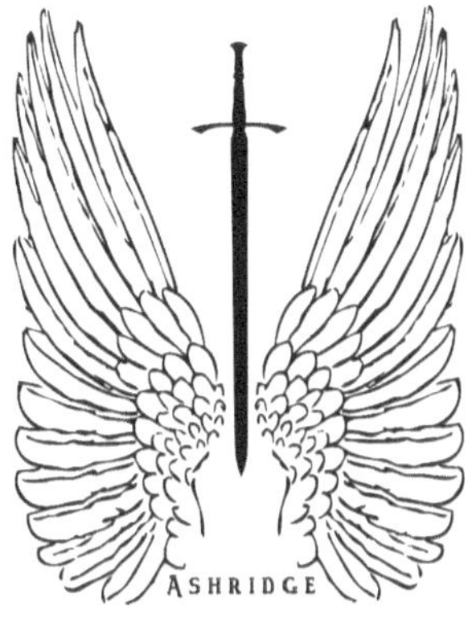

CHAPTER 1

JESSIKA

"Stop slouching," Amala said.

"I'm not slouching. I was resting against the wall. You know how much I hate wearing heels. Why can't I just wear my normal clothes? Why do I have to stand here like I'm ready for this whole thing to turn into a formal celebration?" I sighed.

Amala slid her brown eyes to mine and gave me a sideways look. "Because your mother, the Grand Duchess, required it."

"Is that my best friend talking, or my bodyguard?"

"Both." She elbowed me and smiled.

"Even the Nalrin Guard aren't in their formal attire." I pouted and then saw Janreka of the House of Heros standing about twenty feet away. I smiled, feeling a little better knowing that even one of my best friends, whose mother was Empress of Obsecuritan and Gatekeeper of the Underworld, had also been required to attend in formal wear. Why was she here, though? She couldn't be here to be assigned a Vernadali. Was she? Surely the Therth Guards could keep her safe.

"Jess..."

"Well, Mom just said head to the Curtails of the North; you are getting a Vernadali. No other explanation. There is no telling how many times I will have to come to these presentations. Every month? It could be years before the Angels grace me with a Vernadali." I growled. "So, I ask again, why do we have to be here? They didn't use to make us come to these things."

"Things changed after The Keller War. So, suck it up." Amala's red lipstick smacked with the word. Even though our skin was a luxurious brown that never seemed to dull, she could always pull off the deep red color flawlessly, where I just looked like a cheap whore when I wore it. She had a deep maroon dress on that was so short, I wasn't sure how she could walk without it sliding up her hips, but she looked completely fuckable in it. Even the thigh syth belt didn't prevent at least four different guys giving her a double take as we passed by them in the last hour alone. She could do enough damage without the seven-inch daggers, but they would figure that out soon enough if they pressed too far.

"Lots of things changed after Ansel Keller tore through Nalrin and Obsecuritan." I looked back at Janreka. "I know that better than anyone. Anyone who stayed in Ashridge died when he came through. We were lucky we were in Savanora on holiday when it happened. I still have nightmares about it. Luckily, Lemi wasn't old enough to remember what home looked like when we returned."

Angels, that was over forty years ago, and Ashridge, Obsecuritan, the Seltic Marsh, and much of Nalrin were *still* healing from it. There were parts of the Nalrin City Center that had barely finished renovations. Head Julian had waited until all the residential districts in the center were rebuilt before repairing the main buildings. Decades later, it was only starting to look how it had over fifty years ago.

After defeating her father, Lady Megan Mathewson had dedicated her life to repairing the damage left by her parents. She still felt a responsibility to this world after what her parents did to try and destroy it. While she hated politics, she had taken a special interest in fixing laws that were archaic and "just fucking stupid," as she called them. Her husband, Vernadali CJ, had continued to work within the Vernadali ranks but was never far from her side. They were *the* power couple of the ages, though it helped that Lady Megan Mathewson was one of the most powerful Sangra to have lived in memorable history. She was probably second only to Empress Clarice herself.

"The whole dimension is still healing." Amala chuckled. "Come on, I want to talk to Janreka. You haven't seen her in a while. I'm surprised you didn't run right to her."

We weaved through the crowd of dignitaries and royalty, but it was slow as more and more came into the main hall. It was almost the size of the courtyard in front of the main buildings in Nalrin City and could easily hold a thousand people. The dark-grey marble floors and the tall, thin, blue stained-glass windows were an impressive sight, but that was not what drew my eye. At the end of the room was a raised platform, where the Vernadali would be assigned their Charge. Etched into the light-grey wall was the Vernadali herald.

It was created for the fancy ball that would be taking place tonight for all the Vernadali and their Charges to be celebrated. I did not want to attend and would be spending the evening in my room, reading a good book. Whether I was assigned a Vernadali or not. When Amala noticed I had gone silent, she looked at me, and I sighed.

"Empress Clarice has been doing well in Obsecuritan, and yet Mom and I are struggling to keep the fishing ports open along the coast and the farmers with water. There just hasn't been enough snow in the Black Mountains for the last couple of years to create the needed water supply for Ashridge's crops."

"The Grand Duchess is doing fine, regardless of the empty promises of Kaletta. You know that."

I shook my head at the thought of all those failed and empty promises. Later. I would worry about that later. That was so a future Jessika problem.

Janreka's eyes met mine and lit up when we finally reached her. "Jessika! Amala!" She hugged and kissed Amala then pulled me into a warm hug before giving me Ashridge's customary kiss on each cheek.

"What are you doing here?" I asked, holding her hands.

She rolled her eyes. "Mom says that if I'm going to be traveling the world as an emissary, I need protection, and I refused the Therth Guards. So, she pulled her weight with Head Julian and here I stand, waiting to be assigned a Vernadali. Against my wishes, I might add. It's not like Mom or Head Julian can force an assignment. It's by the Angels. This is the third month that I've attended, and I just want to get started. Trade negotiations with the Seltic Marsh and Cinder have been slow and will go so much faster once I'm able to travel, but Mom won't let me until I have a protection detail. Hence, my presence." She pulled a hand from mine and waved it around flippantly, rolling her eyes.

"Why?" I asked, genuinely concerned. "Why did you refuse your own guards?"

"Obsecuritan was decimated after the war. It needs all the personnel we can afford to stay there. It's been forty years, but there are still limited resources. It's going to take a very long time before we can fully recover. Things are better. Crops are growing, and we aren't so reliant on outside goods, but it's still a slow process. I know you understand. Ashridge has been working just as hard as we have since it all happened." She said it like it was nothing but looked me up and down and scrunched her nose. The small stud in her nose caught the light as she said, "Now, why did your mother make you wear a dress? She knows how much you loathe them."

"Because she is my mom. She can't control what comes out of my mouth, so she tries to control what I wear. There are enough people here that she would know if I didn't." I laughed. It wasn't that the dress wasn't beautiful, because it was. The backless, floor-length, deep-green satin gown not only showed off my Maltal in the center of my back, but the deep V-neck in the front beautifully accentuated my chest. While no one would ever describe my body type as athletic or toned by any stretch, I had learned to love every single one of my curves. It took me years to accept the body I had, and while I detested wearing dresses, and would have preferred my typical black pants and the black corset I liked to wear over my white shirt, I actually liked how stunning I looked in this one.

"Does Empress Clarice know you stole that dress from her closet? I know your mom, and that is something she would wear in a heartbeat. So, did you buy it and hide it, or did you steal it from her closet?" I asked, motioning to her skin-tight white chiffon dress. A silver metal snake gave the illusion of it slithering up her back from the tailbone to the nape of her neck and was strategically held in place by silver chains. The contrast of the white fabric against her dark skin was nothing short of stunning. Her hair was up in a ponytail in small braids, with one larger thick braid circling the base. "You look absolutely amazing! Between you and Amala here, how am I supposed to catch the eye of anyone?"

Janreka laughed. "First of all, you have no shame. I almost feel bad for Jayden."

I rolled my eyes and muttered under my breath, "He's one of my best friends, and you know Jayden and I don't give two shits about each other like that."

"Second, Mom almost required me to wear this dress when she saw it on the hanger." She let out an amused breath and smiled. "I'm so glad that Aunt Megan convinced her to change the dress code in Therth after the war. Can you just imagine me wearing those gaudy relics?"

"I bet Aunt Erida had a fit over that."

"Mom says she did, but Aunt Erida eventually gave in. She still looks at the heritage closets with longing, though. I think she just wants to honor my grandparents' tradition, but you know Aunt Megan."

"Fuck tradition," all three of us said in unison.

I did know her Aunt Megan, pretty well, too. For six years, I dated their son Aiden, that is, until he shattered my heart. Angels. That was almost five years ago. He broke it off, saying he was a Vernadali and there was no way he could be with me while I ran my territory. Then there was the complication of him being assigned to someone else and having to stay with them full time. I understood the logic behind it, but my heart still ached at the thought of him. I had tried moving on, but no one could satisfy me in and out of the bedroom like Aiden could.

I knew there was a remote chance I could see him here, but the last I heard, he was months away, somewhere near the Slumbering Expanse, so it was unlikely. Much to my relief and dismay. There were parts of me that wanted to see him again, but…

"So, how are things with Jayden?" Janreka asked, nudging me with her elbow and bringing me out of my own thoughts.

"I don't know. I think he's in Cinder on some mission." I shrugged nonchalantly.

"What do you mean you don't know? You *think* he's in Cinder? Shouldn't you know where your betrothed is?" She was teasing me, and I just shook my head at her.

I snorted. "We are friends, but neither of us actually *want* the marriage. You know that. We keep trying to convince his father of that, not that he will listen to either of us. Mom told me she would sign off on the nullification, citing that Ashridge doesn't need the support anymore. We may be struggling, but we can manage without any of his help, not like he's given us much, if any, since the agreement."

"His father won't nullify?" Janreka said, her eyes bright with a million thoughts. She lifted her hand, looked to Amala, who met her smile before she looked back at me. I saw the grey smoke of her power curl through her fingers. "I could help with that particular issue."

"No. No. No," I said, pointing a finger at her. "You are not..." I gave them both looks that meant that if either of them killed the Grand Lord of Kaletta, they would be sorry.

"Ahhh, you're no fun!" Amala chuckled beside me. "You know Princess Janreka could make it look like an accident." I saw Janreka wince at the title, but I gave them both another stern look.

"Amala," Janreka warned.

"I know. I know. You hate honorifics." Amala looped her arm through hers. "Your mom does, too."

Amala's eyes lit up a bit before her voice dropped a little. "How is Karlo? I haven't seen him at the meetings in Nalrin as of late."

"My brother is fine. Been asking about *you*, though." Janreka gave her a knowing smirk and then poked her in the shoulder. "You need to step up. He loves you. Why you two haven't made it official is beyond any of our comprehension."

"I know, but your brother is just..." Amela blushed. "He's your brother and Empress Clarice's son."

"And I'm her daughter. So? I'm her Suk'Natal, not him. He gets to live a relatively normal life. Privileged, but he's basically equal in status to you, Amala," Janreka said encouragingly. "I think I would like to have you as a sister."

Amela chewed on her bottom lip a bit and nodded slowly.

"You two are great together. You've known each other since you finished schooling, took your testing, and received your Maltals. You deal with him constantly when you go to Nalrin City for me," I said, taking her hand. "Contact him. If you don't, once I'm crowned, I'll arrange your damn marriage."

"Jess! You wouldn't dare!" Amala gasped as Janreka laughed.

"I'll make my mom agree to that arrangement. Bind it in the Underworld's darkness and make you Silnaree." Janreka crossed her arms just as there was a loud drumming sound from the front of the room, commanding all attention to where Head Vernadali Samuel stood. We all put our fists over our hearts and bowed slightly in respect of the Vernadali who strode into the room. These were the Vernadali who would be assigned their Charges today.

As I stood up straight, I couldn't help but scan the ten men and women who were coming into the room. My heart stopped as I watched a man with honey and chestnut locks that were just too long stride across the front of that platform. I knew that the heat through those hazel-green eyes could burn through the ice I had encased my heart in since the day he walked away. It took every ounce of my willpower to pull my attention from them. My body flushed when I remembered how that perfect amount of scruff on his masculine jaw felt as it brushed against my cheek and he whispered in my ear.

Memories flooded my mind of him running that stubble down my jaw and leaving sensuous kisses down my neck as he moved to my shoulder. The deep rumble of his voice in my ear as he told me how I was his good girl. The feel of the calluses on his palms as they ran down my side, across my bare hips and thighs. The way his fingers would dip between my legs... Angels, my knees almost gave out under me at the thought of it.

"Oh, the Angels are fucking with us, aren't they?" Amala said, bringing me out of the memories. She slowly slid her hand into mine and gripped it tight. She knew how hard this was going to be for me to see him. To see him tied to someone else for life.

"Amala!" Janreka hissed, but out of the corner of my eye, I saw her watching me for how I might react. She took a hold of my other hand and ran her thumb along the back of it for support. The well of emotion that sat at the base of my throat was thick, and I was not sure I could have said a word, even if I were required.

Each Vernadali stood at attention at the front of the room, and there was this tug for me to look at Aiden, but I stood, looking straight, and kept my eyes on Vernadali Samuel. The problem was Aiden was standing only two down from him, and I could see Aiden's eyes flick to me repeatedly.

Not everyone in this room was being charged with a Vernadali this evening. For all he knew, I was here to support Janreka. I was standing right next to her. This was the third month in a row Janreka had been here, and I could come every month for the next five years before I was assigned.

I squeezed on Janreka's hand and tried very hard not to think too much about it. She squeezed it back, and I swore I felt some of her power flow into me and help loosen my chest. I had to remind myself that not even the Vernadali standing there knew who they would be assigned to today. The only one who knew who was receiving assignments tonight was Vernadali Samuel.

"It is with great honor I announce these Vernadali will be assigned their Charges this evening. Each of them graduated in the top five percent of their respective classes. Once their assignment has been given, they will immediately receive their name scroll. Full-time duties for each Vernadali upon their Charge will begin in the morning."

"Princess Janreka of the House of Heros," Vernadali Samuel stated as Janreka moved toward the front of the room. As her hand left mine, I felt that tightening in my chest return, and I struggled to keep my breathing normal. Vernadali Samuel bowed to her, as well as every Vernadali in the room. There could be a very clear argument made that she outranked everyone on this blasted island. The Curtails of the North may be a long way from Therth and the gate to the Underworld, but she still radiated power that could rival even the Mathewson family.

Vernadali Samuel reached over to a pile of envelopes and slowly lifted the seal, breaking the bright blue wax. Unfolding it, Vernadali Samuel said, "Vernadali Natasha Kapinov will report to your quarters first thing in the morning and accompany you back to Therth. Please accompany Vernadali Kapinov for her to receive your name scroll," he said, bowing one last time.

"Thank you, sir." She turned toward Vernadali Kapinov, who had stepped forward and formally bowed to her. Vernadali Natasha Kapinov raised her arm, and as Janreka took it, she looked at me and gave me a reassuring smile.

As Janreka passed Aiden, I swore she narrowed her eyes at him before she was led out of the room. Amala chuckled and whispered, "Reka will handle him."

"Duchess Jessika Valenti of Ashridge," Vernadali Samuel said, and my heart thudded. I squeezed Amala's hand one last time before letting go. Slowly, I moved toward the front of the room. My eyes flicked to Aiden, and I couldn't help but swish my hips and lengthen my stride. For once in my life, I was grateful for the fucking ridiculous high heels I was wearing. I smirked when his attention traveled up the entire length of the thigh-high slit in my dress. Aiden's hands clenched into a fist, and there was a sharp inhale as he fought to maintain his stoic composure. I resisted the urge not to smirk at him. I was more than happy to show him just what he walked away from.

When I bowed to Vernadali Samuel, my long white hair slid over my shoulder, thankfully creating a barrier in front of Aiden. I saw the blue wax crumbling to the floor, and a moment later, Vernadali Samuel's voice rang through the room, freezing me in place.

"Vernadali Aiden Mathewson will report to your quarters first thing in the morning and accompany you back to Ashridge," Vernadali Samuel said.

It took entirely too long for my heart to start beating again.

Remembering where I was, I slowly stood, and my eyes flicked to Aiden's. His eyes flashed in surprise before returning neutral, but I saw how his jaw had slackened in shock. He stepped forward, and at least *he* remembered we were standing in front of a very large crowd, who had started to murmur.

I had to swallow a few times before I could say, "Thank you, sir." I turned toward Aiden, and when his eyes met mine, there were so many emotions going through them, I couldn't read them. He blinked, and I bowed toward him.

"Please accompany Vernadali Aiden Mathewson for him to receive your name within his scroll," Vernadali Samuel said, as if he hadn't just turned my insides to soup. He bowed to me and turned to retrieve the next envelope.

Aiden lifted his arm, and I took it.

"Just breathe, Jess," he said, hardly moving his mouth.

"Aiden." I breathed his name. His hand tightened slightly around my fingers. The heat of his skin on mine sent a wave of all those old feelings through me, and I didn't know what to do with any of it. Fear and confusion were both very clearly present and battling for the top spot in my emotional turmoil.

When we cleared the room and the door shut so that we were the only two in there, I slowly lowered my arm, but he didn't release my fingers. No, instead, his thumb ran over my knuckles as he stared at where he held my hand.

"Aiden," I said, my voice stronger this time but still shaking. My heart pounded so loud I wouldn't be surprised if he could hear it. "Does Vernadali Samuel know? About our history?"

"No. We did a really good job of hiding that aspect of it. Mom, Dad, and the Grand Duchess made sure of it." I took another step back from him, letting our hands drop, and he ran his hand through his hair, a habit he picked up from his dad.

"Angels. What are our parents going to say about this?" I said as I started to pace. I felt a zap and a tug deep within my chest, and out of the corner of my eye, I saw him rub the area over his heart.

"Our parents?" he said, half laughing in frustration. "Jess, what are *we* going to do?"

My eyes snapped to his. Anger fueled by all that hurt rose to the surface as I turned to him, my power causing my hand to glow purple. Aiden looked at it carefully and winced. He had been on the receiving end of it many times and knew that anything I touched with my power would feel like being vibrated with hot spikes.

"Jess," he said carefully, "calm down."

"You haven't learned a damn thing since you left, have you?" He winced at my words, but I continued. "First, I don't give a damn if you're my Vernadali, you *never* tell me to calm down. It is the one surefire way to make me angrier. Second, you and I both know that once a Charge has been assigned, the only way out of it is death. I have no intention of dying, and even though there were times I have wanted to kill *you*, I don't want you to die, either. Right now, it's probably out of respect for your mom and dad more than anything, but..." A lump formed in my throat because the fact was, it hurt to even think about him dying. "I don't want you dead."

"Well, that's something, at least."

I took a few deep breaths and paced a few times across the room, his eyes trailing me the entire time. I faced him, held my head high, and crossed my arms. "So, we are going to be professionals about this."

"What about once you marry Jayden?" His voice was low, but there was something else there. I thought I might have imagined it, but I could have sworn his throat bobbed as he said it.

"We will do what Dad and Uncle Mickey did. You two will work it out." I would have to tell him eventually about how Jayden and I didn't want to marry and that we were trying to get his father to agree to nullifying the agreement, but that was a future me problem. Right now, I had a very real drop-dead gorgeous, six-foot-three problem.

A door on the other side of the room opened, and a petite woman who looked to be about thirty-five, though she was probably about a hundred, walked in and gestured for us to walk through the door. "Vernadali Aiden and Duchess Valenti, this way, please."

Chapter 2

Aiden

As we walked through the doors, I didn't know what to feel. I was assigned to the woman I had always known I would give my life for. Was that why the Angels assigned me to her?

I could feel her behind me. Even without her name scroll, I already knew exactly how she was feeling: scared, anxious, terrified. I didn't need the fucking Vernadali bond to know that. I knew this woman from the inside out.

When I looked at her again, her eyes narrowed, and I shook my head. Professional. I was an Angels Blessed Vernadali's son. I was a Vernadali by right and blood. I had trained for thirty-five years for this moment. Regardless of whose name was there, I would serve and protect them. I had made that decision long ago. I glanced at her, where she was chewing on her thumb, and I shook my head.

"Vernadali Aiden, please sit here, and Duchess Valenti, you need to sit and hold his hand while your name scroll is placed." She quickly tightened the straps across my chest, thighs, and ankles. When she got to my wrists, Jessika flinched.

"Why are you binding him?" She chewed on her bottom lip, and it took everything I had not to focus on that singular movement.

"It's fine," I said, breathing in deep.

"When the scroll is placed, it will bind you two. You will feel a tightening in your chest and a pull toward him," the worker said, and Jessika's eyes met mine. Something in that gaze told me she already felt the pull between us. How could she not? I'd felt it the second I'd marched into that ceremony.

"I didn't ask what I would feel. I asked what Vernadali Mathewson would be going through that you feel it necessary to bind him." Jessika's tone was all regal duchess. It was commanding and everything I remembered about her.

"He will become permanently bonded to you. It is not easy, and we don't want anyone to get hurt," she said as she lined up the machine on my forearm just under the Vernadali herald. I grew up with that herald being so predominant in my life, and now I was getting Jess' name on mine. So many times, I saw Mom lovingly caress it on Dad's arm. He always smiled when she touched it, whether he realized it or not.

Jessika stood up abruptly and paced.

"Will you stop pacing? Your anxiety is making my skin crawl," I said, leaning my head back.

"You can already feel her?" the worker asked as her eyes flicked between the two of us.

Jessika turned toward me and said, "Vernadali Aiden Mathewson, are you sure of this assignment?"

"The Five Angels have deemed me your Vernadali, Duchess Valenti." I met her gaze. I would not back down from this.

"That is not what I asked," she gritted out through her teeth.

"I know that isn't what you asked, Duchess. Now sit your ass down. I am tired and want to get some sleep tonight before making the long trip to Ashridge," I demanded, feeling the Charge within me feed into the command, and she narrowed her eyes at me, knowing exactly what had happened. Slowly, she walked to the chair and sat back down.

The worker's mouth opened and closed, her eyes flicking between the two of us, before saying, "Be right back."

"Aiden," she breathed after the worker had left the room.

"Jess?" I asked, almost mocking her.

She reached over and moved a strand of hair from my face. "Angels be, Aiden."

I resisted the urge to lean into her light touch and just stared at her. Her face was still soft and round, her lips kissably plump, and she was soft and hard in all the right spots. Her long white hair was done half up in a multitude of different braids then let to flow loose down her back. My gaze ran down her body, and I couldn't help but remember how it felt to run my hands over the soft rounded places of her belly. I pulled my gaze back up to hers to keep from thinking of things that I really shouldn't be. Wide, almond-shaped onyx eyes met mine, and I took a deep breath. I always knew I would die for this woman, but to have it decided by the Angels felt like a cruel twist of fate.

I had let her go.

I had let her move on with her life.

I had walked away—for good reason too.

A moment later, the door opened, and the worker, Vernadali Samuel, and two people who had hardly changed their appearance since the day of my birth walked in.

"Aiden," my father said, which was quickly followed by my mother saying, "Jess."

Jessika stood immediately and bowed to them. "Vernadali CJ and Lady Megan."

"You two already know each other?" Vernadali Samuel said. He then turned toward the worker and ordered, "Undo Vernadali Aiden's wrist and chest straps so he can at least sit up to speak to us."

"Everyone knows Lady Megan and Vernadali CJ." Jess' reply was all duchess.

"Mom. Dad. What are you doing here?"

Dad was in his Vernadali uniform, and Mom was in her personal uniform of jeans, white T-shirt, and blue Nalrin issue jacket. Eight-inch daggers with a curved tip, her syths, were sheathed at her thighs, and she was probably the only one who would have been allowed to walk around the complex geared the way she was. I half wondered if they had been in the crowd as I was assigned to Jess. Angels. What did *they* think of all this?

I felt my heart start to race again. As I sat up, I rubbed my wrist and said, "You aren't reassigning the Duchess, Vernadali Samuel."

My parents looked at me and raised an eyebrow. I almost laughed. That was usually a look they reserved for Owen and LJ. "Don't look at me like that. The Angels assigned the Duchess to me, and I will protect her."

"You have never been one to test authority, Aiden," Vernadali Samuel said.

"That was always the twins," Mom declared.

"Don't compare me to them," I said through my teeth. "I am not Owen and LJ. I am Aiden. I will always be different from them. I am a Vernadali. I am the son of an Angels Blessed Vernadali. I will *not* have my legacy tainted by them. I am my own man, with my own life to live, just as they have theirs." I had always been held to a higher standard here in the Curtails of the North, through the rankings, even after finishing my schooling, just because of who my parents were. I was Vernadali CJ's Vernadali son. It put a spotlight on me, one that I would always have to endure.

The twins were my older brother, Owen, and sister, LJ. Everyone knew them. They were special. Elementals born from that Angels Blessed Vernadali and the most powerful Sangra power couple. My whole life I had been compared to them. Would I show the same powers as them? Would I show complementary powers to them? Mom and Dad were pretty good about it, but I heard it from every tutor we had in Nalrin, and even overheard Head Julian talking to Dad about it once. Dad had said it was fine if I didn't develop any power other than the Vernadali traits. He and Uncle Logan could train me.

"Of course. Of course," Vernadali Samuel waved his hand in dismissal. "That wasn't in question. Chantel here said that you two already felt a connection?"

I looked over to Jess, who just met my gaze. It was she who spoke first. "What do you mean 'a connection'?"

"A connection between the two of you. As you know, Duchess, Vernadali have an emotional connection to help assist in their abilities to protect their Charge. They can feel their Charge's fear, for instance, so they know that they are in need of assistance. The bond," Vernadali Samuel said.

"I'm aware," she whispered, turning to look at my dad.

"There is more here, though."

"*Answer him, Aiden. Don't make Jess do this on her own.*" My mother's voice rang through my head, and I turned to glare at her. She stood there, arms crossed and an eyebrow cocked. *Now.*

Mom was rare not only for her power, but because she also had Congiti powers, meaning she could talk to people without actually speaking. On more than one occasion, the twins and I would be standing in front of a crowd getting lectured for our behavior, sputtering excuses, Mom just staring at us. She would be, of course, ripping us a new one mentally, but to the public, we were the ones who sounded like we couldn't get a coherent thought out of our head.

"I'm not eight anymore, Mom. I may look to be in my twenties, but I am forty years old," I said and rubbed my face. Jess giggled next to me, and when I looked at her, she was closer than I expected.

"I guess we have to tell them, Aid." She tucked a strand of hair behind my ear, and I once again resisted the urge to lean into her touch.

"It's not their business," I said through clenched teeth.

My mom sighed, and I knew that she had pushed to both of us when Jess winced. "*Aiden Chatwell Mathewson and Jessika Petra Valenti. If you two do not come clean and tell them about your relationship, Dad and I will. Jess, your mother is not going to be happy if I have to be the one to tell them.*"

Jessika turned to my mom and, with narrowed eyes, stuck her tongue out at her. I hadn't seen her do that since our trip to the Manusia to see Grammy and Pa almost six years ago, and I couldn't help but chuckle. Mom shook her head and smirked, while Dad flat out laughed. Vernadali Samuel, however, looked horrified.

"Vernadali Samuel, a few years ago, Aiden and I dated. We ended it four years and eight months ago." My head snapped up to look at Jessika. She said the time period so specifically and firmly. Her eyes flicked to mine before she looked away, stood up straighter, and said, "We ended things. Our lives were... heading in separate directions."

Vernadali Samuel looked at my mom and dad. It was my mother who spoke first. "The Grand Duchess knew, we knew, and so did Head Julian. Due to the history of CJ and I, we have worked very hard to keep our children's lives private. Most of what is public knowledge of Aiden and the twins is because *they* have allowed it."

"What does any of this have to do with the fact that I can feel her already?" I asked, desperate to change the subject. "What is in the past is in the past. Did the Angels decide my Charge, or was it made by you, Vernadali Samuel."

"The Five Angels have chosen her to be your Charge, Vernadali Aiden," Vernadali Samuel said carefully.

There was a flicker of doubt in his eyes, and it made my anger rise. "Swear it."

"I swear it," he said, standing straighter, and I felt the words in my very bones.

"The Angels have chosen her to be my Charge. Regardless of any history, which can only be to a benefit in my opinion, I will do my duty, and I will live by my oath to Duchess Jessika Valenti," I said, sitting up straight and pressing my hand to my chest.

"Do you have any objections, Duchess?" Vernadali Samuel asked her.

"If the Angels have chosen him to be my Vernadali and not a being, I have no objection," she said in all regal professionality. Jess looked at my parents, and I swear Mom was having a one-way conversation with her before she turned her head sadly toward me. I didn't miss the small nod she gave as her eyes met mine.

"Very well. Continue."

The worker came over, strapped me back down at my chest and wrists, as Jessika walked over and took ahold of my hand. When the machine was repositioned above my forearm, the worker said, "Recite your Vernadali oath, and take a deep breath."

"*Missi sumus a tenebris ad tuendum ab angeli pergemus ad mortem tueri lucem.* From the Angels, we are sent to protect from the dark. To the death, we will march to protect the light. I swear to protect and defend to my dying day, to my last breath into the dark, Jessika Petra Valenti."

My eyes met Jess', and there was that warm tenderness in them that made me catch my breath. Purple flashed before my eyes, and my chest constricted tightly as I felt every muscle in my body go taut. Then there was a pressure in the hand she was holding, and I gripped it tight, unable to see past the purple lights flashing before me.

I felt like my chest was going to cave in as sharp jabs of pain struck my heart. Moments later, I felt the hard pounding in my chest, but as it grew louder, I felt the *thump thump* in my ears. Another heartbeat joined it, just off kilter from mine, beating throughout my body. My chest pulsed in pain as those beats slowly became more and more in sync. Purple fireworks erupted inside me, but when those heartbeats finally synced, all the weight and pain vanished.

I panted, trying to catch my breath. Worry filled me, and when I looked to Jess, she was holding her chest and squeezing my hand. Her lips were moving, but I couldn't make out what she was saying.

"What?" I said, too loud for my own ears.

Another flood of worry flashed through me, and I blinked.

"*Are you okay?*" she asked with a scratch to her temple.

I blinked at her, not believing what I saw. I just needed to catch my breath. "Yeah."

From the corner of the room, I heard Vernadali Samuel say, "Well, it seems your son is better than you, CJ. He didn't pass out."

Dad just laughed and said, "He is a strong man. He will do the Vernadali proud."

I WATCHED AS JESS made her way into the main room. When Amala reached her, she pulled her into a hug and her eyes met mine. I just gave her a small nod before she pulled back. I couldn't help but watch as they headed toward the back of the main hall. That dress hugged every luxurious part of her, and I wanted nothing more than to push her against that wall and kiss her.

When she walked out the back doors, she stopped as if she knew I had been watching her every step and gave me a small smile before Amala took her by the hand and pulled her out of sight.

"Aiden." Mom's voice was soft next to me.

I breathed a heavy sigh and pinched my nose. "Mom, what am I going to do?"

"I don't know, sweetheart." She rubbed my back quickly and said, "Do you still love her?"

"The Angels are fucking with me, right? Why would they do this?" I turned toward her; my eyes wide.

"Let's get back to your room and talk," Dad said behind us. He was right. There were still a lot of people in the main hall, and this was not a conversation for open ears.

I strode straight for those doors she had gone through, knowing my parents were hot on my heels, practically kicking the door open in frustration. I rushed by the game room and the kitchens before turning to the left down the hall for the higher ranking Vernadali.

Two hallways later, I made another left and had to weave through a crowd gathering near one of my friends. As we neared my room, I kept getting waves of sadness, trepidation, and exhilaration. I shook my head and arms out, rolled my shoulders, and shook my legs at the last moment before we got to my room. My dad giggled, and when I looked at him, he was smirking.

"Takes some getting used to, Aiden." He giggled. "Your mom used to drive me crazy. Granted, I realize it was different, but just wait till she has PMS."

"Asshole," Mom said, punching him in the arm. I just rolled my eyes.

When we got to my room, I bounced back onto the bed and leaned against the wall, knees up and arms resting on them. Mom sat in the chair next to my makeshift desk, and Dad sat at my little dining table. The room wasn't much, about five hundred square feet with a small kitchen, bathroom and living/bedroom area. It was more than enough for what I needed every day.

"So again, Aiden, what are you going to do?" Mom asked.

"I don't fucking know." I leaned my head back. "You know I broke it off with her because she had to stay and run Ashridge. I could have been assigned to anyone. I wouldn't be able to fulfill my duties and she hers. They can't both happen."

"Do you still love her, Aiden?" Dad asked carefully.

"Dad, I've known since the first time I laid eyes on her that I would lay my life down for Jess. I love her to the very core of my being." My eyes were closed, head still leaning back against the wall. It hurt to admit out loud. "Now the Angels say I'm supposed to protect her? I would do that, regardless." I looked at them both and wasn't surprised to see my own heartbreak reflected in their eyes. We all knew I was in a no-win situation. "You know she's promised to Jayden Panahov, Lord of Kaletta, right? I have to watch the woman I love with every fiber of my being marry someone else."

"Do you want me to talk to Vernadali Samuel about forcing a new Charge?" Dad asked.

"No," I said, knowing that he would pull what weight he could. "I've been dealt a real messed up emotional soup, but the Angels want me at her side to protect her. I'll figure it out. Being a Vernadali is about thinking of your Charge before yourself."

"I shouldn't have preached that to you growing up," Dad said slowly, but there was a sadness I rarely heard in his voice.

"Whether you did or not, they drilled that into us here. We always think of our Charge before ourselves." I sat up straighter. "It's about Jess' well-being. Not mine."

My parents looked at each other, and I could tell Mom was pushing a whole discussion to Dad. For a good five minutes, they just looked at each other. They had this whole silent language thing down.

I huffed a laugh and said, "Mom, why couldn't I have inherited your Cogniti trait? It would be so beneficial."

She turned toward me with a smirk and said, "Sorry, sweetheart. If it makes you feel better, the twins don't have it, either. It ends with me."

"Just saying, Mom." I sighed. "So, what caused you to be in the Curtails of the North?"

"Julian gave us the heads up you would be assigned tonight, and we thought we could surprise you since we haven't seen you in a year. We didn't expect..."

"I know. None of us did. Since Vernadali Samuel didn't know of Jess' and my history, there was no way for him to give Popa warning either." I took a deep breath and let it out slowly. "It was nice to see you guys again. I'll see if I can get away this year for Christmas in Seaside. I'm still sorry I couldn't come last year. The rioting in Cinder—"

"We know, Aiden. We almost didn't get to go because of it." Mom smiled. "Oh, and Uncle Mickey says hello and that he loves you."

"Back at him." I rubbed my face.

"Are you okay with us going to see Jess before we take off? We are taking the midnight ferry back to Nalrin," Dad asked.

"Why would I care? That's her decision. Something tells me she would be thrilled to see you two."

"It's your decision because you are our son first, and if you want us to keep our distance, then we will. You are also her Vernadali and have a right to say who she sees and who she doesn't." Dad was trying to be supportive and respectful.

"Like I said, Jess would love to see you." Crawling out of the bed to say my goodbyes, I said, "I am glad to see you. Thank you for coming all the way up here."

Once I was on my feet, my mom had me in her arms and pushed, "*If you need anything, let us know.*"

"Yes, Mama." I held her tighter and felt her power wrap around me. I gave her a quick kiss on the cheek as my dad clasped me on my Vernadali tattoo then pulled me in for a tight hug—respect as one of the Vernadali, but also, still being my father.

Dad reached over and took Mom's hand, and I just said, "I love you," as they walked out the door.

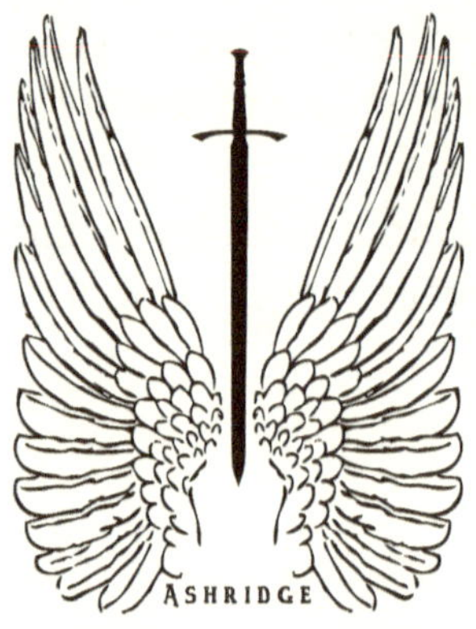

CHAPTER 3

JESSIKA

JENREKA HAD COME IN just after sunup, screaming, "Aiden? Seriously? Aiden was assigned as yours?" Amala stood at the door to the bedroom, in a spaghetti-strapped silk nightgown, shaking her head.

"What?" I looked at her, not sure what she was doing screaming at me this early in the morning.

"Aiden! Aiden was assigned as your Vernadali?" she said, flopping onto the bed.

I took a deep breath and let it out slowly, throwing my arm over my eyes. "Yes." I looked up quickly. "He isn't in here, is he?"

"Not in our rooms, no. Janreka gave her Vernadali instructions that no one was to come into your room until we walked out. That included him. Especially him," Amala said, eyeing Janreka carefully.

"Good."

"He was already stationed outside. I came over this morning to find out who had been assigned to you and was only partially surprised to find him leaning against the wall across from your door, staring at it. I mean, of course he would come to see you while you were here." She waved her arms like it was no big deal. "But then I saw his bag at his feet, and he told me that you had been assigned as his Charge? Be glad you were in the back room. I woke Amala up with my screaming. It isn't his fault, I know, but we had words."

"Meaning she threatened to cut his balls off if anything happened to you." Amala smirked at Janreka, but there was admiration and pride in her eyes.

"He only listened to me because I'm practically his sister," Jenreka said. The Mathewson family had spent much of the twins and Aiden's childhood in Therth with her mother, so yes, Jenreka and her brother were all one big family.

"I talked to his mom and dad for a few minutes last night," I said, smiling. "It was nice to see them again. I hadn't realized how much I missed them."

"What did they say about the whole situation?" Janreka asked.

"They were surprised. Worried about Aiden. I tried to tell them that Aiden wasn't going to be a problem, that because he broke it off with me, he had clearly moved on." I played with my fingers and a loose thread on the blanket, then sat up and crossed my legs, pulling the blanket back up close to me. "They said they hoped we could work through it. I laughed at them because we have no choice but to work through any problems we have. I mean, he is literally bound to me for life. One of us would have to die for this situation to go away, and I'm not too keen on either of us dying."

"And Lady Megan also said to let her know when Aiden pisses Jess off or does anything stupid, so she could whoop his ass," Amala said, laughing. "Makes me wonder what in his future she saw that confirms Aiden will fuck up."

I smiled at them. "He is their son. Of course, Aiden is going to fuck up. She doesn't need her visions to tell her that. You have met Uncle Logan. Stupidity runs in their blood. Hotheadedness, too, but that's more on Aiden's mom's side."

"Aunt Megan has always been protective over you. I saw them last night, too." There was a whisper of something else on Janreka's face, but then it fell. "Jess, what are you going to do?"

"Outwardly? I'm going to be a collected and polished duchess around him. I'll ignore every feeling I have for him and do whatever I can to ignore him, too." Amala and I had talked about it late into the night, and when I looked at the clock, I moaned. I had only gotten four hours of sleep, and I suspected Aiden was going to want to head out soon.

"Outwardly," Janreka scoffed. "I know that in public you will keep it professional. You did that before. What in the Underworld are you going to do about the rest of the time? Are you going to be okay? *Are* you okay?"

"I don't know." I looked at my two closest friends in the entire dimension, and I realized just how much I didn't know what I was going to do. Neither were looking at me with pity. No, they were genuinely concerned.

"Amala. Janreka. What *am* I going to do?" I pleaded, trying to keep the tears from falling. "For almost five years, I have tried to hide the hurt. I have tried to avoid him, which was easily done when he got stationed to the Lansker Frozen

Isles. Then, when he got sent to Nalrin for a while, that… Well, you two know how much I avoided those areas of the city."

"Now he's literally been assigned by the Angels to be up in your business. He will be in every room you are except for, well, I guess you could let him in the bedroom." Amala winked at me and I glared at her.

"Please don't remind me how good the sex was. I tried very hard last night not to think of that, and I wasn't super successful in that endeavor." She only smiled brightly at me.

A knock on the door sounded, and Janreka went to answer it. She came back with a message in her hand and gave it to me. I looked down and saw my mother's elegant script.

"Great. Where am I going?" I sighed heavily, flipped it over, and saw the silver wax with the tips of a feathered angel wing on it. I saw Amala and Janreka give each other a look.

Ripping through the wax, leaving pieces scattered all over the blankets, I read her note:

JESSIBESSIE,

SILENTPORT IS BEING PLAGUED WITH CUT LOCATION MARKERS FOR THE CRAB POTS. FISH ARE BEING POISONED, AND THE GRAIN IS BEING WATERED TO SPOIL BEFORE EITHER CAN GET TO MARKET.

GO AND SEE WHAT YOU CAN FIND OUT THEN MEET ME IN ASHRIDGE IN FIVE MONTHS.

MAY THE ANGELS GIVE YOU WINGS, AND I LOVE YOU.

♥ MOM

"Where are we going?" Amala asked.

"Silentport." I wrinkled my nose. It would be over a hundred degrees, and the whole town would smell horrible. "Their food is being sabotaged, and dear old Mom is tasking us to find out who and why. I'm sure she will want us to handle it as well."

I looked to Janreka, who shook her head. "I'm sorry. Wish I could go with you, but I got orders from Empress Clarice—" She said her mom's name with a dramatic eye roll. "—that my presence is required in Therth."

"It's fine, Janreka. I'm so glad I was able to see you, though." I reached up and pulled her practically into my lap for a hug. "Write more, bitch."

"Fine. Fine. You know how horrible I am about it."

"Weekly," I said, knowing I'd be lucky to get one a month.

"I'll try." She gave me a look then and said, "Keep me updated on the Aiden stuff, okay?"

I nodded and she kissed me before heading out the door.

"You know, if I wanted to settle down with a woman, Janreka, that kind of kiss could have led to something else." I winked at her.

"You don't know what you are missing, love." I could have sworn her hips swayed with a bit more determination as she strode out the door.

"Be nice to your Vernadali!" I shouted, but then there was a male hand at the door. I could tell he was preparing himself before he came in.

I looked to Amala, and she raised eyebrows as if to say, "Up to you."

"Come on in, Aiden." I surprised myself, and apparently even Amala, when I said it just as I had all those years ago.

He came inside but stood by the door. My stomach did a little flip as I took in his stance. He was the Vernadali standing guard, and I hated it.

"Aiden," I said, steeling myself, but his eyes jumped to mine immediately. "Come and sit down. Amala, go get packed and ready. I'll jump in the shower once I'm done with this."

She nodded and gave me a small smile before heading back to her room. I watched her, but I also noticed that Aiden's eyes never left my face.

When I looked back to him, his eyes flicked to the message from my mom. "We aren't heading home to Ashridge?"

"No." I shook my head as my heart did a small leap. Home. He called Ashridge home. "But that isn't what I wanted to talk to you about."

He tilted his head, and I smirked. "Are you okay? How are you feeling this morning?"

"Exhausted, if I'm being honest," he murmured, sitting down in a chair a few feet away and sitting forward to lean onto his knees as he pressed his hands together.

"Honesty is good." My voice was way too small for the conversation I wanted to have. I wanted to sit here and draw boundaries, to know where he stood. Where we would stand.

"How are you?"

"You can't feel how I'm feeling?" I smiled at him. Teasing. Teasing was good.

He smirked. "Jess, I'm getting all kinds of things from you, and I'm not sure what some of them are. There are... a lot of contradictions."

I took a deep breath to settle myself because he wasn't wrong. I wanted to push him into a river, but I also wanted to pull him onto this bed and show him exactly why he never should have left. I wasn't going to do either, but that wasn't the point.

His eyes closed and his shoulders relaxed. "Thank you."

"I'm sorry. I'll try to stay as neutral as possible."

"Why?" His head snapped up. "You wouldn't be you if you did that. We just need to sort out what I feel with what you feel. That takes time together, Jess. We will figure it out. In fact, by the time we get to Ashridge, we will likely have it pretty much down."

"Time together," I whispered, scooting to the edge of the bed. His eyes froze on where I sat, and I quickly realized I still only had my sleeping shirt on and it was pretty much around my hips. I tugged it down, and there was a smirk on his face and a heat in his eyes I remembered entirely too clearly.

"Never bothered me before." His eyes twinkled.

I rolled my eyes. "Perv."

He just shrugged and said, "You were saying."

"Time together. Right." My cheeks were red and hot, and I asked, "Will you have quarters next to mine on the trip back, or will we be required to share a room?"

"Guess that depends on availability. Are we going north by sea, or are we going to go through the Grasslands and through the Black Mountains?" There was a glint in his eye that dulled as we talked business. His eyebrow cocked up, though, as he said, "I guess that depends on where the Grand Duchess has told us to go."

"Silentport," I said apologetically, and he had the same reaction I did, wrinkled nose and all. I couldn't help but laugh. "I had the same reaction. It's going to be so hot and stink like the bowels of the Underworld!"

"Why are we going to that Angels-forsaken fishing hole?" he asked, sighing to the ceiling.

"Excuse me. That is part of your home now, Vernadali Aiden. I expect a little more respect for that Angels-forsaken fishing hole," I teased him. He chuckled and waited for me to continue. "It does provide us with almost forty percent of the fish for the territory. It is also operating as the main port for most of the grain we are receiving from Savanora."

"Why aren't you growing your own grain?" His eyes narrowed in question. "Why do you have to get it from Savanora? They will be charging you entirely too much for it."

"They are, and it's being sabotaged by someone before we can get it to market. It checks in fine at the port, but before it can be distributed, it is being watered down to rot and spoil. The Grand Duchess wants us to go find out who and why. She doesn't specifically state anything, but I suspect she wants us to put a stop to it as well, considering our skill set," I said, running my fingers through the ends of my white hair.

His eyes focused on that motion, and I stopped. He had loved running his hands through my hair. The memory of him doing just that made heat swell between my legs. He licked his lips, and I saw his fingers twitching. There was that heat in his eyes again, and I swore I saw him take a shuddering breath.

I blinked. Why was he acting like this? He left me. I didn't leave him. Yet, it seemed like he was almost holding back from me. Unbidden, and with a strength I didn't know where it came from, I whispered, "Aiden, please stop."

His eyes met mine. "What?"

"Stop looking at me like you want to thread your fingers through my hair and fuck me into oblivion," I finally said sharply. "You left me. I can't have you looking at me like that if we are going to be working together. You. Left. Me. There has to be a hard line."

I couldn't look at him. I was a mess, having him this close. The smell of him permeated the room. Small longing looks, the comfort of us, it was just so easy for us to slip into those old habits.

Why did the Angels do this? Why Aiden? Of all the Vernadali on this island, why the one who shattered my heart on the floor by walking away after I had given my heart so fully to him?

It was only a half moment before he was crouched before me with my hands in his hands. "Jess," he practically begged. His voice was a loving and needy sound that speared my heart.

He took one of those hands and gripped my chin to make me face him. When my eyes met his, there was that old emotion in them. I wanted to take it and make it mine again, but he had said that wasn't what he wanted. He had walked away, and I had found a way to move forward. At least I thought I had, but staring into his eyes… I didn't know anymore.

A shadow crossed his face, and he stepped back. Keeping my head down, I saw him ball his hands into fists a few times before standing at attention and saying, "Duchess, I am ready to depart when you are. I will await you and Lady Amala in the hall."

A lump formed in my throat, and I nodded. When he got to the door, I felt the tears slip out, and a small hiccup squeaked out of me.

"Jess." Aiden's voice was pleaful.

I just rolled over to face the opposite direction, curled up back underneath the blankets, and when I heard the soft click of the door, I didn't try to hold back the sobs.

CHAPTER 4

AIDEN

I DIDN'T KNOW IF what I was feeling was my own or if it was hers. All I knew was that it fucking hurt. My chest felt like someone had ripped my heart out and put syths through it.

I was trying. I was trying to control my emotions and reactions, but when she climbed out from under the blankets in nothing but that T-shirt that had ridden up to her hips, it was everything I could do to stay where I was.

I ran my hands through my hair and growled in frustration, just as Vernadali Samuel walked around the corner.

"Vernadali Aiden," he said as I snapped to attention. "Why are you not inside with the Duchess?"

"She requested I wait outside while they finished packing up, sir." I tried to sound as professional as possible. My chest still hurt, and I had to hide it.

He raised his eyebrows at me and said, "Problems already?"

"Nothing we can't work through, sir."

"Aiden," Vernadali Samuel said in a tone that was much more fatherly than anything else. "Do you still care for the Duchess?"

I blinked. "Sir?"

"I will amend my statement. You do still care for the Duchess, don't you?" He gave me a small smile, and when I didn't answer him, he put his hand on my shoulder and said, "I'm sure the Angels know what they are doing."

I couldn't help but huff a laugh. "I think the Angels are playing a sick joke at my expense."

"If you care for her...," he trailed off as he looked to the door. When he looked back at me, his eyes were pained and sorrowful. "I can't reassign a Charge. The Five Angels give the assignments. You know the Vernadali laws. Your parents were, are, different."

"I know my parents are a special situation. Everything has always been different for them. I have no expectations, sir. Besides, the Duchess is betrothed to marry the Lord of Kaletta."

"Aiden," he said, and I slowly slid my eyes to him. "Just protect her. Be there for her."

"To my dying breath," I said firmly. He nodded and strode down the hall. Once he was out of sight, I relaxed and took a few deep breaths. My chest felt like it was in a vice.

I looked to the door, and it took everything I had not to charge through and go to her. I could feel her pain, her sadness, her confusion. I knew that part of that was me, but I knew with every fiber of my being that it was her, too.

Angels, Jess.

I didn't even realize I had reached for the door until it opened and Amala was standing there.

"Aiden," she said quietly. "Jess is in the shower. She will be ready to leave in about fifteen minutes."

"Yes, Lady Amala." My eyes flicked behind her, and I saw Jess step out of the bathroom wrapped in a towel. As she turned to close the door, I couldn't help but see how red and puffy her eyes were. "I'm sorry, Amala. I thought I was holding it together. I thought I was hiding it."

"You still love her," she said, cocking her head to the side.

I leaned against the wall and nodded slowly.

"Aiden."

"I know."

"As your mother would say, well, that sucks royal monkey balls!"

I laughed. "Royal, indeed."

"What are you going to do?"

"What I'm assigned to do. Protect her," I said, still staring at the closed door that Jess had gone through. "I know all the pitfalls. I know about the Lord of Kaletta. I know they are scheduled to be married sometime next year. I just don't know the details. I have avoided the details. I... I thought I was protecting her when I walked away. Protecting us, by walking away."

"You know you shattered her heart when you did, right?" she said with a voice that was both hard in fury and soft in kindness.

"Jess' wasn't the only one that shattered that day. I haven't felt whole since I walked away from her. When Vernadali Samuel assigned me to her, I didn't know what to feel. I'm terrified of what is going to happen in the future…. But now, I also have a reason to be by her side."

"Would you marry her, though?" Amala's voice was so low that no one else could have heard her.

"It isn't a matter of would. I can't. Not only because she is to marry Lord Jayden, but also because a Vernadali is not allowed to marry their Charge. It is an ancient law."

Amala looked toward Jess' door then turned back to me, eyes narrowed. "Aiden, can I tell you a secret?"

I looked at her and urged her on.

"I'm sure she will tell you at some point, but the Grand Duchess has been trying to get his father to sign off on a nullification agreement, but he won't." She stepped closer to me so that there was no chance of anyone else hearing.

I stood there shocked. "Why? What does Jess think?"

"You need to know, there are only a handful of people who know that information. As her Vernadali, I thought you should be one of them. Because of that, Aiden. Not because of everything else. Give us a few minutes," Amala said, and she stepped back just as Jess opened her door, and my eyes snapped to hers.

She was dressed in tight blue jeans, black knee-high boots, a loose white shirt, with a black corset overtop of it that only went to under her breasts. Her hair was back in a long braid, and I shuddered at the thought of threading my hands through the plait and undoing those long tresses. I closed my eyes and shook the thought before noticing she had put on some makeup to help cover the redness around her eyes, but it didn't do much to cover the puffiness.

I wanted to go to her and tell her how sorry I was for hurting her, for making her cry, but I steeled myself and stayed in place. I could see her do the same.

"Ready to head toward Silentport, Duchess?" I said, becoming the Vernadali I was supposed to be.

"Yes, Vernadali Aiden." Her voice cracked a bit at the name, and Amala went to get a few bags of her own.

"Do you need help with your bags?"

"No, thank you. I only have the one." She picked up a large duffle bag and slung it over her shoulder.

I nodded and grabbed my duffle and uniform bag from by the door. When Jess and Amala came out of the room, I stepped back and allowed them to lead the way toward the boat.

AMALA AND JESS SHARED a stateroom, which had a small, adjoining cabin. The one benefit was that it had a door that joined the two rooms but allowed us to have our separate quarters. If there was any trouble at all, I could easily gain access. She had threatened to barricade it shut when she first saw it, but I just laughed and showed her how it swung into my room, and Amala laughed when Jess had noticed it only locked from my side as well.

Since then, we had settled into an easy rhythm of professionality. It was a lot easier to do since there wasn't much time for us to be alone. She was in meeting after meeting regarding the issues in Ashridge. Not to mention the meetings I had to attend once she was secure in her room each night. As long as there were other people around the Duchess, Lady Amala, and myself, there were no issues to speak of. It was just like old times.

Two months later, we were closing in on the small stretch of water between Kaletta and Savanora. We would be passing closer to Kaletta tonight, and it was expected that Jess would stand on the deck and watch the city as we passed. I had been meeting with the ship's security team on the regular about it, and while there didn't seem to be much in the way of risks, I was still on edge. It would be her first public appearance with me by her side as her Vernadali. Whether that edge was there for Vernadali reasons or personal reasons, I didn't know.

There was one conversation I had been putting off with her. We needed to sort out a way to communicate silently without alerting others. It was a conversation that would bring back old memories, but I needed to see if she would implement some of that old dynamic for security measures. I had already talked to Amala about it, and she had encouraged me to have that conversation with Jess. Now I was staring at the door that separated us and that conversation. Sighing as I knocked the secret code that I had always used when we were together, she knocked the response, and when I opened the door, she was sitting in the reading chair with a book.

"Good afternoon, Vernadali Aiden," she said carefully. "What can I do for you?"

"Afternoon, Duchess," I said, smirking at her. Her cheeks were slightly pink, and I noted the glass of red liquid next to her. "Just how much wine have you had this afternoon?"

"A few."

"Glasses or bottles?"

"Does it matter?"

"It does, because we need to discuss security, and I need your head clear. If you are drunk, I can't talk to you." I was eyeing her carefully. She was either horny as hell or a fuck around and find out kind of drunk.

"BAH! This is only my second glass," she said, lifting the drink and almost spilling it. Second drink, my sister's purple-haired ass. "I wanted to get good and drunk before having to stand before Kaletta tonight. I hate that city. All its glittering gold, opulence, and riches that don't go to its people. The Grand Lord himself is a right asshole." As if she just realized what she said out loud, she cupped her hand over her mouth quickly, and her eyes went wide.

I burst out laughing. "Now really, Jess, tell me how you really feel?"

"I'm sorry, Aiden." She looked at her glass of wine and then at me. It was just like old times. I wanted this easy conversation. I craved frank, open discussion that was easy. I had hated every moment since we left her room at the Curtails of the North because of how strained our conversations were.

"So, *not* wine if you're only two glasses deep, or have you forgotten how to count?" I smirked at her and crossed my arms over my chest.

"Okay, so, it's kilra." She sighed and leaned back in her chair.

"Jess," I said, drawing out her name. "You know what kilra does to you."

There was a sparkle in her eye that brought back very specific memories of her drinking the whiskey... and us. All in a night that ended with her father walking in on us, shaking his head, and walking out. The next morning, I had a very uncomfortable discussion with the Duke of Ashridge. I took a very deep breath, pinched the bridge of my nose, and let it out slowly.

When she saw the look on my face, she said, "I'm not going to like this conversation, am I?"

"I have been avoiding it for a few reasons. You not liking it is one of them."

She took her glass, threw back the last sips of the red whiskey, and sat up straight. "Alright, Aid. Hit me."

I shook my head and huffed through my nose. "I knew I should have talked to you about this before. You've only ever called me that while drunk or during... other times. I need you to have a clear head about this, Jess. You need to remember."

She got up and stood before me. Angels, she was much less stable on her feet than I had anticipated. So fully drunk, not just buzzing hard.

"No. I'm fine. I am the Duchess, and you, my Vernadali." She hiccupped then and started giggling. I raised my eyebrow at her and sighed.

"Yeah, no. You need a nap. Where is Amala?"

"She went to get laid," she said and then muttered under her breath. "Lucky bitch. I want to get laid." Her eyes flicked to mine quickly.

I was watching each twitch of her body, waiting for her to pass out. A wave of heat flashed over me, and when I felt it center near my pelvis, I shifted. Okay, horny Jess it was. Angels.

I took a step back from her. I was trying, damn it. "Jess, go lie down. I'll come to talk to you in a couple of hours."

"Aren't you supposed to protect me?" she said, turning on me, and I narrowed my eyes at her. Her lip protruded slightly as she gave me a pouty look I knew all too well.

"Don't... Jess," I said, taking another step back. My pants were growing tighter, and she knew it. I took a deep breath and very carefully put my hands on her shoulders. "Stop. You gave me crystal-clear instructions that there was a line. If I have to abide by that line, Jessika Petra, then so do you."

Her face cleared slightly at that statement. "Jessika Petra?" she said carefully, and I gave her a stern look. "You only call me that when you are trying to make a very clear point."

She took a deep breath and then said, "You are right. I'm sorry, Aiden. I crossed a line. It's hard. It's easy to slip into old habits. Have a seat. Let me splash some cold water on my face, sober up a bit, and we can talk."

She disappeared into the small bathroom, and I heard the water running. The boat rocked, and I heard her cuss as something large fell to the floor.

"Everything okay?" I asked. There was a weird feeling coming from her right now, and I couldn't exactly place it. Please don't tell me she passed out in the bathroom. These bathrooms are too small for her to be sprawled out.

When she didn't answer me, I went to the bathroom door and asked again, "Jess, is everything okay?"

"Shit." I heard her mutter. "Yeah. No. Come on in."

I slowly opened the door, and when I saw her, I started to laugh. "You stand there and tell me that you are not drunk, but then the boat rocks just a bit, and you fall and get stuck in the shower?"

"Asshole. I thought you were supposed to protect me?"

"Protect, yes. Even if that is from yourself, but there is nothing in the Vernadali code that says I can't laugh my ass off at your stupidity."

"I say again, *asshole*." She tried and failed once again to get up. "Are you just going to stand there and laugh, or are you going to help me?"

Moving around the toilet and closing the door to the bathroom, I reached out my hand and pulled her up and out of the shower.

"I can't believe you sometimes, Jess." I smirked at her. She came up faster than I intended, and I had to catch her as I stumbled back against the opposite wall.

The feel of her body against mine did nothing to hide the erection that had come on earlier. She ground her hips against me, and I groaned. There was no way to hide how hard I was for her. "Humm."

"Jess." I moved her a step away from me, opened the bathroom door, and walked out.

"Aiden." There was something broken in the tone of her voice, and there was a sharp zap of something that hit me in the chest.

"You wanted lines. I'm giving you those lines." I couldn't look at her right now. "I came in here for Vernadali business, but that can't happen right now. Let me know when you sober up, and we can talk."

When I got to the door that separated our two rooms, I said over my shoulder, "You need to figure out what you want, Jess. When you figure it out, let me know."

My voice cracked at the last part. I might as well have told Jess I loved her, but I couldn't have this Vernadali responsibility, be told that is all it is going to be, and then have her do this. I closed the adjoining door and locked it.

Just as I knew she would, she tried to come after me to fight over it. I had to keep her at arm's length until she was sober. If I let her back in here, there was only one way the day would be spent, and I knew she would regret it.

I sat in the lone chair in my room and mumbled, "When did I become so fucking self-righteous?"

She was banging on the door, crying my name, trying to get in. I knew she wasn't mad. That damn link told me everything. It told me things I didn't want to know, and it hurt.

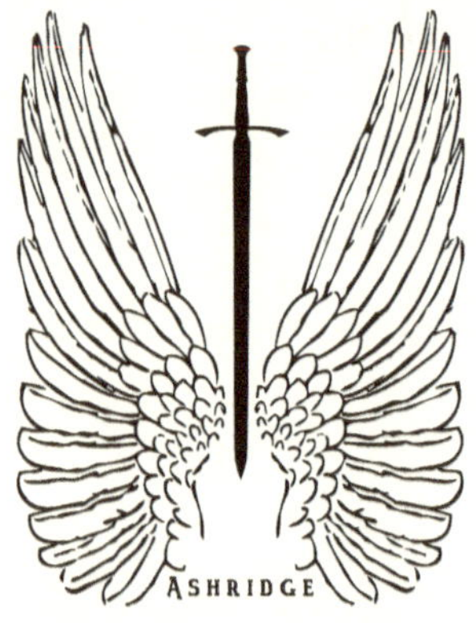

CHAPTER 5

JESSIKA

I WAS DRESSED IN the outfit I was expected to wear on deck as we sailed past Kaletta. Floor-length and bloodred, the dress had a full set of skirts, sweetheart neckline, and small cap sleeves. Amala had put simple, clear stones around my neck, complete with matching earrings and bracelets. She fixed my hair up in a relaxed bun with small curls falling loose around my face, and even placed a crown upon my head. I hated the damn things. They never fit right, had to be pinned into my skull, and still managed to poke in other places.

There was a knock on the hallway door, and when Amala answered it, she said, "Aiden. Why are you coming this way?"

"I am here to escort Duchess Jessika to the deck. We are approaching Kaletta, and we have been informed that the Grand Lord is stationed on the dock to witness the Duchess passing by the city," he said formally.

"I am ready," I said, adjusting the skirt. I hadn't looked at Aiden yet, but when our eyes met, there was a cold stony expression on his face.

"You look beautiful, Duchess. I'm sure the Grand Lord of Kaletta will appreciate you wearing the territory colors." Each word was specifically chosen and formal. He bowed slightly at the waist as he moved out of the doorway to allow me to walk through. Once the guards were walking in front of me, Aiden stepped beside me as we headed down the hall. Amala was just behind us and had ensured the door was locked before following.

"Aiden, I'm...," I started to say, but he interrupted me.

"Later, Jess. Now is not the fucking time."

My stomach roiled, and I was very glad that I had eaten some of the flatbread to soak up some of the alcohol. I was still a little buzzed and a lot ashamed at what had happened earlier.

Angels. I had practically begged Aiden to sleep with me. It wasn't fair. I had told him exactly where that line was, and I blew over it like it wasn't even there. All I could hear was, "You need to figure out what you want, Jess." The problem was, I knew I wanted him, but he didn't want me. Sure, I still turned him on, but that was just physical attraction. That had never been an issue for us. No, I knew I still wanted Aiden's heart.

I glanced in his direction, and he was all Vernadali. If you looked at him, you would think we were strangers walking down the hallway. There was no emotion on his face. What was he thinking? Now that he was assigned to me, would he rethink our position? He had put his duty before us five years ago. He had said it would never work because he would be assigned to someone that would take him far from me, and... Angels, now he was assigned to me. Could we make that work? Would he even want to try? Does he even still care?

I stifled a sniffle as I tried to hold back the tears. There was a sideways glance at me, and just before we entered the deck, Aiden put his hand on my forearm. "Are you okay?"

I blinked the tears away and sniffled again. "Nothing that can't wait until later. We do need to talk, Aiden."

"We do. About security," he said, still being all bodyguard.

"That..." I shook my head and looked down, nodding. "About security. Yes. About what you wanted to discuss with me earlier."

"Ready?" he said, indicating the door. I nodded and headed for the spot against the railing they had set up for me to stand. There were guards on three sides of me, plus Aiden on my right, and Amala on my left. I saw movement from Aiden, who was having a near-silent conversation with Amala. She patted her thigh and moved the slit of her dress just slightly to show him she was indeed wearing a few syths in case something were to happen. What he didn't know was that I had this dress modified so that there were hidden slits in the folds of the skirts to allow me access to no less than three syths around my waist.

I looked out over the water and saw the cesspool that was Kaletta coming into view. I saw the palace as we came around the corner with its shining golden roofs and spearing towers, but then slowly, the bright blue buildings against the white sands and terrain could suddenly be seen. People lined the water bank, waving and shouting at us as we went by.

"This is so stupid. Even after I marry Jayden, it isn't like I'll be their Grand Lady. My priority will always be to the people of Ashridge," I mumbled, and Amala poked me hard. "Tell me what I said that isn't true?"

"Besides the point, Duchess," she said, smirking as a bird came to land on the top deck.

When we came parallel to the city, loud horns sounded, and I had to cover my ears.

"What the Underworld is that for?" I said as the ship slowly came to a stop.

"Why is the ship stopping?" Aiden asked beside me.

"The horns are a command to stop," one of the guards said.

"Again. Why are we stopping? This is not in the schedule. We were to be told of any changes," Aiden demanded.

A boy around ten came up with a message and handed it to Aiden. "Vernadali Aiden, from the palace."

Aiden tore through the seal and read the note. There was a burst of power that wrapped around me, his Charge. It felt warm and comforting but edgy at the same time. I almost smiled at him for it. Aiden, though, sighed and rubbed the bridge of his nose.

"Vernadali Aiden, what is the cause of the delay?" I asked.

"We are receiving an additional passenger and his guards." There was a tone to his voice I didn't like. It was almost like he craved delivering death. His Charge wrapped tighter around me as he said, "Guards, stay with the Duchess. I will be back in a moment."

After taking a couple of steps, he gave a backward glance to Amala, tapped his elbow, and Amala gave him an imperceptible nod. I blinked. Was he using our old hand signals? A tap on the elbow meant "protect."

A few minutes later, Aiden returned without saying another word, but his lips were tight. A boat jetted toward the ship, and when it reached the bow, a covered walkway for whoever it was that was joining us rolled out from the hull. Once that person was on board, the boat sped away.

"Can we go back to my room now, please?" I asked. My feet hurt in these heels because, well, heels sucked. Whoever thought they were a good idea was probably a man who never had to wear them for long periods of time. That man should be brought back to life and shot repeatedly.

"No. As Duchess, you must welcome the guest on board," Aiden said through his teeth.

I reached over and put my hand on his forearm. "What's wrong?"

His eyes slowly tracked the deck, but he just said, "I'm your Vernadali, Jessika. I need to know these things. You could have warned me."

"Warned you? About what?" I asked.

"That I was coming on board," a familiar voice said.

My head whipped around toward that voice, and I saw a man who was just shorter than Aiden dressed in an opulent silk suit striding toward us. I plastered a smile on my face. His black hair, porcelain skin, and almond-shaped brown eyes hadn't changed in the last six months since I saw him. He had let a scruff of a beard grow in since then, and I was still deciding whether it suited him or not.

"Jayden? I thought you were in Cinder. I had no idea you were even back in Nalrin at all. Let alone in Kaletta."

Jayden smiled a bright smile but didn't answer me at first. Instead, he bowed deeply and said, "Good evening, Duchess. May I come on board?"

Formalities first it was then. Add in the fact that the ship would not continue on until I did accept the new arrival... "How many accompany you, Lord Jayden?"

"It's just two guards, Ilris and Killy, and me, Duchess Valenti," he said, indicating the men standing just to either side of him in the red and gold uniforms. Flashy and fully pressed, it was a hideous thing to look at. Not to mention the golden embroidered wolf over the right breast.

"Lord Jayden Panahov, you and your two personal guards may board and settle in."

Once the message had been received that I had accepted his presence on the ship, we were underway again. We stood there for a long moment before I realized that Aiden and Jayden were sizing each other up. I sighed deeply.

"Lord Jayden, this is my assigned Vernadali, Vernadali Aiden," I said, but the next words were lodged in my throat. Aiden's eyes flicked to mine, and there was a quick nod. He knew, but also knew that I had to say them. "Vernadali Aiden, this is Lord Jayden, my betrothed."

Aiden bowed slightly to Jayden, and Jayden just waved him off. "If you are protecting Jessika, then you will never bow to me."

"You are a lord, sir. It is customary to greet you as such," Aiden said. I studied him for a moment, and his hands were in fists at his side.

"Vernadali Aiden, please, I ask it as a favor to Jessika that you don't." Jayden was very relaxed about it. After another long look at Jayden, Aiden looked to me, and I shrugged.

"Very well, If the Duchess requests it."

"Let's meet in my stateroom, and we can talk. Both of you." I gave them each a meaningful look that meant that this wasn't going to be a fun discussion—for either of them.

When Jayden held out his arm, I took it, ever the obedient fiance.

"Very well. I would like to hear of your travels." Jayden turned to his guard and said, "Please go and get our things settled."

"Do you request adjoining rooms with the Duchess, sir?" one of the guards inquired.

"No. I believe her Vernadali is stationed next to her, if protocol is being held. The Duchess' protection is more important than being with my betrothed. Also, if I am not mistaken, Lady Amala is staying with the Duchess," he said then looked at me for confirmation. I nodded.

"Very well, sir."

We made our way back to my room, and when we did, Aiden shut the door and locked it once the four of us were inside. As soon as the lock clicked, Jayden and I dropped each other's hands and sighed a breath of relief.

"I'm sorry, Jessika," Jayden said, taking his overcoat off and tossing it on one of the chairs.

"Your father?" I said, almost growling the words. He nodded.

"He heard that the Grand Duchess had ordered you to Silentport and wanted me to go with you." He flopped back into one of the chairs, arms and legs spread wide. "Then he found out that you would be coming the northern route through the straight and thought it would be *a good way for us to spend time together*. Don't worry, I fought him on it, said there were things I needed to do in Kaletta, but you know my father."

"He's an asshole, Jayden. I haven't made it unknown to you how I feel about him." My eyes flicked to Aiden, who raised an eyebrow at me, and I just smiled.

"So, what's the deal with you and Vernadali Aiden?"

"Jayden," I admonished.

When I didn't answer, he turned to Amala. "Amala, what's the deal with her Vernadali? Are they fucking each other yet?" Then he leaned toward her and whispered loudly, not really trying to keep his voice down, "Or are they still trying to play hard to get with each other."

I burst up laughing, and I saw Aiden stand up straight and physically hold himself back.

"Asshole," I spat at Jayden. Then I turned to Aiden and mouthed, "It's fine." But if looks could kill, Jayden was not winning any points here with Aiden. This is not how I would have liked their first encounter to go.

"Nah. They aren't fucking," Amala said, giggling and giving Jayden some kilra. Then she gave him a conspiratorial look and winked at me before saying, "Not yet, anyways."

"Amala!" I said, heading over to Aiden. I took a hold of his hands, forcing him to release the very tight ball that he had made with them. "Aiden, I'm so sorry."

His eyes were trained on Jayden, and I thought I could see murder there. Jayden, however, was tilting his head to the side and was trying to figure Aiden out. Slowly, Jayden set his glass down and came to stand next to me.

"Jessika didn't tell you, did she?" he asked quietly.

"I know that you two are betrothed," Aiden said, his voice expertly hiding the rage. I could tell he was pulling on years of training not to rip Jayden to pieces right now. He had one hand conveniently next to one of his syths, and the other was still in mine. I ran small circles across his knuckles, and I felt him grip my hand that much harder.

"No, the conditions of our marriage," he said.

"I know that your father promised aid to Ashridge in exchange for the marriage. He promised to provide food, silks, cotton, and military support if needed. None of which has come to light since the betrothal almost two years ago," Aiden said.

Jayden scoffed and threw his hand in the air. "Not all that political bullshit." He strode back to the chair he previously occupied and carefully sat down, taking a deep breath. Taking a drink of the whiskey, he said, "Jess, am I telling your Vernadali or you? He needs to know everything regarding our arrangement. Otherwise, he can't do his job, regardless of whatever else is going on."

"Jayden, there isn't anything going on between Aiden and me. He is my Vernadali."

"You keep telling yourself that." Then he looked at Aiden and said, "You too, pretty boy."

Aiden flinched, and I grabbed him by the waist and said, "Stop it. Both of you."

"Start talking, Jess," Aiden said, softly stroking my hand in that silent language from so many years ago. *I'm good.*

I realized that my arms were still around his waist and Jayden was looking us both up and down. There was a twinkle in his eye, and I just said, "Jayden, you can be such a dick."

He took another long drink from his glass, and I pulled Aiden in farther down the room and said, "Aiden, I should have told you earlier, but considering, well, everything, I couldn't."

"Seriously, Jessika, do you want me to tell him?" Jayden offered. The smile was slight and friendly.

I played with my bottom lip, and when my eyes met Aiden's, he said, "Jess." There was fear and hurt in his eyes, and I didn't know what to do. The whole situation sucked.

"I don't want to marry Jessika any more than she wants to fucking marry me," Jayden blurted.

"Well, that's one way to put it," Amala said, draining the rest of her whiskey.

Aiden's Charge was a powerful wave that surged through the room. There were arms around me, Aiden's arms, and in that moment, I knew I was safe and secure. When the heat left me, Aiden had me behind him and five feet away from where we previously had been in a matter of moments. "Excuse me?"

Jayden's eyes were wide at how quickly we had moved, and frankly, I was still trying to catch my breath.

"Aiden!" Amala said. She shook her finger at him, saying, "You don't need to protect Jess from Jayden. He would die for her, just as much as you would."

I ran a single finger down his back, and I felt Aiden shudder under my touch. I hoped it conveyed the message I wanted to give him, since I couldn't reach his hand, but he took another shuddering breath like he was physically trying to calm down. Amala stepped up to him and said, "Your eyes are purple. Calm your shit down."

I came and stood in front of him, taking his hands in mine.

"Aid, look at me," I said carefully. He closed his eyes, turned his head away from me, and tried to take a deep breath. "Vernadali Aiden Mathewson, I command you as your Charge to look at me."

I heard Jayden gasp behind me, but I kept my eyes on Aiden. He slowly turned back to me and opened his eyes. Those hazel-green eyes I loved so much had been replaced with bright purple ones that almost glowed. I took a deep breath and said, "Jayden is not going to hurt me. I am safe. I am in no danger."

I lifted our clasped hands to my chest and laid it above my heart. He didn't need it to know it was still beating, but

I said, "Feel its physical beat. I know you can feel it, but I am safe."

"I know you are safe. I will keep you safe," he muttered as a promise. I held his gaze as he took a deep breath, and the purple in his eyes started to fade. "What I want to know is, what is Jayden talking about? Until he answers and I am satisfied with that answer, I do not care how many times you and Amala sit there and tell me that Jayden is safe. I will protect you, even from him."

Anger flowed through me. "Aiden, that barely made any sense. You need to calm your shit down and stop being an overprotective, territorial asshole."

Jayden slowly sat down and said, "I appreciate you want to protect her, and I appreciate that you want her safe. However, I am not someone you need to keep her safe from. I care for her very much, but what I said was that I don't want to marry Jessika, any more than she wants to marry me."

Aiden's eyes, while back to his own color, had flashed again before he took another deep breath.

"What is the Duchess Jessika Petra Valenti to you, Vernadali Aiden?" Jayden said, sitting back a tad too cocky for the situation.

"The Duchess is my Charge. Nothing more."

I flinched at Aiden's words. It hurt to hear him say it.

"Oh, for Angel's sake. Will you both stop trying to out dominate each other?" Amala said.

"What?" Aiden and Jayden said.

"You two are fighting for dominance, and the prize is Jess. Knock it the fuck off," Amala said. She looked at me, and I gave her a short nod. "Look, here is the bottom line. Aiden and Jess used to date. *Used* to being the keyword there,

Jayden. Too much to unpack there right now. Aiden, Jayden doesn't want to marry Jessika because he's bisexual."

"Bisexual, leaning male," Jayden said then brazenly looked Aiden up and down. Jayden blinked a few times, fidgeted with his hands, and I couldn't help the huff of a laugh that came from me. Jayden was nervous as hell, and then he started to ramble. "And if you didn't look like you were about to kill me right now, I'd tell you just how sexy you are, but you do look like you are going to kill me, so I'm going to shut up. Amala, can I have more whiskey, please?"

"Aiden," I said, putting a hand on his face, and making him look at me. "Do you need a few minutes, or are you okay?"

"More and more people are finding out about our history, Jess." Aiden's voice was filled with concern and uncertainty.

I looked at him incredulously and backed away from him. "Seriously, out of everything that just happened in the last five minutes, *that* is what you have to say?"

He gave me a look that clearly meant he was very serious.

"Aid, we just told you that one of the most powerful lords is engaged to marry one of the most powerful duchesses in Nalrin, that said lord prefers men, but he's being required to marry that duchess for political reasons alone, and you grasp onto the fact that Jayden now knows we were together?" I threw my hands up in the air, took Amala's whiskey from her hand, and downed the entire thing in one foul gulp. It burned the whole way down, and my body shivered as it settled over my stomach.

"I don't care that Jayden is bisexual. That is his business," Aiden said.

"Seriously?" Jayden said, blushing as a broad smile came across his lips. He gave a hesitant whisper, "Thank you."

"See, not everyone is like the people in Kaletta, or like your bigoted fuckhead of a father," Amala said, refilling Jayden's glass.

"Wait," Jayden said, his head flipping up to Aiden. "She called you Vernadali Aiden Mathewson."

I froze, realizing what I had just done, and I slowly turned to Aiden, giving him a pleading look. His returning gaze clearly said, "*See. This is why I try to keep my private life just that.*" Then he walked over to the bar, poured himself an oversized glass of whiskey, and tipped back half of it before turning around and saying, "Yes. She did."

"*The* Aiden Mathewson?" Jayden said. "Lady Megan and Vernadali CJ's youngest son?"

"Yes, and if you say one word to compare me to LJ and Owen, you won't leave this room. If you say one word about anything that is said tonight in this room, you won't wake the morning after I find out." Aiden's eyes were full of wrath and fury.

"Oh, trust me, I think you have more on me than I do on you," Jayden whispered.

"What do you mean?"

"The dimension finds out you dated Jessika, and its news for a few months. You two are inconvenienced, it causes some political tension, and frankly, could probably help Ashridge in its reconstructive efforts. Just knowing that she's linked to them, I'm sure, would send people flocking to help."

"Jayden, it's not happening. We worked very hard in the past to hide our relationship, and we don't want it getting out now for many reasons. We won't be using his parents as a way to better Ashridge. We will do so through hard work and perseverance. Now, stop rambling and just tell Aiden the rest. He needs to know," I said, staring him down.

"My secret gets out, I'm a dead man. Doesn't matter that I'm his only son. My father doesn't know my sexual preferences. He is a fucking bigot, and it's going to be the first law I change once I'm Grand Lord of Kaletta," Jayden said, staring into his drink.

"Wait, I thought Mom got all those laws abolished twenty years ago." Aiden took the chair across from Jayden. He looked at me for a moment, a confused look on his face, then back to Jayden as he started talking.

"Lady Megan did. Everywhere except for in Kaletta and one small territory at the top tip of the Savanora island. My father calls it an abomination to the Angels. Believes that the Angels put us here to spread our seed and procreate. That can't happen if beings do not have sex in a way that allows for procreation to happen. Anyone who is found with the inappropriate sex is put to death. No chance to explain, plead, or beg to relocate out of Kaletta."

"Fuck," Aiden said, blinking. "How have you escaped your father?"

"I'm meticulously careful. It took a long time for me to open up to Jessika about it," Jayden said, tipping back the last of the kilra in his glass. "It wasn't until I had a long discussion with Princess Janreka about it that I knew I would be able to safely tell her. Jessika and I were not on the greatest of terms at the time."

"So, you know Princess Janreka well?" Aiden asked.

"I knew her better than Jessika. Knew she had ways of knowing things that aren't public."

"That Reka does." Aiden drained the rest of his glass.

"How do you know the Princess?"

"She's basically my sister. Mom and Dad had us in Therth a lot of our childhood. The Empress and Grand Duke are family to us. So, their kids might as well be my brother and sister."

I went over to Jayden and rubbed his shoulders. "Anyway, the day he told me, everything changed about our relationship. We really resented each other up until that point, mostly because we didn't have a say in our future and we were taking it out on the other. Once I knew, we decided that there would be nothing wrong with having a friendship. We would put the front on, like we were expected to in public, but we would be friends in private."

"But to have to hide who you are? That is bullshit. I don't understand it. Why should this matter to anyone other than you and your person?" Aiden said.

I smiled at him. This was just one of the many reasons I loved him. He didn't care about anything that made us different on the outside. It was all about what was on the inside. He was just a good being.

"Having to hide who I am is... Well, let's just say these scars on my wrists would have done the job if Jessika hadn't found me." Jayden looked up at me and gave me a sad smile.

"What?" Aiden asked, genuinely confused now.

CHAPTER 6

AIDEN

I BLINKED AT THE Lord of Kaletta sitting there, looking at Jess like she was his pure damn savior. Yet, that overprotectiveness that had overtaken me earlier, sparking the Charge into full effect, didn't rise.

"Seriously. You need to explain yourselves," I said, looking at the three of them. "Jess, I am your fucking Vernadali. You can't keep secrets from me."

I was very careful not to put any of my Charge into it. I had to keep control. We never knew when there would be a situation, where we would need to defend our Charge. I had to save my power and Charge for anything that might arise at any moment. That was what we were trained to do.

My eyes flicked back to her, and I drew out her name slowly. "Jess."

"Aiden. That isn't my story to tell." She rubbed Jayden's shoulders again. "Only Jayden can tell that story, and only if he wants to, but Jayden and I have an understanding."

Realization hit me hard in the chest as her sadness flowed through me. My eyes flicked to the scars and saw how they lay across his wrist. They were scars meant for one thing and one thing only. It had not been a cry for help. They were an escape from the pain. "Things got bad, didn't they? So bad, you wanted to end it."

Jayden looked up to me, silver lining his eyes, "I had been forced to watch my father and his guards stone a woman to death just because of who she was. I knew that if my father found out, it would be me on that pole."

A single tear had slipped out and was running down his cheek. He sat there silently, as if remembering much more but was unwilling to voice it. "Jessika had been in Kaletta to meet with one of our suppliers. That night, the three of us were supposed to go to the theatre, but I sent them off without me. While she and Amala were out, I went into the bedroom, locked the door, and took my syths to my wrists."

He took another sip of his whiskey before saying with a thick voice, "I woke up to Jessika using her power to try and stop the bleeding, screaming at me for being an idiot, and that I wasn't allowed to die on her. I kept passing out from the blood loss, but she kept zapping my head with that power of hers. She spent hours by my bedside after she and Amala healed me. Then she made me travel with her for three months before she felt comfortable enough to allow me to be on my own again. Lied to my father and said she wanted time with me to get to know her betrothed." There was a smirk and a gleam in his eye as he looked at Jess. She winked at him, and then her eyes were focused on me. She was leaning against one of the side tables, feet crossed with a drink in her hand.

Smiling at Jess because that was exactly something she would do, I met Jayden's gaze which was fierce and determined. "Vernadali Aiden, when Lady Amala said that I would die to protect Duchess Jessika, she isn't wrong. I literally owe her my life."

Blinking, I studied the man across from me. Jayden had been someone I had spent the last few years disliking just because he had the one thing I wanted so badly. He still did, but to see the pain in his face and to hear why they were on such good terms, in the face of everything else, had my head spinning.

The amount of respect that I had growing for this man was huge. "You have the strength of the Angels, Lord Jayden."

A long silence hung in the room before Jess said, "Jayden and I talked it through, and we care for each other very much, as friends. It will be nothing more. After many late-night, long talks, we went to Mom, who worked so closely with Lady Megan in the fight to get those laws nullified. She immediately asked what we wanted to do. We told her that we preferred not to marry just for political reasons. Certainly not for political reasons that were not even coming to fruition."

"The Grand Duchess said she would work with my father to get it nullified, but he won't agree to it. Says our territories will be stronger as one. That Kaletta can fix what is broken in Ashridge." Jayden rolled his eyes at the last of those statements. "The only thing that Ashridge needs is Jessika. Everything she does is for her territory. Underworld's being, she is willing to be in a loveless marriage with me just for the good of her people."

My eyes flicked to Jess. She was staring at me, and while the woman on the exterior was strong and assured, I knew her better than that. There was hurt and something broken within her. I felt her sadness wash through me, and I honestly didn't know if it was hers or mine because I knew, just knew, it was there because of me. I looked down to my clasped hands as I leaned forward with my elbows on my knees.

"So, Jess and Jayden keep the ruse up," Amala said, shrugging and breaking me from my thoughts. "At least, until they can get it nullified. His father keeps pushing for them to set a date and to start planning the wedding, but luckily, we have been able to push that off."

"Not anymore." Jayden flinched at the words. "He's pushing it, again."

"How much?" I said, anger and a dose of fear lacing my words.

"Father says that if we don't wed by the end of the year, he will go to Head Julian for breach of contract. That could force our hand. The contract is pretty straightforward. We might not be able to fight it."

I looked down and studied my feet. Could I go to Julian for that kind of assistance? He was for all purposes a grandfather to me, but to mix family and business? Could I do that? Would Jess even let me?

A pit sat hard and fast in my stomach, and I looked at Jess. Her face had gone white, and she started to shake. Sending my power to wrap around her instinctively, I whispered, "Jess."

"Shit, you move fast, man," Jayden said.

I was standing before her now, but her eyes were staring off toward my chest. Putting my hand on her cheek to make her look at me, I fought every instinct in me to hold her close as my fingers touched her clammy skin. Even though I knew the answer, I asked, "Are you okay?"

Her hand went to her throat and then made a fist. *I'm scared, but I'll behave.*

I pulled her into a hug this time and nodded. She wrapped her arms around my waist and gripped the back of my shirt in her hands.

My heart raced. She was scared to follow through with it, but she would. The full realization she was using our old signals unfurled something in me. She remembered them and was using them. That was going to make our next conversation easier. I had gone to her earlier to ask her to start using them but was so afraid that she wouldn't just because of what they meant in our history.

She unclenched her hands from my shirt but still held me tight. "Jayden, I'm not mad at you."

"I know, Jessika. I know," Jayden said.

I looked over at Jayden, and he had a sad smile on his face. He saw right through both of us. The only thing I could think was, *Shit. This whole thing is fucked.*

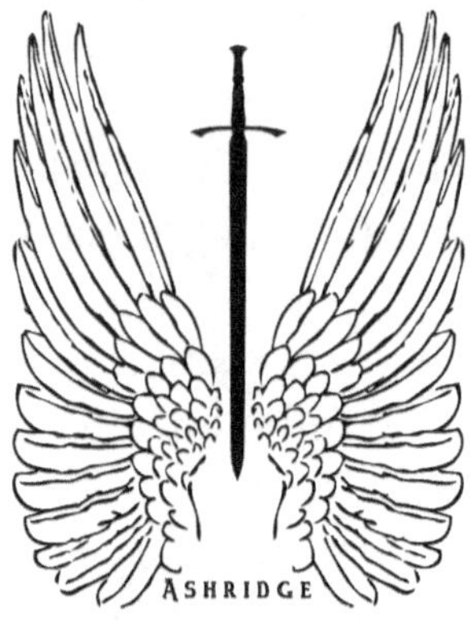

CHAPTER 7

JESSIKA

AIDEN KNOCKED ON MY door, and I responded in that same code we had always used. I didn't know how to feel right now. It was so easy to slide into those old habits, but what would that matter if I had to marry Jayden?

Underworld, Aiden knew I was engaged and still didn't back down to being assigned as my Vernadali. Vernadali Samuel had even tried to give us an out, and he downright refused.

He turned the handle and stuck his head in. "How are you feeling?"

"You know exactly how I am feeling, Aiden. That's why you are here." My words were biting and hostile, but I was holding back tears, so he could get over it.

He was in front of me instantly, and the second he was kneeling, my hands in his, he brought them to his lips. There was a small push of pressure, and my tears started flowing.

"I seriously thought Jayden and I would be able to hold his father off. That we would find a solution," I said, hiccupping through the words.

"Jess." He reached up to wipe the tears from my cheeks. His hands moved to cradle my head, and the feel of his thumb crossing my cheeks as he swept the tears away soothed something in my soul. He had always taken care of me. His mouth opened, then closed.

"What?"

"I could talk to Popa Julian."

"I'm not even sure Head Julian can get us out of this. We would have to prove that he isn't giving us the required assistance as dictated in that contract. The problem is, we are getting supplies. They are just sabotaged before they can go to the people."

"Let me see the contract. Let's send it to Mom, let her look at it. See if there are any loopholes," he offered.

I thought about it, but I had never wanted to use his family's influence. I stated as much just earlier tonight. "Let's keep the family ties as a very last resort, okay? I know your mom and dad would do anything they could to help, but I can't rely on your family, Aiden. I will be Grand Duchess someday, and I need to be able to handle these situations. I've known since I was a little girl that I wouldn't have a say in most things in my life."

I cut my thoughts off, though, because if I didn't, then I was going to tell Aiden everything, and I couldn't do that. There were lines I needed to stop crossing.

"Okay." He crawled up onto the bed with me, leaning against the headboard and sitting on top of the blankets. He reached over and pulled me to sit next to him, wrapping his arm around me.

I chuckled and snuggled up next to him. I smiled as I rested my head on his shoulder. "You have always been able to make me feel better."

He flinched, but then, after a long moment, said, "Maybe it's always been a predetermination that the Angels would assign me as your Vernadali. Vernadali or not, I'll always protect you, Jess. Always." Then he gave me a quick kiss on the top of my head.

That coated one of those broken parts within me. Aiden just sat there and held me for a long while. When I started to doze off, he moved the blankets and tucked me in.

"Don't go." I reached out for his hand when he made for the door.

"Jess. I don't think that is a good idea. Tonight was good. Let's not test it, okay?" His voice was pained, but he stood tall.

I reached up and put my hand to my throat. I was scared. I was terrified of so much: Jayden's father, the welfare of my people, how I was going to run an entire territory, and worst of all, I was scared of losing Aiden.

He came over and sat on his knees before me at the bed. "So, you do remember all the hand signals we used to use?"

"Yes," I said, my voice shaking, just above a whisper. I remembered everything we used it for. All those silent commands both in public and those in the bedroom.

He reached up and put a strand of hair that had fallen out back behind my ear.

"That was what I wanted to talk to you about. Before, I mean. I want to use them as a way for you to check in with me and tell me what you need if we are in public," he said, his eyes warm and soft.

"I saw you give Amala the command to protect when Jayden first boarded. When did you teach them to her?" I asked. Our voices were barely a whisper, but we had been so quiet tonight, that it was almost as though we were yelling.

"Back when we were together. I wanted her to be able to help if I wasn't able to."

"So, not for the same reasons?" I asked, a little embarrassed.

"No. Not for the same reasons. There were plenty that we used just in the bedroom she doesn't know, Jess." Aiden had a small smile on his face. My insides swam at the memory of our time in the bedroom. He really had given me the best sex of my life. After we broke up, I tried to fill that hole, but it wasn't something anyone could ever fill.

Aiden closed his eyes and took a deep breath. "Whatever thought went through your head, I just got very warm and tingly."

I giggled. "Oops."

He shook his head and gave me a small smile. Then he gave me a small, meaningful look that meant we were teetering on the edge of that line.

"Thank you for coming and calming me down tonight, Aiden."

"Anything for you. Get some sleep. We have a LightCall with your mother in the morning," he said with a wink.

"Great. That sounds exactly how I want to spend my morning." I rolled my eyes. "Goodnight, Aiden."

He reached down and gave me a quick kiss on the top of the head. "Goodnight, Jess."

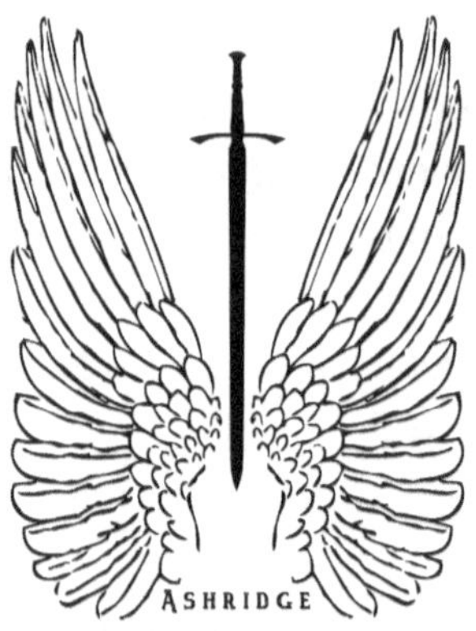

CHAPTER 8

JESSIKA

I GRABBED MY DUFFLE and met Aiden and Amala in the main room, who each had their bags.

"Ready to go, Duchess?" Aiden said.

I nodded and took a quick look around the room. Since the night that Jayden had arrived on the ship, the four of us had spent every night here strategizing and trying to figure out what was happening to our food stores. Jayden had given us some updated information on a few things, including a rumor he had heard about soldiers above Ashridge in the Black Mountains. Why Kaletta soldiers were in the mountains above the capital, he had no idea. Then there was the fact that Aiden saw some strange ships off the coast the closer we got to Silentport. Something was brewing; we just didn't know what.

"Duchess?" Amala said, bringing my thoughts back.

"Sorry, just thinking things through. I can't wait to get off this damn boat. It's been a long two and a half months." Aiden gave me a look, and I rolled my eyes. "I know it would have taken four if we had gone through Bellstar and then through the Black Mountains. Not really the point, Aiden."

Amala laughed and just said, "Well, at least it gave you two a chance to work through some things."

Aiden and I looked at each other, and there were a lot of unsaid things between us. Yes, we had held the lines, but it didn't mean it was easy to do.

There were three distinct thuds from above us, alerting us that we had arrived. Aiden led the way out, I followed, and Amala took up the rear. I tried hard, but I failed horribly in not watching Aiden's ass sway from side to side as he strode down the hall. His syths were strapped to his muscled thighs, and I couldn't help but bite my bottom lip.

I felt heat pooling in my core, and when I took a deep breath to calm myself, Aiden's head shook from side to side. SHIT. I was still not used to him knowing how I felt. Even after two and a half months, I was not used to this. How did his dad handle it? How were we going to handle it?

"Future you problems, Jess. Future you problems," I muttered to myself as we reached the plank to walk down to the dock. As I looked down the ramp, which only had rope along the sides, I froze. Aiden stopped and looked back at me as I slowly closed my eyes to steel that fear and shove it down. I had been eight when I fell off the plank and into the ocean. There had been rough seas, and the ship had slammed into the dock as I hit the water. I had been trapped for only five minutes under the dock while they got me out, but I'd been scared of falling off the planks ever since.

Aiden reached up and, with a single finger, itched his temple. *Are you okay?*

Giving a small, curt nod, I slowly lifted my foot, but I hesitated again.

I must have taken longer than I thought because Aiden was there, taking my hand and leading me down the plank. Looking over my shoulder behind me when we reached the dock, Amala, Jayden, and his guards were right behind me, as if nothing had happened.

Jayden smiled at us as he went to the carriage and loaded our things, Amala and his guard right behind him.

Aiden looked at me and squeezed my hand. "Breathe, Jess."

I blinked and slowly blew out.

"You good?"

"Yeah. Sorry. Took me by surprise is all. I've done really well in the last couple years. I swear."

"It's okay," Aiden said. He released my hand and said louder, "Duchess, the carriage is ready for our departure."

I mentally shook off the image as we made our way.

The sheer number of shouting press was overwhelming, but Aiden's hand on my elbow guided me to the awaiting carriage. When we got there, Jayden and Amala were already inside. I glanced at Jayden, who stepped out quickly and helped me in. It gave the illusion of the dutiful fiance for the papers that I was sure would be on the Grand Lord's desk by midday tomorrow.

Aiden, however, asked Jayden's guards to ride on the back. "Keep an eye out behind us. I will ride with the driver."

"Yes, Vernadali Aiden," they said as he closed the door. The carriage jostled a bit as the guards and Aiden climbed up, and then there were two quick knocks on the roof. I answered them, letting him know that we were settled, and the carriage started to move.

"How did the press know we were here?" I asked, looking outside as we sped down the street.

"Who knows. That large of a ship had to be carrying someone of importance. I have no doubt the reporters were thrilled to see us walk down that plank, though."

My eyes narrowed on four men trashing vegetable stands as we slowed and waited to cross one of the main streets that intersected the side streets. "Jayden?" I growled.

His eyes followed to where mine were, and I looked back at him. He was just as shocked as I was. Anger rose, and I fisted my hands in my lap, feeling the vibration of the fabric of my pants more than realizing my power had appeared.

"I don't. Jessika, I swear." He was stumbling over his words, shaking his head from side to side, and looked back out toward the men, who wore red and gold uniforms as they destroyed stalls in the market.

The carriage moved, and we lost sight of them, but Aiden was sticking his head in the window. I didn't look at him, but Amala said, "Nothing that Jessika can't handle until we get to the house, Aiden." Her voice was laced with violence, and I swore I saw her syth in her hand. "We will talk when we arrive. Jayden has some explaining to do."

I hadn't taken my eyes from Jayden, but out of the corner of my eye, I saw Aiden nod his head once and climb back up to the top. "Jayden, don't say a fucking word until we are settled. You have about ten minutes before Aiden rips into your ass."

"Aiden isn't the one I'm worried about," he said, looking at me carefully.

"For anything you think I might do to you, Aiden will do tenfold. He is my Vernadali. I swear…" I stopped talking, and he opened his mouth, but I cut him off. "Shut up, Jayden."

Eight minutes of complete silence followed. The entire time, I watched Jayden. I couldn't believe that he was behind it, but *someone* was in Kaletta colors. His eyebrows were pinched, and he would scratch at his beard then look off far into the distance.

Fear. Confusion. Betrayal. They each flowed through me in quick succession. I knew that Aiden would be fighting himself to stay in that seat, but… Jayden? Jayden wouldn't be behind this. He would have said something if he knew anything, right?

Two minutes later, we were standing in the living room of the house, and Aiden's Charge was flowing through the space, wrapping tight around me.

Aiden stood in front of me, arms crossed and looking like a mountain. "What the hell is going on?"

"Why don't we ask Jayden?" I said through my teeth. "Explain to me what we saw."

"I swear I don't know, Jessika," Jayden said, voice shaking.

"What happened? Someone needs to start talking." Aiden's voice was low and demanding.

"When we stopped at Crosswell and Talen, we had the perfect view of the marketplace, and persons in red and gold uniforms were destroying the produce stands." I felt my power flowing down my hands. I raised one hand and said, "So tell me, Jayden, why were there soldiers who appeared to be Kaletta Guards in my town? Why were they here destroying my produce?"

Aiden's head flipped around to him, and I felt more than saw his power ripple through viciously. Both Amala and Jayden winced as it flowed over them. "Excuse me?"

"I swear, Vernadali Aiden, I had nothing to do with this." He didn't break Aiden's stare.

"Then answer the Duchess." Aiden's voice was one I hadn't heard in years, and when I had, his big brother Owen had ended up pretty bloody after that fight.

"I don't know." He started pacing and jerked his jacket off, throwing it on the couch across from us. "I've been trying to figure it out the whole way here."

"I want to believe you, Jayden, but what we saw today speaks to the contrary."

"I swear it." Jayden's eyes were wide and pleading.

"Red and gold uniforms. Who else on this continent has those colors? No one," Aiden said.

"I would never hurt Jessika. I've done a lot to help her rebuild Ashridge. I want Ashridge to thrive. I told you as much on the fucking boat."

"Aiden." I knew that there couldn't be an ounce of mistrust between us. If Aiden was constantly wondering if or when Jayden would turn on us, then this was going to be a long lifetime. Sighing and knowing that Aiden would be pissed as hell at me, I said, "Test him."

"Jess." I heard the pleading in his voice not to ask him to do this. It wore on him. He would be out for hours afterward.

"I believe him, but you need that proof. I know the side effects. If he isn't lying, then you will be fine in a couple hours. I'll have Jayden and Amala to protect me until then."

Aiden looked to Amala who said, "I've got her while you're out."

He pinched the bridge of his nose and sighed. "Fine."

"What is he going to do?" Jayden stopped his pacing, and even his guards looked carefully to Aiden.

"This is going to hurt like the Underworld's depths," Aiden said, but before Aiden could give any further instruction, Jayden's guards were standing before him with syths out.

"Stand the Underworld down." Aiden rolled his eyes dramatically. "It's going to hurt me like the Underworld, not Jayden. At least, not if he is telling the truth. Jayden, tell them to stand down."

"Vernadali Aiden, you know the laws," one of his guards said. Jayden was standing very still, looking at all of us.

"I do, and if I am protecting my Charge, your laws cannot do shit to me. I stand above them." Aiden's voice held back rage. His eyes circled with purple, and I felt his Charge wrap around me. For as long as I'd known him, I had rarely seen him like this.

It was Jayden who spoke next. "Stand down. Whatever it is that Vernadali Aiden is going to do, I will endure it to prove to not only him, but also to Jessika, that I am not lying."

CHAPTER 9

AIDEN

"Sɪᴛ ᴅᴏᴡɴ ɪɴ ᴛʜᴇ chair." I pointed to the black oversized chair near the fireplace, where he slowly crossed the room and sat down. I stripped off my jacket and pulled my boots off. Luckily, the floor was hardwood, which would ground me as I did this.

I walked around to the back of the chair, rolled my head and shoulders, and took a deep breath.

"What do I need to do?" Jayden asked, his voice calmer now. I thought the fact that Jess trusted and believed him made him feel better, but Jess was doing this for me. I could tell in her eyes. She knew we had to have complete trust in the four of us to make this work.

"The things I do for you, Jess," I muttered under my breath, and there was a knowing smirk on her face that was then followed up with a warmth and tingle up my back. "Not now, for Angels' sake, Jessika Petra."

Her eyebrows shot up in surprise, and Amala huffed a laugh. Jayden just looked between us, confused.

I took a quick breath and said, "Just answer my questions with the truth, and you will only feel weird."

"Okay." Jayden sat up straighter in the chair, and I placed my fingertips on his forehead and pulled his head back to lie in my other hand, fingers at the base of his skull and the heel of my hand at the crown.

Slowly, I fed my power into him. The response from him was warm and smelled of... "Peppermint?" I whispered. I released his head and looked at Jess, whose eyes were questioning, but she smiled. She knew that if I was getting a smell or flavor from them, they were going in with openness.

Repositioning my hands on his head, I asked, "What is your full name?"

"Jayden Pasquel Panahov, Lord of Kaletta. Sole son of the Grand Lord of Kaletta."

"How old are you?" I felt him relax under my touch.

"46 years old."

"Your power?" I asked, more because I was curious than anything.

"Nothing special like Jessika's. Standard Sangra test results, higher healing scores."

I blinked. I looked to Amala and Jess who were just staring at Jayden.

"What do you want from Duchess Jessika Valenti?" I asked and saw Jess' eyes narrow at me. I tried to ignore the irritation I felt from her.

"Friendship, Vernadali Aiden. Only friendship."

"Did you lie to us the first night I met you?" Angels, I felt like a right asshole for going down this road. I had no doubt that he was telling the truth that night, but it was a way for me to verify the truth through this connection.

"No, sir. If you want verification, you may conduct this test on the two guards that accompany me."

My eyes flicked to them, and they stood at full attention. However, the one on the right had narrowed his eyes slightly, and I swore that was love and concern in that look.

"Pick one," I said, knowing exactly who he was going to pick.

"Ilris," he said without hesitation, and that same guard stepped forward.

"Lord Jayden, does the other guard know of what I speak?" My head was starting to tingle at the base of my neck, and I was very grateful that he wasn't a fighting interrogation.

"He does. You need not ask him to leave," Jayden said as I rolled my head, trying to fight off the tightening in my shoulders, and took a deep breath.

"Ilris, put your hand in his. I will channel through Lord Jayden," I commanded, meeting his eyes. Ilris reached out and put his hand in Jayden's.

"I'll prove a point," he said as he threaded his fingers through Ilris' and, without me saying a word, said, "Ilris is my partner. He accompanies me always and has been my lover for the last ten years."

My eyes met Ilris', and there was a dose of fear in them, but I said, "Is your relationship what Lord Jayden states?"

I felt that fear flood through, and the jolts of pain hit both Ilris and me, but when he looked back to Jayden, it soothed out. There was a small smile on his face before he said, "His relationship status with myself is accurate and true. Lord Jayden has my heart."

"Thank you, Ilris. You can stand back at your station."

I waited for Ilris to take his position back by Killy before asking, "Why did the Grand Lord send you to meet us in Kaletta?"

"The Grand Lord told me it was to impress upon the Duchess that we must marry by the end of the year. He also wanted me to tell the Grand Duchess he would not be signing any nullification of our arrangement, and that if she refused to follow through, he would go to Head Julian for enforcement."

"Did he tell you to deliver any other messages while you are in the Ashridge Territory?" I pushed.

"No," he said, but a spear of pain went through my head, and Jayden winced.

"Jayden?!" Jessika said, taking a step forward, worry in her voice.

"My father didn't give me any other messages to deliver," he said, but then he stiffened, and pain lanced through my hands, down my back, and to my legs.

I looked to Jess, and Amala had already taken a defensive position next to her. I looked at the guards, and while they were standing at attention, they both had a look of confusion on their faces.

Jayden's head turned toward Ilris, then toward Jess before saying, "Why does it hurt?"

"Because you didn't state the truth," I said, gritting my teeth through the pain. "What message other than marrying Jessika Valenti sooner did the Grand Lord tell you to deliver?"

"Nothing!" he said, but the pain speared through deep and true.

"Jayden, tell him. Tell him what you know," Ilris whispered.

I looked into Jayden's eyes, and there was confusion laced throughout them. I studied them more, sending my power through the neural pathways, searching.

"Aiden, it hurts," he said through a whispered plea.

"Shhh. Hold on." I found a strange thread in the recesses of his mind. I closed my eyes and concentrated on it, Jayden twitched, and then white-hot pain flashed through me. As slowly as I could, I backed away from its source and asked, "Does the Grand Lord have a witch in his employ?"

"Yes," Jayden said, that warmth and peppermint flowing through me at his answer.

I looked at Jess who asked, "Since when? There is no record of any witch assigned to your territory."

"She wasn't assigned through normal channels. My father found her in the underground. Why does that matter?" Jayden asked.

"Swear that you know of no harm to come to the Grand Duchess, Duchess, or her brother." I said, gritting my teeth.

"I swear I know of no harm to come to the Ashridge royal house," Jayden said, and there was just a twist of pain in that statement.

"Clarify, Jayden," I growled. His eyes met mine and were searching for what I meant. "You suspect something?"

He blinked twice, swallowing. "I swear I wasn't hiding anything. I just don't want to be the rumor mill." Swallowing hard again, I felt him relax and smelled peppermint through the connection. "I walked in on my father talking about removing some competition. I wouldn't normally consider that an issue, but with what I have seen today, I am second-guessing myself."

"Did the witch see you before you left Kaletta?" I asked, gritting my teeth at the needles that were pressing through my brain.

"Yes. When I met with my father. She usually lurks in the shadows."

I could feel Jess' and Amala's eyes on me, but I didn't break eye contact with Jayden. "Did you feel strange leaving that room?"

Jayden blinked and nodded. "I had a headache until about an hour before we got to the docks. So, for about four hours."

My shoulders were killing me, and the pain in my head was starting to throb. Not to mention that my knees were locked into place, and I hadn't been able to move them since that first spear of pain lanced through me.

"Do you know if the Grand Lord is at the cause of the issues in Ashridge?"

"Before today, I would have said no. However, after what I saw in the market, I wonder if the Kaletta soldiers in the Black Mountains are blocking supplies and if they are also at fault for what is going on here in Silentport."

It was all warmth and peppermint. There was a bitterness there, but I wasn't sure whether that was coming from Jayden or me. "Not to mention that Ashridge has had water problems. I also suspect those soldiers in the Black Mountains are doing something to redirect the snow runoff."

My eyes flicked to Jess, who was now chewing on her thumb, deep in thought. Slowly, I pulled my power from him and laid his head gently on the back of the chair. "Sit here. You are going to feel lightheaded for a few minutes while your brain becomes your own again. Ilris, Killy, can you please get him some water to drink, too?"

"Yes, Vernadali Aiden." Killy turned to the kitchen, while Ilris took large determined steps to Jayden, knelt, and took his hand, kissing it softly. I couldn't help the small smile that crossed my face.

A deep throbbing settled hard and fast into my head, making all the lights in the room way too bright. I flopped onto my stomach onto the couch, and promptly put Jayden's jacket over my head to block out the light.

"Aiden?" Jess asked, rubbing small circles on my back.

"Jess, just leave me alone. I really hate you right now." I groaned, but there was no bite to it. "Just get me something for my head and let me rest."

"Okay, Aid," she said with a gentle laugh.

CHAPTER 10

AIDEN

I QUICKLY DRESSED IN black pants, boots, and a long-sleeved shirt. For two days, we had been wandering our way through the city, gently asking what people knew about the attacks on the supplies, but we were not finding out much of anything. The marketplace continued to be vandalized, but they never did it while we were near. If we were at the marketplace, they were across town at the warehouses. If we were checking out the warehouses, they were wreaking havoc on the marketplace. Even the vendors were unable to tell us if they were actual Kaletta soldiers or not. Sure, the uniforms looked similar, but they said they couldn't be sure.

"You're going out," Jess chastised. I had to blink. She had her long white hair completely down and was standing there in just a tank top and short sleeping shorts.

Holy Angels in the ether. I swallowed hard to gather my wits. "I'm going to do some looking around. I've asked Amala to keep watch for a few hours." I turned back to my bag, pulling my syth belt out and fastening it around my hips. I rolled out the extra dagger and syth roll that I had and slid my syths into the sheaths on my thighs.

"Let me come with you," she begged, leaning against the door jamb. "Amala, too."

"No," I said, shaking my head. "What if something goes wrong? I can't chance you getting hurt."

"Aiden. You know I'm trained."

I turned to face her. "I do. And I know you are a damn good fighter, too, because, yes, there is a difference. But the answer is still no."

"Aiden. Between your Uncle Mickey, Uncle Logan, your dad, and the guards at Ashridge, you know I can take care of myself," she whined.

"Did I not just say that I know you are a damn good fighter? Angels, Jess. I know you can take care of yourself. Doesn't matter. I am responsible for your safety, and I say you aren't going." The woman was more stubborn than Mom.

"Is this my ex-boyfriend talking or my Vernadali?" she said, narrowing her eyes.

"Duchess Jessika Valenti, I am your Vernadali first and foremost. The rest is history and plays no part in this decision." Well, okay, it played a part. If something were to happen to Jess, I didn't know what I would do. "I swear you have cotton in your ears. You aren't listening to me."

"Your parents...," she started to say, but I cut her off before she could really raise my blood pressure.

"My parents are wholly different," I said, pointing a finger at her, then crossed my arms and, with my voice tight, said, "My mother was fighting her parents. My father was literally part of that fight. You know how much I hate how everyone brings them up. I love my family and would do anything to protect them." I stopped and took a deep breath. It wasn't like we hadn't had this discussion before, it was just that she needed to be reminded.

"LJ, Owen, and I have been compared to them our entire fucking lives. We are not them. Granted, the twins got elemental powers, and I got to carry on the Vernadali line, but we are not them. Mom and Dad got to play by their own special rules. We don't have that luxury. There are laws, rules, and a certain way of doing things. Don't make this harder than it needs to be, Jess."

She had the good graces to flinch at that. "You are right. I'm sorry."

I slid a couple other weapons into my belt and extra syths into my boots, the entire time feeling just how worried and concerned she was, but when the heat hit, I looked up at her and gave her a shake of my head.

Only, when my eyes met hers, she was biting that lower lip, and I could tell her mind was racing fast and furious. Slowly, I strode over to her, my heart beating quickly. "Jess."

Her eyes flashed with heat, and I saw her bite her lip harder as I stood in front of her. I lifted my hand to rest it on her cheek, and just when she started to lean into it, I reached back and pulled on her earlobe.

"AIDEN CHATWELL MATHEWSON!" she screamed, swatting my hand away and rubbing at both of her ears. "You know how much I hate that."

I howled in laughter and just said, "I'll be back in a few hours. Keep your mind out of the gutter, and try not to get yourself killed while I'm out."

"Asshole," she muttered.

"But I'm *your* asshole, and one that you are stuck with for life," I said, winking at her. I walked quickly out of there to give myself space, because I was sporting a massive hard-on from the way she was looking at me. That woman… ANGELS! I tried to discreetly readjust myself as we walked down the hall, but one of the servants at the house was holding back a smile.

Walking into the living room, Amala and Jayden watched us carefully, and I started chuckling again. Jess, on the other hand, kept muttering what an asshole I was and rubbed her ears as she shouldered past me.

Amala smiled through a fake groan when she saw Jess. "Aiden. Do you think you could not do that to her? She'll be jumpy for hours now."

"I haven't done it in five-and-a-half years. Give me a break. Besides, she deserved it."

"What did she do to deserve it?" Amala asked through her giggles. At the same time, Jayden questioned, "What did you do?" The way Jess continued to rub her ears and make a scrunchy nose face even had him giggling.

"You are all assholes," Jess mumbled.

"Don't make me repeat myself." I smiled at her, and this time she gave me a small sideways grin.

"What did you do?" Jayden asked again.

"Jess hates having her earlobes pulled. Puts her into a fit for a long while. What I want to know is, what she did to deserve it from Aiden," Amala said.

"She, umm, had inappropriate thoughts that were making it hard for me to concentrate. So, I fixed the problem," I said, running my hand through my hair, but continued, "Amala, as we discussed, I'm going out for a few hours. You've got Duchess duty."

"I'm not a child." Jess sulked, pulling her knees up to her chest, and resumed rubbing her ear.

Amala nodded in confirmation, and before anyone could call me an asshole again, I walked out, waving my hand quickly over the front door, putting a sealing spell on it. I didn't want anyone but Amala going in or out of that place. The only way Jess was leaving that building was if it were on fire.

TWO HOURS LATER, I was perched on the roof over the marketplace when I heard someone behind me. Slowly, I slid my syths out, and was just about to whirl around on the person behind me, when Amala said, "Easy, Aiden."

"Angels, Amala." I hissed, and then I looked at her and moaned. "Please don't tell me Jess is with you and that's why you are here? I spelled the house."

She shook her head. "Playing board games with Jayden. His guards are watching her. Yes, she tried to follow me and ran into a wall. Cussing your name, by the way."

I pursed my lips and gave her a look. She just rolled her eyes and moved closer to whisper in my ear, "I've been following four people dressed up in older Kaletta uniforms. They should be coming around that corner in just a moment." She pointed in the far-right direction, and just as she said, they came through.

Using their power, they smashed produce, tipped casks of wine, and overturned baskets of grain into the wine spilling into the street.

I motioned for her to follow me, and we jumped across a couple of homes before descending down a rain pipe to the ground in an alley. When they were at the stall just at the end, I looked to Amala, and we threw our power out at them, pinning them against the far wall. I felt them push back against ours, but I took a roll of rope that was in another stall and brought it up to hog-tie them in the air before dropping them in the middle of the cobblestone street.

"Neat trick," Amala said.

"*She* taught me all kinds of things that aren't in the records at Nalrin." I smiled at her, and when I looked back at the four pigs in the street, I crouched down next to one and looked at the uniform.

Cocking my head to the side, my eyes flicked to Amala, and she noticed the same thing. These were the old Kaletta uniforms. The Grand Lord changed them out about ten years ago for the fancier ones. "Who are you?"

The one before me spat at me, and when it hit my shoulder, I cringed.

"That is really gross. You know that, right?" I said, rolling my eyes. "Didn't anyone teach you anything about respect?"

"I'm not going to tell any Ashridge scum anything."

"Good thing I'm not Ashridge scum then." With a wave of my hand, two of the guards that were trying to worm their way away were flung back toward us and to Amala's feet. "Keep an eye on them, will you, A?"

She gave me a deadly smile, her eyes turning the poison green that meant true death if she willed it. When she reached forward, I saw that same green haze flow through her fingers in the night and the men's eyes go wide.

Amala just leaned forward. "Tell us what we want to know or you become a vegetable. Much like the ones you destroyed at the end of the street."

While my hands radiated a blue purple, the men in front of Amala looked to the man in front of me before looking back at her. "We won't tell you anything. If we talk, we are dead."

There was one just to my left who hadn't moved an inch since landing on the ground. Using my power to drag him in front of me roughly across the cobblestones, I crouched before him but paused. He was a lot younger than the rest. Thin and scrawny too. "Where did you get the uniform, kid?"

He shook his head in terror, looking at my hands.

"He won't talk. He can't. The Ashridge Guards cut out his tongue. You are just a bunch of fucking bastards," the one in front of me said again.

My head flopped in his direction, and I gave him a droll stare. "Will you please shut up?" With a flick of my fingers, there was a gag in his mouth. "Much better."

I reached over to the young kid and forced his mouth open. No tongue. "Did the Ashridge Guards do this?" I asked, but the kid looked at the others. "No, kid, look at me. I'm the only one who you need to be worrying about."

He shook his head.

"Kaletta soldiers?"

He looked away and gave me a small nod. "Is that why you are helping them?" I asked kinder this time, trying to suppress my rage. Another small nod.

"Don't move from that spot. Understand?"

Firm nod, yes.

I turned back to the piece of shit in front of me, then I looked at the two that were before Amala. Her hands were getting closer to the one on her right, and I cleared my throat. She turned toward me and narrowed her eyes. Raising an eyebrow, I asked, "Don't you think you should be asking them questions instead of just turning their brains to a pile of slime?"

"Fine. Take all the fun out of it," she said then looked at one of them and jumped back when the front of his pants had a very wet stain spread across the front of him. His eyes rolled back, and he started foaming at the mouth.

Then the other two older men followed suit.

"What the fuck, Amala?" I scolded. "We needed them alive."

"I didn't touch them," Amala said in defense. She looked over to the kid who spit out a tooth onto the street, and I sagged.

I gave her an apologetic look before saying, "Suicide teeth." The kid nodded. The poor kid was scared, and he really didn't look like he had anything to eat in days. "Are you going to cooperate with us? I'll get you some warm food and some blankets for tonight."

His eyes lit up, and I swore I heard his stomach growl at the promise of food. Angels, it may have been days since he ate last. I flicked my wrists, and the ropes around his feet fell to the ground. I left his hands behind his back just in case we were being played, but I did loosen them slightly so they didn't pull so much at the shoulders.

Amala went to work positioning the three men back-to-back and wrapping their bodies with a note for the guards in the morning. I pushed the kid along, and he looked up at me, trying to hide the fear that was flowing through him.

After we made it down about a block, Amala came and walked on the other side of the kid. It was another two blocks to the kitchen, and when we arrived, we were greeted by a tall burly man with a pot belly and long greying beard.

"Can I help you?" he said, putting his hands on either side of the door frame.

"I am Vernadali Aiden, Vernadali to Duchess Jessika Valenti. I'd like to ensure this boy gets food and a warm bed to sleep in this evening." I looked to the kid and, with a commanding tone a parent would take scolding their child, said, "But he gets the warm bed only if he answers my questions while he eats."

The guard at the door looked at me, then to the kid, and then to Amala and ran his eyes up and down, giving her a little smirk. "You can put that smirk away, big boy. Not interested."

"Shame," he said, shrugging it off. "Who are you?"

"Amala Jilnore." It was like she could care less who she was talking to. She didn't even give him a title. I huffed a laugh. She really didn't give two shits who he thought she was. And if he thought he would have a chance with her, good luck. She should already be Silnaree to Reka's brother, if either one of them would pull their heads out of their asses.

"And you are in the company of Duchess Valenti's Vernadali?" He raised an eyebrow at her, and she smirked as she looked him up and down before saying, "Yeah."

He gave us a quick nod and then led us to a corner booth where Amala and I could sit on either side of the kid, blocking him in. "I'll have one of the girls bring you a plate." About five minutes later, a strawberry-blonde girl who couldn't be more than twelve came up and gave us a plate of crumbled steak and rice.

I held it away from the kid for a moment and said, "You promise to tell us the truth?" He nodded and looked at the plate. His stomach growled loudly, and I slid the plate over to him.

"Since you can't verbally answer, you will have to clearly nod your head as we question you." Then I said, feeling like a right shithead, "If I think you are lying to me, I'll take the plate. Understood?"

He nodded.

I let him eat about half the plate before I started to ask questions, because he really did need the food. No kid should be this hungry. I asked him to slow down a bit since I didn't want him throwing it back up from eating so quickly.

"Did those men give you this uniform?" A nod indicating yes as he took another bite of rice.

"Did those three cut your tongue out?" I asked as softly as I could. He shook his head.

"Someone in Silentport?" Another shake of his head.

His hands motioned above his plate, pointing to the area just above it. I studied him for a moment, pointed to the plate, and asked, "Ashridge?" He nodded and pointed to a spot above the plate and then his mouth.

"Kaletta?" His head nodded quickly up and down.

I looked at Amala, whose eyes were big and round. "The guards in Kaletta did this to you?"

Shaking his head, he indicated someone wearing a crown.

"Ah, fuck. The Grand Lord?" His head nodded slowly. His hand moved in a gesture to indicate that he wanted to write something down, and Amala went to the guard who let us in, returning with a pad and pen. She slid it over to him, and the kid actually pushed the plate away and started writing quickly on the pad.

This kid was literate. His letters were well formed, and he wrote quickly and with purpose. There was no hesitation. This kid was raised with an education. I looked at Amala again, and when her eyes met mine, I knew she had realized the same thing.

When he was done, he pushed it between us. "Cut it out for talking in the hall outside of a governor meeting. I was sent here to follow Jared's directions."

"Jared was one of the ones who died tonight?" He nodded his head and smiled.

"Where are your parents?" Amala asked.

The kid's head hung low, and he ran a finger over his neck. He reached over and took the paper and pen again and scribbled, "I was a page at the palace. One of the guards is a friend. He helped me after they..." He froze and looked up at us, gulping. He didn't need to finish.

"Angels," I said, running my hand through my hair.

"Tell us everything you know about what the Kaletta Guards are doing here in Silentport."

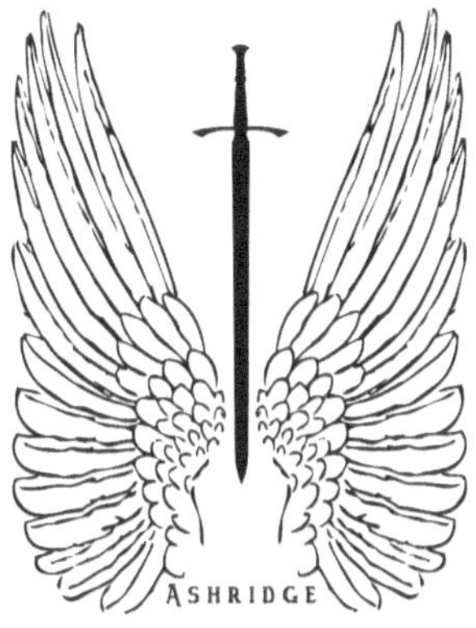

CHAPTER 11

JESSIKA

It was the middle of the night, and I was pacing the living room in nothing but a pair of booty sleeper shorts and a tank top. Aiden had left hours ago, and Amala an hour after that.

"Jessika, Amala is one of the best fighters we know. She will be fine. Aiden's a Vernadali. Not only will he protect her, but he can damn well take care of himself. Angels. On top of that, he's a Mathewson Vernadali. Have you seen Vernadali CJ fight? If Aiden can even remotely keep up with him, you have nothing to worry about," Jayden said.

"I know they can take care of themselves," I ran my fingers through my hair and completely undid the loose braid. I cussed and pulled at one of the tangles when my ring got caught. Jayden walked up, chuckled at me, and stopped my hand from moving.

"Jessika, take a deep breath," he said, untangling my hair from my fingers. Then he took the tie from the strands and said, "Now, put it back up and stop pulling at it."

I glared at him and threw my hair up in a messy bun. "They should have been back by now. Not to mention that Aiden... that fucking asshole, spelled the manor against me leaving. Before you come to his defense, yes, I felt the loopholes. I know I could leave if something major happened, but that's not the point. What if they are hurt? What if he needs our help?"

"Again, he's a Vernadali and one of the most powerful, badass bodyguards in the entire dimension. Amala graduated in the top two percent of her Nalrin Guard class. She specifically requested to be at your side. Head Julian has you protected better than even himself at times."

"Jayden," I said, flopping onto the couch.

"Jessika, I need you to be honest with me about something. I think I already know the answer, but we haven't had much time to ourselves to really talk because, well, Aiden does his job well."

I glared at him and said, "No. Aiden and I are not having sex."

"Angels, I know that. You would be in a better mood if you were getting laid on the regular. Which I hope you do soon, because you are wound up tighter than a top," he said, smirking at me.

"In what other arrangement does a fiance tell the other to go get laid?!" I was almost laughing at the craziness of it all.

"You are right. It does sound crazy, doesn't it? Let's be real though, if I weren't with Ilris, I would be all over that man.

How you even remotely resist is beyond me." He laughed as I tried to stammer out a response, but he cut me off, "Jessika, you know I find you beautiful, and I am attracted to you—"

"You have Ilris." I smiled warmly at him. "Jayden, I do not fault you. In fact, I am so glad you have someone who cares for you the way you deserve to be cared for."

"Which is sort of what I wanted to talk to you about." Jayden took a deep breath before he said, "Amala said that you and Aiden had been together before."

I nodded.

"How long ago?"

"About five years at this point." I was playing with my fingers and not looking at him. I knew where this was going, and I wanted to put it off.

"I'll be blunt," he said, coming to stand before me and taking my hands in his. "Jessika, look at me." I felt the tears in my eyes, and I tried to blink them away. When I thought I had them contained, I looked at him as he said, "Well, I guess that answers that. You are still in love with Aiden, aren't you?"

I couldn't speak. I just nodded.

"Oh, Jessika." He pulled me into a tight hug and we stood like that for a long time.

Jayden's guards came around the corner, and when I saw them, I stepped back. "Thanks. Go ahead and go to bed. I'll wait up."

Jayden looked to the guards, and through some silent command, they simply turned and went upstairs. "No. I'll wait here with you."

An hour later, the front door flew open, and Amala was half carrying Aiden through the door. Aiden's hand flung out, and one of the chairs slid across the floor to where they were standing just inside the room. I was there instantly, helping Amala get him settled.

His entire right side was saturated with blood, and it was seeping through his fingers as they pressed against the wound. Aiden was breathing in short quick breaths as I used my power to cut through what was left of the shirt he was wearing. When I saw the deep slash and two puncture wounds in his side, I hissed. The gash was deep, and you could see the fatty bits and muscle tissue pushing out.

"I already tried to heal it with my power," Amala said. "He just moaned in pain, and I couldn't get it to close."

I looked at Jayden, and we both put our hands over the wound, muttering the incantation to heal it in low tones. Aiden hissed and writhed, and I stopped when a yellow and green ooze came out.

The warmth of a summer breeze flickered through the house, and I looked at Jayden, who smiled and sent his power out again. A minute later, his guards were there with the med kit they always traveled with. There was a flurry of action, where Jayden pulled me back and his guards went to work on Aiden. They tore his shirt completely off, and my breath hitched when I saw the blood seeping into the chair and pooling onto his pants.

Jayden made me turn to face him as I heard Aiden grunt and moan behind me. "Don't look at him. Look at me. You need to calm down. He can feel your panic and can't concentrate on healing if he thinks you're in danger. I need you to calm so that when Ilris and Killy work on mending his wounds, he will actually heal. Deep breaths, Jessika."

He was right. That was how I could help him. I could control my emotions. I took short breaths at first, but slowly, they became longer and deeper.

Mmm. Longer and deeper. That single thought brought one of my favorite memories with Aiden when we were back at his parents' house near the forest. We had snuck off, and once we got to the waterfall, he dragged me back behind it to our secret little place. The way he had pushed me against the wall and kissed me was demanding. I had my legs wrapped around his hips, grinding against him in seconds.

"Jayden, I appreciate what you are doing over there to calm her anxiety, but change her line of thinking." I heard Aiden say behind me through gritted teeth and hissing breaths.

My eyes flashed open, and I flushed red as Jayden smirked at me. "Well, she isn't anxious and terrified anymore."

"Yeah, but she keeps that up, and I'm going to have a problem over here that I can't really—" He hissed and bit his lip as Killy sprayed something on his side and it foamed up. "That I can't really deal with."

"Aiden!" I shouted at him.

"Not my fault that your thoughts are giving me the warm and tinglies that settle at my dick," Aiden said through hissed breaths as Killy chuckled while working on pulling the discolored goo from the wound.

"Way to go, Jess. Give Aiden a hard-on while he gets tended to from being stabbed," Amala said, snickering.

"Speaking of. What the Angels happened?" I demanded of Amala.

"We caught some guys in the marketplace. One of them was a kid who hadn't eaten in days. We went and got him some food and a warm bed and he gave us some information." Amala was pacing across the room. She limped slightly, but she was ignoring it. Then she looked at Jayden. "They were wearing the old Kaletta uniforms. Most of Ashridge is used to seeing your soldiers in those colors, and they have always looked the other way. They don't look close enough at them to see how much they have changed. These are about ten years old. Your father has gone to a flashier set more recently, and these are faded and worn."

"I thought all guards had to turn in the old ones and they had been burned," Jayden said and looked to his guards who nodded.

"There shouldn't be any that are still out and available," Ilris muttered. "The orders were given, and I watched ditches full of old uniforms burn."

"What happened to Aiden?" I let some of my frustration flow through.

"He got stabbed." I wanted to knock the smile off her face.

"No shit. Really?" I rolled my eyes. "Now is not the time for your smart-ass comments. Now, tell me *how* Aiden got stabbed."

"After we finished talking to the kid, who gave us some extremely interesting info about your Grand Lord, Jayden, we left after ensuring the kid was taken care of for the next week. The guard said he could have him do some work as well to, and I quote, '*Earn his keep,*' even though Aiden paid him very well for the boy to stay there," she rattled off while removing her boots.

She leaned back on the couch and continued, "We were about halfway back when we got jumped. It was men dressed just like the ones at the marketplace, in the same ten-year-old uniforms. They are all lying in the sewer now, but not before one of them pulled a syth from his boot and got Aiden. They didn't say anything. Just jumped us and..." She raised her hand to her cheek and winced a bit when she touched it. "We will be bruised in the morning, but we lived. They didn't."

Ilris saw Amala wince and came over to take a look at it. "Looks like there might be a small break in the cheekbone. Hold on a second." His hand glowed a bright pink, and she winced as he ran his finger over a few spots on her face. "That fixes that one. Fixed a small hairline at the top of your eye too. What else hurts?"

She repositioned herself on the couch, but flinched at the movement, and I sent my power out to her. "She won't tell you, but her right knee, left hip, and left wrist." I tipped my head to the side. "Oh, and she has a few slices down her back."

"Bitch," she said then turned to Killy. "I'm fine. How's Aiden?"

"I'm fine," Aiden said, his rough voice closer than I expected. I turned my head to find him standing not a foot from me. I whirled around to him and took in the cut that Killy had cleaned up. It was stitched, and Killy was trying to put a patch over it, but Aiden kept batting his hand away. I grabbed his hand and narrowed my eyes at him. He sighed and then reached up to touch my cheek. I stepped back but kept a hold of his hand.

"No way. Last time you got near my face, you pulled my ear," I said sternly. He giggled but winced. I pulled him toward the couch and made him sit next to Amala. "Rest. Both of you."

As he turned, my hand grazed over his Maltal, and Aiden froze with a hiss through his teeth. "Is there a slice across my back too?"

"What?" I had him turn toward me, and his Maltal seemed to be shimmering. It was an intricate design to start: waves with an open-mouthed skull and ravens. The way it shimmered almost gave the skull and ravens movement. I ran my hands along the waves at the bottom, and he murmured how that felt cold, but when I moved to the skull that flowed out of those raging waves and ran my other hand along the ravens cawing next to it, he hissed.

Killy was there looking over it and running his hand just over the surface. "Vernadali Aiden, just how much of your power did you use tonight?"

Amala looked at him, and I saw Aiden's eyes meet hers. Not caring for the look between the two of them, I commanded, "Aiden. Answer him."

"I almost expended it all. It wasn't an easy fight tonight," he muttered. Killy was studying his back as the waves moved with the skull and ravens.

"Your power is regenerating quickly then," he said almost in awe as he ran his hand over it. "Is that normal for you? How are you feeling?"

"Stronger, but the wounds aren't healing any quicker."

"You are a Mathewson, so the standard rules don't always apply to you," Killy muttered as he looked at some of the other wounds on his back.

"The rules apply to me more because of my last name. The rules don't apply to my parents," Aiden said.

"Not when it comes to your genetic makeup. Who knows what you received from your parents, genetically speaking. Your father is the first Angels' Blessed—" he started to say, but Aiden cut him off.

"If anyone mentions my parents again, they are going to have a broken jaw." He growled and then practically plopped onto the couch and hissed when he leaned back.

"Stubborn ass," I muttered. "What Killy means is that your body may react differently because you are descended from Angels Blessed parents, you shit. He wasn't claiming you are special or have special abilities. He is simply stating that your body may react differently than every other Sangra in this dimension because of it."

His only response was a groan as his head hit the back of the couch, and he closed his eyes.

It took Aiden days before he would stop wincing at every little movement. His power returned, for the most part, by the next morning. It was faster than the usual Sangra, but I was still worried that he and Amala had been caught by surprise. I had also had a little bit of a shouting match with him that he could have been killed if Amala hadn't been there with him. He told me not to worry and that it was just part of the job. He left hours ago to do some more scouting, and I was a bundle of nerves. Now I was pacing in the upstairs lounge while Jayden read the local news.

"What is going through that head of yours, Jess?" Jayden said.

"Just worried about Aiden." I chewed on my thumb. "And the fact that he and Amala got jumped."

His head tilted to the side, and he studied me for a long moment. He turned and closed the doors behind us, ensuring we were the only ones in the room.

"What?" I growled.

"Cool yourself, girl."

"Sorry. What do you need to talk about? Rarely do you close the door so we are in a room alone," I said, then a smile crossed my face. "Usually that is only when there are appearances to be made."

"Aiden's out checking on some of the leads we have gotten lately, but just in case he comes back, I don't want him to hear this," Jayden said, scratching his beard. He kept it trimmed and short, and it did give him a bit of a distinguished look.

"I do like the scruff on you, Jayden."

That scruff couldn't hide the blush that filled his cheeks as he said, "Ilris asked me to try it, and as it turns out, he absolutely adores it." His eyes met mine and narrowed. "But you are trying to distract me."

I feigned innocence. "But I don't even know what you want to talk about?" He laughed before I said, "Should I be distracting you from this discussion? Is this one I don't want to have?"

"Oh, you are going to hate it," he said, smirking. "My father. I got a message this morning, saying he wants the wedding to occur earlier. Claims Ashridge is in dire need of Kaletta support and moral correctness."

"I'm sorry. What?" I said, blinking at him.

He just nodded at me.

"He can't be serious. He knows we are not in agreement." My heart started to race, and I heard Aiden come back and Amala ask how things went. I couldn't exactly hear his response, but I heard his footsteps come to the door.

"Jess? You okay?" he said, knocking on the door.

"Fine, just having a conversation with Jayden. We will be out in a few. Go get a drink. We will meet you in the living room." I tried to take a deep breath to calm myself, and once I heard his steps go back down the hall and down the stairs, I looked at Jayden.

"Jess," Jayden said, looking back at the door as if he were watching Aiden's back as he walked away. "Why aren't you trying to mend things with him so you two can be together?"

His voice was so quiet, I almost missed it.

"Aiden." I sighed and said, "Aiden decided to break it off with me, not the other way around. I think he knows how I feel. He has to. I mean, it's no secret he still turns me on."

I was staring at the door now, too, and when Jayden opened his mouth, I interrupted and said, "But that isn't really a possibility for me. Between his decisions and the situation with your father, even trying with Aiden isn't remotely feasible."

"Why not? You know I'm with Ilris," he said, shrugging. "Even if we were to marry, we would just have our separate relationships. We would have to produce heirs, but you know I wouldn't hold you to any oaths."

"I couldn't do that to Aiden. I mean, at the very least we would have to consummate the marriage, and while the thought of sex with you isn't a problem..." I looked him up and down and waggled my eyebrows and smirked. Jayden rolled his eyes and smiled at me in response. "The problem is that I couldn't keep Aiden in the shadows. That isn't how our relationship would work."

"That's one benefit to being in a relationship that is socially acceptable and not against the very laws of your lands," he said sadly.

"Jayden, that isn't what I meant."

"I know it's not, Jess. You have always been completely accepting of who I am, and I love you for that. I know that you are happy for my relationship with Ilris, but it isn't the same. My relationship can get me killed." His voice cracked at the end.

"Not in Ashridge, it wouldn't. Jayden, if we were to marry, you would be my duke. You would outrank your father in Nalrin. You could have Ilris as your official consort by law. Your father wouldn't be able to do shit," I said, trying to help.

"Except that if that were to happen, I would never be able to help the people of Kaletta or go back there ever again. And if you think that my father wouldn't go to very large lengths to murder me and Ilris in Ashridge, think again." His eyes were very hard at that statement.

"I'm sorry, Jayden." I took his hand and kissed his cheek.

"Back to the discussion at hand though. What did you mean when you said that your relationship wouldn't work if you named him your consort."

"Aiden and I had a certain dynamic." My cheeks reddened, but I also sighed defeatedly.

His eyebrows raised, then his head ticked to the side and he smiled in understanding. "A dominant and submissive relationship. Which is why you already had public hand signals to communicate."

I simply nodded.

"He was your dominant, which is why he couldn't be held to the shadows," Jayden said in understanding. Then he snickered, saying, "Part of me is surprised you are the sub, though."

"Really?"

"Yeah. You are the Duchess. You dominate any room you are in, just with your presence. I'm amazed you don't demand that in the bedroom as well."

"It's the release of that power for me. The liberation I feel when I can, albeit temporarily, hand over all the decision-making to someone else is amazing. However, that isn't the point of the discussion. There are so many other reasons why we couldn't be together. Him being a Vernadali being one of them. So, it doesn't matter." I unraveled part of the threading on my vest and tied a knot in it. "My very soul is in love with Aiden. I'm not sure I will be able to love another as deeply. Feelings aside, Aiden chose being a Vernadali over being with me."

"Vernadali marry, though," Jayden said just as a power rippled through the air.

We both looked at the door and back at each other before I said, "They can marry, but it's very hard on the family as the Vernadali has to stay with their Charge. If they weren't allowed to marry, then they wouldn't be able to continue the line, or well, I guess they could, but that isn't really the point. However, it is very strictly against all Vernadali rules to marry their Charge. Now that I am his Charge, there is no option for us."

A knot in my chest was forming as I went to the door and opened it, only to have Aiden standing there, his eyes filled with tears as he held a single sheet of paper.

"Jess," he said slowly. I took it, not taking my eyes from his. This was not good. Not good at all.

CHAPTER 12

AIDEN

THE MESSENGER WAS BANGING on the door and I was only two drinks in. I needed a whole lot more after tonight's scouting. Jess and Jayden were having a private discussion, and I had an uneasy feeling about tonight. Something was wrong or was going to go terribly wrong.

It didn't help that I felt this tightness in my chest and feeling of hopelessness from Jess. I wished she would just talk to me. Tell me what was going on. We really needed to work on our communication. Only, if I locked us in a room to hash everything out, I knew it would touch on subjects I really didn't want to talk about. We needed to, but...

I opened the door to a small page boy who couldn't be more than eight who said, "Message for the Duchess Jessika Valenti. Urgent. Must deliver immediately."

"I am the Duchess' Vernadali. I will deliver the message," I said as I reached down to take it from the kid. It had a high-level enchantment placed on it to ensure that only she received it. If that had been the case, then why not just send a Lark Messenger? Lark Messengers were used just exactly for that. Only she would be able to hear its song and the message it carried.

Closing the door, I looked at the writing and recognized it as the handwriting of Noah Husen, the Grand Duchess' personal secretary. I sent my power into it, breaking the spell. Being her Vernadali, the incantation would recognize the association, unless specifically protected against me. Opening the message, I read it once, stumbled back against the door, read it again to make sure I'd gotten it right, blinked, and then read it one more time. "No."

Amala was there instantly and took it from me. She read it, her hand covering her gasp, tears instantly streaming down her face as she read the words again and again. She looked up at me, then up the stairs to where Jess and Jayden were. "Jess."

"I'll tell her," I said, drawing up my power.

"Are you sure?"

Nodding, I took a deep breath to keep the dam from breaking within me, and without conscious thought, my Charge flew through the house. I had to protect her. She was the...

Looking up toward the room, I could tell by the way my power flew back to me that she was still with Jayden, but he was just going to have to deal with the intrusion. I took another breath to box away the devastation that was coursing through me and to gather the strength to do my duty.

"Yeah. Go have a drink, Amala. I'll send Jayden down and let him know. Tell him that we need to be packed and ready to head to Ashridge in two hours. We can use the horses to ride hard and fast. Get his guards to pack all their shit. We won't be able to take it all via horseback. They can ship it to Ashridge if they want." My voice cracked, but each word still came out a Vernadali order. "We leave in two hours. We have to get her back to Ashridge before word spreads."

She nodded. "Yes, sir."

I looked to the staff that had gathered in the kitchen. The cook's gaze met mine in confusion, but he nodded and said in an accent that was deep in the back of his throat, "I will prepare food so that you can eat well on the road, sir."

"Thank you." I looked up the stairs and took a deep breath. A single tear fell down my cheek, and I angrily brushed it away.

I took the stairs quickly, but I dreaded having to give her this news. When I reached the door, my Charge flung out again and searched for her. I visualized it wrapping around her.

"Protect her." Every fiber in my being recoiled from having to do what I needed to do next.

Protect her.

How was I going to do this? I looked down at the message, reading it again. A part of me wished I could change the words. I looked up at the door, bound to knock, when Jess opened it.

"Jess," I whispered through the lump in my throat.

She looked at me, then at the paper in my hand, and back at me.

"What has happened?" she said, standing tall and becoming the Duchess.

"Jayden. Go downstairs and Amala will bring you up to date. I need to talk to the..." I paused, because the title wasn't right anymore. "I need to talk to Jess."

He gave me a worried look as he walked by, but my eyes didn't leave hers. When his feet hit the stairs, I took Jess' hand and led her back into the room, closing and locking the door.

"Aiden," she said, blinking at me.

"Kotě." I swallowed hard.

Her hand tensed around mine, but she choked out, "What happened?"

I blinked, drew up my power, and became the Vernadali, the friend, the protector, she needed right now. "The Grand Duchess was found dead in her rooms this morning."

"What?" She took a step back, shaking her head. It was like the distance between us would somehow change the devastation that was settling into her.

"The Grand Duchess was found dead in her rooms this morning with a black snake head attached to her neck. Whoever it was allowed the snake to inject the venom and then killed it. However, they left its head still attached to her," I said, but my voice was all wrong. My voice was still holding that tone of a Vernadali, even if it had cracked in a few spots.

"Stop. Stop being a Vernadali," she said, tears filling her eyes. "Mom... Mom is dead?"

I nodded, and the next moment she was in my arms, sobbing. Picking her up, I carried her over to the couch, sitting her across my lap. I thought the pain I felt when I walked away from her was going to be the most painful thing I had ever experienced. I was wrong. So, so wrong. That was nothing compared to what was coming through the Vernadali bond from her now. The emptiness, the sorrow, the pure loss...

"I'm sorry, my kotě," I said, holding her to my chest as she cried. "I'm so, so sorry."

She sobbed for fifteen minutes before movement thundered around the house. Her head popped up, and she stared at the door before she burrowed back into my chest and arms. From behind the door, I heard Jayden's guards packing and ordering that the horses be prepared.

"What is going on out there?" Jess mumbled into my chest.

"I've given the order that we are leaving in..." I looked to the clock on the mantel. "...an hour and a half. We need to get you back to Ashridge before word spreads." I wouldn't tell her that there would be chaos in the streets, and there were going to be lots of people questioning her power. She would be tested over and over again during the coming months.

Jess' tear-filled eyes met mine, and another wave of grief rolled through her. I laid a hand on her head, pulled her toward me, and tightened my other arm around her, holding her tight. She cried on and off for another twenty minutes before she looked at me and said, "Thank you for letting me break down." She wiped her face, and what was left of her eyeliner smeared across the side of her cheek. I tried to clean it up with my thumb, but I just made it worse.

Sliding her off my lap, I went to the bathroom and grabbed one of the silver-colored hand towels. Wetting it, I went and knelt before her. Jess looked at me with red, swollen raccoon eyes, and I couldn't say anything. I just swallowed.

My thumb rubbed across her cheek, and she leaned into my touch. I felt warmth throughout my body and smiled. "May I?" I asked, holding up the wet towel.

She nodded her head, and I went to work cleaning the tear-smudged makeup on her face. If my time with her taught me anything, Jess would want to look more put together in front of her people. Sure, the puffy eyes, the occasional tears, the hitched voice, and the sadness on her face would all be expected. But Jess wouldn't want to look like a hysterical mess. She would likely be going without any for the next week while we rode hard toward Ashridge, anyway.

The tears continued to fall, but the sobbing had stopped for now. She would break down again, and I would be there for her every time. There was a primal satisfaction in that. I took a breath to shove that thought down, because all I wanted to do was take care of her, and here she was, finally letting me.

Jess reached out and took my hand. "Aid, who would do this?"

I shook my head. "I don't know for sure, but once we get to Ashridge, I'll meet with the Nalrin Guard stationed there and we will find out."

She moved to stand, and I asked, "You sure you are ready to move? Once you get off this couch, we need to get going, and there's no stopping after that." She nodded and stood, but she pulled me into a huge hug.

"I'm glad you were here when I found out." Jess reached up and kissed my cheek as she pinched my hip.

I blinked and slowly turned my head to look at her. She smiled sadly, pinched my hip once more, and strode for the door without looking back.

My heartbeat drummed in my ears as I watched her step out toward the stairs. Did she?

She just told me twice that she loved me. I took a shuddering breath, not only to calm myself, but also at the wave of sheer determination that flowed through me. There was that need to have her again, to make her mine. I took another deep breath when her voice echoed from the top of the stairs, "As Vernadali Aiden has commanded, we leave in 30 minutes. Understood?"

"Yes, Grand Duchess." The house sounded off. There was a pain in my chest that came from Jess at hearing the title, but I slowly turned toward her as she stood, back straight and tall, at the top of those stairs.

"Vernadali Aiden," she said, pulling on all her royal training.

I opened my mouth, but I had to swallow first before I said, loud and clear, "Yes, Grand Duchess." The words felt wrong in my mouth, but that was her title now. I had tried to say them earlier, but they had gotten stuck in my throat.

"Time frame confirmed?"

"Confirmed," I said loud enough for the house to hear. Then she strode down the stairs calling for Amala.

"Lord Jayden." His red and glassy eyes met mine from the bottom of the stairs. We all had known the Grand Duchess. We had all loved her. There was pride and pain in his face for her, and it confirmed how much he cared for her. He stood there, all regal lord as he faced me.

"Yes, Vernadali Aiden?" As Jess passed him, she reached out and squeezed his hand for a moment, and she let it go as she turned toward the bar room.

"Will you and your guards be ready to leave when we do?" I asked as I reached the bottom of the stairs.

"Yes, sir. We would like to request that we accompany the..." He paused for a moment and swallowed thickly before saying, "Grand Duchess to Ashridge. I would like to offer my guards as additional protection while we travel."

"Much appreciated," I said, sagging. "Now that the formalities are over, are you okay?"

"Heartbroken for Jessika. She's going to be okay, though, right?" His eyes flicked toward the bar room where she was holding Amala. The tears were flowing again. Her shoulders shook, but I knew she would pull herself together.

"She will be, but she didn't just lose the Grand Duchess. She lost her mother, and not two years after losing her father," I said. "They loved each other fiercely. Now she has to get back to Ashridge and somehow pull herself together between here and there over the next week to become her mother."

"Any idea who did it?"

We had both been watching Jess, but when I looked at him, Jayden's lips thinned. "Yeah. That was my first guess too."

"Jayden." I jerked my head toward the corner next to the stairs. We tucked ourselves into the corner, where it was a little more secluded, and I lowered my voice so that only he could hear me, "Tonight I found eight Kaletta soldiers watering down the grain and smashing the produce in the warehouse near the docks. I also have been receiving reports that it has been Kaletta ships cutting the crab pods and fishing nets offshore to cripple the supply here in Silentport."

Jayden leaned against the wall with a heavy sigh. "I was going to tell you when you got back tonight. I've been working with a network of spies here in Silentport. They said the same thing. That they have actually seen Kaletta soldiers, in current uniform, sabotaging the fishing boats and gear."

"What is your father playing at?" My anger was rising.

"I don't know. I really don't know," he said, scratching his beard, then his eyes went hard and cold. "All I know is that if he killed Jessika's mom, I will kill him myself."

"You will have to get in line. I will relieve him of his head so fast, he won't know what hit him, but only after I've used some special torture methods that only the Vernadali know." My eyes flicked back to Jess, who had pulled herself back together again and was giving orders to one of the house staff. "But that woman in there? She gets first go at him. We will be lucky if she doesn't vibrate him to a pile of goo without so much as a bone fragment left for us to torture."

Jayden's eyes met mine, and there was a smile on his face that promised death. "Glad we are on the same page, Aiden."

WE WERE MINUTES FROM leaving when a high-pitched chiming sound came from the back of the bar room. "I'll be back in a minute." Amala and Jayden's guards immediately circled Jess.

I pushed on the hidden door at the back of the bar, and the chiming got louder. Before I hit the button, I closed the door behind me. The room was completely soundproof, and we had only heard the chiming because of the speaker system in the house.

"Aiden."

"Dad?" I said carefully. His voice sounded much how I imagined mine did: rough, emotional, and worried. "Are you okay? Mom?"

"We are fine," Dad said, but then the screen panned over to where Julian was. They all looked like they had been crying.

"Head Julian," I said, putting my fist over my heart.

He rolled his eyes and waved his hand in dismissal. "Bah!"

"I'm with the Grand Duchess. We are heading back to Ashridge immediately," I advised them.

Julian released a breath. "You received word."

I nodded. "Has anyone notified Duke Lemi yet?"

"No. We are working on it, though. Last we heard, he was on assignment with his family in Cinder," Julian said.

I thought for a moment. "I'll have Jess LightCall him if you can give me a secure location for it once we are there. We should be in Ashridge in about a week." Julian nodded, and then I looked toward my mom.

"Auntie Clarice left a couple of prowlers here in Nalrin. We are taking them to Ashridge tonight, and we should be there this time tomorrow. We will hold things down until you and Jess arrive." I took a deep breath, then another when my mom's eyebrow cocked up. "Aiden, we are not testing you. We will only be holding down the fort until you and the Grand Duchess arrive," she said, forcing out the last few words.

I closed my eyes and leaned my head back. Of course, they would be sending Mom to Ashridge. Who else would they send? I shook it off. My personal issues had no place here. The only thing that was important was safely delivering Jess to Ashridge.

"Why aren't you and Dad just teleporting to Ashridge? Why take Auntie's prowlers?" I asked.

"You know Julian likes to have us make an entrance." She rolled her eyes and smiled.

"And you like making them." Popa Julian chuckled back, to which Mom just shrugged. "Besides, this was an assassination. The dimension heads locked things down again. I'm sorry, otherwise I'd set provisions for you to transport directly there, Aiden."

I nodded and looked toward Jess as if I could see through the wall and into those onyx eyes. "Will it be safe there?" My head whipped back toward the screen, and in a voice that was pure commanding Vernadali, I said, "The main hall and residence buildings must be secured before she arrives. Find the persons who did this before I get there if you can."

There was a slight narrowing of Mom's eyes before Dad put a hand on her shoulder. "And just what do you think we will be doing there, Vernadali Aiden?" Mom said, her tone thick with anger.

"I would like to hope that you will be making sure that the Grand Duchess will be safe when she arrives there, Lady Megan," I said, matching her tone.

"Babe, he's doing his job." I heard my dad say. "He is a Vernadali protecting his Charge."

"He's back talking his mother," she complained, but her eyes had softened.

"And I wonder where he learned how to do that?" Dad smiled at me. "He is demanding that we do our job and ensuring that Jess is safe when they arrive in a week." He kissed the top of her head and she dropped it.

I shook my head. "We were just about to walk out. Do you have any other information for us?"

"Any idea who it might have been?" Julian said.

"I do," I said, letting out a long breath and running my hands through my hair. "I think it's the Grand Lord of Kaletta."

Stares and slack jaws met me on the other side of the LightCall.

Julian recovered the quickest. "Aiden." Then he blinked again. "Any proof as to that?"

"Not yet, but considering what I've seen here in Silentport..." I hesitated for a moment but continued. "His ships and soldiers have been seen sabotaging the food production and stores here. Lady Amala and I caught some soldiers in the marketplace. They had suicide teeth, so we weren't able to get much from them. One, however, was a small boy who had his tongue cut out by them. He gave us a bunch of information that we have confirmed since then."

"Those are large allegations, Aiden," Julian said carefully.

"I know, but when Lord Jayden asked me who I thought it was, his only response was that he was thinking the same thing. I'm not sure—" Mom cut me off.

"Lord Jayden? He is with you?" she asked, surprised, and she looked back to my dad who had the same confused look on his face.

"Yes. He met us on the ship in Kaletta." I looked to each of them through the portal and said, "What don't I know? What aren't you telling me?"

"Nothing," my father said, looking off to the side.

"Don't you nothing me. This is Jess, Dad. What aren't you telling me? Do I need to be worried about Jayden being around Jess?"

"Calm down, Aiden. No. We just thought he was still in Cinder. Honestly, none of us knew he was back on Nalrin soil, let alone had joined back up with you and Jess, clear across the continent."

"Is she safe with him? In your opinion?" I felt weird even asking that question. Everything Jayden had done and said around her made me believe he would protect her to his dying breath. Just as I would.

"Jayden, yes. What guards did Jayden bring with him?" Julian asked.

"Killy and Ilris. Killy is a damn talented healer, too. Got into a bit of a scuffle the other night, and he healed me up pretty good."

"Just Killy and Ilris?" Julian said, cocking an eyebrow. I nodded, and he said, "Then you and the Grand Duchess are safe. Angels, I can't believe I'm having to call Jess that," he said, shaking his head.

Dad was whispering instructions to someone off screen, and I narrowed my eyes at him. Mom elbowed him, causing him to narrow his eyes at her.

"Who else is there?" I growled.

A curtain of bright purple hair jumped in front of the camera and I groaned, fully annoyed now. Her bright blue eyes smiled at me. "Hi, Aiden."

"Let me guess, Owen is there, too." I rolled my eyes. "Hi, Lindy Jean. Hi, Owen." Then my brother's head popped into view, and they waved. "Great. Let's just have a fucking family reunion," I muttered. "The only ones missing are Uncle Logan, Aunt Amber, Auntie Kait, and Uncle Mickey."

"Mickel is currently working on getting things ready for us. He's here, but just not right here. He's staying in Nalrin, though," Mom said, glaring at Julian, who muttered, "We will see about that."

Only Mom could push Julian. I huffed a laugh and ran my hand through my hair again. "You know, I don't want this to be a family affair. Just because I am a Mathewson, doesn't mean that the second my Charge is possibly threatened, I call in the clan. Yes, I will admit, some of it is pride, but I have trained for thirty-five years to be a Vernadali, one of the most badass fighting forces in the realms. Dad, Uncle Mickey, and Uncle Logan trained all of us to be able to not only take care of ourselves, but those we love and care for. Why do I feel like I'm still being treated like a three-year-old who isn't even able to take care of a pet fish?"

"Aiden, that isn't what we are doing. We are not challenging your ability to protect Jessika," Mom said carefully. She used that same tone on Dad many times when his Vernadali was coming out. I almost chuckled at it.

"Jess doesn't want to use the Mathewson name to fix things in Ashridge. She wants to do this on her own. She doesn't want our help."

"We are only ensuring that Ashridge stays stable while you two are enroute. You know as well as I do that there is likely already chaos in the streets right now. Governors and other officials are hoping to use this opportunity to take over," Mom said. "You aren't using the Mathewson name, Aiden. Julian is ordering Lady Megan there to handle the Governors until the rightful ruler arrives and instills unity and solidarity."

"Just don't go all Bellstar on them, please?" I said, pinching the bridge of my nose. That had everyone huffing a laugh, except for Julian. Back in the Keller War, Mom had removed Bellstar of its existing management quite violently. "I don't want to have to help clean that mess up."

"Me, either," Julian said under his breath.

"Seriously, Aiden. This is Jess. We all love her. Let us help." LJ's voice was full of the sadness everyone was feeling at the loss of the Grand Duchess. "I... We know you are her Vernadali. We won't get in your way of that. In fact, I will defer to all your commands in regard to her safety because of it. While Owen and I are in Kaletta, we will keep in contact. You run point on all of this. I know we have had our differences and you want to prove yourself. More than that, I know you want to keep her safe because you still..."

"That's enough," I said, growling through my teeth.

"Let me make something clear." I looked them each in the eye as Owen and LJ stood next to Mom and Dad.

Jess.

I had to remember they were trying to help Jess.

Put your fucking pride aside, Aiden Chatwell Mathewson.

Taking a deep breath, I redirected my thoughts. "LJ and Owen. While in Kaletta, be careful. The message we received from the Grand Duchess' secretary was that she was killed with a black chiklory, and its head was left in her neck."

"What?" Julian said. Well, they had heard she died, but not how.

"A black chiklory snake. That means that they imported it through the underground. They don't want it tracked." I watched as they realized the most venomous snake in Nalsar had been used to kill her. "If it is the Grand Lord who did this, he will be covering his tracks. Follow the breadcrumbs. Be careful."

"Of course," the twins said in unison.

"Mom. Dad. I'll see you in Ashridge in a week. Popa...," I said, realizing how true the words were. I met his eyes, which were big and soft. That little man had the heart the size of the Underworld. "Thanks for the help in protecting Jess. Thank you all."

"Of course, Aiden. Swift travels, and may the Angels give you wings," he said before the LightCall blinked out.

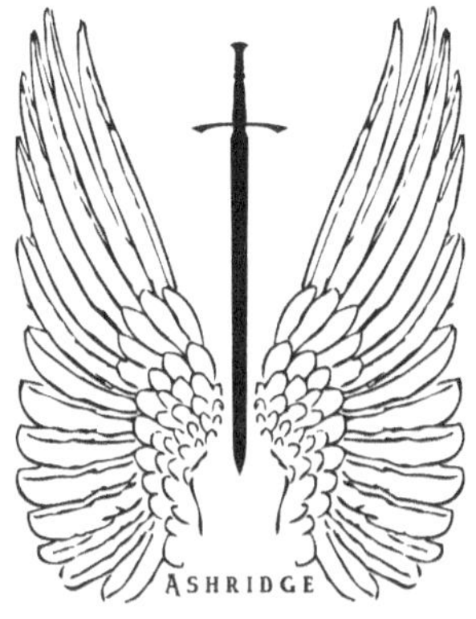

CHAPTER 13

JESSIKA

MOM WAS GONE. SHE was really gone. The tightness in my chest threatened to strangle me as we bolted across the countryside, but then Aiden told us that the entire Mathewson family was helping on this assignment. I knew that would be grating on him, and I worried more for him than I did for me. I couldn't change the fact that someone killed my mom.

"Aiden, you okay?" I asked when we stopped just outside of Greenvale. He had bitched about the whole family coming to help but said that he realized that this was bigger than his pride. He had always struggled with being the youngest in the family, and it was a powerful family at that.

Dawn was breaking behind us, and we had to let the horses get some water. Maybe we could get some fresh ones. I dismounted and looked at the entrance to the general store, where the storekeeper had just flipped the sign saying they were open. Jayden's guards went straight in and started picking out some supplies. Luckily, none of us were dressed in uniform. I didn't want to cause a scene in case someone recognized me and had heard about my mother.

Jayden and Amala were talking in low whispers, so I turned back to Aiden. "Seriously. Are you okay?"

"Jess, don't worry about me. I will always have this family drama. I'm much more worried about you right now," he said, dismounting and coming to stand before me. "I'm really concerned about you, actually. I'm not getting much of any emotion from you. Are *you* okay?"

I nodded my head. He studied me a bit more, and I pulled him close for a hug. I just needed his arms around me. "I'm not sure what to feel. I'm a little numb. Almost like I won't believe it until I get to Ashridge, have to preside over her rights, and light the pyre." Angels. I'm going to have to light her pyre. Would my brother even be there? "Aiden, do you know if word has gotten to Lemi yet?"

"When I talked to Head Julian, he said he didn't know. They are in Cinder, so Julian will secure a LightCall so you can talk to him when we get home, okay?" he tried to assure me.

"I'm going to go get some more water for the day. Refill the canteens. We should find shelter tonight. I overheard the guys say there were storms rolling in," Jayden said.

Nodding, I looked around at the sky, trying to get a sense for just how soon those storms were coming. Things looked a bit dark in the horizon, but it was still a ways off. "Let's see if we can make it to Santalava. It's a small enough town that we should be able to hole up for one night undetected before we head for the mountains. I don't suspect anyone will think we would have made it quite that far yet. Plus, I instructed the ship we were on to sail at dawn. Most will think we left on the ship."

I ran my hands along the zipper of his jacket, looked down between us, and smiled. He was in a pair of jeans, riding boots, a T-shirt, and the sexier than hell leather jacket. My gaze slowly roamed up his neck and along his jaw before meeting his eyes. Angels be. Five years had done absolutely nothing to loosen the hold he had on me. My hand lay over his heart, and I felt its consistency thrumming underneath.

"Jess, you keep looking at me like that, and I'm gonna start thinking other, less honorable things," he said with a knowing look.

"Aiden, I know there are a lot of things we still have to talk about. Things we are both too fucking chicken shit to say. I know that there are things we have to work out, but I am eternally grateful that the Angels assigned you as my Vernadali. There isn't anyone else I would rather have here."

His heart jumped at my words, and he gave me a quick kiss on the top of the head. "I'm glad I'm here for you too, my kotĕ."

I smiled. The first time he had called me kitten, I had wrinkled my nose at it. Then he said that kitten was too long, so, we took the old Chantil word for it and adopted it. Still to this day, it made my heart skip when he called me that.

Jayden and Amala came back with the water, and his guards worked to secure the canteens to the packs.

"The horses need some more rest," Amala said with a sigh. "Greenvale doesn't have any for us to switch out, though."

"Aiden can fix that," I said, giving him a look.

"I can?"

"You can." I smiled and crossed my arms, letting him figure it out. He had done it so many times when we were way too far away from our parents to get back in time without getting in trouble.

"I can?" Aiden said again, still confused. He stared at me, and just when I saw Jayden from the corner of my eye start to open his mouth, realization dawned in Aiden's eyes, but he rolled them dramatically.

"Angels, that took you way too long to remember." I chuckled.

Amala looked at me and then to Aiden, and then she figured it out. "The travel incantations."

"The travel incantations?" Jayden asked.

"Empress Clarice used it on Vernadali CJ before they knew he was a Vernadali during the Keller War. It is an incantation that helps with energy and endurance. Lady Megan also used it on some horses coming back from her honeymoon, and then on some of Empress Clarice's prowlers," Aiden explained. "Lady Megan ensured the three of us knew how to use and cast them in case of emergency. Vernadali CJ was particularly tedious with me about it. Especially once I was classified as a Vernadali."

"Well, that would be helpful," Jayden said.

"Horses and riders?" Aiden asked.

I thought about it. Since we rode most of the night, we were all going to be tired, but we were all highly focused on getting home. I looked at each of them and noted the bags under everyone's eyes. "Yes, both please."

Aiden stood back, took a deep breath, shook his hands out, and then looked at me. I nodded in reassurance. Closing his eyes, he brought his hands out to his sides, up over his head, and then back down into a prayer position. His eyes popped open as he moved his hand to form a triangle and then flat again repeatedly as he mumbled, "*Gil mah re spree en phis.*"

A blue-purple film layered over each horse, then he turned to each of us, repeating the incantation with the movements. When it lay over me, I closed my eyes. It felt like small jolts of electricity flowing over me from the tip of my head to my toes.

I sighed when it settled within me and smirked.

Amala started giggling. "Is this what your mom feels like all the time? I feel like I've had about eight cups of that Manusian drink she loves so much. Coffee. That's it." Jayden and his guards giggled as well. Even the horses seemed to huff at the comment, but then my chestnut gelding pawed the ground and rubbed against my hip.

"I swear Mom lives off that stuff," Aiden said. "Come on. We have a lot of ground to cover before nightfall."

SANTALAVA WAS A CUTE little town up on a cliff overlooking the ocean. It was one of the few places that could grow produce successfully. I wasn't sure why, but Santalava had escaped a lot of the sabotaging of goods. The only reason we could think of was that it was up on the bluff on the east side, and along the west was a cliff made from the sands of the desert between here and Ashridge, therefore leaving it protected and hidden.

We would be continuing south to avoid wearing out the horses getting across the desert. Camtulas, a giant lizard made for traveling across sand, would have been better, but I hadn't seen any at the stable as we entered town.

The gelding I was on was slowing, and I was feeling the fatigue start to wear on us. We had been going for a full day. Thirty-eight hours straight of hard riding, with small breaks for food and water, was not the ideal way to spend the day. I looked at the hotel with longing and tipped my head toward it when I made eye contact with Aiden.

He put his heels to his horse and went to secure rooms for us. Instantly, I was surrounded by Jayden and Amala on either side as well as Jayden's guards in front and behind me.

"I don't need to be surrounded. You leave me alone when Aiden's here. What's so different?" I said quietly so no one on the street could hear.

"Aiden is your Vernadali, Grand Duchess. We are your guards," Killy said, turning back to smile at me.

"No, you are Jayden's guards," I said, raising my eyebrows.

"Not until we deliver you to Ashridge," Killy muttered.

Jayden turned toward me and said, "When we found out, I offered my guards as additional security. That includes myself."

"Jayden, you need them."

"They will protect me if I'm in danger, but I've also given them orders that if it comes between the two of us, they are to protect you first and foremost." His eyes flicked to Ilris, then back to me.

"I'm going to assume one particular guard fought you a bit on that order," I said, hearing a nervous chuckle behind me.

Jayden's smile grew, but his eyes met Ilris' and warmed when he said, "You could say that. It took a bit of convincing, but he will protect you, just as Amala and I will."

"All I know is that right now, I could use a good night's sleep," Amala said. "The incantation was great. It got us here, but I'm crashing. I'm not sure I'll remember much after my head hits the pillow."

Killy laughed, but it was a weary sound. "The bed will be lucky if I get my boots off first." He made his point with a huge yawn that sounded like a wild beast's mating call.

Twenty minutes later, we had unpacked and each had our own assigned room. Aiden had insisted upon everyone eating, but the most he got was a loose promise from the rest of us to put something into our stomachs before crashing for the night.

"I'll eat with you, Aiden. I'm dead tired and sore, but I don't think I can sleep yet." I was exhausted, but I knew I needed the food. It would make Aiden happy, too.

A few minutes later, he came in with a tray of food that smelled divine. When he lifted the cover, he revealed a roast stew. Warm comfort food.

"I could kiss you for this, Aiden." The words flung from my lips before I realized what I had said. I froze, but then I just reached over to take his bowl and spoon. I could feel his gaze on me and the redness in my cheeks. "Just shut up and eat, asshole."

There was a huff of a laugh, and when I lifted the first spoonful to my lips and tasted it, I moaned. Its calming heat spread through me as I took another spoonful. I stopped and looked at him with narrowed eyes, "Did you enchant the stew?"

There was a sideways smile from him, but he said, "No. I swear it. I should have thought of that, though."

I took another spoonful and kept my narrowed gaze on him.

"I swear it, Jess." He narrowed his eyes at me mischievously and said, "If I had enchanted it, I would have done something much more entertaining than just warming you from the inside out in comfort."

"Oh, really?" I teased back. "And just what in the name of the Angels would you have done?"

"Something to warm you, alright, but it would have been concentrated on a very specific location of your body."

"AIDEN!" I exclaimed and started laughing as he joined in. Everything about this conversation was easy. It was almost as if nothing had changed, though everything had.

"I have missed this," I said, finishing off the bowl of stew. "Just us, giving each other a hard time and enjoying the company."

He looked down at his bowl. "It is nice." There was a small smile on his face, but I could tell his mind was racing.

I reached over and put my hand on his knee. He leaned back and put his hand on mine. A small smile crossed his face as his head rested on the back of the chair, and he ran his thumb across the back of my hand.

Warm admiration spread through me. I could sit like this all night, and we stayed like that for a few minutes before he said, "Come on, Kotě, let's get you to bed."

CHAPTER 14

AIDEN

I SAT THERE, STARING at the bathroom door, the entire time she washed up and changed for bed. That woman was something else. I had felt the devastation and pain in the breakdown she had as she cried in the shower. It was everything I could do to keep from going to her. The thing was, I also knew she did it there because no one could see her and she wanted to appear strong, even in front of me. She was the Grand Duchess now. If things were complicated before, they sure as the Underworld were an even more tangled mess now.

I blinked, and she was humming to herself as she exited the bathroom. How long had I been zoned out? I shook my head but then looked her up and down. She was in a short silk night dress, and her long white hair was up in a messy bun. Angels. That greedy part of myself wanted to push her against the wall and make her submit to me like she had so many times before.

"Fall asleep?" she asked carefully.

"Just thinking, I think," I said, getting up and striding across the room to the door that adjoined our rooms before I did something really stupid.

"Aiden?" Her voice was tentative and low. I turned to her, and she said, "Can you stay until I fall asleep? I know that sounds childish, but..."

"No problem," I said, not letting her finish. I gritted my teeth for restraint but tried to smile at her. Once she was under the covers, she sat against a bunch of pillows and patted the space beside her. I sat down, and she snuggled up next to me.

"What do you think waits for us in Ashridge?" she asked, her voice almost trembling. I looked down, and her face was wet again. I ignored it but moved the strands of hair that were sticking to her face back behind her ear. I swore I felt a tingling of her power flow through that touch.

"I don't know." Taking a deep breath, I said again, "I don't know, Jess. I don't know a lot of things right now. I know that isn't what you want to hear from the person who is supposed to protect you, but I can't lie to you, either."

She nodded against my shoulder. I felt her face move and twitch, and at one point when I looked down, her brows were furrowed in concentration. I rubbed them smooth, and she looked up at me, smiling, before laying her head back down on my shoulder.

"Aiden?" Her voice was thick, and I pulled back to look at her. "Why did you leave me?"

I blinked. Well, there it was. The dragon in the room.

"Jess, is now the time for this conversation?" Yes, I was a chicken shit. Yes, I was avoiding the whole discussion completely and would continue to do so for as long as she would let me.

"If not now, then when?" she said, sitting up. She wasn't angry. There was nothing but sadness, which was a constant since we left Silentport, and now there was also a thread of confusion.

"I told you why, Jess. I'm a Vernadali and you are the Duchess. Grand Duchess now. How was that supposed to work?" My voice was half stuck in my throat at saying the words. "You have an entire territory to run. I have one person to protect. I would have had to stay with that person always. I couldn't be there to help run a territory and be a Vernadali. I can't change who I am, Jess."

She snuggled up next to me again, and I wrapped my arm around her.

"That isn't the case now, though." Her voice was so small, it broke my heart.

"I know, my kotě," I whispered. Now it was so much worse. She shuddered next to me, and I pulled the blanket up closer around her.

"Now you are *my* Vernadali."

"Exactly." I breathed the word more than said it. She didn't understand that it wasn't going to be viewed the same way that I saw it. She saw it as the solution. I knew that. I, however, still saw it as a very real problem.

Her hand was running up and down my thigh, and we both knew what she was doing. It wasn't fair, but I couldn't bring myself to stop it.

"Now you have to stay with me." She was leading this conversation toward another one I really didn't want to have with her.

"Jess," I said, hissing her name as her fingers ran just a little too close to the hardness she was creating. She didn't stop, though, and a second later, I was lying on top of her, pinning her hands to her sides.

The heat in her eyes as she looked back at me almost melted any and all self-control I had. My hips still moved without conscious thought against her as I growled at her in frustration and excitement. When her moan hit me, I was up and off the bed instantly.

I couldn't do this. I couldn't do this to her.

"Aiden?" The worry and touch of disappointment in her voice hurt.

"I want nothing more than to bury myself within you, Jess. Please do not tempt me." My hands were tight fists at my sides.

She put a hand on my shoulder and said, "Stay with me tonight, Aid."

"I can't." The words burned as they flowed up my throat. I turned to face her. "Jess, I didn't want to leave you. You keep saying I left you, and I did, but it was to protect you. To protect us. I'm still trying to protect you. Vernadali law strictly forbids a Vernadali marrying their Charge."

"CJ did." Her voice was hard and determined.

"My parents have never played by the rules that apply to everyone else. You know that. What was Julian or the Vernadali going to do when he was Angels Blessed and she Angels Touched. They could walk in, take out Julian, and no one would say anything because of it. They can do whatever they want. Just because I am their son, doesn't mean I can."

"I will petition everyone I have to, to keep you, Aiden." She would, too, and it would fail. It didn't matter who I was. It had been made clear to me when I was eight years old that I was going to be following the same rules and Vernadali laws that every other Vernadali followed, regardless of my parentage. At the time, I was fine with that. I had been fine with that until I met Jess. She turned my whole world upside down. It was the only time in my life that I ever considered petitioning for a release from the Vernadali. It would never be granted, though, and I would be seen as weak. Insert family drama here, as they say. But, Jess wanting to keep me? That would be too much to hope for.

My hand reached up and cradled her cheek. "You already have me." I swallowed hard. "I am your Vernadali. I will never leave your side. I have always known that I would die for you. That has not changed."

"No, Aiden. That isn't what I mean and you know it. You know I am still in love with you. You. Know. It." She punctuated each word with a hard poke of her finger into my chest. Her words were stern, but there was a softness to her face that was just us.

"So, you really did pinch my hip twice then?" My heart skipped a beat. I didn't imagine it. While I had recognized it, I...

She nodded. "I love you, Aiden Mathewson. You. Not the Vernadali trying to play by the rules. I love everything about the man underneath."

I took a step back and felt my breath hitch a few times as I tried to gain oxygen. What were we going to do? I wanted to take that step back and kiss those beautiful plump lips. I wanted to go to bed with the taste of her on me.

"Stay with me tonight, Aid. You can't stand there and tell me I don't still turn you on. You can't stand there and tell me that you feel nothing for me. You wouldn't still call me your kotě if you didn't." She was staring me down, but vulnerability shone in those eyes. She was standing before me heart wide open, and I couldn't do this. I couldn't go down a road that would only lead to her heart being completely shattered. I would deal with mine. I had always been and would always be hers. She, on the other hand, could move on. She had to marry and produce heirs. The thought sent a bolt of rage down my spine, but I tapped it down.

"Jess, I have never stopped loving and wanting you. So yes, I'm hard for you, because you will always have that effect on me." I turned my back on her and, once again, went to the door that adjoined my room. Looking back at her, I felt another piece of my heart crack and flake off into a pit of loneliness. "If I stay, I'll kiss you. If I kiss you, I won't stop kissing you. But we can't. There is no happy ending here. I don't want to break your heart all over again, I love you too much to do that." My voice cracked at the words.

The look on her face made me want to take it all back. I could feel how I just took the air out of her lungs. How I broke her all over again. I crossed into my room and quickly shut and locked the door.

This time it was me that couldn't hold back the tears. What had I done? I wasn't going to tell her. I didn't want her to know how much I still wanted her. I didn't want her to know how much I loved her.

I went over to the small bar that was in my room and tipped back two quick shots of tequila. The burn down my throat only served as a reminder of the pain in my chest. I picked up the bottle and threw it against the opposite wall. As I watched the amber liquid flow, I slid to the floor, put my face in my hands, and let the tears flow.

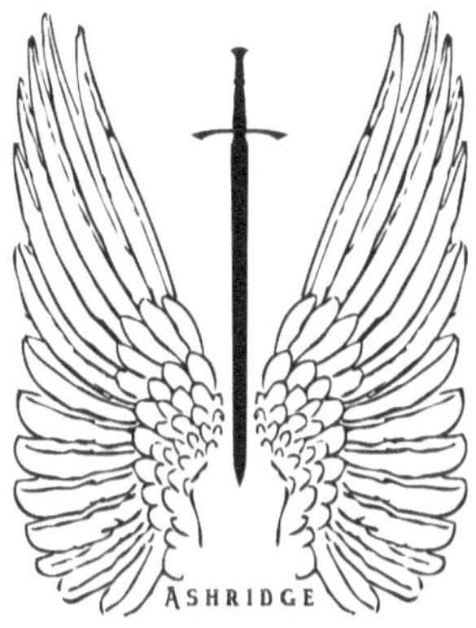

CHAPTER 15

JESSIKA

I STARED AT THE door as he closed it. He still loved me. There was a crash in his room a few moments later, and I ran to the door. I was about to push it open when I heard him crying. I sank to the floor and just stared.

Did he seriously just tell me he still loved me and then walked out? He was supposed to stay. He was supposed to stay with me tonight. Either as my Aiden or as my Vernadali, but he wasn't supposed to walk out.

Nothing happened the way it was supposed to. Yes, I wanted to have that conversation with him. Yes, I wanted to tell him exactly how I felt. I knew he still cared, but ANGELS. Aiden just said he still loves me. I had hoped, I had hoped he did, but...

Then why in the Underworld was he in there and not in here putting me on my knees and telling me to suck his delicious cock? If that was how he felt, he should be in here, fucking me against the wall and commanding me to do what he wanted, what we both wanted.

What the actual fuck, Aiden?

I wasn't sure how long I sat there staring at that door. I knew he eventually stood and got in the shower, but when Amala came in, that was where she found me: knees to my chest on the floor, crying next to the door that Aiden and I shared.

"Fuck! What happened?" She gathered me into her arms. "Jessika?"

She was right in front of me, but I didn't see her. I saw Aiden standing there, telling me he still loved me. It should have filled me with joy. With happiness. But it didn't. I was numb.

Then her hands were on my face, and she was slapping my cheeks. "Jess, answer me."

"He loves me," I whispered, so light that she didn't hear me.

"What?"

I slowly moved my eyes to meet hers. "Aiden said he still loves me."

There was no shock on her face, no fear, only resignation. "Well, anyone could have told you that."

"You knew?" I said, a little surprised.

"Grand Duchess—" she started to say.

"Don't you fucking dare, Amala. We are too close for that bullshit. You knew Aiden still loved me?"

"I did. Janreka, too. Oh, and Jayden, Lady Megan, and Vernadali CJ." She sighed. "Jess, anyone who has seen you two together can tell there is something other than him being your Vernadali going on."

"That's just it, though, there isn't," I said as she hauled me off the floor and to the large red chair in the seating area.

"Sure, there is," Amala said dismissively.

"No. There isn't. I tried. Angels, I wanted to." I flushed, remembering what he said. "Aiden did, too. He admitted it."

She looked to the door, whispering something about "*Why did he send her in here?*" before she turned back to me. "So why aren't you two in here fucking like laphorns?"

"Because he says there is no happy ending for us, and that he is still trying to protect us. Protect me. That is his job. Apparently, he thinks that includes protecting me from him," I said, my voice hitching.

"He is quoting old Vernadali Law, isn't he?" Amala grumbled.

I nodded.

"He doesn't know. Vernadali Samuel didn't tell him. That fucking bastard. They aren't spreading the word at all." She stood and angrily laughed at the room. "They aren't telling the Vernadali."

"Amala, what are you talking about?"

"The dimensions abolished that law, and a few others, after his parents married. While yes, they were Angels Blessed, they saw Lady Megan and Vernadali CJ were able to keep their marriage happy, healthy, and still do everything they had to. There was a strong argument for keeping the law in place, but the law was antiquated and was overturned. There are a ton of rules that have to be followed, and there are multiple high level sign offs that need to be done."

"Like?" I forced myself not to let hope bloom in my chest.

"The Vernadali and their Charge would have to petition the Vernadali Council for approval to marry, the Head of the Realm would have to sign off, and if they were within a territory, then the head of that territory would also have to give permission. There are also other conditions that have to be met." She started thinking and smiled. "Which you two have already met. The biggest being that he has a lifetime assignment to you and wears your name scroll."

"Why didn't you tell us that? Will you go in there and tell him that?" I was trying not to yell at her, but there was disbelief and astonishment that there was a real possibility, and he wouldn't listen to me.

"He won't believe me if I tell him. When we get to Ashridge, I'll send a message to the Vernadali Council on your behalf," she said, taking my hands in hers and squeezing them tight.

"Why didn't you tell us that before?" I repeated.

"I didn't realize that was what was holding him back. Didn't know he didn't know." Then she cocked her head to the side and asked, "But even if you do get back with Aiden, what about Jayden? His father isn't going to let you out of that contract. Not now that you are the Grand Duchess."

I sighed. I just wanted Aiden back for one night. To know that he still loved me and to be able to show him just how much I loved him. I wanted my heart back.

I got up and started pacing the room. "I know there are obstacles, but we can get through those. I know we can."

"Only, it appears the biggest one is the bonehead next door," Amala said.

I laughed outright at that.

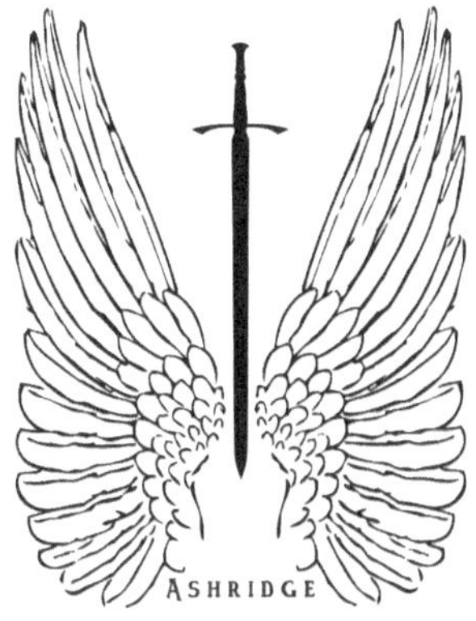

CHAPTER 16

JESSIKA

THE NEXT MORNING, WE were up, dressed, and packing the horses an hour after dawn. I had slept like the dead for the four hours I did sleep. Outside, everything was wet, the ground sloshed and splashed under our feet, and it didn't look like the clouds were done, either. I could still smell the rain in the air and knew this was going to be a long, wet ride.

Aiden wouldn't look at me, and Jayden had given me a questioning look to see what was wrong, but I just shook him off.

"Lord Jayden," a man with a huge bulbous nose said.

Jayden turned to him and stood tall before saying, "Yes?"

"Message for you, sir." The man bowed low as he handed Jayden a piece of parchment. His head stayed up, and he made contact with me as he handed it over. I straightened, feeling my power rally under my skin. I looked him over and noticed he didn't wear the standard issue syths, but instead wore a pair of short swords at his hips.

"Excuse me, sir," I said, not breaking his gaze. "I notice you have short swords and not the standard syth."

"Yes, Duchess, I mean Grand Duchess." I winced but hid it well enough that he continued, "Me hands are so large, short swords fit better. My family can't afford to custom a syth."

"Thank you for delivering the message." The messenger nodded his head and headed down the street. I watched him as Jayden opened the message, and the messenger kept looking over his shoulder.

"Underworld's darkness," Jayden said, rubbing his face. I looked back at him, and he was looking at his guards, then to Aiden, then back to his guards.

"What does it say?" Aiden asked.

"It's from his *Grand Lord*," Jayden said, each word through his teeth. I could tell he really was feeling torn.

"What is it, Jayden?" Aiden asked. Yup. Still cranky in the morning when he gets blue balls. There was a part of me that snickered at that. It was his own damn fault.

"He commands me to go to the ridge to moderate the turmoil that is rising. He says I will get more information when I arrive." Jayden was looking at Killy and Ilris for a long moment, as if they were having their own discussion, before turning to Aiden. "Vernadali Aiden, I defer to you. Do we continue on to Ashridge, or do I break off and head to the ridge?"

I blinked and looked at Jayden. His gaze didn't leave Aiden's. My eyes flicked between the two of them. "Jayden, it's your Grand Lord commanding you. Of course, you have to go. Why are you even asking Aiden?"

"Aiden is an A class Vernadali. He outranks not only both of us, but also the asshole that is my father, the Grand Lord of Kaletta." The two of them were still staring each other down.

Finally, Aiden groaned. "Go. Maybe you can find out more about why the Grand Lord is sabotaging Ashridge's production. Killy and Ilris can go with you. I don't want you unprotected."

"What about me?" I said defensively. It was selfish, but I didn't want any of them to go.

"You have Aiden and Amala," Jayden said without hesitation.

"I'll put the travel incantation on the horses again, and we will ride straight through to Shuset. Then we'll make the long push across the sands to Ashridge," Aiden commanded, but he ran his hands through his hair from back to front, making it stand up and fluff unnaturally. He looked like a welter, with their full mane surrounding their heads.

I covered my mouth as I giggled, and Amala straight up laughed. Aiden just glared at us.

"Hey, you are the one that made your hair stand up straight like that." Amala cackled.

"I know you are frustrated, Aiden. The three of us are very well trained. We will be fine." I turned to Jayden. "Be careful. If he finds out we suspect him, he will use you against me. You are too important to me and Ashridge to lose, Jayden." I pulled him close and gave him a quick kiss on the cheek.

"Please be careful. I'll meet you in Ashridge as soon as I can."

"Don't chance written communication. Use Lark Messengers." Aiden was nervous about this. I reached over and took his hand and squeezed it. His body froze for a moment, but then he settled. He squeezed it again and said, "The Grand Duchess is right. If there is any sign of danger, I want all three of you to get the fuck out of Kaletta and get back to Ashridge."

"Yes, sir," Jayden, Killy, and Ilris said in unison as they mounted their horses.

I stepped back as Aiden took a step toward Jayden. There were some whispered instructions that I couldn't hear, then Aiden cast the travel incantation on Jayden's group. Just before he left, he looked at me, smiled, and said, "Be safe, Jessika."

"May the Angels grant you wings."

Aiden turned and cast the incantation on the three of us and our horses as I watched Jayden go. There was a bad feeling sitting in my stomach, and I took a few deep breaths to release it. I felt my power swimming under the surface, but I also knew I was feeling too much right now. I had to box it away and just let it sit until I had the time to be able to unpack it all.

Aiden's voice was closer than I expected when he said, "We need to hurry. Shuset is a ways off."

There was a crowd gathering outside, and there were murmurs about how the Grand Duchess was in town. Taking a deep breath, I pulled on the façade that was my royal heritage and glanced at Aiden and Amala. Both were staring at me like they couldn't believe what they were seeing. Aiden scratched his temple, and I winked at him in answer as I put my foot in the stirrup and mounted my horse. Once I was settled, he pawed the ground, anxious about getting on the road.

"Grand Duchess," Aiden said, every bit the protective Vernadali. I felt his charge wrap around me as I smiled at him, gave them each a nod, chirped as I put my heels to my horse's side, and took off before the crowd could surround us.

WE RODE HARD AND pushed the horses for hours. We had stopped at one of the oases on the desert's edge before angling straight for Shuset. The sun had gone down, and we were trying to reach the small town and gain lodging before the rain came and we lost all our light. We had all turned in our saddles to watch the rain line behind us. It was moving fast, but luckily, it only took another thirty minutes before we rode into town, just as the wind rolled over us.

Shuset wasn't much more than a pitstop on the road. There was a hotel, stables, message center, and a general store. Few homes surrounded the stead, and the family that had run the town for the last 200 years was sweet and accommodating.

"Grand Duchess!" the short plump woman said from behind the counter. Her dress was simple, but it only emphasized her dark brown skin and black hair.

"Hethlene. It's been so long since I've seen you," I said, giving her two quick kisses on the cheeks.

"Our family extends its sadness to you for the loss of your mother," she said easily.

"Thank you," I replied with the same ease. It was all the years of training that allowed me to take it without the emotions welling up. "Could you give us rooms tonight?"

"I have one. Do you mind sharing?" I shook my head, knowing the three of us could work it out. "Bit of a full house tonight with the storm. I'll have Mennes get the horses settled for you in the stable."

A woman who appeared to be a little older than myself came out, and I gasped, putting my hand over my mouth. When Aiden and Amala saw, they did as well. "Bevy, you're pregnant!"

"Jessika!" she said, waddling her way to us. "I mean, Grand Duchess, welcome." She tried to curtsy, but I pulled her up.

"Don't you dare. You might fall on that ass of yours." Aiden was chuckling at her.

"I haven't seen you all for what, seven years?" Bevy's eyes were a little astonished to see us all standing there together. "Wait? I thought you two broke up, and you—" She pointed to me. "—were engaged to the Lord of Kaletta, Jayden Panahov."

"You are right on all accounts." I rolled my eyes and gave her a small smile.

She looked at Aiden carefully, and then back at me, before her eyes popped wide. "Don't tell me you got assigned to Jess?"

"I did." He was beaming. He lifted his arm and showed her his name scroll, and I couldn't help but blush. It was almost as if he were showing it off like a prize.

"Don't ask, Bevy. It's totally and completely complicated. Starting and ending with stubbornness," Amala said, stopping any further digging. I wanted to smack her. "What we want to know is if Blaise is now your husband and the father of that babe, or if you conned someone else to take pity upon your beautiful, stunning carcass."

"Bitch," Bevy said and stuck out her tongue. "Of course, it's Blaise. You think I would like anyone else near him? He's mine."

"We really need to get out here more often."

Hethlene came over and put her arm around Bevy and said, "Didn't Blaise tell you to stay in bed. You are ready to have these babes, and you are coming down to the kitchens?"

"Mama, I'm fine. I just needed to stretch, and I wanted a snack." Bevy turned to us and said, "Twins, so they are a bit overprotective."

"Room is on the top floor, last door on the right. You should be able to listen to the storm tonight," Hethlene said, leading Bevy to the kitchens.

"Thanks," I said. "Oh, Hethlene? I know it's a lot to ask, but any chance we can get something to eat? We've been on the road all day."

"Of course, Grand Duchess, we will bring something up."

Heading upstairs, we opened the last door on the right to see that the room was small. Really small. It was just big enough for the queen bed that was pushed up against the far wall, and a small path to the bathroom that was just around the corner. On the far wall was a tiny window that we might be big enough to crawl out of if it even had a mechanism to open it. There was enough room for the door to open, but other than the path along the bed to where the entrance to the bathroom was, there wasn't really enough space for someone to sleep on the floor.

"Well, get comfy girls," Aiden said, laughing a bit. He looked at me apologetically, but I smiled at him.

I toed off my boots and let my syth belt clammer to the floor. I climbed up on the bed so that they would have some room to at least get undressed. Amala and Aiden striped down to the driest part of their clothes, and I just flopped back.

"I'm exhausted," I grumbled to no one in particular.

"The incantation wore off a few hours ago. Doesn't surprise me you are getting tired," Amala muttered, her voice sounding just as worn as my own. "I feel like every muscle in my body is sore. My legs are pulsing, they are so tired."

"My feet are pulsing," I muttered, throwing my arm over my eyes.

"You two are such babies." Aiden chuckled, took my foot, and started massaging it. I moaned at the instant relief I felt.

"Oh, I love you, Aiden." He froze, and I realized what I said. "Did I say you could stop?" I said, trying to cover it up.

I could just see him from under my arm, and he was shaking his head back and forth, trying to suppress a laugh. There was a trace of that smile on his lips for a minute before his eyes met Amala's and he shook his head quickly. Then he hit a spot on my foot that I felt all the way up my legs and released into my hips. I moaned a satisfied sound, and it was Amala who laughed that time.

Aiden switched to the other foot, repeated the motions, and just as the tightness released in the other hip, there was a soft knock on the door. Aiden got up before Amala and I could move, and a kid no older than ten or twelve came in with a tray of food for us.

"Hethlene apologizes for not having anything warm, but promises a warm, full breakfast for the Grand Duchess in the morn." He bowed low before he ducked out quickly.

I sat up and looked at the tray of thinly sliced meats, cheese, and dried bread. My stomach growled in response, and I saw Aiden eye it. "Go wash up, and then we will dig in."

We took turns in the bathroom, and while I was in there, I took the chance to wipe down the worst parts of me. I didn't fully bathe, but it felt so good to be able just to remove a layer of the dirt and sweat. I stuck my head in the sink and rinsed my hair out quickly. Once I wrung most of the water out, I combed through it with my fingers and went to braiding it as I opened the door using my power. When I came out, they were licking their fingers over a mostly empty tray. "Angels, did you leave me any?"

"Yes," Aiden said but smirked. "But don't mouth off or I'll take it. You can be stuck with what is left in the pack."

I pushed him out of the way and took the tray before moving to the other side of the bed with my bounty. Once I took a bite, I knew why it hadn't taken them long to devour how much they did. It was deliciously salty and savory. Not five minutes later, I was giving Aiden the tray to sit outside for them to collect.

"Massage Amala's legs. Then let's get some sleep."

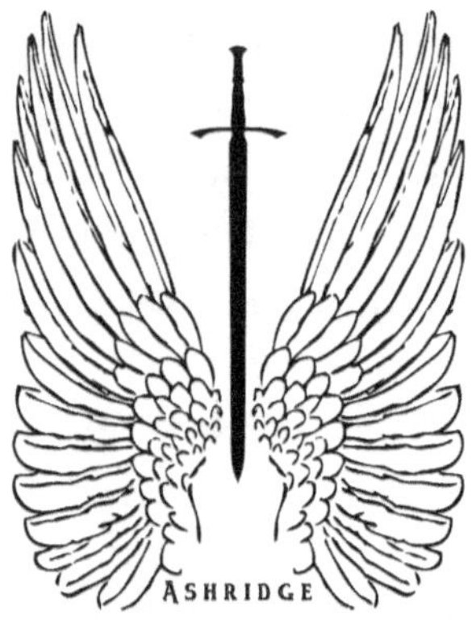

CHAPTER 17

JESSIKA

I WASN'T SURE HOW long I was asleep before I woke to Aiden's arm firmly around my waist. I tried to turn toward him, but he whispered in my ear, "Shh. Amala went to scout."

"What do you mean?" I said as I let my power flow through me and into the room. There was something off in the air. Something crisp, and it tasted like metal in the back of my throat. That in itself should have put me on edge, but when my power reached the door, it felt like someone had put a silence incantation on the room, in reverse. I turned my head to look at him.

"It woke me up." He was so quiet I didn't even feel the breath of air on my ear as he said it. "Amala felt it the second I woke her. Where is your syth belt?"

"In my boots. By the door."

He uncoiled himself from me, and then jerked his head to the door, put his finger to his lips, and motioned for me to get my boots and syth belt on.

I gave him a look and rolled my eyes. Of course, I was going to do so as quietly as I could. I pushed more of my power into my muscles and twitched my fingers, silently casting the incantation for silent feet. Once they were on, I slid my syths out and whirled them in my hands while rolling my neck.

Something hit the door hard, and the enchantment keeping the noise out failed. Aiden turned toward me and ran a thumb across his jaw. *Behind me.* I nodded and followed him out.

When I saw what was before us, I stopped for a half second, but Aiden was already halfway down the hall and engaged with one of the many Kaletta soldiers. At the far end near the stairs, Amala was already fighting and had just used her power to push one of the attackers back and down the stairs. He didn't get back up. I took three strides down the hall, and when Aiden presented a soldier's back to me, I reached out, grasping the base of his spinal cord, and sent my power vibrating through him. A high-pitched scream filled the room, and I felt the bones shatter within his body and blood vessels pop. When I let go, he fell in a heap on the floor.

Aiden didn't even flinch as he turned on another one of the soldiers. Just as his back was turned, strong arms circled my waist, lifting me so my feet were no longer on the ground.

I took a deep breath and reached behind me to grasp the head of my attacker. I sent my power into his skull and gritted my teeth as I felt the shaking in my bones, but the scream in my ear made everything fade to crackling muteness. It had only taken moments for his brain to turn to goo. As he crumpled to the ground, I landed awkwardly and felt my ankle roll.

I hissed but caught myself before I looked to Aiden, who was sticking his syth up into a soldier's rib cage, into his heart. Pushing him up and over the railing, he turned toward me and itched his temple. I gave him a quick nod and went to help Amala.

Making our way down the hall, more soldiers seemed to materialize out of thin air, but they all fell to my touch and power as they reached me. I could feel my power starting to drain, and that was unsettling. There were still so many soldiers. I could probably kill one, maybe two more before I would be unable to use it for much more than opening a door.

I felt, more than heard, the soldier behind me. I whirled around, sticking my syth into his neck. I hadn't moved quite quick enough, and he sliced into my hip as he went down. I knew it wasn't life threatening, but it was going to hurt like hell later. I kicked the soldier I had just stabbed, who was dead before he hit the ground, off my syth and turned to hear Amala. "If you are done dancing with them, Jess, I could use some help."

I took off running. Aiden, busy with two of his own soldiers, whirled toward me, and I felt his Charge wrap around me again. I stopped, turned to face him, and he nodded toward Amala. Quickly, I pushed my power toward the one with his back to me, and he stumbled forward, right into Aiden's syth. I huffed a breath and realized my well of power was much lower than I thought.

Aiden, without taking his sparkling eyes off of me and smirking, jabbed his hand backwards and into the gut of the

Kaletta soldier behind him. He turned, taking his syth with him, effectively gutting the man.

Knowing Aiden was safe, I turned toward Amala, and when I saw the soldier sneaking up behind her, I pushed what was left of my power into my fingers and gripped the back of his neck. I felt the pain in my throat as the soldier went down before he had a chance to touch Amala. I let out a hard sharp huff of air. "Angels."

Amala pulled her syth from the one she had been fighting and, as she turned toward me, pushed him down the stairs with her foot.

"I'm out. No more goo brains for me," I said, leaning forward and putting my hands on my knees. I rubbed at my ear, grateful that the hearing was coming back, but not at how slowly it was happening. I looked back down the hall and was surprised at the number of them on the ground. There had to be at least twenty Kaletta soldiers. All in the current opulent uniforms. "What is the Grand Lord up to?"

Aiden was there seconds later, and when his hand touched my back, I felt the pain running from my shoulders to my knees release. It also felt as though he had pushed air back into my lungs. "I don't know what you just did, Aiden, but thank you."

He smirked, but there was a satisfaction that gleamed in his eyes that warmed a deep part of me. I held that gaze a moment longer before we heard screams from downstairs. All three of us ran down the stairs to the main room. There were at least thirty more soldiers, but my eyes were only on the one who had Hethlene against the wall, hand at her throat.

"Let her go," I growled, twirling my syths in my hands.

"By whose command?" the soldier said, without even bothering to look.

"The Grand Duchess of Ashridge, Jessika Petra Valenti, and the betrothed to your Lord of Kaletta, Jayden Panahov." I tried to push my power into my tone, but it was hard to keep the breathlessness at bay.

"We do not take orders from Lord Jayden, nor you." He finally turned to look at me and smirked. Then, licking his lips, he brazenly looked me up and down. I heard Aiden growl next to me, but I clicked through my teeth, and he stopped. "Duchess, you haven't been crowned. Your dear mother hasn't even been sent to the Angels yet. There is no formal title upon you."

"Watch yourself, you piece of dragon shit." Amala hissed.

He smirked and then turned back to Hethlene. He leaned closer to her and brought his body up against hers, grinding slightly.

"Release her now," I said again. When he repeated the motion, I let one of my syths fly, and it landed in his upper thigh.

The room exploded into motion. I went for Hethlene, and when I reached her, she assured me, "I'm fine."

"Get out of here now. Lockdown." She nodded, and I turned back to the shithead who had been holding her by the throat.

He pulled my syth from his thigh and moved quicker than I had expected. One moment, I was standing there watching Hethlene run out of the room, the next, he had me pinned under him on the ground, with his leg between my thighs.

I could hear the fight going on in the rest of the large room, but I couldn't see anything. The man's large body covered every inch of me. I tried to keep my emotions in check, so that it wouldn't set Aiden off, but I didn't think I was having much success. Anger was at least at the forefront.

"See here, little Duchess, you won't be in power much longer. Our Grand Lord has plans," he whispered into my ear.

I threw all my weight into him, in an attempt to dislodge him, but he might as well have been a mountain. I used every maneuver I could think of that I had been taught, but I couldn't overpower him. I pulled into the shreds of my power, and when I bucked one more time, I threw the last dregs of my power into him, focusing on the bones at the base of his back.

It wasn't much, but it was enough that he moved and I was able to get out from under him. Just as he lifted from me, Aiden was there slicing through his throat. Hot liquid sprayed across the front of me, but I didn't take my eyes off his until the light had faded from them. Even though I knew he was dead, I stood and kicked him in the balls out of pure spite.

Turning, I shouted, "Amala, watch out!"

As she dispatched a soldier on her right, another came up behind her, kicked the back of her knee, causing her to buckle, and he sliced through her throat as she fell to the ground. Her eyes had just met mine before they went blank, and she crumpled to the floor.

I swear every particle in that room seemed to freeze midair. Everyone stopped as Amala's body hit the ground and she bled out. I could feel dozens of eyes on me, but everything in my head had gone completely silent.

Arms gripped around my waist and forced me to turn away from where my best friend lay, dead.

Aiden.

It was Aiden.

His mouth was moving, but I couldn't hear or comprehend a word. My eyes met his and refused to move.

Amala.

Amala was dead.

What was I going to do without Amala? She had been by my side most of my life. She was my anchor, my friend, my confidant.

Kaletta soldiers were disappearing through whatever exits they were able to find, but before they got through the doors, they were dropping motionless to the floor. Aiden, on the other hand, had my head in his hands, trying to get me to do something, but I didn't know what.

His gaze searched the room, and again, his mouth moved, but I didn't make out the words. Aiden's hazel-green eyes met mine again, scanned my face, and widened slightly.

I blinked as he ran his thumbs across my cheeks. There was a wave of love that flowed through that touch. I concentrated on the movement of his skin against mine. Aiden was here. Solid and here. As long as Aiden was here, I was safe. As long as Aiden was here, I was protected.

His thumbs trailed once more across my cheeks and then down across my jaw before they were under my chin, and he forced my mouth closed. When my lips met, there was a hollowing out in the room, something popped deep in the pit of my chest, and the room went black.

CHAPTER 18

AIDEN

I LET THE SOLDIER that had Jess pinned under him drop to the floor and turned just as Amala fell to the ground, her throat cut from ear to ear. As she fell, she kept tapping her elbow. One last command between us. *Protect.*

Then it started. A hollow feeling opened up inside of me as I heard a high-pitched screech fill the room. Instantly, I was standing before Jess, pulling her to face me and putting her head in my hands. The sound... It was coming from her.

My eyes flicked to her ears as I noticed them sharpen at the tips, just the slightest bit. When I looked at her open mouth, I saw her canines sharpen slightly as well. I studied the rest of her face as her cheekbones became slightly more predominant, her cheeks thinning slightly. Angels, all of her features had shifted, but only just enough to make her look as if she were just a few years younger.

"Jess, look at me. Listen to me." Her eyes met mine as I pushed my Charge into the command. "Look at me. Jessika Petra Valenti. Look. At. Me."

I knew the moment she felt the command in my tone. Her eyes snapped to mine and didn't leave. My heart broke for her as I noted how they were filled with sadness, fear, and emptiness. Only, she just kept making that noise. Shit. I had to get her to calm before things got out of control. My eyes flicked around the room, and the Kaletta soldiers were falling whether they stood or ran for their lives. Each and every one other than the two of us fell to the ground, dead.

"Jess, what are you doing?" I breathed, but then my eyes widened as I realized what was happening to her. Her mom had told me something years ago. Something important that I had forgotten until I saw what was happening before me.

"Oh, my kotě." I ran my thumbs over her cheekbones. She finally blinked then. Slowly, I repeated the motion, this time running my thumbs down to her jaw and gently forcing her mouth to close. When she did, the noise stopped, and she collapsed in my arms.

Catching her, I found a spot against the wall a few feet away and leaned against it for support. Sliding down the wall, I set her in my lap and held her for a long time as my eyes flicked from her to Amala.

Amala.

We were so royally fucked. The Grand Lord of Kaletta had done this. He had sent his soldiers after Jess. After my Jess. She was mine. Mine. He wasn't going to take her from me.

I looked down to the woman cradled in my lap. Blood coated her long white hair and completely covered the T-shirt and sleeping shorts she had on. Blood ran down her full thighs and soaked into my pants as she sat there. Cuts covered her body, and I couldn't help my eyes flicking to Amala before they settled back on Jess.

Dammit. We were truly, so royally fucked.

All those years ago, her mother had warned me they had Irvian blood in them. I had prayed she would never experience the event that would set off the transformation, but here we were.

The Irvians were an elven race that had long since gone extinct in pureblood, or even recorded mixed blood status. Many great grandfathers ago, on Jess' father's side, there had been a mixed-blood bastard-born child. The ruling line had been eradicated to the point that he was the only living blood heir to the territory, and thus Irvian blood was brought into Ashridge ruling line.

Jessika's family line didn't carry any of the attributes, and it was mostly forgotten to history. Only, her mother had wanted to make sure that Amala and I knew it was the cause of her unique power. That vibrating power had only shown up in ancient textbooks in the ancient lands of Irvania. Not to mention Jess' ability to move really fast, and how her hearing and eyesight had always been better than most.

One of her mother's concerns was that Irvians would transform from their humanoid form to their elven form during traumatic events. If that happened while I was around, she wanted me to know, just in case. She had told Jess, of course, but none of us ever truly expected it to manifest.

I looked down at her in confusion. The thing was, though, that a transformation should only happen if she was completely drained of all of her power. She wasn't out. I would have known. She had been low, real low, yes, but she hadn't been completely out.

"Jess," I whispered against her cheek. I looked at her again and wiped away some of the blood on her face. Angels. We both were covered in it.

My eyes looked back to Amala and stayed there for a long moment. She was really gone. She wasn't coming back to Ashridge with us. She wouldn't be there to be the buffer between all of us. She wouldn't be there to pull our heads out of our own asses when we needed it most. What were we going to do without her? We needed her.

"Aiden," Hethlene said, her voice cracking at the sound as she came back into the room. "Is she…?"

"No. She's alive. Just resting now." My vision was going blurry, and my voice was thick as I said, "Amala. She's gone, Hethlene."

Tears finally fell from my eyes as I tipped my head forward toward Jess. I couldn't see straight enough to see what Hethlene was doing, but as I brought my knees up, I pulled Jess closer to my chest. I held her tight and pushed what power I could into her, muttering every healing incantation that came to mind to heal the small cuts and wounds she had. There was one near her hip that I hadn't noticed before, and I placed my hand over it, muttering the incantation again. I felt it seal up but knew there would likely be a scar once it had fully healed.

There was a loud three-bell ring, where I instinctively brought Jess even closer to my chest as I looked around the room. Blinking my eyes clear again, Hethlene was kneeling before me. When I stiffened, she said, "That's the all-clear signal, hun."

I sniffed and nodded. "Amala. We need to send her to Ashridge."

She nodded.

"Send a note spelled only for Lady Megan Mathewson or Vernadali CJ Mathewson to read. They are overseeing things in Ashridge until we arrive. Let them know we will be delayed as well, and that it was Kaletta soldiers who did this today."

"Yes, Vernadali Aiden."

That title.

I blinked.

Vernadali. You were an Angels-be-damned Vernadali, for fuck's sake. Your Charge is in your arms. Protect her.

Flashes of Amala falling to the floor and tapping her elbow played on quick repeat in the span of only a few seconds.

Protect her.

Protect her.

Protect her.

"Hethlene," I said, my voice becoming that Vernadali I needed to be. "Are you okay?"

"Yes, sir." Her voice was strong, and I admired her for that.

"Is the house clear of everyone but family?"

"Yes. It's just Bevy, Blaise, and me. Shanlik won't be back for a few more weeks," she said, and I pulled on my power again, muttering the specialty incantations only the Vernadali used to protect a location.

"Are they injured? Are Bevy and the babies okay?" I asked, meeting her eyes.

"They are, sir. Blaise instantly stood guard in front of their door. There was no harm to any of them. They only went for you three." She let out a long breath. "What are your orders, Vernadali Aiden?"

"No one will be able to enter or exit the house without my approval or knowing. I need her to be safe until we are able to travel. I also need to examine the soldiers to see if there are any clues as to what is going on." I used my power to help me up smoothly with Jess still firmly in my arms before saying, "I am going to get her cleaned up and in bed. Get Blaise up here to help with the soldiers. Lay them out, and I'll be down in a bit."

I carried her up the stairs, into the room we had been sharing, and laid her on the bed. I ran my hand through my hair, dried blood flaking off, and I winced at the cut that was on my shoulder I didn't even know was there. Waving my hand over it, I sealed it up before looking back at Jess.

"Jess, I'm so sorry," I muttered, holding back tears. "I'll get you home safe. I promise."

I leaned over, kissed her forehead, and went into the bathroom to get the bath started. Once the water was warm and the tub was filling, I went back and stripped Jess of the soiled clothing. As I carried her to the bath, her hand moved, and she snuggled up next to me. I felt something zap in my chest and her twitch at the same time. I took a deep breath and gently sat her in the tub.

Grabbing one of the cups, I started rinsing the blood from her hair, which was no easy feat when I was trying to keep her sitting up enough to do it. I needed about three more hands. Once her hair was no longer red, now just a dingy white, I drained the tub and let the hot water run from the faucet. Hethlene came in and brought some towels in for us along with a plate of meats and cheeses.

"Blaise and I have sent Amala to Lady Megan and Vernadali CJ as instructed, Vernadali Aiden. Is there anything else you need?" she said, sticking her head into the bathroom as I started washing her hair again. I had to get it back to white. Rinsing helped, but she needed her white hair again. I had to get it clean.

"No, Hethlene. Thank you. I'll be down after I get both of us cleaned and her settled to inspect the Kaletta soldiers," I said and went to scrubbing the blood off Jess' body.

"Very well, Vernadali Aiden," she said, but she paused at the threshold. "I'm so sorry for the loss of Lady Amala." Then she turned and left the small room.

I scrubbed the remaining blood from Jess' body and healed any other wounds that I hadn't already. Every once in a while, there was that zap again in my chest that coincided with her body twitching. What was happening?

Eventually, I finished cleaning her up, and when I went to stand, I leaned her against the back of the tub, stripped off the sodden bra and underwear, and tossed them into the corner.

"Please don't wake up right now, Jess," I said, half giggling at the situation. I could just see the expression on her face, my leaning over her in just my jeans and her sitting in the tub, naked as the day she was born.

I looped my arms around her legs and back and lifted her from the tub, and my foot slipped on the wet floor. I flung my power out to keep from falling, and once I was stable on my own two feet again, I used my power to pull back the sheets and laid her down.

Zap.

"Fuck, Jess. That hurt," I said rubbing my chest.

I took her hand and ran my thumb across it, sending my Charge wrapping around her. I knelt there at the side of the bed, holding her hand, and wondered what she was going to do when she woke. For the first time in a very long time, I had no idea how she would react.

Sighing, I kissed her hand and stood. That was when I realized I was soaking wet. *First things first, get all this blood off me. Second, go downstairs and see what I can find out* from the dead soldiers. Third, when Jess woke up, we ride hard and fast for Ashridge.

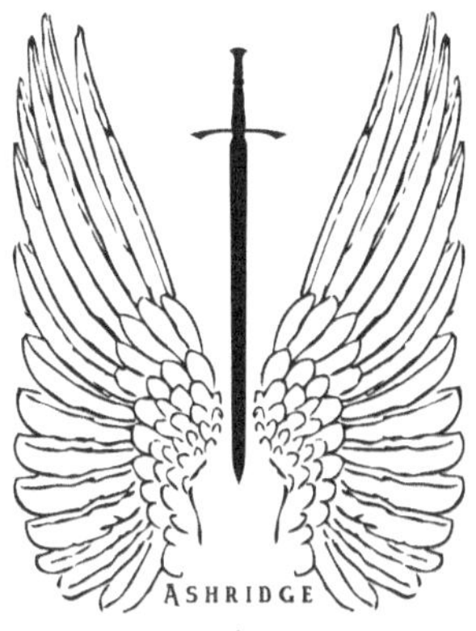

CHAPTER 19

JESSIKA

Zap.

I sat straight up, clutching my chest. The pain was quick and hard. My breath was rushing in and out quickly, and when I blinked, I realized I was lying in a bed, a bed that Aiden, Amala, and I had been sharing.

We were in Shuset... where we were attacked.

Amala.

Amala had died.

I looked around the room, panic building in my chest. Aiden. Where was Aiden? My feet had no sooner hit the floor when he burst through the door.

"Jess." His Charge flew through the room, and I winced at the power of it. My eyes met his, and his cheeks reddened.

He was making a concentrated effort not to look down, and only then did I realize why.

I was naked. Completely naked.

I put a hand on my hip, popping it out slightly, and smirked. It wasn't anything he hadn't seen, or worshiped for that matter, but he was doing everything he could to only look at my eyes.

"Jess...," he admonished.

"Aiden?" I teased, but when he didn't break his stare, I climbed back into bed and pulled the sheets up to cover my breasts. He really was trying to hold that line, even if I didn't give a shit about it. Who was the idiot who drew that line? Oh, right. I was that idiot.

He reached down to bring me my backpack with clothes and handed it to me. When he did, his throat bobbed before he reached up and scratched his temple. My heart sank.

"Every inch of me hurts, inside and out," I muttered as I clipped my bra on and reached for some panties at the very bottom of the bag. "Even my bones hurt. How is that possible? I knew I ran my power out, but I feel like I had to... regrow myself."

"Not surprising." Aiden's voice was harder than I expected.

"What do you mean?"

"Jess," he said, just as I slipped the T-shirt over my head. He took slow deliberate steps toward me before he took my hands and pushed his power into me, calming me instantly.

"Well, that's not a good sign," I said, but the look on his face was strange. Memories of before I passed out flooded back, and a knot sat in my throat. "Yes, I... I... Amala? She's really dead?"

He nodded, and my breaths started coming in sharp gasps. His hands tightened around mine, and I felt his power flow into and around me to sooth me. To calm me down. My breathing evened out, and after a few moments, I tipped my head to the side. "How do you do that?"

"What?"

"Push your power and calm me down."

A small smirk appeared at the corner of his lips before he let out a quick sigh. "It's one thing that was passed down from Dad. The Five Angels blessed him with the affinity to sooth without pain back when he and Mom were in the Manusia."

"I know the story."

"What is told publicly isn't necessarily what happened. Publicly, the council says that the Five Angels blessed Dad with the affinity to soothe or relinquish pain at any time, but it only works when Mom uses the Golden Medallion of Sa Ra." I narrowed my eyes at him. "Not what your parents told you, huh?"

"No. They said that when they were married, he was given his Angels Blessed status," I said, completely confused.

"Angels, no. He was already a full-fledged Vernadali then. Mom and Dad got married after he finished training at the Curtails of the North. He... Mom and Dad don't talk about it much, but I remember them telling LJ, Owen, and me when we received our Maltals the true story of the Keller War. That what they taught wasn't the whole truth, and the timelines were all wrong. We were explicitly told not to correct it publicly, and if we had questions, to go to them."

"Why do they want to control the narrative?" I asked.

Aiden's eyebrows shot to his hairline. "Why do they want to control the narrative? Jess, you've been involved in politics your whole life, and you really have to ask that question? Power wants to control and keep that power."

I took a deep breath and said, "You are right about that, but you didn't answer my question."

"I did. Were you not listening?" He reached up and twirled a strand of my hair around his finger and played with it as he said, "It's one of the things I inherited from Dad. Owen, LJ, and I can all do it. It's easier with you, though. Always has been. Like my power always knew we would be forever connected." He froze at those words, and his cheeks reddened slightly as he let the long white strands around his finger unwind.

We sat like that for a moment, where he actively avoided looking at me. I could see his mind working, and I half wondered what he was thinking when a shadow crossed his face. His shoulders tightened, and he took a deep breath before he looked at me. "Do you remember what happened after you watched Amala die?"

I blinked, not knowing exactly what he meant by that. "What do you mean what happened? I passed out."

"Do you remember screaming in a pitch that melted every Kaletta soldier's brain that was in that room? The only ones immune were you and me. It's a damn good thing that Hethlene had already fled." He squeezed my hands tight and pushed more of his power into me.

"Aiden, stop trying to calm me. I need to fucking process, and I can't do that if you are trying to protect me from freaking out. I think what you just told me entitles me to a little bit of freaking out." I pulled my hands back and started playing with the ends of my hair. His eyes fixed on that movement, but I pressed, "Now what in the fuck do you mean, I screamed and melted the brains of the Kaletta soldiers?"

He let out a huff and ran his hands through his hair.

"Aiden." I growled at him. "Tell me what happened."

"I didn't fully understand everything at the time, okay." He turned toward me. "Only after I got you settled here and I went down stairs did I put together what happened."

"Aiden." My heart was racing now, my chest constricting and my power humming in my chest.

"Deep breath, Kotě. Deep breath." The sound of my nickname instantly helped calm me. Whatever it was, he wasn't mad at me for it. I felt my chest loosen, but my heart was still racing. "Good girl."

My whole body reacted at those two little words. I felt my stomach drop, heart skip, and heat settle deep in my stomach. Aiden smirked and shook his head. "Seriously?"

I just lifted a shoulder. My mind really was all over the place. It was like I could concentrate on a few things at once, which was an odd feeling. I could feel and concentrate on the loss of Amala and my mom, the panic that Aiden obviously felt for what he was trying to tell me, and all at the same time, I could picture tracing every muscle on his body under me.

"With everything going?" He shook his head but then his face fell. He took a deep breath and let it out slowly. He met my gaze with a seriousness he hadn't given me in a long time. "We lost Amala. I've already sent her to Ashridge. Well, Hethlene did while I tended to you."

"Aiden, what did I do after Amala died?" I said, bringing the conversation back around. He studied me for a long moment before he explained.

"You killed them all. Even with little to no power left, you killed them all."

"Don't sugarcoat it. I remember the look in your eyes. I remember you looked around the room trying to sort things out. I remember you fixing me before I passed out. What did I do? Other than melt their brains."

"You let out this screeching noise. I think that was the remnants of your power vibrating their brains to mush. There isn't a piece of glass left in the room that didn't shatter and turn to dust. Jess, you wouldn't stop screeching. I had to use my Charge on you to get you to look at me." He winced at his words. I knew he wouldn't use it unless it was absolutely necessary. He would carry more guilt for that than I would. "As you melted their minds, you..." His eyes met mine, and even though I felt my heart race like it was going to thump out of my chest in fear, the look in his eyes was one of love and adoration. "You transformed."

"What?"

"Jess, you transformed." He reached over and ran his thumb along my cheekbone, lighting a fire on my cheek. "Here."

Then at the tip of my ears, "Just a tad sharper here."

Then he looked at my mouth as he ran his thumb across my bottom lip. There was a heat in his gruff voice as he said, "And here."

I felt pulsing heat gather between my legs, and it was everything I could do not to just pull him against me and kiss him. His eyes hadn't left my lips as he licked his, but then the full force of what he had just told me hit me like I had been dumped in the oceans of the Southern Isles.

"I transformed? As in that tiny drop of Irvianian blood in my veins ran true?" I said, letting my tongue run over my teeth, and I felt it. My canines were just slightly longer and delicately pointed. It wasn't much, and if I was careful about how much I opened my mouth, no one would probably ever notice.

Aiden nodded gently. "It ran true."

"Anything else change?" I pulled my hair down and noticed it was still as snow white as it had always been. It was a rare thing to have hair this white your entire life, and I really didn't want to lose it. I loved my hair.

"That is all that I noticed. You look a couple years younger, but I think that's just the slight shift in features. You are just as beautiful as ever, Jess."

"I always thought Mom was being silly. Just telling me stories. I didn't think any of it was really true." I pointedly ignored his compliment.

"I had hoped it would have just been a good story, or at least, I had seriously hoped you would never go through such a traumatic event that it would trigger the transformation." He paused, and all that wicked excitement in his eyes faded to sorrowfulness. "As your Vernadali, I should have been able to prevent it. I should have been able to prevent you from ever having to transform, even if the line ran true."

"Aiden, you couldn't have prevented this. You did everything right today."

"Two days ago," Aiden said slowly. "Jess, you've been sleeping for two days."

"I'm sorry, what?"

"It's been two days. I've been corresponding with Mom and Dad through the messenger office. Things are fine in Ashridge. They are working on trying to rush a coronation for you to be formally recognized as Grand Duchess, but everyone seems to already be using the title. There is no pushback from anyone on the ruling council. That could be because, well, it's Lady Megan running the show, but they are concerned that we haven't been able to move since the event." He was rambling, and I couldn't help but think how adorable he looked. "I told Dad I used the special incantations to protect the building, and he approved of us staying put until you were ready to go. Mom, on the other hand, was pissed at him for not telling her about those protections."

"Vernadalis have their own secrets," I said nonchalantly. "You don't mind I keep tricks of the trade to myself?"

"Nah. If everyone knew them, then they could anticipate how you would protect your Charges, and that would negate the Vernadali being able to do their job." It was true. Not knowing everything made it easier for them to do their job. Sure, there were lots of people who still tried to learn all those little tricks, but they weren't all going to be found.

He looked at me again and, knowing what I was avoiding asking, said, "Empress Clarice, Grand Duke Alexei, and Princess Janreka arrived in Ashridge yesterday. No, I don't know how they got there so quick, but you know Empress Clarice has her own secrets." He shrugged with a small smile and said, "They want to be there for the Grand Duchess' pyre and for you. Lady Amala is being tended to, and her parents have been notified. They will be in Ashridge tomorrow but will wait for you to arrive before they light her pyre. Princess Janreka demanded being present for both lightings."

I nodded but started crying again. I hadn't missed the fact Aiden was using formal titles. This was hard for him, too. "She's really gone."

Aiden was there instantly, wrapping his arms around me and pulling me into his lap. "I know."

I sat there, crying into his chest, for a long time before I felt antsy. Pulling away, I reached up and kissed his cheek before getting up and going to the bathroom.

I turned the faucet on, splashed cold water on my face, and rubbed it into my eyes. Reaching over, I didn't find the towel, but Aiden was there handing me one. "Here. I should have replaced them, but I forgot."

"Thanks." I patted my face dry, and when my eyes met my reflection, I froze. The changes that Aiden had mentioned were tiny, but noticeable. If someone hadn't seen me in more than ten years, they probably wouldn't notice right away, since I hadn't really aged much in the last twenty years. Just as Aiden had said, my cheekbones were more pronounced and my ears had sharpened just a bit at the tips. It wasn't much, but... How would the people of Ashridge see me? Would they think I'm a freak? Would they even recognize me as the rightful heir to the throne if they knew I had transformed as part of the drop of Irvanian blood in me?

I lifted my lips and ran a finger over one of my canines, and my entire line of thinking shifted and suddenly wondered what Aiden would think of me running them along his skin. Would he like the tease of sharpness against his skin... against his cock? I took a ragged breath to try to stop that line of thinking, because what if he was disgusted by me now?

"Whatever you just thought of..." His voice was a heated warning.

I shook my head and turned to him. "Aiden, answer me something, seriously."

"Of course." His eyes narrowed in confusion and then scanned my face for any indication of my thoughts.

"Do you think me a monster because I've transformed?" My eyes dropped to his chest as I waited for his answer.

He took a step toward me and lifted my chin with a finger. "Look at me, Kotě."

My gaze met his lips then slowly lifted to meet his eyes. I blinked as I realized they burned with lust and love. "Never.

You will never be a monster. You are still just as beautiful as the day I met you, Jess."

"Are you saying that because that is what I need to hear, or because that is what you feel in here, Aiden?" I poked at his heart through his chest.

"You are my kotě." His voice hitched, as if he were trying to hold something back. "You will always be the most beautiful thing to me."

Without thinking, I pushed up on my toes and kissed him. There was a split-second of hesitation from him before he moved and kissed me back with enthusiasm. His fingers threaded in my hair at the nape of my neck, and I moaned into the kiss. It was everything I remembered. It was light. It was breath. It was every tingling sensation from my fingers to my toes.

I fisted my hands in his shirt, pulling him closer as our tongues danced. The taste of him was nothing but power. Our power. I felt stronger in his arms. I hadn't felt like this in years.

When the kiss broke, we were both panting, and he was whispering my name, reverently, over and over again as our foreheads rested against each other.

I opened my eyes and saw the concentration on his face. I had a feeling he was trying very hard to convince himself not to just pick me up and take me to bed. I, however, concentrated on breathing in through my nose to calm myself. I would take the kiss. I would take it and try for more later. I didn't want to push him. I knew how Aiden was, and I wanted it back. I wanted it all back. I had to give him time. I had to be patient.

"Let me finish getting dressed, and then we can head downstairs," I whispered as confusion flashed across his face. "I need food." He blinked and smirked. "Aiden, I want nothing more than you for dinner, but I need physical sustenance. Real talk."

I felt his chest expand as he took a deep breath and saw the concentration in his eyes where he hauled rational thought into his brain. I was making him think of my needs, and it worked. "You transformed, and therefore your metabolism has sped up. You also have had nothing to eat or drink for two days."

I nodded as I slipped my pants on. He watched every movement, right down to me buttoning the fly on my pants one by one. When I reached for my boots, he didn't move. "Aiden, I need my boots, and you are clearly blocking the way."

He smirked and reached behind him, producing my boots for me. "Sit down. I'll put them on for you."

I sat on the bed across from the doorway to the bathroom, and he knelt in the doorway to put them on. As he slid the zipper up, he let the other hand caress my thigh. He repeated the motion with the other boot and then lifted me by the hips up into his arms. His hands moved to under my ass and squeezed.

"You are still the same boy, aren't you?" I kissed the tip of his nose.

He growled in frustration, but then he sighed. "You need to eat."

"I do." And as if on cue, my stomach growled. "Proof, I really do need to eat something of substance, Aiden."

He set me down and took my hand to lead me out. I hadn't realized just how long the hallway was that we had initially fought through. When we got downstairs, I stopped, looked around the large bar room, and Aiden turned to face me as our arms became taut.

Everything had been cleared out, and there was no visual trace of blood anywhere. With my new heightened senses, I could still smell the residual tang of it in the air, but the place had been well scrubbed.

Two days, and they had been able to get it all cleaned up? I blinked, but when I opened my eyes again, they moved of their own accord to where Amala had fallen, and a pit opened in my chest. Aiden wrapped me in his arms, and we stood there for a long moment. He didn't pull back until my breathing calmed, and he ran his thumbs across my face, wiping the tears away. I didn't even realize I had been crying.

Unable to speak, I simply reached up and caressed his hand. *I'm good.* He nodded and took me to a table that he and Hethlene had been using while I'd been recovering.

There was a chirping musical song that for some reason, put my nerves on edge. When I saw the bird in a cage, I stopped and looked at it. A bird that was a foot-and-a-half tall, with a bright gold chest that matched its beak, and a white band around the neck looked back at me. The upward crest on the top of its head grazed the top of the cage, but I couldn't help but appreciate the beautiful red markings on the wings and tail. Its big blue eye held my gaze, and I sighed.

"It came yesterday. It must be from Jayden." He sent his power out into the hall, and Hethlene came out with a plate of meat and ketsh.

"Should I listen to it now?" I asked.

"No, you need to eat. Then we can deal with whatever it is that he is telling us. It's been driving Hethlene a bit batty just tapping the side of the cage to the same beat, over and over again."

"I've seriously thought about just putting it in a stew, but if it's from the Lord, then you likely need to hear what it says. It would defeat the purpose if I ate it," Hethlene mocked, but she narrowed her eyes at the bird.

I cut a piece of the meat off and moaned when it hit my tongue. It fell apart in my mouth and was just plain delicious. "Hethlene, I don't know how you cooked or seasoned this, but it is wonderful."

I proceeded to dive in, and in what seemed like only a minute, I was all but licking the plate clean. When I looked up, Aiden and Hethlene were looking at me, both with wonder and admiration. "What? I was hungry."

Aiden shook his head at me and went to finish his meal.

"Do you want more?" Hethlene asked.

"No, thank you. Since I haven't eaten in a couple days. I should probably pace myself and not eat too much."

I did, however, get up and head over to the Lark Messenger and let it out of its cage. It circled the room twice, and just when Aiden finished his last bite and stood, it landed on my hand.

Jessika,

The Grand Lord is behind everything plaguing Ashridge. Orders come through every couple of hours for where soldiers are supposed to go and sabotage your production. It spreads from Silentport to the Black Mountains back to the coast. They are even re-routing the water in the Black Mountains to keep it from the farmers.

Jessika, the soldiers talk how the Kaletta Assassination of the Grand Duchess of Ashridge was a success. Please be careful. They have orders to storm Ashridge if his demands are not met by you. I don't know what those demands are, but I will meet

I instructed the bird to repeat the message, and it did. Then I put it in the cage. I wanted to send one back to him. One they wouldn't be able to intercept.

"What is it?" Aiden said, standing tall.

"*He* is behind everything. They are bragging in the camp about killing my mother." My voice hitched as a ball of emotion climbed up my throat. "Jayden said he will meet us back in Ashridge, but *he* has demands, and Jayden doesn't know what they are."

I paced through the room for a few minutes, and when I landed on the spot that Amala fell, I knelt in that spot and ran my fingers across it. Warmth met me. I took a deep soothing breath. I had her in my heart, if nowhere else. Now, I had to stand up and be the Grand Duchess.

So, putting my power into my legs and standing tall, I felt a new sort of power settle within me. In a voice I only used before the ruling council, I said, "Vernadali Aiden, please prepare our things and our horses. I know it is midday, but we must reach Ashridge immediately."

"Yes, Grand Duchess," Aiden echoed before striding from the room.

"Hethlene, I am sorry for the chaos and devastation we have caused upon your home. Once I reach Ashridge, you will be compensated. Thank you for the hospitality."

"Of course, Grand Duchess. Always a pleasure to have you in our home," she said, curtsying. I couldn't help the eye roll, and I saw a small smile on her lips as she rose.

"Now, please open the cage. I have a message to send." Hethlene turned toward the cage, and the bird shot out toward my outstretched hand.

Placing my palm facing its head, it rested its beak against the palm of my hand as I spoke.

Once it was imprinted upon the bird, it squealed and took off into the skies.

As I watched it fly off, I sighed. It was time.

CHAPTER 20

AIDEN

JESSIKA WAS COMPLETELY FOCUSED. When we stopped at an oasis to let the horses rest and get water, she hopped down and asked, "Cast the incantation so we can keep going."

"Jess, I know you want to get to Ashridge and put an end to all of this," I said, "but the more I cast it, the more it is going to wear on us."

"It's been days, Aiden, please."

She was ordering me just by being the Grand Duchess, and I knew that if I pushed her, she would relent, but I just looked at her and said, "I'll do it once on this three-day trip. I won't chance it on you more than that. I don't know how it is going to react to you since you've transformed."

The look she was giving me should have had me begging for forgiveness on my knees, but I wouldn't let her win this. "My kotě," I said carefully. "You will inherently be able to travel longer, harder, and faster. I will put it on the horse, but not you."

Her eyes were narrowed to slits. "And what about you?"

"I'll be fine," I lied. I would be exhausted, but I had one job. I had to get her to Ashridge safely.

"Thought you said you wouldn't, no, I believe the words were, *couldn't*, lie to me, Aiden." She walked toward me, swaying her hips, and I narrowed my eyes at her.

"You may be Grand Duchess, but I am your Vernadali. My priority has always and will always be your well-being." I put my hands on her hips as she pressed against me. The little vixen was doing everything she could to get her way. The line had greyed out after that fucking, mind-blowing kiss, and I was trying to hold back. Fuck greyed out, that line almost disappeared when I kissed her. All I could think about was taking her to bed since that kiss. Bending down, I whispered in her ear, "Which means, I'll cast it once on you when we get closer to Ashridge. No cheating. No amount of teasing, my little kotě, is going to change my mind."

I pulled back, and the look she gave me instantly made my cock hard. Damn this woman. So, in the voice I had only ever used with her, I said, "Now, get that beautiful ass up in the saddle. We have ground to cover before nightfall."

With every ounce of restraint I had, I pulled away from her, put my foot in the stirrup, and hauled myself into my own saddle. Holding the reins a little tighter than I should have, which caused the mare to prance, I said, "Move it, Kotě." She blinked a few times and then climbed up on the saddle of her gelding.

I chuckled at the emotions I was getting from her. There had to be a line between us, but each day that was greying and blurring more. I'd already blown past one of them. When she had kissed me, all propriety went out the window. I hadn't been able to think beyond the feel of her pressed against me. I didn't know what I was going to do if she pushed it further, because with that look on her face, I knew that if I had told her to get on her knees right then, she would have and eagerly gone to work. I shifted in the saddle and quickly realized this was not going to be an easy stretch of road. Angels, only Jess could do this to me.

I quickly cast the incantation on the horses and a light version of the incantation on myself. I glanced at Jess, and she had a determined smirk on her face. There was a chirp, and Jess had her gelding dashing across the expanse.

Angels, this woman was going to kill me one way or another.

THE SUN HAD GONE down a couple hours ago, and we were coming to one of the many oases between us and Ashridge City. Since we were taking the southern route, there was nothing but an endless hard-sand desert plain, which allowed the horses to go longer between breaks.

I could feel Jess tiring and knew that we would have to make a quick camp for the night. I hated being so exposed, but at least there would be fresh water for both us and the horses. When we got there, Jess jumped off immediately and tossed me the reins. It was overcast, and I could smell the moisture in the air, even if it hadn't started raining. I tied off the horses under some of the tall leafy trees along the water's edge, where they would be able to reach the water, and stripped to my undershorts. Jess had just pulled off her boots and jacket before she dove headfirst into the water. I didn't blame her. It was hot and sweltering.

If nothing else, we could rinse the sweat and dust off our backs. When I reached the water's edge, she was floating on the surface, and I couldn't take my eyes off the pure bliss and elation on her face. I could feel it through the bond, too, and I couldn't help but smile. Sitting down with my feet on the water's edge, I just watched her. Each of her movements was fluid, and watching the tension release from her face released something within. As if she knew I was watching her, she faced me, her eyes sparkling in the light and a smile on her face. She was a siren song, and I was weak against it. I wanted to jump in after her, pull her against me, and kiss her with everything I had. I wanted to do so much more with her, but there were things to consider outside of us, and neither of us had the luxury to act that selfishly.

Jess dove back under the water and came up with nothing but her underwear on. She chucked her clothes at me, and I caught them with ease. Shaking my head at her and huffing a laugh, I got up and hung them over one of the branches. When I returned to the water, she was floating on her back again, and this time I didn't hesitate, diving in.

The water was cool and instantly diminished the headache that had built from sitting in the heat. It may be night, but damn if it wasn't still hot. I dove deep into the pool of water and hovered near the bottom, where the temperature was significantly cooler, until my lungs burned with the need to breathe. When I reached the surface again, Jess splashed me instantly and laughed.

Angels, I really was in so much trouble. If my heart and soul hadn't already been madly in love with her, I would have fallen right there. Her laugh was such a pure sound, it made my soul lighter just hearing it. I was a lovesick puppy.

She swam over to where I was, and I left all the rules and my sanity back on that horse when I brought her close to me and kissed her. I felt the moan come from her as she wrapped her legs around my waist. There was no way she was missing the raging hard-on I had. The cold water had helped some, but the second her lips met mine, it was just like it was back in Shuset.

She pulled back as we started to sink and unwrapped her legs. I laughed at the sputtering that came from her when her head went under. "Jerk."

"Yeah, well, not really my fault you forgot how to swim."

"You distracted me." She smirked and let her eyes drop toward my waist. "With that hard-on you got going on."

"And whose fault is that?" Her answering smile was bright and her eyes shone in the moonlight. "Fuck, woman. Will you stop being so damn beautiful?" I muttered and dove under the water, scrubbing off as much of the sweat as I could before making my way back toward the beach. I had to get my wits back, only she caught up with me before I was out and jumped on my back, pulling me backwards into the water.

This time it was me clearing water out of my nose and her giggling, but she hadn't let go of me. We were about chest deep in the water, and she repositioned herself to be in front of me, her legs still wrapped tight against my waist.

"Jess." My voice was full of the emotion that I could no longer contain.

"Aiden." Her eyes met mine, and there were a million questions behind them. It took her a moment, but her voice came out tentative and vulnerable. "Can we, for just one night, forget that you are Vernadali and I am the Grand Duchess?"

I wanted to say yes. Angels, I wanted it just to be us, but I wanted so much more than what she was offering. "I can't. That isn't enough, Jess," I said, my voice just as nervous and shaky as hers. I ran a thumb across her cheek, and my chest tightened.

"Aiden, I love you. Only you. I haven't been able to look at anyone seriously since the day you left. And yes, I know we've already had that discussion. I'm not bringing that back up. I'm just saying, there is no one else in this dimension, or any other, for me other than you." She unwrapped her legs but kept her arms around my shoulders. Mine tightened around her, and everything within me shuddered.

"My kotě." My forehead rested on hers, and I felt the growling in my chest more than I heard it. She purred back.

"Aiden, please." She was begging, and that purr pulled on every ounce of restraint within me.

"I want to hold you and never let you go. I've told you before, you are mine. If we do this tonight, if we give in, there is no going back. No one will ever have you again. You will consent to being mine forever."

"That sounds like a marriage proposal."

Staring into her onyx eyes, I steeled myself for what I was going to say. There was no going back. "Whatever you want to call it. If you cross that line, you will consent to being mine forever. Damn the Vernadali Council. Damn the Nalrin Council. Damn Ashridge. I will walk away from everything to stand at your side, but you will still have to run Ashridge and find a way for me to stand beside you and support you. Not from the shadows. Not a dirty little secret. Not second to Jayden or anyone else. It will be a promise you can't break with me. I know Ashridge has to have a ruler since your brother abdicated the throne to marry his wife. You are the Grand Duchess. You are the sole blood heir to the Ashridge territory."

Her eyes cleared from the ecstasy-induced haze, and she looked at me for a long, painful moment.

"Did you hear me?" I asked carefully. I couldn't do this. Not to myself, not to her. I couldn't give in for one night and be able to walk away again. She had to know that.

"I did." She stared at me. "Are you being serious right now?"

"I have never been more serious in my life. I walked away once Jess, and it nearly killed me. I won't be able to have you for one night and walk away again. This time would be worse, because I would still have to see and feel you every day for the rest of my life. That means that you have to make a decision, and quickly. We have at least one more night before we get to Ashridge. One more night to figure this out. I won't have you choose between Ashridge and me, because Ashridge *should* and must always win that decision. I can't have you leave it without a ruler." I kissed her forehead and took a half step back from her, letting out a long breath through my nose, my chest constricting with dread.

"Do you love me, Aiden?" Her voice was small but strong.

"I wouldn't be saying all of this if I didn't. I have loved you since the first time our eyes met, Jessika Petra Valenti. You have owned every ounce of me from that moment on. That will not change, no matter what your decision is. I would never have walked away if we were just two normal beings living in some small town somewhere." I made myself meet her eyes, "But we are not normal people. I am Vernadali CJ and Lady Megan's Vernadali son. You are the sole heir and rightful Grand Duchess of Ashridge."

Her hands trembled as they ran down my bare chest. Her eyes were filled with love, and I thought she would answer right then and there, but I said, "You have to think about this. You cannot make a decision right here and now. There is more than just me to consider in all this. You have to think about Jayden, Killy, and Ilris, too. They are entwined in this mess, and I won't have our decision ruin their lives. They have to be considered. They *deserve* that."

"You know, Jayden told me that I should have you as my consort. He would always have Ilris. He *told* me to take you as my consort, Aiden." She said the words quietly, as if they were too loud for the air around us.

I shook my head and looked away. Consort my ass. I was no one's consort. I wouldn't be deemed second to anyone, especially some other man, even if it was one who had given his blessing. I wanted someone who wanted only me and would claim only me. Others could have that multiple being dynamic. There were Vernadali who had relationships with many people at once, and they all knew and agreed to it. I respected them for that lifestyle, but that wasn't something I could agree to or ever be comfortable with.

"Look at me, damn it," she said, pulling my chin, forcing compliance. "You know what I told him? I told him that wasn't how our relationship worked. You couldn't be someone who sat in the shadows. I know that, Aiden. I would *never* ask that of you. I could never expect that of you."

I could feel her determination. I knew her decision. That made it all so much worse. I knew she wanted me, and only me, but I still had to make her think it through.

"Jayden isn't safe in Kaletta. He has to have a legal place in Ashridge. A legal place to have Killy and Ilris by his side. If not, they are going to be sent home, and I can't have Jayden and Ilris' relationship on my conscience. That doesn't even include the legally-binding marriage agreement you have with Jayden."

"You think I don't know that, Aiden? I've been trying to work that out since Silentport. Jayden and I talked a lot about it." She went and sat down so that the water was still covering her lower half, and I went to sit beside her.

"So, what do we do?" I asked her.

"I want one night with you where it is just us. No rules, no expectations. I still want that. Underworld's darkness, I want that for the rest of our lives, but I understand what you are saying." She laid her palm flat and pushed her power through it. The water hummed and vibrated, and I closed my eyes at the feel of it against my skin.

"Do I have to have answers about Jayden, Killy, and Ilris before I give you my answer?" She looked back at me, and I met her gaze. "I will always choose you. My heart and soul are yours. They have been since that night we were in the Black Mountains and we first decided to try our relationship. When you first kissed me, you owned me. You still own me. I am yours."

I reached over and put my hand on her cheek. My mouth opened and closed. Nothing came out. I knew it wasn't fair for me to demand she had all the answers. Even if she gave me possibilities, that was all they were, possibilities.

"I love you, Aiden Chatwell Mathewson."

"I love you, Jessika Petra Valenti." Then I brought my mouth to hers and kissed her.

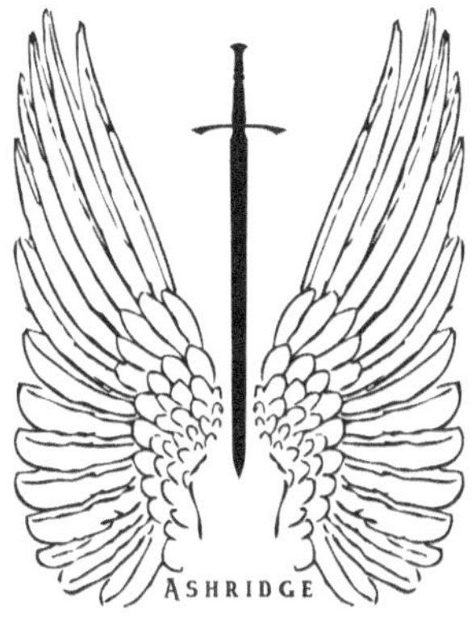

CHAPTER 21

JESSIKA

I WOKE THE NEXT morning wrapped up in Aiden's arms. We hadn't had sex last night, but I still felt raw and open. Aiden stirred next to me, and I untangled myself from him and looked to the sky. The clouds in the distance were dark and heavy with rain. Studying it another moment, I quickly realized there was no way we would be able to outrun that storm. It was going to be a wet, windy, and highly uncomfortable ride.

"Aid," I said, looking at the wall of green more closely. "Aiden!"

He was standing with this syths, Charge wrapped around me within seconds.

"I'm fine, but we need to move to where we will be able to hunker down. We won't be able to outrun that storm." I pointed to the horizon.

"Fuck," he said, rubbing his eyes and looking around. "Avalan is a couple hours' ride to the south. That, or we ride it out on the desert plains."

"Avalan. That is going to cause some serious flash flooding." I pointed toward the wall of clouds. "We need proper shelter. I know it makes us backtrack a bit, but we can't get anywhere else. The other oases between here and Ashridge don't have any cover at all, even if we could get there before the storm overtakes us."

"There isn't enough cover here, either." He weighed our options and ran his hands through his hair. "If we use the incantation, we can still get to Ashridge tomorrow night, weather permitting, even from Avalan." He let out a heavy sigh. "Let's do it."

We both threw on our now dried clothes, because neither of us bothered to get out of our underclothes last night.

The horses were already anxious, and I saw Aiden cast the incantation on both of them as I put the blanket and saddle on the back of my horse. When I pulled on the strap, tightening the saddle, thunder rolled across the plain. My eyes flicked to Aiden, and we both knew that we would have to ride like the wind. Once the horses were saddled and our packs were secured, I pulled myself up.

The rain had started to fall, and I tipped my head back, closed my eyes, and tried to let it calm me as I prayed to the Angels that we would get to shelter before the worst of the storm found us. Under normal circumstances, I would have stood here and danced in the rain, but time was not on my side.

"After you, Grand Duchess." The title alone made my heart hurt. He was trying to put distance between us, and I hated every minute of it. I wasn't going to let him. Call me selfish. Call me manipulative. He still loved me. He may have said I was his, but that was a two-way street. He was mine. I'd be damned to the deepest darkest parts of the Underworld if I was going to let him go now.

I reached my hand out toward him, waited for him to take it, and squeezed it as I mouthed, "I love you." He gave me a small smile and dropped my hand. Taking the reins, I wheeled my horse around and put my heels to his sides.

IT RAINED THE ENTIRE way to Avalan. Both of us kept looking over our shoulders at the storm coming, and it was closing in fast. We were wet, covered in mud, and I could feel dirt in areas that were chaffing. I wanted a shower. That was high on the list of priorities.

We bolted into the small town and went straight for the hotel. Aiden headed inside to get us a room, while I settled the horses in the stable and grabbed our packs. I was making my way back toward the hotel when Aiden met me in the street.

"We got the last room," he said, holding the key in his hand.

"Horses are settled. Stable hand said that they expect the storm to stick around a couple days, but hopefully we can head out tomorrow." I handed him his bag, but my eyes went to the message center as something that Amala had said echoed through my head. Without saying a word, I turned straight for it.

There was a bright, metallic ding as I entered the message center, and a smile crossed my face when I looked up and saw a small brass bell hanging from the door jamb. Aiden's mom had told me of the system back in the Manusia, but I hadn't seen it used here as a way of indicating someone had come in.

A tall brawny man came out of the back room, running his hands through his long hair, and, without looking up, muttered, "What can I do ya for?"

"I need to send a message to Ashridge, immediately," I commanded, standing tall.

His eyes popped up at the sound of my voice, and he immediately bowed. "Grand Duchess. What an honor, of course."

He slid a blank sheet of parchment and a pen toward me and said, "The storm may slow down the communication, but it will get through."

"Thank you. I need to ensure that it is only seen by Lady Megan Mathewson or Vernadali CJ Mathewson. Is that clear?" I wrote down the information I had been given by Jayden. When I handed him the message, he immediately folded it without reading it.

My eyes flicked to Aiden, and before I could think twice, I wrote a separate message to his father. "Please also ensure this is seen by *only* Vernadali CJ."

Aiden's eyebrows knitted together in question, and I shook my head.

"Of course, Grand Duchess. Will you be staying at the River Rock?" he said, indicating the only hotel in the town.

"We are, until the worst of the storm passes." I slid him the kinls to pay for the transmissions, and a few more, since I knew this was going to be the first of many messages bouncing back and forth.

"This is too much."

"I need any and all communications that pass between Ashridge, Vernadali Aiden, and me to be as if they never occurred. Is that clear?" I said, my voice low.

His eyes widened, and he nodded.

"Have a good day, sir." I turned around and walked out and toward the hotel without saying a word to Aiden. I tipped my head back, finally allowed myself to take the previously denied moment, and treasured the raindrops on my face. Aiden had taken my hand to lead me toward the hotel, and when we walked inside, I wiped my face off and looked at him, "What room?"

"3812," he said, looking me up and down. What was he getting from me? He grabbed my hand again and headed for the stairs. When we reached them, we went up two flights before he stopped, pinned me against the wall, and kissed me breathless. Then he moved down along my jaw and my neck. He whispered something, but I didn't hear him.

"Humm?"

"What did you send to my father?" He was not playing fair.

"Aiden," I breathed. "No cheating."

He pulled back and rested his forehead on mine, his breathing just as ragged as my own. Every one of his muscles was tense as he took a step back. His eyes were so bright that I wasn't sure if they were hazel or molten gold. I took a calming breath and said, "I'm not going to tell you, Aiden. I need to talk to your dad. Period. That's it. Okay?"

He nodded, took my hand, and led me up the stairs to the next floor. He looked down the hall before we went through it and quickly pulled us into the room we would be staying in.

This one was bigger than the one in Shuset, but, of course, it still only had one bed. I gave him an even look, and he just smiled innocently. Shaking my head at him, I went to get cleaned up in the bathroom. Even though we spent most of the evening in the oasis pool, it was nice to be able to use soap with hot, running water and really clean myself.

Once again clean, and with white hair instead of a dirty blonde from the dust, I climbed into the soft bed. Aiden kissed the top of my head and headed into the bathroom. The shower started, and I leaned my head back against the headboard.

The comfort of the bed was enticing, and I couldn't help but slide farther into the solid weight of the blankets. The temperature was dropping, and I secretly hoped I could use Aiden as a heater in the middle of the night.

Aiden was still in the shower when there was a soft knock on the door. I swung my legs around to climb out of the bed, but before I was able to open the door, Aiden was there, stark naked, soap from his hair running down his face. I nearly jumped out of my skin but started laughing. I forgot how quick the Vernadali could move if they needed to. He raised an eyebrow at me, and I rolled my eyes and stepped back. He stuck his head through the crack in the door, and when he closed it, he handed me a piece of paper.

"It's enchanted against me. Whatever you asked Dad, he doesn't want me reading it." He smirked.

"Go finish your shower. You are getting the floor all wet." He turned toward the bathroom, and out of playful instinct, I smacked his ass.

One second, I was laughing at the sound it made, and the next, I was against the wall, his lips on mine.

Fuck.

I fucked up. Or did I?

When Aiden pulled back, he gave me a long look up and down and tapped his chin. I raised my eyebrow at him, and he mirrored the movement. Soap was sliding down the side of his face and flowing down each ripple of muscle in his torso. I ran a single finger through the soap, across his chest, and down his abs. When I hit his hip bone, he tapped his chin one more time, and I instantly dropped to my knees, looking up at him. I didn't think I had moved my hand, but when the soap went down his leg, my finger was following it.

He was hard before me, and I licked my lips, biting back a giggle as his hand hit the wall behind me hard and I saw him fist his other. His restraint was one to rival the Angels. I knew I wasn't making it easy on him. I didn't *want* to make this easy on him. His eyes were on mine, and I just said, "Aiden."

I had followed his command. I had honored his request, and I told him last night I chose him. His hand loosened, and he reached over, putting a finger under my chin. As my teeth caught my bottom lip, his breathing went ragged. I sat here, just like he had commanded. My hands were in my lap now, and it was taking everything I had in me not to take him into my mouth.

"Answer now, Grand Duchess." Aiden had not broken my gaze, and I clenched my thighs together, a movement he did not miss if the tilt of his lips was any indication.

"I told you last night, Vernadali Aiden Mathewson. I choose you. I know the challenges. I choose them. I *will* have you at my side. We will figure a way out of the contract with Kaletta and find a way to save our friends and their lovers." I would not say his name in this room. Not now. Not when...

He pulled me up and pinned me against the wall, and his lips were on mine in seconds. My panties were in his hands and burned to ash in the next. I gasped at how quickly he replaced them with his hand and started to work my clit.

CHAPTER 22

AIDEN

"Answer now, Grand Duchess." I had to know. It was now or never. It took everything I had, including using my own Vernadali power, to not push the dominance. She had submitted by kneeling. Sure, she resisted at first, but she submitted. Just like she always did. Ultimately, she was my good girl.

"I told you last night, Vernadali Aiden Mathewson. I choose you. I know the challenges. I choose them. I will have you at my side. We will figure out a way to get out of the contract with Kaletta and find a way to save our friends and their lovers," she said, and I felt the honesty and determination in each word pass through that bond. I knew it, but I needed to hear it. When the last word came out, her eyes went soft and her lower lip stuck out just enough that my cock jumped.

I lifted her and crashed my mouth on hers. I needed her like the air I breathed. I needed the feel of her skin against mine. I needed to bury myself so deep within her, she would never need to doubt me.

Using the wall as a brace, I tore through the G-string she was wearing. The fucking thing had been teasing me the second she walked out of the bathroom. She knew it too. I coiled it up in my hands and burned it to ash.

I reached over, parted her lips, and ran my finger up and down her slit, teasing her. Her hips moved against me, and I couldn't help but chuckle at her enthusiasm.

Pulling back from her, I tried to catch my breath as I slid just one finger up into her, letting the heel of my hand rub against that bundle of nerves. She lifted her leg and wrapped it around my hip, but the soap made it too slick for her to grip.

"Kotě," I whispered as she ground against my hand. I slid another finger up her slick, wet hole, and the sounds she made had me smiling wickedly.

"Aid."

"How long has it been for you?" She was tight. Tighter than I remembered her, and there was no way I wouldn't hurt her if I took her right now.

"Over a year." She breathed as I finger-fucked her while she ground against the palm of my hand. Fuck. A year. I buried my head in the crook of her neck and ran my tongue along it, kissing her softly.

I curled my fingers against her front wall, and she purred like my good little kitten. She was holding onto me around my neck, and I slid one arm under her leg to steady her. When I curled my finger along the front wall again, her teeth scraped along my shoulder and I shuddered at the feel of them against my skin.

Oh, Underworld. I knew that if she transitioned, she may claim her partner, but I couldn't think of that now.

I slid a third finger into her and felt her walls start to tighten around me, but I didn't relent and continued fingering her. Her wetness was coating her entire pussy and down the inside of her thigh.

"Fuck, Aiden. I want to cum. Please, let me cum." She moaned and begged.

"That's my good girl." I smiled and kissed her neck. "Cum for me, my kotě." I finger-fucked her hard and pressed my thumb against her clit. Moments later, her walls gripped ahold of my fingers, and she threw her head back. I leaned back to watch the ecstasy on her face and smiled. I didn't let up, and soon another orgasm washed over her.

I removed my hand, lifted her, and carried her to the bed. When I laid her down, she tried to take me with her, but I just said, "I'm going to rinse the soap off. I'll be back in just a minute. Besides, you need to get your wits about you first."

"Aiden," she said, but it was weak. I kissed her quickly, headed into the shower, and realized I had completely forgotten to turn the water off, which was now ice cold.

I shivered as the near frigid water ran through my hair. I had to work a little to get the soap all out, as it had started to dry. I chuckled. It was so worth it to see her writhing against me.

Grabbing the towel, I sent my power out to Jess and smiled. She had fallen asleep. The cold water had helped settle my erection for now, but I knew it would only take moments in bed next to her before I would be rock-hard again.

Taking my time in getting cleaned up to let her rest, I was just finishing up when another knock on the door sounded. When I answered it, the same little boy who had delivered my father's message was standing there. "Vernadali Aiden, I've been asked to await a response."

Poking my head around the corner, I saw her still sleeping, and I tore through the seal on the back and read the message.

J&A,

JAYDEN IS ON HIS WAY TO ASHRIDGE WITH HIS FATHER. WE WILL HOLD HIM OFF FOR AS LONG AS WE CAN.

EXPECTED ETA?

-MOM

Well, nothing like short and sweet, huh? I quickly wrote back:

MOM AND DAD,

WE WILL BE HERE UNTIL THE STORM PASSES. WE NEED TWO DAYS, MAYBE THREE. PROTECT JAYDEN, ILRIS, AND KILLY. HE WILL TRY TO USE THEM AS PAWNS. PROTECT THEM.

READ THE ASHRIDGE AND KALETTA TERRITORY AGREEMENT, PLEASE, MOM. FIND THE LOOPHOLES. THE GRAND DUCHESS IS MINE. KALETTA WILL NOT HAVE HER. JAYDEN WILL NOT OBJECT.

-A

Handing the message back to the kid, with a few extra kinls, his eyes widened, and I put my fingers to my lips as he nodded again.

I closed the door, and when I turned the corner, Jess was there on the bed with her hand out.

I smirked at her but handed her the one from Mom.

"Both of them, Aiden," she said, only slightly annoyed.

I reached down and picked up the one from my dad and cringed at the prickling feeling that came from it. "He really doesn't want me to read this one."

"Wouldn't do you any good. Knowing him, he had it enchanted so that it would only look to be an empty sheet of paper from your viewpoint, even if you opened it." She gave me a wicked little smile.

I handed it to her and sat on the bed next to her. She snuggled into my side, and I wrapped my arm around her so she was against my shoulder.

She read through the one from Mom and asked, "How did you respond?"

"We will be here until the storm passes. Likely two or three days. I also asked them to protect Jayden, Ilris, and Killy." I stopped and took a deep breath, shifting a little under her. "Then I really stuck my foot in my mouth. I'm sorry I didn't clear it with you first. I should have, and you should have been the one to say it."

"You told them about us." There was no judgment or frustration behind it.

"In a manner of speaking. I told Mom to read through the marriage agreement. She'll find a way out of it. She's my mom. She always does."

She gave me an even look. "What else? That isn't all you said."

I ran my hand through my hair. "No. That isn't all." I let out a long breath. "I may have also said that you were mine and that Kaletta wouldn't have you. I told her Jayden wouldn't object."

I fully expected her to lose her shit with me over that. Instead, she surprised me by turning to straddle my legs and sit on my thighs. Then, in a small voice, she said, "You did?"

"I did. Or was your answer at that wall incorrect?"

"No, I am yours, Aiden. I'm just surprised the first people you tell are your parents."

Gently placing my hands on her hips, I leaned my head back and huffed a laugh. "Yeah, it is a little strange." I looked back at her and said, "Do you wish I hadn't?"

"No, if anyone can find a way out of the contract, it will be Lady Megan. Jayden had suggested it and I blew him off. I don't want to use your name and connections to rule and get what I want." She let out a rough breath. "I'm against a wall right now, figuratively speaking. With my mom dead, it's only Jayden and I who object to the agreement. All four signatures have to be on the nullification, unless the..."

Her voice trailed off as a wicked gleam sparked in her eyes. "Oh, I need to send a message to Janreka. She is going to have so much fun." Then she cocked her head to the side. "You said she's in Ashridge, right?" I nodded, and she crossed her arms, tapping her chin. "She did offer when we were in the Curtails... No. If anyone is going to, it will be Jayden or me."

I looked at her like she was crazy. "Jess, you are speaking in partial sentences. What are you talking about?"

"Taking his head, of course," she said, looking at me like I was now the crazy one.

"Jess, if he gets too close to you, I will remove his head. You and Jayden may not have the chance." I pulled her closer to me, and she wrapped her arms around my neck.

"Is that so?" She smiled brightly, and I marveled at how her small little fangs seemed to taunt me more than anything. Just the thought of her biting me with those made me shiver. The points were small and dainty, and they fit her perfectly. It was like this was who she was supposed to be.

I nodded, remembering I should answer her. "No one will harm a hair on your body and live through it."

"Is that my Dom talking, or my Vernadali?" She nipped at my bottom lip.

"Do you want me to still be your dominant?" I asked, picking up a strand of hair that lay on her right breast. I curled it around my finger and rubbed it with my thumb. "You still followed my commands, and you submitted to me earlier, but do you want that again?"

"Yes. It will have to be a little different from last time, since I'm Grand Duchess. We have to have an understanding that there will be times and circumstances where I won't be able to submit. I have to be able to do that without punishments." Her eyes met mine, and there was need there, but there was also that regal stature that wasn't going to be put aside. "We will have to find other ways to make it work when I have to outright and completely deny and overrule you."

"Things to iron out later, I guess, but otherwise same rules? Same punishments and expectations?" Jess reached over and kissed me softly, shivered slightly, and whispered a soft sweet yes against my lips before leaning her forehead against mine. It was music to my ears.

"Can I ask something?" she asked a moment later, her voice soft but sure, so I nodded. "This time, I want a symbol of being yours, and I want you to have one, too. I'm going all in on this with you. You said that if we did this, I was consenting to being yours forever. That works both ways."

I blinked at her, and my voice shook with the well of emotion that threatened to come out as I said, "You would wear *my* collar?"

"Only yours."

"Okay." I swallowed, pushing down that ball of emotion that jumped into my throat, and smiled at her. "I will find something befitting my Grand Duchess."

"Of course, I'll want a proper engagement ring from you as well." Her smile faltered slightly before she said, "Once we are officially out of the contract with Kaletta, obviously."

I nodded but couldn't help but smile as she ran her fingers over my Vernadali tattoo and her name scroll. She was mine. This was real. She really was mine.

"But our symbols? Those happen before we reach Ashridge. I want to walk into Ashridge wearing something that says you own me. That I am yours. Whatever it is, we both wear it."

I kissed her, hard. I couldn't help it. I swallowed back the tears as it sank in that she was completely giving herself over to me. She pressed her hips and chest into me, and I just revealed in the taste of her. I ran my hands up her back and gripped her shoulders. When the kiss broke, we sat there for long minutes in silence, which allowed my mind to start to roam.

"Have you had other dynamics since...," I said, my voice trailing off.

"I tried twice, but I couldn't give my submission to anyone but you. Both tried to control me. Not dominate. There was no communication. It was not healthy." There was a bitterness in her voice that had me on edge, and I wanted nothing more than to hunt them down and give them a few lessons.

"When you say you couldn't submit to them, what do you mean?"

"The trust wasn't there, so I couldn't give myself wholly to them. There was too much Duchess that wouldn't relinquish the control. I know that you can protect me. I know you will take care of me. I know that if I ask you to stop, you will," she said quietly, but it wasn't weak. Thunder rolled around us, and the rain started pelting the windows.

"Say it, Kotě. Say your safe word."

"Pear," she murmured immediately and met my eyes. The heat in her gaze fueled the spark in my soul that had died out five years ago and was being reignited.

"Pear," I repeated as I felt her pride and certainty come through the bond.

"I want you, Aiden. We can't go back to what things were, but we can start over."

There was a knock on the door again, and with a sigh, she hopped off my lap and swung her legs around to sit on the bed so I could get up to answer it. The message boy was back and handed me two messages.

A&J,

THE GRAND LORD IS ARRIVING WITH A FULL STRINGENT OF SOLDIERS. SOMETHING ISN'T RIGHT ABOUT THIS WHOLE THING, BUT OUR SPIES HAVEN'T GAINED ANY INTEL, YET.

HAS JAYDEN SENT ANY OTHER WORD?

PROTECT EACH OTHER. ARRIVE IN ONE PIECE.

JESS, OFFICIALLY WELCOME TO THE FAMILY.

BE SAFE AND SEE YOU SOON.

-MOM AND DAD

I turned to Jess to let her read it, but she was scribbling a response to my dad. With a few words and a flick of her fingers, she had the ink disappearing so I couldn't see what she had written. I was sure not even my mom would be able to read that message.

"Can you have this sent to Vernadali CJ immediately, please," Jess said carefully. "And the response sent for Lady Megan."

I scribbled that we would be safe and how we hadn't heard anything else from Jayden. There wasn't really anything else to say, anyway. I gave him the response and paid him handsomely for the back and forth. The poor kid was soaked to the bone.

When I turned back to Jess, she was turned halfway away from me and blushing. Jess was actually blushing. I slid my arms around her waist and asked her, "Why are your cheeks that adorable shade of red?"

"Your parents." She had a smile on her lips but jumped when the thunder cracked through the room and the walls shook with the force of it.

"What about them?" I chuckled, nibbling on her ear. She melted to my touch and leaned into me.

"They said, *Welcome to the family.*" Her head leaned onto my shoulder, and she half turned it to face me.

"Yeah." I wasn't exactly sure what that was supposed to mean.

"I'm technically engaged to two men right now, and they just say welcome to the family?"

I sighed and turned her to face me. "Remember, Kotě, you've always been part of this family. You never really left. You still talked to my parents over the years while we were... on a break." The shock on her face was hysterical. "Yes, we were on a break. That is all *we* are going to call it. It was rough, it was brutal, but I'm never walking away from you again."

"I won't let you." She stood on her tiptoes to kiss me. "I'm tired. As much as I want to have sex with you, I'm really tired. It seems like the damn messenger boy shows up every thirty minutes, and we both know that isn't nearly long enough to have you worship me, or me worship you," she murmured against my collarbone.

"Fine. Let's get some rest. Once the storm passes, I'll get you that collar, and then we will ride long and hard—" I smirked at her. "—to Ashridge."

"Hummhum." Jess turned toward the bed and winked at me over her shoulder. She climbed up onto the bed and crawled to the opposite side, sticking that ass out and swaying it back and forth as she went. I was instantly hard for her and groaned in frustration.

"Angels, Jess."

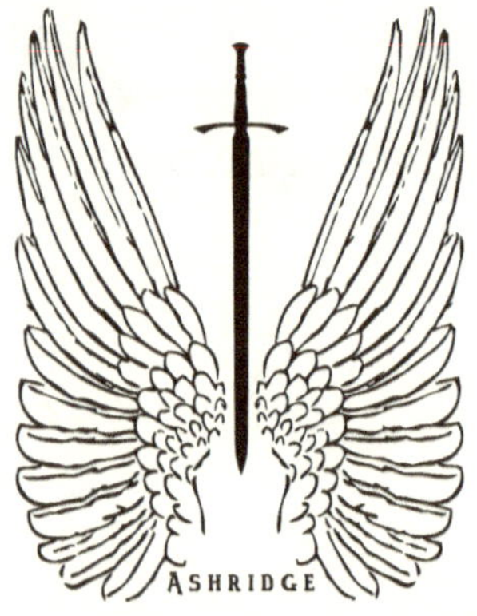

CHAPTER 23

JESSIKA

I SLEPT ON AND off, lying there in Aiden's arms. The messenger came about every thirty to forty minutes to deliver messages, and Aiden kept answering them. I didn't want to move from the bed. When messages came from his dad, I answered them, but Aiden handed them off, and I stayed in my warm and cozy place. Unfortunately, the storm wasn't letting up and actually seemed to be getting worse.

The next day was much the same: rain, wind, and extensive lightning and thunder. The messenger came every hour, but when I asked Aiden what was so important, he said, "I'm trying to see what I can do about us, Kotĕ."

I eyed him carefully but didn't dare let on that I had been doing the same with his dad. I had said nothing, but it warmed my heart to know that he was trying to find a way to make it legal.

"Jess, what is it?"

"I don't know what you're talking about." I snuggled up closer to his chest, and he rolled over on top of me. He used his knee to spread my legs, and I didn't fight him.

"Kotě, you can't lie to me." He sat back on his feet between my legs and ran a single finger up and down the sides of them. I tried not to react, but he knew every inch of my body. "You know how much I love these thick thighs of yours? Your soft curves as they writhe under me?"

"And what does that have to do with me not being able to lie to you?" I said as he trailed his hand from my hip to my knee. My breath was hesitant, and I was trying not to show just how turned on I was by him kneeling between my legs, hands caressing my thighs.

"I can feel you, remember?" He tapped his tattoo and, more importantly, that blasted name on the scroll. My heart leaped, and he chuckled. "Just like that jump in apprehension you just felt."

His voice changed to a rough, demanding tone that instantly had me wiggling my hips and trying to scissor my legs together. My eyes grew when I realized my mistake.

His mouth moved into a smirk, he spread his fingers into a V, and I gave him a narrowed look before I complied.

"Good girl." Heat flooded through me at his tone. "Take them off."

"Aiden," I begged.

He leaned over me, caged me in, and whispered against the column of my neck in that voice that would have me doing anything for him, "Take your panties off. Now, my kotě."

My breathing hitched as I slid them over my hips and kicked them off. I laid my hands at my sides, as I knew I should, and waited for his next command.

Aiden sat back, pulling me with him and lifting my shirt up and over my head. No sooner was the shirt past my lips than his lips were on mine. My arms were out, though he didn't lift the shirt completely off, but instead tightened it across my eyes. I leaned back, bracing myself with my hands against the mattress and fisting the sheets. His fingers made quick work of my bra, and I heard it land somewhere near the dresser across the room.

He broke the kiss and finished removing my shirt. Fisting my hair, he pulled my head back as he looked down at me. My chest pushed out toward him as I watched his gaze take in every exaggerated breath of my chest, lick his lips as he studied my stomach, and how the heat became scorching in his eyes as he reached my core.

"Aiden." I breathed his name like a prayer to the Angels.

"I have missed this view. Fuck, you are so beautiful, Jess." His hand tightened in my hair as he kissed me gently. "Now, I know you want me to fuck you, and I have every intention of doing just that. I plan on having myself buried so deep within you that you won't know where you end and I begin. Do not move. No matter what." His finger ran up the center of me, and I whimpered, chasing his movement.

He chuckled and did it again. Spreading my lips and circling my opening, he pressed his thumb against my clit. When I let out a breathy moan, he plunged two fingers in and split them into a V, where I instinctively moved my legs wider. On his outward draw, he hit that spot, and I clamped around him and moaned.

"Good girl." Aiden removed his fingers and raised them to his mouth where he sucked them clean, all while holding eye contact with me. Fuck, it was enough to have me losing it all over again.

He stood from the bed, removed his pants and shirt, but paused when his eyes met mine. It was only when I licked my lips at the sight before me that he tapped his chin, and my eyes widened in excitement. I bounced off the bed, but before I could kneel, he grabbed my breasts in his hands and tweaked my nipples, bending down to flick his tongue around the erect peaks. When he pulled back, he winked at me, and I sank to my knees before him, biting my lower lip, looking up at him as I waited for permission to taste him.

"Kotě." His quiet voice was laced with need as his hand cradled the side of my head.

"Please, sir?" I begged, my eyes flicking to his rock-hard cock before glancing up again.

"Have you been a good girl today, Jess? Do you deserve to suck my cock as a reward?"

"Yes." My voice was thick, and I could feel my mouth watering with the need to swallow him. My eyes flicked to it again, and it was already wet with precum. I couldn't help but lick my lips. Leaning forward, his fingers were still threaded in my hair, and I moaned at the feel of him pulling it to keep me in place. I smirked.

Taking himself in his other hand, he brought just the tip of it to my lips and ran it across them. Need and heat spread through my entire body. My eyes hadn't left his, and I could see the fire burning within that gaze. With a single wink, he gave me permission.

My tongue flicked out and slowly licked that string of precum from the tip. I let it hang between him and I, and he moaned. It took all my concentration not to close my eyes. He tasted better than I remembered.

I licked around the head of him, took just the tip into my mouth, and sucked in short quick movements. When I felt him twitch and pulse, I slowed and licked from the base of him, up and through his slit again. His fingers tightened in my hair, and he threw his head back and cussed under his breath. Teasing Aiden and bringing him right to the edge was something I had always been good at.

I pulled back, released him with a pop, and the growl that echoed through the room wasn't human. Gazing up to him through my lashes, I couldn't help the smile as I took him deep into my mouth. His hand hadn't moved from the back of my head, but he let me set the pace. After a few shorter strokes, I tipped my head and swallowed him down my throat, holding him there before pulsing three times and bringing him back out to the head of him. On the last pull, I carefully ran the point of my new fangs along the long length of him and felt him twitch and harden even more against my tongue.

"My kotě." He moaned, but I swallowed him whole over and over again. His other hand reached over and cupped the other side of my head. He was deep-throat fucking me, and I felt as if a geyser had opened between my legs. There was nothing more satisfying than the feeling of him taking his pleasure from me.

I pulled back momentarily to catch my breath, sucking the head of him, letting my teeth scrape along the length of him. Swirling my tongue around him as I swallowed him, I winked and he started to fuck my mouth again. There were loud groans, and when I moaned with him down my throat, it took two short thrusts for him to bury himself deep down my throat and release. His power pulsed into the room, and I threw mine out to meet it, sending the air in the room vibrating.

I swallowed every drop before he released his grip on my hair. As I licked him clean, carefully running my canines against him, he started hardening and twitching again. Sitting back on my feet, I looked up at him and licked my lips. His power snapped back into him as he collapsed onto his knees before me, taking my head in his hands.

His breathing was ragged, and his eyes were glazed and big as he stared at me. I reached up to scratch my temple, and a soft smile crossed his lips as he winked at me. Aiden leaned forward and pressed his forehead to mine.

I leaned into him and kissed him. Softly at first, but he deepened the kiss, and I swore I heard his voice in my head say, "*I'll never leave you again, Jessika Petra.*" It was in a soft loving tone, but that was quickly followed with a growling, "*You are mine.*" His hands hadn't left my face, but I swore there was a caress between my legs.

"Aiden, please. I need you inside me," I whispered against his lips. He lifted me and laid me down on the bed, motioning his fingers into a V. My legs instantly spread for him, and as his hands wrapped around the outside of my thighs, I felt my lips part and someone flick my clit.

I jumped, and he chuckled. "Easy, Kotě. Easy." His hands found my breasts, but I distinctly felt fingers also rubbing my clit expertly at the same time.

"Neat trick." I whimpered, leaning back and just savoring the feel of him on my skin.

He leaned down and took a nipple into his mouth and nipped at it at the same time his power flicked at my clit. His power continued to tease and stroke me as he left a trail of kisses down my abdomen to where he was working between my legs. One moment, it was phantom hands, and the next, his tongue ran from one end of me to that bundle of nerves, where he clamped down, sending me into another wave of ecstasy.

When I came down, his tongue ran circles around my opening, his eyes met mine, and I grabbed his shoulders, pulling him up to me. His kiss was light as I wrapped my legs around him, pushing my heels into his ass to pull him closer.

"Kotě." Aiden growled as the head of him slipped up and down me.

"Make me yours," I whispered. "Take what is yours."

His lips met mine as he pushed himself slowly into me. I felt myself stretch, and I had honestly forgotten just how much he filled me. My back arched into him, and I was unable to contain the purr that answered the growl that came from him. His head raised and when his hazel-green eyes met mine, I saw a small ring of purple along those outer edges. He gave me a questioning look as I raised my hand to rest on his cheek, my fingers running circles around his eyes.

"What?" he said, blinking.

"Your eyes are rimmed with purple."

His smile was bright as he whispered against my lips, "So are yours, my kotě."

His hips ground against me, and the smirk on his face as he moved slowly inside me was intoxicating. "Later, we will so talk about that later." I nipped at his lips, and he growled as he rolled his hips again, hitting that spot.

My head tipped back, and I lifted my hips to meet his. He retreated from me, and a smirk was the only warning I got before Aiden slammed back in. He repeated the movement, and when I met him, he groaned.

"I swear, Aiden, if you don't just start fucking me like it's our last day on—" My words were cut off with a kiss as he pounded into me, causing me to gasp at each deep connection.

When he slowed and I reached to pull him to me, he growled and stopped with just the head of him in me. My gaze snapped to his and narrowed. I moved my hips, but Aiden matched each of my movements, keeping just the tip of him within me. In an effort to restrict my movement, he reached for my hip, pressing it down into the bed.

"My kotě." He leaned down and kissed my neck, just under my ear, and I melted into him. As he leaned in closer and continued to kiss my neck, I thrust my hips up, but he was quicker than I was.

Sitting back on his feet, his eyes met mine and he cocked an eyebrow. A smirk and a growling tone that only promised a lot of punishment met me as I said, "You know, I'm not the sweet little fuck, Aiden."

"I've made you purr with a slow, sweet fuck." He pinched my nipple.

"It has been five years since I've been fucked to the point I don't know my name and station," I said, finding some bravery. "Is my dom going to do that or not?"

The look on his face made me want to take the words back. Okay, not really, but the determination and the flash in his eyes had me taking half a movement back before he caught me, flipped me over onto my stomach, and tied my hands to the railing on the top of the bed with his power.

"Aiden," I pleaded.

"What made you think to challenge me?" he said, leaning over me, whispering against my shoulder. I felt him hard against my ass and his chest against my back. "Do you really believe I won't give you everything you want in bed?"

"No."

"When have I ever left you lacking in bed—" Then he growled in my ear. "—my kotě?"

Not being smart at all, I turned my head to look over my shoulder at him and smiled, knowing I would earn a punishment. "Six years ago, in the cave when your father caught us."

There was a chuckle, and I felt his hardness twitch against me before he leaned back. There was a smack that filled the air, and a half second later, I felt the sting against my ass as I moaned. Another smack ran through the air, and then there was the wave of pleasure that flowed through me. I bit my lower lip and felt my canine pinch the flesh of it.

"I made up for it later." He chuckled as he smacked the other cheek. He had made up for it in abundance that night. Underworld, the fact that we had been caught had turned us both on.

"Now, where is this defiance coming from, Kotě?"

Two more quick smacks to my ass, and I could feel myself get wetter for him. I wiggled, but he held my ass there, running his hands over the red, heat now spreading. Leaning down, he kissed both cheeks, and then there was a long languid lick up the center of me that had me moaning his name loudly into the air. I moved against him as he drank me in. His tongue circled every inch of my core, and even as his hands tried to hold me in place, my body moved of its own accord.

His tongue gave two quick flicks over my clit before he came and positioned himself behind me. I was already so close, and he knew it. He smacked each side again, and I quivered under him.

"Aiden, please. Please, let me cum all over your hard cock."

"I don't know, Kotě. You have been a bit defiant. Are you sure you deserve this?" He ran himself along the length of me, and I tried to get him inside me again, but he knew my every trick. Finally, he teased, "Promise to be good?"

"Aiden."

There was a satisfied chuckle just one second before he plunged back into me. Grabbing onto my hips, he thrust into me and proceeded to pound into me relentlessly. I writhed under him, meeting him stroke for stroke.

I felt him twitch within me before he pulled out and released my hands. I looked at him and blinked.

"I need to see you as you cum on my cock."

He rolled me over, and in one quick movement had himself seated deep within me. With every thrust, he rolled against that bundle of nerves, and hit that spot within me, making my toes curl.

I ran my nails down his back and heard him hiss, then growl. Something within me awoke at that sound, and there was a purr that escaped my throat. His chest rumbled deep against me, and as I ran my teeth over his shoulder, the growl deepened into something more primal. I pulled myself away from him. Instinct was having me focus on that spot where Aiden's neck met his shoulder.

He pulled out, slamming back in, which had me running my fangs along that spot. Every part of me wanted to sink my fangs into him. There was something all-encompassing about it. My focus was centered on it. When he slammed back into me, I pulled back to meet his gaze, that purple ring still shining bright. "Aiden."

"What's wrong?" He kissed my nose and rolled his hips against mine.

"I'm fighting every ounce of me to not sink my fangs into you." My mothers' words from all those years ago echoed in my head about the Iviarian's mating claim.

"I am yours, Jess. Forever," he whispered in my ear.

I froze and pulled back just that little bit to look at him. When he stopped and looked at me, he asked, "Do you want a mate?"

"I've already told you that I am yours and you are mine." He rolled against me, and I bowed against him as I said, as seriously as I could, "Aiden, the Irvians mate forever."

Smiling, he slowly pulled out, and in an agonizingly slow manner, he pushed back in. A pleasure bloomed through me as I shuddered against him. "I know. Claim me. I am already yours. You've owned me from the day I first saw you. Claim me when you are ready, Jess."

He kissed me hard and moved his hips to meet mine. He started to slow, but he quickly gave hard, determined thrusts that were meant to bring me back to that edge.

Heat pulsed through my body, and the closer I got, the more instinct took over. My nails were raking down his back again, and my teeth grazed his shoulder. Each time I did that, there was that rumbling growl from deep in his chest.

"Someone really likes the teeth," I teased, nipping at his ear. He jerked deep within me, and I smirked as he finally stopped playing around and picked up the pace, pounding into me. I held him close, and that primal need was fully awake now, demanding that I claim Aiden as my mate. When I opened my eyes, there was a purple film over my vision, and through that haze, I could see where the veins were in his shoulder.

When the next wave of pleasure burst through me, it was raw and pure. Before I realized what I was doing, my teeth sank into him, and I felt the tang of his blood on my lips. His roar of pleasure met mine as we both careened off the cliff and into ecstasy.

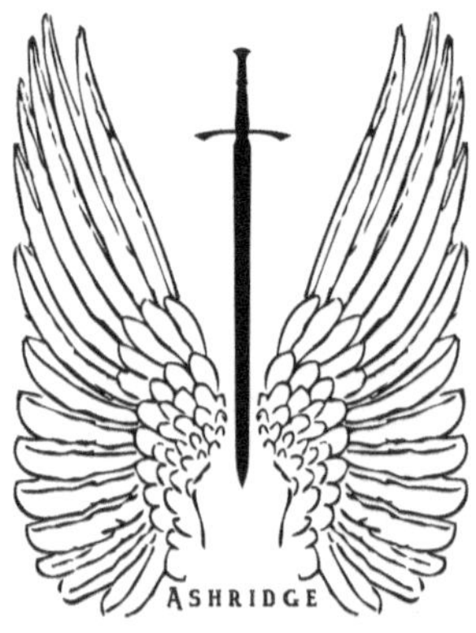

Chapter 24

Jessika

We lay there for long moments, until I removed my lips from his shoulder and my tongue circled the spot where my fangs had dug in. I kissed it gently, feeling him twitch inside me. When he pulled back to look at me, his eyes were still that hazel green I loved so very much, but the ring of purple around the outside edges glowed bright.

"Fuuuck." He leaned down and rested his forehead on mine. He was heaving deep hard breaths, but whispered, "Kotě."

"Aiden?" I asked, a bit hesitant and scared.

His eyebrows scrunched together, and he tilted his head to the side. "Kotě? What's wrong?"

"Are you mad?"

He blinked at me a few times and pulled his head back, studying me. His hand reached up and moved a few strands from my face and tucked them behind my ear. "Why in all the dimensions would I be mad?"

"I... I claimed you. We didn't really talk about it first. We should have talked about it before we had sex. I'm sorry, Aiden." I felt my chest shudder in fear of his rejection, and my hands started to shake and sweat. I quickly moved them from around his shoulders to grip the sheets.

"Why in the world would she think that I would be mad at her about that?"

"Because I claimed you without talking to you about it when we were not mid... Aiden." My eyes widened. "How did I know what you were just thinking right there?"

"Because you know me so well."

"No. I *heard* your voice in my head." I reached up and put his cheek in my hand. He hadn't moved and only now started to retreat from inside me.

"You imagined my voice," he said, sliding off to the side of me, and I rolled over to face him.

I looked at the spot on his shoulder and pondered for a moment. Could it have been the bite? Or was he late to his mom's Cogniti powers?

"If you really did hear me, it was more than likely the bite. There is no way I am coming into the Congiti powers this late in life. Mom's started at a young age. They wouldn't start now." He ran a hand up and down my spine.

"Aiden..." He gave me another questioning look. "I didn't say anything."

"What? Yes, you did."

"Did your mom teach you the golden glow of protection she and your dad used to use all the time? Are you using it now?" I asked carefully, not seeing it on my skin.

"No. She tried with all three of us, but it didn't work." He studied me some more and said, "We don't know what all the Irvains had for abilities. Is this one of them?"

"I... I don't know," I said, snuggling up next to him. I felt my hands shaking, and I pressed myself against his chest. "Aid, we don't know anything about the Irvains other than the few things that Mom told us all those years ago. I don't know what I am, and I'm scared."

"Being scared is okay, but why are you shaking so much?" he said, pulling me close. "Kotě, it's okay. I'm not going anywhere."

I didn't know if he held me for minutes or hours, but eventually the shaking stopped, and I drifted off to sleep.

HE WOKE ME FOR dinner, and to answer more messages from Vernadali CJ and Lady Megan, but there wasn't much more in the way of progress on their end. Lady Megan was still going through the contract, and there were definitely breaches, but she wasn't sure if they would hold up for a nullification. Vernadali CJ had been talking to Head Julian and the Vernadali Council, trying to find a way for us to move forward, but he wasn't having much luck yet. He said the biggest hurdle was that I was still engaged and promised to the Lord of Kaletta. I had sent him a message back, asking if it would all be moot if Aiden and I just married en route, and while I hadn't received an answer back, I could almost hear the frustrated groan he would give seeing that.

I sat there eating, thinking seriously about it, and threw caution to the wind and asked Aiden, "What would be worth declaring war against Kaletta?"

"Excuse me?" Aiden's food fell off his fork when he stopped mid-bite.

"Serious question. If you had to, what would you go to war with Kaletta over?"

"You," he said, dead serious. He hadn't hesitated once he realized that I was asking a serious question.

"Me?"

"Yes. If they were to lay any claim to you. If they were to kidnap you or so much as hurt one hair on that head of yours, I would lay waste to the entire territory to get you back."

Nodding, I took a deep breath and met his stare. "They already lay claim to my hand in marriage." Yes, I was testing the waters with him. He didn't know what his father and I had been talking about, but I had to feel him out on this.

"They may lay claim, but they won't have it. It's mine." He shrugged like it wasn't a big deal.

"Would you go to war over it? Would you marry me tonight and go to war tomorrow over having my hand in marriage?"

"Yes. I don't have to think about that, but why are you asking?" When I didn't answer right away and chewed on my bottom lip, he pushed his plate away and leaned on the table we had set up in the corner. I was using the lone chair in the room, and he sat on the edge of the bed, but only because it boxed me in on the off chance someone came barging in. "By law, I am your Vernadali, and I will always have your safety at the forefront of my mind. As yours... As your mate—" The fact he corrected the statement made my heart jump in excitement. "—I will always think of your well-being and wants first. Kaletta isn't safe for you. It's not safe for Jayden, Killy, or Ilris, either, and we have to find a way to legally get them out. If the Grand Lord gets his hands on you, he will do nothing more than lock you up and have you as his broodmare."

It answered the question but certainly put another long list of questions into play. I chewed on my thumb and thought about it.

"Jess," Aiden said, reaching across and pulling my thumb from my teeth. "What are you thinking?"

I stared out the window and watched the rain fall. "A lot."

"A lot of things that are making you a mess of emotions. I know that. You need to be more specific about what exactly is causing you to feel like this."

"You. My friends. Kaletta. Your dad. Your mom. Ashridge." My hand waved around in small circles as I rattled off the items. I was intentionally being vague, and I could almost hear his frustration. I definitely felt it rolling off him.

"Specifically, Jess."

I looked at him. "If I spew this out, do you promise not to yell or laugh at me? Because I know it's stupid and reckless."

He sat up straight. "I will try. Is this something that is about to make me die an early death from a heart attack?"

"Maybe." I drew out the word, and he closed his eyes, taking a deep breath, and said, "Alright. I'm ready."

"I'm thinking about marrying you tonight to make all contracts for my hand in marriage void. Only, I know that Kaletta would instantly declare war over the contract. There was a lot that Kaletta stood to gain politically from the marriage between Jayden and me. However, I know that also puts our friends at risk, and it only hurts the people of Ashridge. I know that it is not a smart move, and the only thing it would do is cause more problems than it would solve, yet I would do it in a heartbeat."

He started chuckling, and then when I met his eyes, he started laughing hysterically.

"Jess, while it warms my heart and makes me so selfishly proud that you would be willing to chance all of that just to make me your legal mate—" He took a long deep breath to calm the laughing before continuing. "—you are right. It would do a whole lot more damage than it would fix. The only thing it would correct is to take marriage to Jayden off the table."

"I know." I huffed out a breath in frustration.

"That all being said." He had stopped laughing now and was much more serious. "I could never let you do that. I want nothing more than to marry you. You know that. You are mine. That isn't up for anyone's discussion."

I gave him a small smile.

"I also won't let you jeopardize Ashridge or our friends like that. We will find a way to nullify the contract. We will find a way to legally marry. You won't have to go to war with Kaletta. The Grand Lord will lose his head before that happens."

I blinked at him. "Aiden."

"I know you are not asking me to kill him, but if you think for one second that Reka and I won't protect you and Ashridge with our last breath, think again. You said she already offered to kill him for you." I laughed at him, and he continued, "The Grand Lord is up to something. We just need to figure out what it is exactly and how to stop him."

I looked through the window. There was so much to do. "Once the storm clears."

He got up and took our plates and set them outside for someone to pick up. "Once the storm clears, we will head to Ashridge and get everything sorted out, Kotě."

When he returned and closed the door, he locked it. "Go ahead and take a shower, and then come to bed."

I nodded, and as I walked by him, he wrapped an arm around me and kissed me quickly on the top of the head and whispered, "Love you, Kotě."

"Love you, too."

CHAPTER 25

AIDEN

WAKING WITH MY ARMS around Jess was like nothing else in Nalsar. I cherished the long deep breaths that she took, but there were other things that needed to happen today. I carefully disentangled myself from her and maneuvered myself off the bed, doing everything I could not to wake her.

When I got to the bathroom, I closed the door softly, but not without taking another long look at her lying on the bed. She had barely put anything on before we settled in for bed last night. The lightweight tank she wore had settled low across her chest, and I let a long breath out to settle myself before closing the door.

I took a colder shower than I normally would and got dressed as quickly as I could before opening the door to see her sitting up in the bed. I hadn't even felt her awaken. Angels, I really was distracted.

Her head cocked to the side, and she had the cutest look of confusion on her face. "Where are you going?"

"I have a few things to check on. Last night, I asked the messenger not to deliver messages unless they were listed as an emergency. I know that they are all urgent, and usually they would deliver it immediately, but unless they were an emergency, I instructed that they wouldn't deliver anything until after lunch. I wanted to make sure you got some rest." The corner of my lip lifted, and I was sure my eyes matched the heat that was building in hers. "Stop looking at me like that or we won't be leaving this room today."

"Would that be such a bad idea?"

"It wouldn't, but the world is only going to wait so long for us, Kotě." I felt the disappointment in her eyes settle within me as well.

She nodded. "So, what are you doing today?"

"As I said, I'll check for messages while I'm out." I shrugged, and when she narrowed her eyes, seeing right through me, I rolled mine. "We need some supplies for our trip home. I'll also check on how the storm is moving so we can decide if we leave today or tomorrow."

"Tomorrow. I don't care if there are clear skies today. I want one more day. One more day to push the real world away. One more day where I don't have to be the Grand Duchess. One more day to just be your kotě. There's going to be too much to do when I get back home."

"Even after our discussion at dinner last night?"

"Yes." She looked away from me and out the window, but not before I saw the questions and concern fill her eyes.

"As you wish, Grand Duchess," I said automatically. She flinched.

"Please don't call me that." Her voice was low and sad.

"There are times where the title is required." I took her hands, and she squeezed them tight, like she was holding on for dear life.

"Never in our private residence, though. I don't care if we are talking politics, solutions, or of Ashridge." She looked up to me, and her focus was strong and determined. "Unless we are before others, if it is just us in our residence, you will never call me that. Add it to the dynamic if you must, but between Grand Duchess and Vernadali, I command it."

I nodded my head. "Do you want anything while I'm out?" She shook her head, and I leaned over and kissed her forehead before heading out.

HOURS LATER, I CAME back to find her reading a book on the bed. Her long white hair was still wet, and water had created a wet spot on her T-shirt where it was pulled over her shoulder. She was toying with the ends, and when she looked up at me, her eyes were red.

"What happened? What's wrong?" My Charge flew out toward her to get a sense of what she was feeling, and there was sadness, but then amusement. I narrowed my eyes at her.

"The book, Aiden. I was crying over the story in the book." She lifted it, showed me the cover portraying a man with red swirls and stuff around him, and laughed at me. I smiled and shook my head.

"You can't scare me like that."

"Hey, I'm at a really sad part of the story. I can't help it if the author is pulling emotions out of me. Fuck, Aiden. I'm fine, just sad at a character death, okay?" She threw a pillow at me.

Then the notes in my hand burned and I cringed. "Here. Take them before my dad's message starts burning welts into my hand."

She took them and immediately tore into them. There was confusion, then as she opened the last one, an amused smile crossed her beautiful face. Those plump red lips of hers broke out into the largest smile that I had seen from her since the first time I told her that I loved her.

"What has that most perfect look on your face? What did Dad say?" I asked. She crumpled them up and tried to hide them behind her back. "Jess, it isn't like I would be able to read them even if I got my hands on them."

"Nothing." I gave her a look, and she then smiled softly before saying, "Okay, so it is something, but it has to wait until we get to Ashridge. He has... things to do before it will be perfect."

She crawled out of the blankets and came to stand before me, wrapping her arms around my neck. I put the package I was carrying on the edge of the bed, and I leaned down to kiss her.

Her kiss was soft and rattled my already frayed nerves. They fluttered through my stomach, and I was really glad I hadn't eaten. "Did you eat? I asked one of the servants downstairs to send something up for you."

"Yeah, they brought a tray up for me about an hour after you left." She ran a hand down my chest, and I shuddered at the touch. I narrowed my eyes at her. There was a huge amount of anticipation flowing through her, but it had a flirty edge to it.

"What did you find out about the storm?" Her voice was hesitant, almost like she didn't want the answer.

"We should stay one more night to ensure it has passed and we won't be delayed more than necessary once on the road. We will have to stay one night out on the flats, but then should be able to make it by midmorning the following day." We could leave now, and based on my messages from my mom, we really should be leaving today, but Jess said she wanted one more day, so I would give it to her.

She pulled me close and rested her head on my chest. "Thank you."

I wrapped my arms tight around her. When she let out a shuddering breath, I knew what was going through her mind.

"We will deal with it when we arrive, Kotě." She relaxed at that, and when she held me tighter, I asked, "What are you thinking?"

"Nothing specific. Why?" She was smirking, but kept her head down.

"What is it, Jess?" I cupped her chin and lifted her head to force her to look at me.

That smile turned soft and sultry. "Just about you, and how I don't have to let you walk away from me ever again. You are my Vernadali, my mate, and the protector of my heart."

I slid my hand along her chin to cup her cheek. I let out a sigh that was sucked right back up the second she ran her fingers along my side, making me twist out of her grip. "Kotě, you know how ticklish I am there."

"I do, and I plan on torturing you with it for years, because I also know that if I run one finger from that rib down your happy trail and stop, it will make you hard as a rock." She stuck a finger in her mouth and bit the tip of it, twisting from side to side.

"Angels, woman." I let out a shaky breath, and then I was kissing her. It was hard and fast, and her hand ran that line across my stomach, indeed making me instantly hard for her. There wasn't a touch on my skin that didn't make me crave her. If I could spend an eternity touching, holding, and fucking this woman, I would die a happy man.

She pulled back and rested her forehead on my chin. "Told you."

When I stepped back from her, my heart was racing and I couldn't think straight. I took a deep breath to calm and center myself before saying, "Kotě."

She tilted her head to the side and gave me a questioning look. "Aiden."

I wanted to do this right but knew I was likely fucking it all up. There must be a right and wrong way to do this, but I didn't care. I was going to dedicate myself to her. That was what mattered. When I tapped my chin, she gave me another questioning look as she knelt and sat on her feet before me.

"I have a very important question for you, Jessika Petra Valenti," I said, trying to keep my voice strong and steady. Her eyes flicked to the package and then back to me.

"Do you wish to still have me as your dominant and to willingly give me your submission?" I asked, almost in a rush.

Her eyes glazed over before she blinked and, without hesitation, said, "Yes. Always, as previously discussed." As this wasn't going to be a 38-hour, 7-days-a-week submission, there would be limitations to when I could be her dominant. She was the Grand Duchess of Ashridge, after all. There would be times I could not, and would not, take over. We had sorted out many of those details and lines as we lay in bed yesterday.

I reached into the bag and pulled out the necklace I had the blacksmith make for me this morning. Thin, matte-finished, rounded silver steel stretched from one side of her neck to the other, and it had a chain connecting on the back with a small lock. There was a matching one in the bag for me, with one difference. Hers had the rounded steel twisted in the center into a heart.

I heard her gasp as her eyes filled with tears at the sight of it. Her gaze flicked back to mine and held, and I continued, "Will you accept this symbol of our relationship and agreement? To willingly give your submission to me."

"Yes, Aiden. I am yours, always." Her eyes never left mine when I encircled it around her neck and locked the small lock at the back.

Once the click sounded, I was on my knees, kissing her. There. Let the whole world know she was mine. We hadn't done anything last time, and this felt like this was so, so much more.

When our kiss broke, she captured my bottom lip, and the scrap of her delicate canines sent a shudder through me. The memory of them as she had carefully scraped them up my cock was making me hard all over again for her. But Angels, when she had sunk them into my shoulder, the whole world had erupted and there had been that zap to my chest again, but much deeper than those that had settled within us for the Vernadali bond. I knew now that it was the Irvian mate bond, but it didn't matter, I knew this girl. In and out. She was mine. The world just needed to know.

I ran my hands down her throat, to where the heart sat at the base of her neck. My fingers ran over it as it circled against the skin. Her throat bobbed, causing the steel to move, before she softly whispered, "What about yours? Didn't we say you would have something as well?"

I smirked against her lips and reached into the bag to retrieve the matching one. When I handed it to Jess, she smiled brightly and lifted one hand to her throat, where the heart sat right at the hollow at its base. "It matches, except for the heart."

"I said I wanted it to be made clear you are mine. Jess, I promise to protect you. I promise to love, nurture, and take care of you, beyond what is required of me being your Vernadali. I promise you that."

"I accept you, Aiden," she said, tears streaming down her face as she reached over and secured the necklace around my neck.

CHAPTER 26

AIDEN

THE NEXT MORNING, WE got up and immediately started packing and getting ready for the push to Ashridge. I was in the shower when I felt her anxiety spike. Turning the faucet off and wrapping a towel around my waist, I stuck my head out of the bathroom to find her pacing while twiddling with the heart at the base of her throat.

"Done already?" she asked when she saw me standing there.

"Hard to shower when I can feel every ounce of your anxiety coursing through me. It makes things difficult when I'm just trying to get clean, kotě." I raised an eyebrow and smirked at her, and she gave me an apologetic look. "I'm clean enough. Soap is out of my hair this time. What has you torn up?"

She didn't say anything but handed me a sheet of paper. Angels, another message came from Mom and Dad.

GRAND DUCHESS,
THE GRAND LORD ARRIVED THIS MORNING. I'M TRYING TO HOLD HIM OFF, BUT HE IS MAKING DEMANDS THAT I CAN'T AUTHORIZE.
ASHRIDGE REQUIRES ITS GRAND DUCHESS.
MAY THE ANGELS GRANT YOU WINGS.
-LADY MEGAN MATHEWSON

Well, shit. Mom was demanding we get on the road.

"It's never good when Mom signs things, '*Lady Megan*.'" I turned to get dressed.

"Aiden—" She stopped when I threw the towel on the bed and strode to my pack for a clean set of clothes. When I looked up at her, she was chewing on her bottom lip and looking me up and down.

I moved my hips in hope of hiding what that look did to me and blushed. "Jess," I admonished, but she just stood there giving me one of those heated smiles. "Are you packed and ready?"

I slipped my pants on, buttoned them quickly, and finished throwing my stuff back in my pack. When I was done, she was standing in the back corner, chewing on her thumb.

"Seriously, Jess. Can you please calm down? There is only so much that you would be able to grant, and we don't need Kaletta. The bigger question is, just how are we going to save our friends?" I went to stand before her, to make her listen to me. "We talked about this the other night."

She looked up at me and, in a voice of desperation, said, "I know, and that is the biggest problem. How do I get out of the marriage agreement with Jayden and save him, Ilris, and Killy?"

"I don't know. Mom is looking into it. Said she has a few ideas and is trying to go through Popa to see if there is anything he can do, too." She gave me a look, which I knew was a reminder that she didn't want to use my family name to help with Ashridge. "And before you say one word about that look you just gave me, don't forget, you are a Mathewson now. Just not legally, yet. I will have you as my wife, Jess, and we will save our friends too."

She released a long breath and said, "I understand that, Aiden, but you know I need to run Ashridge separate from the Mathewson name. When we marry, you will be Duke Aiden Chatwell Mathewson Valenti. You will be taking *my* name. Yours will be added to mine, but it will be Valenti as the final name. I won't be solely taking yours, as much as I wish it could be that way."

"I know." And I did. I really did, but I didn't want to be Duke. Angels knew I didn't want that responsibility. The only person I wanted to take care of was Jess. I let out a long sigh and sat on the edge of the bed.

"What?" Jess pushed off the dresser. "What is on your mind?"

"I don't want to be Duke," I whined and gave her a crooked smile. "You are the only person I will be protecting, and I will always have your best interest at the forefront of my mind."

She stepped out of the bathroom holding her toiletries, and as she walked past me, she kissed my forehead, saying, "Well, it's a package deal, Aiden."

She froze and studied the wall for a moment before she dropped her things into her pack and turned to face me. "Aiden, it really is a package deal. I have to rule. You becoming Duke is just what happens. I realize you are my Vernadali first, but you will also be Duke."

I closed my eyes and flopped back onto the bed. "I am first and foremost a Vernadali. I was assigned by the Angels to be your Vernadali. Vernadali cannot mix with politics. Can I even be Duke? I mean, we are just trying to find a way for a Vernadali to marry his Charge. It won't matter that Head Julian is also Popa Julian. That is not a line I'll cross... ANGELS. You know I hate politics. I'm a badass bodyguard, Jess, *your* badass bodyguard, not a politician. I will stand by your side in every meeting there is for you to run Ashridge. Ashridge should be your number one priority, but I'm not the person to make decisions."

The bed dipped under Jess' weight as she sat down next to me. Leaning over my chest and supporting herself with her hand, she looked down at me and bit her lower lip. Our eyes met, and I could tell that she was struggling with what to tell me. "Jess, what aren't you telling me?"

"I don't want to get your hopes up, so I'm not telling you. As for all that other bullshit you just spewed, you would make an amazing duke, but I understand. Details to be worked out later, okay?" Her voice was low and tentative, and I could feel something from her, but I couldn't make out what it was. It was warm, but it had a prickly feeling to it.

I narrowed my eyes at her and cocked my head to the side. "What are you feeling right now, Jess?"

"Nervous. Anxious. Turmoil." Then she let out a deep sigh and looked to the ceiling. "Fear. Dread. There are too many feelings within me right now. I feel all the feels. I can't explain it all to you, Aiden. I'm distraught over losing my mom and Amala. I'm scared of what the Grand Lord of Kaletta is going to do. I'm scared for Ashridge. I'm scared of what is going to happen to us. I'm scared I'm going to mess us up. I'm scared that Vernadali CJ won't get the Vernadali Coun—" Then she bit her lip. She was quiet for a long minute before she looked down at me.

"You aren't going to tell me, are you?" I sat up and cupped her cheek. I pushed some of my Charge into her to help calm her, and I saw her shoulders lower just that littlest bit. She took a deep breath before meeting my gaze and shook her head. "Okay. As long as it doesn't endanger your life, I'll allow this one secret, Jess, but no more, okay?"

Her eyes flashed, and when I held her stare, I said, "I am your Vernadali. I need to know anything and everything that can be a risk to you. More than that, we have made a commitment to each other." I slid my hand down to loop my finger through the center of the heart, pulling her closer to me. There was clear understanding there in her eyes now, so I continued, "I will take care of you. I will ensure that you are happy, safe, and well taken care of. I cannot do my job in either facet if you keep secrets. Is that understood, Jessika Petra?"

"Yes, Aiden."

"Anything else we need to discuss? Other than the whole Duke thing, which we will deal with later." I gave her a stern look that she threw right back at me, and she lifted her eyebrow. "Are you ready to depart, Grand Duchess?"

Her eyes narrowed as she said, "What did I say about that, Aiden."

I smirked at her just as the man standing at the door cleared his throat. She took a deep breath and pursed those luscious lips of hers, and I knew there was a twinkle in my eye at the small victory I had just laid at her feet.

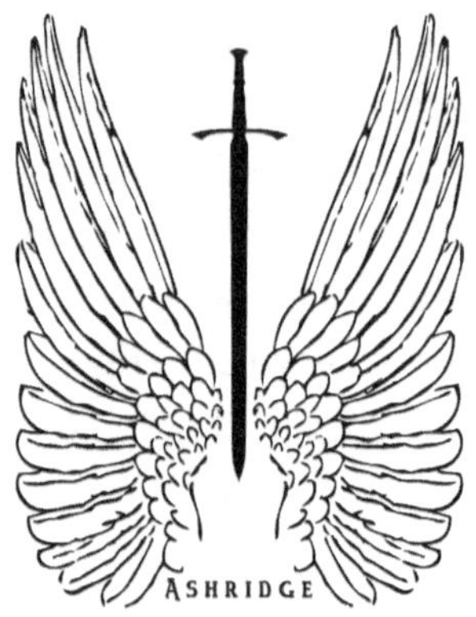

CHAPTER 27

JESSIKA

I WANTED TO SMACK him. He knew there was someone coming, and I was so wrapped up in his presence, as usual, that I hadn't realized there was anyone at the door. There was a twinkle in his eyes that said he knew he had won, and I wanted to kick him in the balls.

"The horses are ready, Vernadali Aiden. The kitchen has provided you food for the trip, and there are a couple extra blankets strapped to the saddles. Now that the storm has moved on, the temperature will be dropping very low, sir," the man at the door said.

Aiden's eyes hadn't left mine, and they stayed on me as he stood, saying, "Grand Duchess, it is time to depart and head back to Ashridge."

"We will depart when the Grand Duchess says it's time to depart," I said, meeting his stare with a fierceness that I knew would end up with me over his knee.

"As you wish, Grand Duchess. Shaleni, please ensure that the horses stay ready until the Grand Duchess wishes to depart." Aiden sat back on the bed and leaned back on his hands on the mattress. There was a look in his eye that meant the second we were in a position for him to reprimand me for that, I wasn't going to be able to sit. Did I really want to sit on a horse, riding hard across the desert plain, with a sore ass? No. No, I really didn't.

Just before the man at the door shut it, I said loudly, "Shaleni, I am actually ready to leave."

"Yes, Grand Duchess," he said, leaving the door open and looking from me to Aiden. "I'll have them out front immediately, Grand Duchess."

Once he stepped out of the room, I took a step back from Aiden, and he smiled at me. I knew that smile. I knew all the ways I was going to *pay* for pushing back on him. I would enjoy every moment of it. If we had the time, I was sure he would have me over his knee. Angels, I hoped he wasn't going to go that route right now. I really didn't want to ride home with a sore rear.

"I am surprised that you aren't begging for forgiveness right now," Aiden said, standing with predatory grace and staying right with me. I scooped up my syth belt and fumbled with the buckles. I was trying not to look at Aiden, but I felt my cheeks heat, and my fingers could not get the prongs through the holes on the stupid buckle.

"I... I don't know what you mean," I stammered, finally getting the one around my waist secured. I reached down to buckle the one on my right side, and Aiden's hand covered mine. His hand lifted and made a fist. *Behave*. I winked at him, indicating I understood.

"You don't, do you?" He knelt before me, and the humor rolling off his tongue made my stomach swim. I took a deep breath to steady myself as he finished buckling the lower strap on the right outside edge.

I couldn't say anything as his fingers ran up my leg across my center and slowly along the seam of my pants. I knew better than to move, but I couldn't help the moan that escaped my lips. I threw my power at the door and shut it, because I wasn't sure just how far he was going to take this. When the door clicked shut, he pushed harder against that bundle of nerves, and I had to grab ahold of the footboard.

"Aiden." I breathed.

"Jess?" he said, in question, as he continued running a finger up and down my center while his other hand worked the straps on my outer left thigh, securing my syth belt fully. He kept it up, and I felt my stomach tighten, the heat in my core pooling right where his fingers teased me. I let my head fall back just the smallest bit, enjoying the sensation he was creating, and as he ran his finger down to my opening and pushed against the bundle of nerves again, I moaned louder, jerking my hips toward him. At that movement, Aiden chuckled and stopped. My eyes popped open, meeting his, which were shining with amusement. He was enjoying this very much. It was that smirk that made me realize I was not going to like what came out of his mouth next. As he stood, in a hushed whisper that was all my dom, he said, "You don't get to cum right now."

I let out a quick short breath and bit the inside of my cheek. I really wanted to call him an asshole, or a whole slew of other names, but instead, I said, "Yes, Aiden."

"Good girl." He reached down and kissed me quickly on the lips and then said, "Get your pack. We need to get moving."

I blinked, took a deep breath, and sheathed my syths. With another deep breath to calm myself and clear my head, I picked up my pack and walked out the door.

WE SECURED OUR PACKS on the horses, and I caught myself automatically looking for Amala when my brain caught up and reminded me she was no longer here. When Aiden came over next to me, he asked, "You okay?"

"Can't you tell? Through the bond?" My words may have come off more clipped than they needed to be.

He sighed. "I can't get a read on any one thing. I just want to make sure you are okay."

"As I said earlier, I'm feeling everything right now. Not to mention the fact that you edged me. Since we've been on the road, we got attacked and had to hunker down because of a storm, thus delaying us from sending my mother to the Angels, so yes, I'm a bit apprehensive." My voice had a bit too much bite, and his hand wrapped around mine as I grabbed the reins to the brown and white gelding I would be riding. His eyes met mine, and I sighed. "I'm sorry. I miss her."

"I know, Jess. I do too."

"I didn't get a chance to say goodbye. There were things to say. I haven't even had a chance to see her body. Stupid transformation." I ran my tongue along my teeth and resisted the childish urge to stomp my foot.

"Those fangs are adorable on you." Aiden smirked at me, and his eyes flicked to my ears. "All of it is adorable on you. I'm sorry you had to go through that. Are going through it, I mean."

I just wrapped my arms around him, and when I felt his wrap around me, a weight lifted off my shoulders. I had Aiden. I would always be safe with Aiden. His Charge pushed into me, and it was like a heavy, warm blanket caressing all my frayed nerves. I lifted my head and looked up at him. His eyes met mine, and he was about to say something when someone cleared their throat behind us.

Turning, I saw a crowd gathering. "Grand Duchess, is there anything else you need for your journey back to the capital?"

"No. Thank you," I said, pulling myself together.

"Grand Duchess." The man standing before me was Sir Ioannis, the overseer of Avalan. I nodded to him. "There have been a lot of rumors going around town since you arrived."

I felt Aiden stiffen next to me, and I wondered just what he hadn't told me. My eyes stayed focused on Sir Ioannis as I said, "Oh? And which rumors do you speak of?"

He ran his hands down his fitted button-up shirt and acted like he was dusting off his hands on his jeans before he scratched his greying beard and said, "There are rumors that Kaletta is positioning for war against Ashridge. That couldn't be true, though, if you are marrying the Grand Lord's son, Lord Jayden. Is that correct?"

"Rumors are just that, rumors. I was with Lord Jayden just before arriving with the storm this week. He was called away while en route back to the capital after hearing of my mother's death. I assure you that we are in an amicable relationship with Kaletta." I tried to skirt around so many of the issues that I knew would be coming.

"Damn, kotĕ, that was impressive. How did they know? How were they getting those rumors?" I turned toward Aiden to give him a silencing look for saying something like that in front of our people, but he was all Vernadali: standing straight up, hands behind him, within easy reach of his syths if he needed them. His eyes were scanning the crowd, no doubt checking for any issues. There was no indication that he had said a word. *It's okay, Jessika. Breathe.*

"Grand Duchess, there are rumors—" he said, but I cut him off.

"They are only rumors. Now, the storm has delayed my trip, and I must return to... I must return." My throat filled sadness, and my mouth was thick and heavy.

I turned and put my foot in the stirrup and felt Aiden's hands on my hips to help me up. I didn't need it, but that simple touch on my hips helped ease the anxiousness flowing through me.

A moment later, he was up on his horse, and I turned without saying another word to the overseer. Putting my heels to the gelding's sides, he took off like an arrow out of town.

CHAPTER 28

AIDEN

THE MOONS WERE HIGH in the sky and nearly full, so we kept riding late into the night. Even once the horses tired, we dismounted and kept walking. Over an hour ago, she had reached over and grabbed my hand, and when her fingers threaded through mine, she let out a small sigh. I could feel her anxiety rising the closer we got to Ashridge, and I pushed more of my power into her to calm her, but it was rising faster than I could calm it.

I pulled her to a stop and made her look at me. "Jess, we should halt for the night. We still have a good six hours of riding tomorrow before we get home. We need a good night's sleep, and the horses need to rest. Once we get there, it's going to be stressful and insane."

She looked out toward where Ashridge was, a swirl of emotions fluttering through her before she sighed. "I can feel the weight of that crown sitting heavier on my shoulders the closer we get." I didn't know how to respond to that, and when I didn't say anything, she looked at me and, with a lift of her lips, asked, "No smart-ass comments or words of wisdom?"

I dropped the reins to my horse, ran my hand through my hair, and shook my head. "Nope. Not a damn thing."

She dropped the reins to her horse as well and wrapped her arms around my waist. Jess' emotions flicked through wildly, and I felt her arms tighten. She was an emotional mess. So much had happened in the last week and a half. I let out a long sigh, and she looked up at me. "*What are you thinking, Aid?*"

I jerked my head back. "Jess, were you just wondering what I was thinking?"

"Yeah."

"Angels. It works both ways. We are gonna have to work on that. It could come in handy. Gonna take lots of practice, I think."

She gave me a strange look. "Aiden, you know how you yell at me about my half sentences and conversations? Well, you are doing that right now."

I ran my hands through my hair and then looked at her. Fuck. I reached forward, cupped her face, and kissed her.

"What in the Underworld was that for?" she said, smiling brightly.

"You are fucking amazing!"

"Well obviously, but why this time?" There was a lightness to her voice that I was happy to hear, even though I knew it wasn't how she was really feeling.

"I think that the Irivian bond allows us to talk to each other through it. You've been hearing me, but I just heard you wonder what I was thinking." When she just continued to look at me, I kissed her again and continued, "Jess, we have not only the Vernadali bond that gives me those ever so frustrating emotional feelings, but if we can master this Irivian bond, then that can be so helpful. Think about it. We can have whole conversations in a crowded room."

"What, and get rid of our hand signals?" There was a pang of worry in that statement.

I reached over, put my finger through the heart, and pulled her to me. "No, Kotě. Those are wholly separate." Relief rushed through her, along with a heat that even I felt settle between my hips, making my cock twitch. I smirked and leaned in to kiss her softly.

"So, rest tonight, and the world tomorrow?" she whispered softly against my lips.

"Yeah. The world tomorrow."

"WILL YOU PLEASE JUST settle down and sleep?" I pulled Jess tighter against me and nuzzled into her hair, but she just ran her hand along mine. "Bullshit, you are okay."

"Aid." Her voice was tired, and I wanted to take it all away. "I'm fine. Go to sleep."

I sat up on my elbow and rolled her onto her back to face me. She reached up and rested her hand on my cheek. There were so many emotions coming through the Vernadali bond, and even with what I saw on her face, I couldn't figure out exactly what was going through her mind. "What are you thinking, Kotě?"

She giggled at me and then flashed a bit of fang. "Who would have thought that name would have been so fitting. Now I even have the fangs."

"You've always had fangs and sharp claws. Just because you couldn't see them, didn't mean you were any less of a kitten. Now, you just have the fangs to match. Which are adorable, by the way."

"Did you know then?" She rubbed my cheek and tongued that canine in a smirk.

"Know what?"

"When you nicknamed me *kitten*, did you know then that I had the Irivian blood in me?"

"I didn't." I let out a quick breath. "And once I did, I didn't even think about the correlation. I told you before, I hoped you never had to go through something traumatic enough to cause the transformation."

"One would think losing my parents would have caused it."

"Jess," I said, waiting for her to look at me. "We expect to one day lose our parents. While it wrecks us, we know that someday we will have to light their pyre. We don't expect to lose our best friend. Let alone in a way that you did."

"I knew I could lose her one day, though. Amala and I had discussed it. She had laid a vow at my feet the day she got assigned in Ashridge. She said she would lay down her life for me and Ashridge. So, I knew it could be the case, I—"

"You didn't believe it would actually happen," I said, cutting her off. I felt her grief and anguish over having to light that pyre.

She shook her head. "But that isn't what I was thinking about while lying here. You mentioned that you thought we might be able to use the claiming as a way to talk to each other?"

"I did."

"We have the hand signals, though. Aren't they discreet enough?"

"They are, but there will be times when people will be paying too close attention. More so now that you are Grand Duchess." I thought for a moment and said, "What I don't understand, though, is that if it is the claiming, then wouldn't that only be between two Irvirians?"

"Lady Megan is Cogniti, though. Could the claiming have attached to that?"

I blinked at her. "Maybe, but I don't have that ability. We will need to find out more about all the little things that are you now. Talk to people. See what traits, exactly, other than those sexy ears and fangs, you might come into." I studied her for a long moment. "Since we aren't sleeping, do you want to try?"

Her eyes lit with a hunger that sent a shiver down my spine, then the little vixen ran a finger along the length of me. I would have been fine if she hadn't sent a thread of her power along her finger, vibrating her touch along the way.

"Angels be," I said, jerking my hips away. "That is not playing fair."

She reached up and nipped at my lips. In a flash, I grabbed the heart on her necklace, where she instantly stilled.

"Now, Kotě," I purred at her as I sat up, taking her with me. She sat on her heels and put her hands on her lap. "If you are good, I will let you have what you want."

"Yes, Aiden." Her voice was submissive, but then she smirked and looked up at me through her lashes before saying, "But are you punishing me or yourself?"

A simple raise of my eyebrows had her biting her bottom lip. "Let's try this claiming thing. Then we can talk about your punishment."

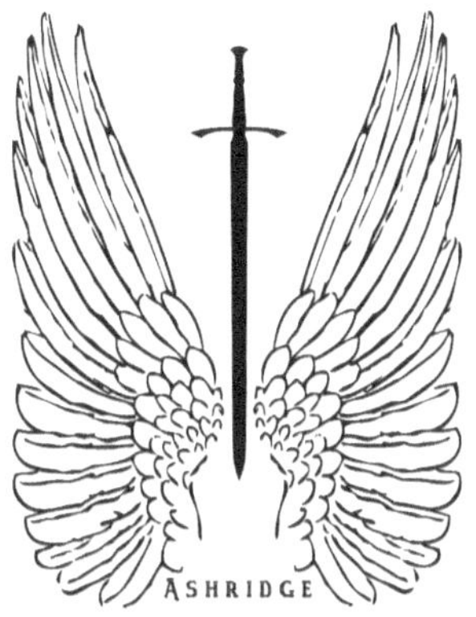

CHAPTER 29

JESSIKA

SWEAT WAS TRICKLING DOWN my back as I concentrated. We could feel the claiming linking us now. I could latch onto it without much thought, Aiden, too, but to actually get a thought to push through that connection was not happening.

Every once in a while, I would swear I could hear his groan of frustration down it, but I could have just imagined it. He thought he had heard me, but what he heard wasn't what I thought, so the Angels only knew if this could even work.

"It's worked on accident a few times, though, so it works. It just, we just...," Aiden said, letting out a tired huff of breath.

"We have to figure it out," I finished for him, sitting back on my heels.

When he was studying me, I reached up and scratched my temple, and he winked back. "Swear it."

"What is there to swear? You asked if I was okay; I said I was." He chuckled and took my hand, rubbing my knuckles and then kissing them softly. "Tomorrow, all of the Underworld is going to break loose, and I would be lying if I said I did want to go back to Ashridge tomorrow, but I also know we *need* to get you back."

My heart sank. That crown indeed felt heavy on my head, and it wasn't even there. Aiden's finger was under my chin and pulled me to look at him.

"Tomorrow. That is a future you problem," he whispered so close that I could feel his breath on my skin. He kissed down my jaw, and when he got to my ears, I tensed, remembering what he had done back in Silentport.

"Aiden, if you pull my ear right now, I will zap you in the crotch. Not vibrate like I did earlier, straight up zap you to the point you will have welts."

There was a husky huff of laughter there "Would that be a fitting punishment?"

I tried to turn my head to glare at him, but his thumb and finger held my head in place. He rubbed the scruff of his beard against my jaw line, I felt myself coil tight deep within me, and then there was that soft growl that I felt into my core. I couldn't help but purr back to him.

I felt the smirk against my cheek. "I love the way you purr at me."

While his fingers firmly held my chin, his other hand ran down my side, and his fingers were running along the seam of my pants. This time, however, he was noticeably avoiding that bundle of nerves I needed him to push against.

I moved my hips, and he tsked in my ear. "Now, now, Kotĕ. What do you think you are doing?"

"Aid, please." I was begging because he knew exactly what he was doing to me, and he was enjoying every minute of it.

He let me go, and I nearly fell into him. "Please what?" he asked, crossing his arms. I glared at him, and the right side of his mouth twisted up while a sparkle of amusement lit up his eyes. My eyes traveled down his body, and he didn't even try to hide the fact he had a raging hard-on.

I sent my power through my finger, and his moan rolled between us. I stopped, my eyes flicking to his in question.

"What?"

"I... I think I felt that." I looked to his chest, which was at least two feet from me, and blinked as I stared at it.

"I wasn't touching you, Kotĕ."

"I know that, dumbass." My eyes flicked back up to him, and when they met, understanding finally settled within those hazel-green eyes.

"You felt me along the claiming?" He was rubbing his chest, and then there was a small tug on it. We had figured out tugging, but it was the talking down the claiming that was a problem. Then there was a harder tug that made me want to pull into him.

When my eyes met his again, there was a heat in them that I was sure matched my own. "I believe you were about to give me my punishment?"

"And what do you think would be fitting?"

"Since you have been edging me since before we left Avalan, I think making me forget about tomorrow sounds like a good start."

"Angels, woman. You think that I'm going to let our last night alone not be spent worshiping you?"

"Well, you were trying to get me to sleep earlier." I had my head down, and he set a single finger on the heart at the base of my throat and said, "Doesn't mean I'm not going to claim what is mine before we reach Ashridge again." Then he leaned in and kissed my jaw, down my neck, and when he reached that heart, he kissed it and then looked at me, his lips a hair away from mine.

"I am yours. Always," I whispered.

There was a rumble that I felt deep within me. I smiled, knowing that was sent down the claiming, just as he said, "Yes. You are. Now I'm going to ensure you never forget it."

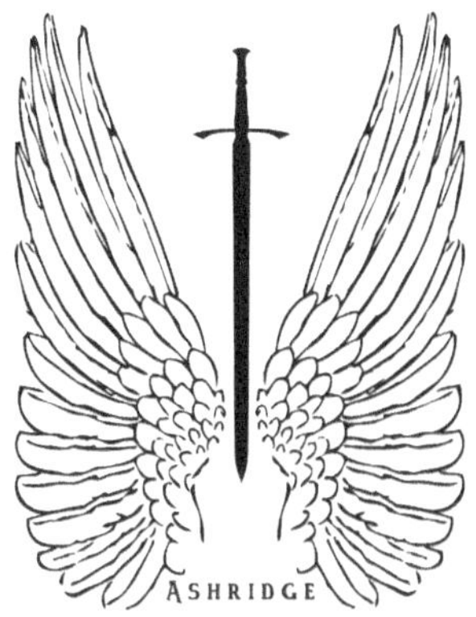

CHAPTER 30

JESSIKA

WHEN I WOKE IN the morning, I just lay there. I refused to open my eyes because once that happened, real life would come back with the oppressive weight of protecting all of Ashridge and finding a way to save our friends.

"I know you aren't asleep," Aiden muttered as he pulled me closer to him. I nuzzled into his chest and wrapped an arm around his waist to hold him. "I have felt your anxiousness and frustration for hours."

"I love you, Aiden."

"I love you, too, my kotě." He kissed the top of my head, just as my stomach growled.

"Sorry." I giggled at him. "Guess no matter how much we want to lie here and ignore the world, it isn't going to let us."

He let out a huge sigh. "That it is not. Stay here, I'll get you something to eat and some water."

"I'm not thirsty." I pouted once he was standing, and he turned toward me and raised an eyebrow. I repeated, "I'm not thirsty."

"Listen." He tapped his chin and I sat on my knees. "You rode long and hard over the last 38 hours. You have a long day on the plains today before getting to Ashridge. Who would I be if you arrived dehydrated?"

"Can you make me some coffee instead?"

"Coffee is not water. It won't hydrate you the way you need to be." He crossed his arms and looked down at me, and I intentionally swept my eyes up to look at him through my eyelashes and stuck my lip out.

"Jessika."

"Aiden."

"No coffee. Water." He turned and went to the horse, and I chuckled. I was intentionally giving him a hard time, and he was letting me. I wasn't sure if that scared me or not. I knew he had my best interest at heart, but I would love some coffee right now. Lady Megan had insisted I try it when I was at the house years ago, and I was now thoroughly addicted to the stuff.

Aiden returned and handed me a canteen. "Drink. You do need to rehydrate. Regardless of all that show you just put on, you need to stay hydrated." He crouched down in front of me and ran his fingers along my jaw. "Seriously, Jess. Drink. I'm not trying to be a dick."

"I know." I lifted it to my mouth, and I didn't know how he did it, but it was ice cold and tasted delicious. I didn't realize how parched I was until I had finished the entire canteen. I handed it back to Aiden and tipped it upside down to prove to him I had drunk the non-happy non-bean juice.

He smirked at me as he took it from my hands and handed me some bread and cheese. "Sorry. It's all that's left. Avalan didn't have much we could travel with."

"It's fine." I nibbled on the cheese as he pulled on the claiming. I looked up at him, and I could see through the façade he was giving me how much he didn't want to go home today. "I know, Aiden, but we have to save our friends. You were right in that I can't leave Ashridge without a ruler."

It hurt to watch that façade flake away. "We have our work cut out for us when we get home, don't we?" He was slowly pulling himself back into the Grand Duchess' Vernadali.

"Aiden," I said, feeling a very tight knot sit at the base of my throat. It hurt to swallow around, but I knew I needed to say this. "When we get to Ashridge, I need you to be strong for me. I know that makes me sound like the weakest Grand Duchess ever, and it is totally and completely unfair of me to ask this of you, but I need you to be my rock. I need you to keep me sane. I need you to hold me, and when I fall apart after lighting my mom's pyre, and then Amala's..." Tears ran down my cheeks, and I couldn't make them stop. He was instantly there, holding my face in his hands.

"Jessika Petra Valenti. My kotě." He took a deep breath and gave me a lingering kiss on my forehead again before putting his forehead to mine and saying, "As your mate and as your Vernadali, I will always be here to pick you up when the pieces need to be put back together. You are mine, but I am also yours."

I wrapped my arms around him and let the tears fall. It wasn't fair of me to ask, or to beg him to do this, but he was. He had always thought of me before himself, whether that was because he loved me or because he was a Vernadali, or whether that was just who he was. I didn't know, and right now, I didn't care.

AIDEN LET ME CRY myself out before giving me one hell of a searing kiss, helping me up onto the horse, and leading us toward Ashridge. We could see the Black Mountains now, and I knew that within hours we would be within the halls of Ashridge. I pulled on the claiming, and Aiden looked at me as we came to one of the ridges surrounding the city.

I reached up and put my hand to my throat. His eyes were soft as he reached down and pinched his hip, and I tried to smile at him as I pinched mine in return. Taking a deep breath and climbing down off my horse, walking up the ridge, I was about to see Ashridge for the first time in months.

For the first time as Grand Duchess.

Taking a few determined steps, I crested the hill and froze. "Aiden!"

He was instantly there. "Wha..."

I looked up at him and then back to the camp of Kaletta soldiers that were stationed there. Behind them was the final ridge before it extended to the view of Ashridge City. The city never ceased to amaze me in its beauty, but I couldn't take it in as I studied the thousands of soldiers who had made camp, intentionally just out of sight of where the guards would be able to see them from the rise and towers.

"What is the Grand Lord demanding of Lady Megan and Ashridge that would require this kind of a showing of his might?" I muttered as Aiden took my hand. He squeezed it, and I turned to look at him. His eyes were scanning the soldiers, and when they settled on one spot in particular, I felt his Charge wrap around me.

"Aiden." I winced. "I recognize you are being my Vernadali right now, but that hurt."

"Sorry. The general's tent is on the back edge, nearest us."

"Do you think Jayden, Killy, and Ilris are in there, or do you think the Grand Lord took them into Ashridge with him?"

Aiden ran his hand through his hair and scanned the army between us and the main gates. "I don't like this."

"Well, let's just go down there and find out what in the Underworld they are doing in my territory." I took a few steps but got launched back when I neared the end of Aiden's reach. He caught me before I landed flat on my ass, but when he set me up right, I turned to glare at him. "Aiden, I have the right to demand them to leave. The armies of Kaletta have no legal right to be here."

"You are right, Grand Duchess, but listen. There are thousands of soldiers down there. If you think for one moment I'm going to let you go storming in there, ordering opposing soldiers around, think again. They are going to laugh in your face. They are not bound to your rule. They are bound to the Grand Lord of Kaletta. They made oaths to Kaletta, not Ashridge. You could just as easily end up their prisoner."

"I dare them." I felt my power rise to my fingertips, and I wanted to send the sand under their feet vibrating, turning it all to quicksand.

The look Aiden gave me was nothing short of vicious. "Grand Duchess, it is my Angels bound duty to ensure your safety. Do not make me use those abilities against you to keep you safe from yourself."

"Is that my Vernadali speaking or my mate?" I spat as my lips lifted and showed him those fangs he loved so much.

There was a softening in the lines of his face, but the fear and determination were still there as he lifted a hand and ran his thumb across my bottom lip. His eyes froze on my mouth before he looked down at me and said, "As adorable as it is to see you this angry at me, and rightfully so, you can believe that this is your Vernadali speaking to you right now. I am Angels bound to protect you with my life. I will gladly do so as your mate *or* Vernadali, but as your Vernadali, I will not allow you to walk into enemy hands. Are. We. Clear?"

"We are." And we were. I knew he was right, and he was only doing his job, but how dare Kaletta have such a large amount of their military at the gates of the Ashridge capital. "Do you think Kaletta is truly our enemy? Yes, they are making it harder on us to stand on our own feet, but isn't that just a political ploy to have Jayden and I marry sooner? I know Jayden heard rumors and boasting of Kaletta killing Mom, but do we know for sure that they did? It was just a rumor around camp, right?"

"If the Grand Lord of Kaletta murdered the Grand Duchess, then that is an act of war. That would be solidified by the showing before us." Aiden pulled me and the horses down below the ridge, so we wouldn't be seen, and then paced a few minutes before saying, "If Kaletta moves those forces against Ashridge, could the capital defend itself?"

"Before I left, there were about ten thousand troops in the capital." I took a deep breath and let it out slowly. "But I don't know if Mom sent them out. Your parents didn't say anything about a shortage of troops, but it never really came up. So, I don't know."

He faced toward the camp and stared in that direction like he was looking for answers before he said, "Let's get you back on your throne, Grand Duchess. We will have to go around, but we should be there in short order."

This time I looked toward where the soldiers were. "If the Grand Lord is responsible for Mom's death, I will turn him to goo before his armies."

"Yes, Grand Duchess."

CHAPTER 31

AIDEN

THE ANGER IN WHICH she had said she would turn the Grand Lord to goo gave me immense satisfaction. She had turned on her heels and all but leaped onto the back of her horse before swinging him around and heading toward the gates. I wasn't even sure she had used the stirrup to get astride the gelding. All I knew was that she had instantly taken off, and I was left to catch up, again.

The rough stone walls of Ashridge were taller than I remembered from the last time I was here. Jess had slowed to a walk as we approached the gates of the capital, and I studied her as she tied off her reins on the horn and turned in the saddle to face backwards as she searched for something in her pack. When she found what she was looking for, she kept it hidden from me.

"Jess... what are you doing?" She only winked at me with a smirk before turning back around. How she did that without falling on her ass, or revealing what she had pulled from her pack, I didn't know. There was a playful tone to her anxiety and anticipation now, and I narrowed my eyes at her.

We stopped just before the gates and heard one of the guards yell, "Identify yourselves."

Before I could say one word, Jess revealed what she had been hiding by putting a crown on her head and spoke with a strength I had always admired, "Grand Duchess Jessika Valenti with my Angels bound Vernadali Aiden Mathewson. Open the gates so that I can meet with Lady Megan and Vernadali CJ who have been overseeing the capital since the Grand Duchess' murder."

Silence filled the parapet, and I saw the guard quickly line the front and stand at attention. Footsteps scurried across the stone, echoing down toward us. Silent signals were no doubt flowing through the city for each and every guard to stand at attention as she passed. The gates opened, and when it was barely open wide enough for us to pass through, she put her heels to the gelding's sides and took off, once again leaving me to chase after her.

Wicked satisfaction came bursting through the Vernadali bond, and I shook my head, smiling. As we raced through the walls, I ran my fingers along the rounded steel at my neck and smirked as I tugged on that claiming. She tugged back and reached down to pinch her hip as she rounded the bend and went up the triple wide street to the main hall.

She rode that gelding straight up the stairs to the main hall, and when the guards saw her, there was only a moment's hesitation before they saw the crown on her head. The doors swung open, and she burst through into the main hall. The Grand Duchess of Ashridge jumped out of the saddle, just as I cleared the doorway. Moments later, I was standing next to her, my Charge flowing through the room and creating a bubble around us.

A quick sweep of the room indicated most of the Capital Council and guards all at attention, weapons drawn. When I looked to the front of the room, I let out a breath in relief and felt Jess do the same as we saw my parents and Jayden, Killy and Ilris next to them.

"Grand Duchess. Welcome home." My mother's voice rang through the room as she stepped out front of the table, and everyone at the front table fell to one knee with a clenched fist out toward her.

My gaze encircled the room, and I took a step closer to Jess before the council and guards dropped to one knee. Jess froze, taking in the sight of everyone instantly bowing before her. Anxiety, fear, and waves of loss flowed through her, but when I put my hand on the small of her back and pulled at the claiming again, she let out a long breath through her nose. Lifting her chin slightly, she commanded, "You may rise."

Guards behind us came and took the horses, and we were almost to the front of the room when a tall, dark figure came running out of the hall from the right, long ponytail swaying in the shadows, instantly putting me on guard.

"Jess!" the voice called out, and I relaxed as the figure pulled the shadows back. Reka stepped into the room wearing tight fitted pants, a white button up, rolled up to the elbows, and short black boots with heels so high I wondered how she walked in them.

"Janreka!" Jess ran to her best friend, tears already running down her face.

I looked to my parents, who were smiling. It was then I realized that Auntie Clarice and Uncle Alexei were standing in the entrance to one of the hallways. I let Jess have her moment with Reka and headed toward my family.

Standing before them, I bent at the waist with my hand over my fist. "Empress Clarice, Grand Duke Alexei, welcome to Ashridge. I apologize on behalf of the Grand Duchess that she was not here to greet you upon your arrival."

I heard my father chuckle and, out of the corner of my eye, saw Mom roll her eyes.

"I don't know, CJ, should I just send him to the Underworld now for not anticipating that Jess wouldn't be here and it would take time to travel here after getting word of her mother's death?" I heard the teasing tone, lifted my eyes, and narrowed them at her. "Vernadali Aiden, rise and come and give your aunt a hug before I zap your ass."

I stood and whined, "Yes, Auntie Clarice."

I felt Jess behind me, and after giving Auntie Clarice and Uncle Alexei a hug, I turned toward Jess. "I'd like to formally introduce you to the Grand Duchess of Ashridge, Jessika Petra Valenti."

Everyone at that table from Killy to Reka, who was now standing next to Uncle Alexei, bowed. Jess turned to me and whispered, "Did you have to do that, Aid? It isn't like everyone here doesn't already know me."

"Hey, when else are you going to get the Empress and Gatekeeper of the Underworld to actually bow to you?"

"You have always been a sassy shit," Uncle Alexei said.

"And I wonder where I learned that from?" My eyes bounced between my mom and him, only to have the entire table chuckle.

There was a knowing cough behind us, and Jess took a quick breath before turning to the hall of council members. "You are all dismissed. I have much to discuss with my..." Her eyes flicked to me and sparkled for a moment before she said, "Family before I will be in a position to discuss any legal matters with the council. Please return after we have lit the pyre for the deceased Grand Duchess. Understood?"

"Yes, Grand Duchess," the room said in unison.

As soon as the council members were out of the room, Jayden was there giving Jess a huge hug and said, "Family? So, does that mean that you two finally pulled your heads out of your asses? And please tell me that he has fucked you silly, because if I have to endure anymore of the tension we went through at Silentport, I might kill you, Jess, and only feel bad about it for half a minute. Angels!"

"Jayden...," Jess tried to admonish, but it was Reka who squealed in delight behind me. "Seriously?"

"Yes, Janreka," Jess muttered, but she turned to smile at me, touched the heart at the base of her throat, and winked. "He still owes me an engagement ring, though."

"But I can't do that until Mom finds a way for us to nullify the agreement with Kaletta." I looked around the room again and sent my power out to see if the Grand Lord was lurking in any corner, but I didn't feel anyone other than those standing with us. "We can't just outright refuse, because as part of that nullification, we will have to find a way for Jayden, Killy, and Ilris to have legal standing within Ashridge," I said, running my hand through my hair.

Jayden blinked at me, looked at Jess who nodded, and then to Killy and Ilris. "I'm sorry, what?"

Jess took Jayden's hands and said, "I will protect not only Ashridge, but also you, Jayden. That includes Killy and Ilris."

"Jess." His eyes were filled with tears. "You..."

"Shut it, asshole. You know Jess isn't going to leave you to *him*," I said, half laughing, then sobered. "Where is he anyways?"

"Said he didn't need to be here." Mom shrugged. "He made a bunch of demands I am not agreeing to, nor have the right to, and when I told him so, he demanded an audience with you immediately upon your return. Now he is basically pouting and won't leave his room until you arrive."

"He is going to wait a bit longer," Jess bit out, and I felt the dread filling her.

"It will be okay," I said, making her look at me.

She nodded and then turned to Mom. "Lady Megan—"

"Oh, for fuck's sake. Please call me Mom or Megan when we are with family. I've always hated the title." She shuddered and then Dad put his arm around her and kissed the top of her head before adding, "Ditto."

It was Auntie Clarice who chimed in, "Why do you even have to say that? I mean, Jess, you've always been part of this family. You better start calling us the same thing that shithead you're attached to does."

"Empress," she started to say, but the look Auntie Clarice gave her would have had anyone less on their knees begging for forgiveness. "Clarice," she amended quickly, "it might take some time to call you Auntie Clarice, but I will try to just say Clarice."

"Not sure why it is so hard. The twins and Aiden have been doing it for ages. Logan's kids, too."

"Why?" Jess' shock made me giggle. "You are the *Gatekeeper to the Underworld*, one of the most powerful Sangra *or* beings this side of the Nalsar dimension, and I'm just supposed to go from calling you Empress Clarice to Auntie? You have to see how absurd that is, right?"

Reka started chuckling and said, "Jess, think of it like how you call me Princess in formal settings and Janreka when it's just us."

"But we've been friends forever."

"Exactly!" Auntie Clarice said. "It is no different. You've known Alexei, Megan, CJ, and me for just about the same amount of time. It's no different. Don't make me command you."

"Yes, ma'am," she said before turning to me, trying to look formidable, but there was a smirk sitting in the corner of her lips. "I may have to rethink this whole marrying you thing if they keep this insistence upon making me one of you."

"You already are, and you know you love it," I said, reaching down and kissing her quickly. She melted under me, and I tightened my hold on her a bit. She just looked up at me, those onyx eyes warm and endearing in a way that made me hard instantly.

"Angels, I thought I would never see the day," Jayden said. "Jess rendered speechless. If we had known that it just took Aiden kissing her to do it, I would have called you in sooner." I glared at him, but he just beamed back at me.

I looked back at Jess and felt exhaustion weighing heavily on her. "Do you want to get cleaned up before we really dig in, or do you want to get started now?"

She looked at Mom, who said, "There are a couple of things to discuss, but the main one is do you want to see your mom? We have the pyre ready. She is being held in state downstairs. We can have her moved and ready for the pyre at dusk tonight if you wish."

Pain lanced through her, and she wrapped an arm around my waist tight. "Tonight," she said barely above a whisper, and then louder said, "Tonight, please. Mom has waited long enough to be sent to the Angels."

"As you wish, Grand Duchess," Mom said.

"If you are going to require me to call you Mom or Megan, then please don't Grand Duchess me when we are not in formal settings. You can speak formally if you must, but..."

"Of course, Jess."

"What of Amala's parents? Have they arrived? When is her pyre scheduled?" Jess' eyes were lined with tears, and when my eyes met Reka's, I saw her trying to hold them back as well.

"They arrived last night. They wanted to wait for you to arrive. If they agree, we can have Amala and the Grand Duchess' pyres both tonight," Dad said, and Jess only nodded. When she didn't say anything else, Dad said, "I'll go speak to them now."

"Any word on Lemi?"

"A LightCall is set and ready for your use to call him at any time. I spoke to him a couple days ago to let him know," Mom told her.

"Karlo?" Jess looked over to Auntie Clarice.

It was Uncle Alexei who said, "He won't leave Amala's side. Reka told us after you all left the Curtails of the North, you two threatened to make them Silnaree. I think there was already that bond, even if not solidified by the darkness."

A tear fell from Jess' cheek as she nodded and turned to me. I reached out and wiped it off with my thumb. "Jess, go get cleaned up, do what you need to do, and I'll meet you in our residence when I'm done. I need to talk to Jayden."

She nodded, and Jayden said, "There is a lot to go over from our time in the camps."

Not taking my eyes off Jess, I said, "Reka, can you watch over her and ensure she gets some food and water. Water, not coffee." I felt Jess chuckle, and Reka laughed outright at that. "She hasn't had much more than a few bites of cheese and bread since we got up this morning."

"Of course, Aiden."

Jess held me tighter for a moment, and I pulled her in close, whispering in her ear, "I'm going to talk to him about his claim regarding the Grand Lord and the army stationed outside of Ashridge." She nodded, pulled on the claiming, and pinched my hip before taking Reka's hand and striding away.

I watched as Reka put her arm around her shaking shoulders. The wave of sadness that hit me was a punch to the gut. I took another deep breath and forced myself into that Vernadali that she needed me to be. She needed me to take care of things while she got her bearings here. Reka was with her, and there was no one else I trusted more with my mate than her. When she disappeared around the corner, I took another moment to center myself before turning toward the rest of my family.

"Uncle Alexei, can you finalize the pyres for tonight, please?"

"As you say, Vernadali Aiden." He gave me a quick bow, and I shook my head at him. That was going to get some getting used to. As he rose, he smirked at me, and Auntie Clarice smacked him in the ass as he moved out. He jumped and gave her a look that I really didn't want to read too much into, because damn, if they didn't look like Jess and me.

"Jayden, we need to talk. Mom, Auntie Clarice, care to join us?" I was in Vernadali mode. I needed to know what had been going on and get updated quickly. "But we need somewhere private to talk with no chance of people overhearing."

"There is an enchanted meeting chamber we can use," Mom said.

"Lead the way."

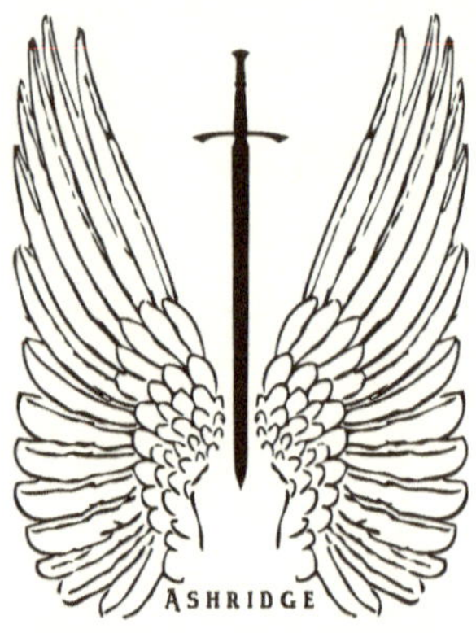

CHAPTER 32

JESSIKA

SLOWLY, I WALKED INTO what used to be my mom's office. The walls were a pale grey, with hints of pale blue throughout. I smiled. Blue had been her favorite color, and I couldn't help but see different memories from my past in this room as I looked around it.

My eyes focused for a minute on the desk, and all I could see was her long brown hair in a messy bun on the top of her hair, sleeves rolled up to her elbows, and a hand on her forehead as she scribbled notes over whatever she had been looking at that day.

"Mama?" a small voice said.

"Hey, JessieBessie. Bad dreams again?" Her head popped up, and her gaze met my wide-eyed, fear-filled one. Her expression instantly softened as she smiled. I nodded my

head. "Come here, sweetie." I ran over to her, my feet padding across the soft carpet in the room to her open arms.

She gathered me up and let me cry as I told her about the monsters that attacked the city. Mom kissed my temple. "It's okay, JessieBessie. That particular monster has been taken care of and will never hurt anyone again.

"But what about other monsters like that?"

"There will always be monsters in this world. It is our job to protect our people from them as much as we can."

My voice cracked. "But we didn't save our people from the monster."

Mom let out a heavy sigh. "We didn't. Ashridge has a hard road ahead, but with people like Head Julian, Empress Clarice, and now Lady Megan and her Angels Blessed Vernadali..." She wiped my hair back from my face. "We can rebuild. We can start over."

I shook my head to clear the image. No matter how much work she had to do, she had always made time for my brother and me if we needed her. I took a deep breath and let it out softly. It was strange that particular memory hit me. I rested my hands on the edge of the desk and let out a long breath.

"What just went through your mind?" Janreka asked as she sat in the chair in the corner.

"I was three when we were in Savanora on holiday and Ansel Keller came in and overtook Ashridge City. Lemi was an infant. Yet, I still had nightmares of seeing what Ashridge City looked like when we returned."

"Okay." She let the words drag out.

Turning to face her and leaning against the desk, I said, "When I walked in, I saw Mom sitting in her chair, and she instantly dropped everything to just hold me. I was six or seven at the time of that particular memory. Had those nightmares until I was twelve or thirteen. Even though she was literally having to build the city from the rubble up, she had still made Lemi and me her number one priority."

"I sometimes forget that you are older than us." A large grin crossed her face. "You will technically be my older sister now."

"LJ, I think, will enjoy having another sister. Owen, on the other hand…" I couldn't help the chuckle that bubbled out of me.

Janreka's face lit up. "Hey, we just evened out the score! Three girls and three boys."

"Only because Aiden is the first one to commit to anyone. I was hoping it would have been Karlo and Amala that were the first. Maybe Owen."

"Nah, he's too much of a fuckboy still. He likes to be free, much to Aunt Megan's chagrin. The number of times that she has laid into him about that behavior is endless. She's always telling him she knows she raised him to treat women better than that. He usually ends up with zaps to the ass, but he's just a shithead." Janreka chuckled. A blue light came on over by the bookshelf and I sighed. "Go and talk to Lemi. I'll be out here when you are done." Janreka nodded to the bookcase and leaned her head back, closing her eyes. My dearest friend patted me on the shoulder.

Making my way over to the bookshelf, I pulled on the fifth book on the right, causing a scan pad to slide out from the shelf underneath the book. Placing my hand on it, there were small vibrations as it sensed my power and scanned the pointer finger and pinky. There was a soft beep, and a door to the right popped open.

Sliding into the little eight-by-eight-foot room, I looked to the wall next to the door, lined with dark- and light-grey chiffon, showcasing a large crest of Ashridge in the center.

I ran my fingers along the upturned wings and had to swallow another sob. Turning to the desk on the other wall, I sat down and punched in the code CJ had given me to connect the LightCall system to Cinder.

I had put off calling Lemi in lieu of a shower and a cup of coffee, that Janreka had promised she wouldn't tell Aiden about, before I sent word to Noah, my Secretary of Territory Affairs, that I needed the call to connect and headed over. As I waited for Lemi to pop up, my eyes scanned the room, noting the areas where the cleaners had missed and shaking my head. It took a few moments, but then Lemi's face filled the screen.

"JessieBessie." His voice was relieved.

"Hey, Lems."

"How are you holding up?" His eyes were swollen, and there were shadows under them.

"I have Aiden holding me together." I shrugged. "How are you? Are you going to be able to make it tonight?"

A tear fell from his left eye, and he shook his head. "It would take three months to get back to Nalrin soil. You know that Head Julian has transport locked down. He tried to get approval from the dimensional heads for an exception, but they wouldn't approve it. Said it's protocol for full lockdown upon a Head of Territory assassination. I'm stuck. Not to mention that Katerina is stuck working with the Duchess here." A shadow crossed his face, and he wiped at the tears. "Angels, I tried anyway, Jessika, but hit a wall and was back here. I'm sorry I can't be there."

Tears fell down my cheeks at the realization I wouldn't have Lemi with me tonight. I would have to stand there alone.

"Wait." He sat up straighter and leaned against the desk. "Did you say Aiden? As in your asshole ex who shattered your heart? *That* Aiden?"

I laughed and touched the necklace. It was a nervous habit now. Knowing it sat there gave me a lot of comfort. A full smile crossed my face when I said, "Yes, Aiden Mathewson."

"Well, shit! No wonder everything went through Vernadali CJ. What else aren't you telling me?" He raised an eyebrow, but then his eyes narrowed as he studied me. "Oh, fuck. JessiBessie, you transformed."

I nodded my head, and a new wave of grief fell through me. Fresh tears streamed down my face as I told Lemi the short version of what happened. "Amala was killed when we were en route back to Ashridge from Silentport. I watched the Kaletta Guard slice her throat. It triggered the transformation."

"You would have had to have been without your power. Just how long had you been fighting? You know how to pace yourself."

I did know how to pace myself. Well, I should have been able to. I looked down and picked at my nails. They had grown and become more claw like in the last week. As I blinked, another round of tears fell down my face. "Apparently, I didn't pace myself properly. I was fighting for my life, Lems. I just turned everyone to goo as they touched us." Sighing, I looked up at him, "Things were complicated. I was already grieving Mom, Aiden and I... Well, that is a bit of a long discussion. I don't know Lems. I just ran out."

He nodded but just said, "The ears look good. The fangs too. It suits you."

Then his head tilted to the side as he picked up on one detail. "Kaletta Guards attacked you?"

I let a long silence hang between us as I thought how I was going to tell him that the territory that was supposed to have our back may be the one destroying us.

"Lems, we think it was the Grand Lord who killed Mom. I haven't declared war yet. When I have the proof, I will, and the Grand Lord will lose his head for killing Mom and Amala."

"Are you just going to remove it, or turn it to goo?" he asked carefully, but there was a bit of an amused, evil smirk that crossed his lips.

I raised my hand as it coated in purple, and the room hummed. "I want him to feel it. I'll make it so slow and painful, he will beg for my mercy." His eyes were focused and deadly as I said, "I have no mercy to give him."

"That's my big sister." He studied me for another moment before he said, "I know you said it's a long story, but just tell me one thing. How did you and Aiden cross each other again, and why was he traveling with you in the first place?"

My eyes narrowed at him, "Seriously? Head Julian or Vernadali CJ didn't tell you?"

"Tell me what, JessieBessie?" There was the protective little brother I knew, and I couldn't help but smile.

"Aiden is my Angels deemed Vernadali," I said, smiling brightly.

"You are fucking kidding me."

"Nope. Trust me when I say, it was a bit of a shock to us, too. If it makes you feel any better, Janreka has been threatening him on a consistent basis, but he isn't going anywhere," I said with a glint in my eye.

He blinked, and recognition flicked in his dark-brown eyes. "You completed the claiming!"

"Still working some things out, but we did." I smiled and couldn't help the heavy sigh that left me when I said, "Like

I said, Lems, there is still a lot to work out, namely the contract with Kaletta."

"Are you willing to go to war over it?" Lemi asked, a twinkle in his eye. I knew he would have my back in any decision I made. "I can come back to help with that if you wish. You know how much I loathe the Grand Lord."

"I don't *want* to go to war, but this is about more than Aiden and me. Aiden is mine and I am his. That doesn't change. You know Mom, Jayden and I were trying to get the agreement nullified." He nodded and so I continued, "We are still working on that. First, we have to ensure that Kaletta stops sabotaging our supplies, because they have been, by the way. Second, we have to make sure we can stand on our own. I think we can. We don't need Kaletta. They have breached the agreement in minor ways that I'm sure he'll just correct for a time, but we have to have an unforgivable, unfixable reason for that agreement to be nullified." There was a surge of pride that went over Lemi's features that made me smile, but then I remembered the biggest hurdle we had. "We also have to find a place for Jayden and two of his guards. It's about their safety as well. It really is much bigger than just Aiden and me. We have to be smart about this."

"You are going to be an amazing grand duchess, Jessy."

"Well, Mom and Dad did a lot in training us for this, but I just wish they were here to help advise." I sniffled, and it was wholly ungrand duchess like, which caused him to chuckle.

"When Katerina finishes here in Cinder, I'll get back as soon as I can, okay?" His head turned in the other direction, and I saw Katerina poke her head in.

"Hey, Jess." Her voice was full of sorrow.

"Hey, Kat."

"I'll send his ass home. He needs to be there. Even if he can't make it in time for the pyre or the coronation, you could use an extra Ashridge hand." She put her hand on his shoulder, and I saw him wince as she squeezed it tight.

"I think I like her more and more," I said, laughing, but then asked, "Would it be okay if the kids stayed with you? I'm concerned this might get ugly here."

"No problem, Grand Duchess. The kids love Cinder." Katerina nodded. "They are giving us the full royal treatment, so I have lots of help. Lemi here is bored anyways, so I'll get him on the next boat to Nalrin. There is one that leaves in the morning. I'm sorry, Jess."

Nodding at her, I let out a long breath. "I'll ask Head Julian to see if continental transportation can open up so that Lemi can teleport once he's on the continent."

"Is he there?" Lemi asked, and I nodded. I had been told he arrived an hour ago, even though I hadn't seen him. "Tell him I said thank you." There was a beat of silence before he asked, "Have you seen Mom yet?"

"No, I'm heading down after we finish here to see her and Amala."

He nodded. "Give her a parting kiss for me, please?"

"Of course. I love you, Lems. I'll see you soon."

"Love you too, JessieBessie." He clicked the call off, and I used my power to allow the door to open. Another wave of grief racketed through me and I took a deep breath to settle myself.

Janreka was there leaning on the desk. I wiped my eyes and blinked because I didn't even realize I had started to cry again. Once I got to the threshold, her arms were around me, and I sobbed into her chest.

I STOOD AT THE stone door that led to the chamber where my mom and best friend lay waiting to be sent to the Five Angels. I pushed on the door, but it didn't budge. A small pad popped out of the side, and I placed my hand on it. Just as it had to let me into the LightCall room, it vibrated as it scanned my pointer and pinky before the door popped open and a soft ten-second countdown started to occur.

I looked at Janreka, who grabbed my arm and pulled me in right behind her. Half a second later, the door was shut. Once the door shut, the room's temp dropped another few degrees, and I sighed as I turned and saw them both lying there, Karlo's head popping up from beside Amala.

"Karlo," I breathed.

"Jess... I mean, Grand—" I gave him an even look. "Jess." He stood, and I ran to him, throwing my arms around his shoulders. He was a little taller than me, and his long dark hair was pulled back into a bun in the back, with pieces sticking out all over the place. He held me tight, and I felt how his strength had waned, but he still picked me up, holding me with my toes barely touching the ground. The shuddering breaths I felt against my chest brought more tears to my eyes.

"Put her down, Kar. Don't think Aiden would appreciate you breaking the Grand Duchess," Janreka said from behind me, as he gently set me back down.

Karlo's head popped up, looked at her, and then back at me. "Aiden finally pulled his head from that tight Vernadali ass?" He looked at his sister who nodded, rolling her eyes. "It's about time. So, you are officially family now?" I nodded, and then he noticed the changes in my features, looked between my mom and Amala, and asked, "Which one caused you to transform?"

I looked down at Amala. "She died fighting for me, Kar."

"And she would do it a thousand times over to make sure that you survived. It was just who she was." His voice was sad but proud.

"I'm sorry."

"Don't be. I knew when I fell in love with her, I could lose her like this." I wrapped an arm around him again, and his voice was thick when he said, "It just doesn't make it hurt any less."

"When was the last time you really slept?"

"Night before she died." His voice was so weary and tired that I felt my chest tighten.

"Go, get some sleep."

He shook his head. "I can't leave her until we light the pyre."

"Which will be tonight." His head turned to me, then his eyes shifted to where my mom lay. "Seriously, Kar. Go shower. Get cleaned up."

"Is that my new big sister talking or the Grand Duchess?" He raised an eyebrow.

"Don't make it have to be the Grand Duchess. Besides, Amala wouldn't want you showing up smelling the way you do. When was the last time you showered or ate?" I raised an eyebrow at him, and he looked to Amala and shrugged. Reaching out to take his hand, I squeezed it. "They will be coming to get her in a couple hours to take her to the pyre. Go get cleaned up for the ceremony. You will need your strength for that tonight."

He looked down at Amala again and nodded. "Okay, Jess."

I gave him another hug and watched him walk out the door.

"How did you do that?" Janreka asked. "Mom ordered him as the Empress and he wouldn't budge."

"That was his mom. You are blood. It's not that my word means more. I'm just a different person who loves her as much as he does."

I was still staring at the closed door when she said, "Go see your mom. I'm gonna talk to Amala."

"Can you... like Empress Clarice?"

"No." She let out a weighted sigh. "Won't get that ability until I take over for her, and trust me when I say, I really don't want to do that any time soon. There are days she comes upstairs and is so grey and worn. I worry about her," she said before squeezing her hand and heading to the other side of the room.

"Hi, Mom." They had dressed her in a solid black satin dress and laid grey and blue daisies in her hands. I ran my hand along the lines of the stone bowl they laid her in, until I got to her face. She really did look like she was sleeping. They had even painted her face, so she didn't look so pale.

Her long brunette hair flowed around her in elegant waves, and my breath caught when I saw that they had placed the official Ashridge crown on her head. A large single clear stone with peppering throughout sat in the center as silver wings feathered out to either side of the head, dotted with smaller peppered stones throughout. Along each tip of the feather was another small peppered stone.

"Mom, can I even bear the weight of that crown? There is already so much going on. The Grand Lord is the cause of our destroyed shipments, he's likely the cause of the water shortage from the Black Mountains, and..." I looked down at her neck, to the two bruised puncture wounds. My breath caught, and anger mixed with that lump in my throat made the words come out strained "We strongly suspect that he is to blame for your death."

I felt a tug along the claiming and sighed. I tugged back to let him know I was okay, and I looked around the room. There was only the soft whispering from Janreka as she spoke to Amala. There was a stack of chairs against the wall opposite the door, and using my power, I sent a chair over to Janreka, who turned and nodded her thanks. Then I summoned one for myself. I sat there, folded my arms at the edge of the bowl, and laid my head down.

Another small tug on the claiming had me smiling. "Oh, Mom. If you didn't know, I, um, transformed. And Aiden is mine. Okay, so that isn't exactly how I should probably say that. Where do I even begin? Aiden and I worked through a bunch of things, and we promised ourselves to each other. And Amala died, and I transformed. Mom, Amala lies with you here. She died trying to protect me. Can you help her in the Underworld when you get there, please?"

Fresh sobs wracked through my chest, and I couldn't stop them when they flowed. I let them pour down my face, not even trying to wipe them off or wipe my nose.

"Momma Grand Duchess, did Jess tell you she and Aiden are back together?" Janreka came over and rubbed my back after who knew how long. "Yeah, they both finally pulled their heads out of their asses and decided to the Underworld with all that bullshit."

"Janreka!"

She looked at me and smiled. "They are ridiculously cute together. You would be proud of your daughter, Momma Grand Duchess. Don't worry. Us Mathewsons stay together, so we will find a way to make sure they get married. We will find a way through the old antiquated Vernadali laws *and* get out of that ridiculous contract with Kaletta with the fewest casualties."

I laughed at that, spurting snot everywhere. Janreka handed me a handkerchief, and I thanked her through my attempts to blow my nose.

"Go and say goodbye to Amala. I have some things to discuss with Momma Grand Duchess." The way she had said that made me wonder if she actually could talk to the dead like her mom. Maybe not exactly like Empress Clarice, but if there wasn't some way for her to still do it.

Getting up, I kissed Mom on each cheek and whispered, "I love you. Lems, too."

I met Janreka's gaze, and her face was streaked with tears as she looked at my mom lying there.

I took a moment before crossing the room. Taking those steps to Amala felt wrong. When I saw her lying there, my eyes immediately went to where they had slit her throat. Someone had done a really good job of sealing it up, but the mark was still clearly visible.

I looked down at the rest of her, in a pair of dark jeans and a loose-fitting shirt, and smiled. "Let me guess, Janreka dressed you. You look comfy there, you know, if you hadn't died." The words sounded harsher than I intended. "Why did you have to die, Amala? You are one of the best fighters I know. You weren't supposed to die. We were supposed to grow old, get married to the men that love to drive us crazy, have kids together, and complain about Aiden and Karlo not changing enough diapers. Where do you get off going and dying on me?"

A sob sat in my throat, but I didn't think I had anything left in me. I started laughing at the stupidity of my anger toward her. "I know it wasn't your fault, Amala. Doesn't mean the other stuff isn't true. You *were* supposed to grow old with me, have kids and change diapers because Aiden and Karlo wouldn't." The tears did flow then, because now I was mad at myself for being so mad at her. I wasn't sure how much time had passed, but a sick kind of laughter bubbled up through me, and when Janreka came up next to me, she asked, "What's so funny?"

"I was telling Amala that she was supposed to grow old with me and complain about how our husbands didn't change enough diapers."

"And that is funny?"

"Can you see Aiden changing diapers?!" Now the tears were coming out in hysterical laughter.

"He'll be a great father, and he *will* change the diapers." Janreka sputtered the words through her own laughter now, because I thought she saw exactly what he would be doing. "But of course, he'll be gagging at each one from the smell."

"Right?"

I was laughing again, and feeling much lighter, when I looked over at Amala and saw her lying there. For a moment, it was like old times. The three of us sitting somewhere, laughing and having a good time with each other.

"I'll miss her, too, Jess," Janreka whispered.

"I watched it all happen. I know exactly how she died, and she was fighting those Kaletta soldiers to keep *me* safe. I'll carry that guilt for the rest of my life."

"The Grand Lord will suffer for ordering the attack."

"What would have been the point, though? There are a million and one ways for him to be able to take over, or whatever it is he is trying for. Is he trying to control me?

Does he think I'll be impressionable as a newly crowned Grand Duchess?" My eyes hadn't left Amala.

"We don't know, and trust me, Aunt Megan and Uncle CJ have been trying to figure that out." She sighed before saying, "Jess, we need to get you upstairs and ready for tonight. We've been here a lot longer than you think."

"I want to stop by and see Amala's parents first, okay?" I asked, looking at her like if she told me no, I would understand.

"Of course. I know they would like to see you, too."

Turning back to Amala and kissing her on each cheek, I rested my forehead to hers and said my final goodbye. "Thank you for keeping me safe, Amala."

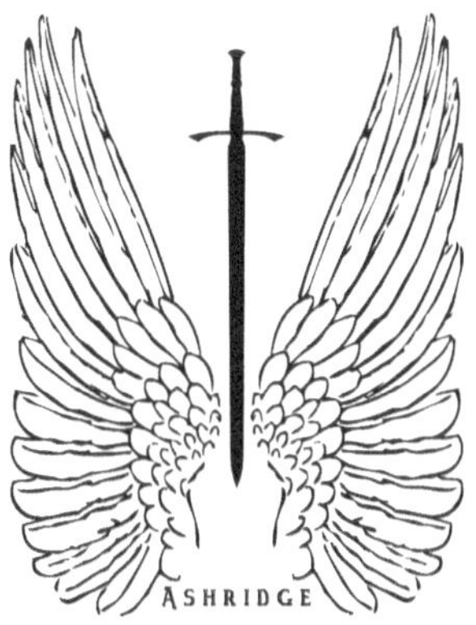

CHAPTER 33

JESSIKA

I STARED AT MY reflection in the mirror as I sat there. After saying my goodbyes to my mom and Amala, I went to see Amala's parents, and I wasn't sure which was harder: being in that room, talking to my mom who just lay there looking like she was sleeping, saying goodbye to my best friend with that slice across her throat, or having to face her parents who were having to say goodbye to their daughter because she was protecting me. I was so emotionally raw; I could feel myself going numb. My eyes burned, and my throat was sore from the crying I'd done today.

I heard Aiden turn the shower off and went back to getting my hair ready for the pyre. He finally made it to our quarters after hours of meetings. When he walked into the room, he kissed my cheek, pinched my hip, and got right into the shower himself. I looked back toward the bathroom as I pulled forward another section of hair and started braiding it.

Aiden had left me alone for hours. I had felt him tug on the claiming when waves of grief washed over me as I was sitting there with Mom and Amala. I let a small smile cross my lips as I realized he had let me process, while he made sure that things stayed in motion here. Lady Megan could still make decisions for me, but I could always overrule anything I didn't agree with.

What all did they talk about? Was the Kaletta Army still here? Would they stay? I sighed. "Angels, I'm so stupid sometimes."

"And why is that?" Aiden said, coming out of the bathroom, and when I looked over at him, my breath caught. His hair, still a little wet, went in just about every direction, but it was the towel precariously wrapped around his waist that caught my eye. More importantly, that little trail of hair that led to some of my favorite parts of him.

"Aiden..." I drew out his name as heat flooded every inch of me.

I took a lot of satisfaction in the deep breath he took as he tried to ignore everything he felt from me and then tried to calm his own emotions. "Why are you stupid?"

I blinked and then looked up at him. "Stupid?"

"I mean, other than the fact that you look struck stupid sitting there looking at me."

"Well, you would be, too, if I walked out of the bathroom looking like your own personal buffet," I said without thinking twice.

"You always look like my own personal meal, Kotě." He stepped back into the bathroom, and a moment later walked back out in a pair of pants before kneeling before me. "Now. I'm only going to ask one more time. Why do you feel so stupid?"

I shook my head to clear my thoughts and tried to remember what I was even thinking about. "Oh! The Kaletta Army."

"What about it?"

"The army was there because the Grand Lord is here. Of course, he would bring an entire army with him. He would want his visit to Ashridge to be a show of Kaletta's strength."

Aiden tilted his head slightly and scrunched his eyes as he thought about it. "Jayden said he wasn't sure why his father had moved half of what was stationed at the ridge with him, but if what you are thinking is true, then it would make sense."

"He is making demands. Whatever it is he wants from us is big. It has to be." I picked up the three strands of braided hair and braided them together behind my head. "If he can bring this many soldiers to Ashridge, then it will give the impression that he has so many soldiers, he can afford to have this many as his personal company. It's a boasting of strength, whether he has it or not."

Aiden thought for a moment. "Only Jayden said that the rest at the ridge are ready to move on a moment's notice."

There was a knock at the door, interrupting us, and he got up and was halfway to the door when a wave of power hit me, and I chuckled softly. Aiden stopped and just said, "We are dressed. You can come in, Reka."

The door swung open, she came in with three different crowns, and I groaned as I took Aiden's hand and stood. "Really? You know how much I hate those things."

"Jess, you are Grand Duchess now," she admonished but then said, "And why are you complaining now? You literally galloped through Ashridge and into the main hall on horseback wearing yours."

"You did," Aiden said, smiling. "And, she's right. You do have to wear one tonight."

I couldn't help but smile at that. It had been worth it to see the shocked expression on his face and then watch him chase after me down the streets. "Doesn't mean they are comfortable. Regardless, it served a purpose. The people of Ashridge had to know their Grand Duchess was back, and besides, it made for quite the impressive entrance."

Janreka and Aiden just looked at each other, shrugged, and turned back to me. I beheld the crowns sitting on their individual pillows on the tray in Janreka's arms and sighed. All I could see was my mother wearing each of them at pyres I had previously attended. The first was for my grandmother, then my grandfather, then my father. Now I was having to wear one of them for my mother.

"The Mourning Crowns," I said under my breath. "Why these? There are eight of them, so why these specifically?"

"They pair with your dress," Janreka said quietly as she looked me over from head to toe. I looked down at the black chiffon dress that faded to a light grey at the floor. Its deep V-neck stopped at the jeweled belt just under my breasts.

"Is it too much?" I sighed, but Aiden's eyes twinkled. "I'm not asking you. You wanted to use your power to keep my boobs up and on display."

He shrugged, but then Janreka spat, "Perv."

"What? They are spectacular boobs. Besides, she's mine. I can be pervy with her."

"She isn't owned."

"Well... actually...," I started to say, and the knowing smirk on Aiden's face had me suppressing a giggle as I touched the rounded metal at my throat.

"That isn't what I meant and you two *both* know that." Janreka rolled her eyes dramatically and put the crowns down on the vanity dresser I had been sitting at. "As for the dress, it's fine. I love the added silver chains underneath. The Grand Duchess would be proud, Jess." Her finger ran across one of the silver chains that circled around and between my breasts in an intricate pattern.

"I'm going to finish getting dressed," Aiden said, kissing my temple and walking off to the other room.

I turned to look at the Mourning Crowns and then toward the mirror. I didn't even think about it. I knew I needed to wear the one Mom wore to Dad's, so I reached over, picked up the middle one, and placed it around the intricate braid I had at the crown of my head. I had opted to let the rest of my hair flow loose because Mom had always loved my hair down. Placing it on my head, the crown was stark against my white hair with the large black stones, an inch between the five of them, which were held in place by sweeping dark silver swirls, where each of the points above the large stone had a small cluster of black ones.

I felt a sob rise in my throat, but Janreka was there a moment later, straightening it and pinning it to the braided coil. She waved her hand, snapped her fingers, and a decorative webbed chain appeared lined with small peppered stones. She attached it to either side of the crown and looped the nearly see-through cord over my hair to help keep it in place.

When I turned to face her, her eyes were mixed with pride and sadness. "Did you at least use waterproof cosmetics?"

"Of course," I said, sniffling. She reached up and wiped a tear from just under my eye and said, "You seem to be holding it together pretty well, considering, but I have to ask, Jess…" I waited, and when she went to speak, she had to clear her throat, "I love you, and I want to understand, but it's rude."

"Janreka, everything's fine. Just ask."

"Your features have changed." Her eyes flicked from my ears to my mouth, to my face.

I laughed. I genuinely laughed for the first time in over a week. "Seriously? That's what you want to ask about? After everything we have ever talked about, you think mentioning *that* is rude?" I heard Aiden laughing in the other room, and when I pulled on the claiming, he instantly stopped, shouting, "RUDE!"

"Jess, you have slightly pointed ears and fangs. REAL FANGS. Not your usual metaphorical ones." Then she stopped, blinked, and turned to look through the wall to the room where Aiden was getting ready. "What? How?"

When she turned back to face me, her eyes were wide. "The claiming. You two completed the claiming!" She jumped and clapped. "So, you are family now by right." She stuck her tongue out at me, and I shook my head.

"I hate you," I mocked.

"No, you don't. I'm your sister. Can't get rid of me now." I rolled my eyes at her, because of all the things that were going on, she was as giddy as the day after a Maltal ceremony.

When Aiden walked out of the other room, my eyes swept up the length of his body, and he shifted under the scrutiny. The Vernadali uniform of black pants, boots, and shirt were stunning to say the least. The velvet and satin cape over his right shoulder was secured with a silver braided cord, only accentuating his height. How had I not noticed that when we were at the Curtails of the North? How could I not have noticed just how amazing he looked in it? "Aiden, I swear."

"What?"

"Every time you've walked into this room today, I have wanted to push you down and fuck you," I said, my cheeks reddening when I remembered that Janreka was there. I turned to her and smirked. "Sorry."

Laughing, she just said, "No, you are not, but you are right. I mean, if you weren't practically my brother, I'd also admit you look scrumptious, Aiden."

I raised an eyebrow at her, and she giggled. "He's all yours."

"Damn straight he is."

"Angels and Underworlds being. You two are ridiculous."

Then Janreka was taking long determined strides toward Aiden, and with a flick of her wrists, his syths went from sitting on the table to her hands. She handed them to him and said, "Please protect her."

I watched them as they looked at each other for a long moment before he said, "With my last breath, Reka. I promise you that."

"As will I, brother," Janreka vowed, and they both turned to face me.

I stood there staring between them as Aiden secured his syths. As one, they came to stand before me, and it was Aiden who broke the silence. "Shall we send Momma Grand Duchess and Amala to the Angels, my kotě?"

I looked out the window, running through everything that I had to say tonight. Some of it was scripted, but most of it just needed to be said. The sun was fully down now, and I knew there would be throngs of people outside, waiting to give their respect. "Aiden, remember your promise to me this morning?"

When I didn't turn to face him, he pulled on the claiming. I forced myself to look at him and saw him holding out his arm for me just as he had when he was first named my Vernadali. This was who he had to be tonight. He was my Angels bound Vernadali.

Taking a deep breath, I looked up at him and tried to push down the claiming, "*I wouldn't want to be here with anyone else. Thank you.*" A sad lift of his lips told me he heard me. He reached up and touched the matching rounded steel around his neck as he said, "Always."

I pulled every ounce of strength I had in me and laid my arm over his. His hand twisted a moment to circle mine and gave it a quick squeeze before we nodded to Janreka.

Janreka opened the door, and I heard the guards' feet scrape against the floor as they snapped to attention down the hall. She took a step back and against the wall opposite the door, her Vernadali right next to her, and nodded. "Grand Duchess."

I took one last deep breath before stepping out and turning down the hall to light Mom and Amala's pyre. I just had to get through the next couple hours, and then I could come back and cry myself to sleep.

CHAPTER 34

AIDEN

WE MADE OUR WAY through the main hall and toward the building that connected to the field where the pyre had been constructed. It took us about ten minutes to get there, but when she saw the pyre with the Grand Duchess and Amala atop, Jess pulled on my arm to stop.

I looked at her because I couldn't feel anything from her. Nothing. "Jess?"

"I'm numb right now, Aiden, but I'm okay. I just need to get through this so I can mourn more in private, alright?"

I squeezed her hand in confirmation, but Janreka moved in front of us. She nodded her head toward someone just outside of my field of vision, and Mom's voice was in my head.

"The Grand Lord is here, as he should be. But just a warning, do not act now."

"The Grand Lord is here. Just ignore him," I whispered as quietly as I could. Her head whipped around to me. A flash of anger flew across her face, and I felt it through the bond. "Do you want me to have him removed?"

She took a very large deep breath and let it out slowly. "No, I'm both surprised and not that he came. While I understand it's a political move, I'm still surprised I haven't seen him yet." She was biting her lip, obviously pondering something. When her eyes flicked to mine and then back out toward the pyre, I had a feeling I wasn't going to like what she had to say. "Aiden, I know you aren't going to like this, but I need you to let me do something."

"I'm listening." Janreka turned toward us to check if we were ready, and I signaled for her to hold off for just one moment.

"I need to walk out there with you as my Vernadali, at my back but as close as possible." I could feel her anguish over asking this of me. Her eyes finally met mine. "Everyone except our family believes I am still to marry Jayden."

Pride, not disappointment, filled me. This. This was the Jessika I had dedicated myself to. "Jess, if we were alone right now, I would kiss you," I muttered. Surprise covered her face, and I simply reached over and pinched her hip. She returned the gesture and then looked out toward the pyre.

"Mom, I wish you could see just how wonderful Aiden is as my Vernadali."

I smiled at her again and asked, "Ready?"

"Not in the least bit, but here we go."

I nodded to Janreka, who nodded to someone else. Then I heard Auntie Clarice ring out, "Grand Duchess Jessika Petra Valenti."

With a quick release of breath, Jess stood straight and walked out to the throng of people who, when she came into full view, instantly fell to one knee, thrust one arm out, and slammed their other palm to the ground. I stood maybe two feet behind her and looked at who was on the rise with us.

I was surprised to see that it was only Auntie Clarice and Janreka standing to the left of us, and Amala's parents were to the right. I looked past Jess to just below the rise and saw that Popa Julian, Mom, Dad, Uncle Mickey, Aunt Kait, LJ, Owen, Uncle Alexei, Karlo, and even Uncle Logan and Aunt Amber were lined up before us. I felt the tightening in my throat. The entire Mathewson family had rallied to be here for this. While I knew they were here to honor Momma Grand Duchess, I knew they also came for Jess. When did they all arrive?

"You think we wouldn't be here for Jess?" I heard Mom say, and when I looked at her, there was a small smirk on her face.

My gaze crossed over where Momma Grand Duchess and Amala lay on top of the pyre. In the front row to the right side the Grand Lord of Kaletta, Jayden, Ilris, and Killy knelt before us. Jayden's eyes briefly met mine, but they were filled with tears.

"You may rise," The Grand Duchess of Ashridge commanded. I sent my Charge toward her and wrapped a close-fitting bubble around her. Her shoulders lowered just the slightest bit when it brushed against her skin. I added a double layer of my power in front of her. My shoulders twitched at how she was unprotected and exposed at the front.

The sound of the Nalrin Guard and Vernadali alike snapping to attention rang around the thousands of people who now stood before us. It took everything I had, and all those years of training, to not go stand at her side. I took a long slow breath through my nose and let it out slowly. I moved to stand next to Janreka and Auntie Clarice, who had discreetly given me a comforting touch on the arm.

"Thank you," I said, trying not to have it noticed by anyone else. There was the smallest of nods from her before Jess started addressing her people.

"For many, the Grand Duchess was a strong, fearless, and devoted woman who fought through every roadblock that was thrown at her to help rebuild Ashridge after the Keller Wars." Her eyes shifted to the Grand Lord who had the audacity to smirk at her.

I felt rage flow through her, slow and steady. That scared me more than any sudden burst of emotion. I pushed some of my power into her, hoping it would reel her back in. She took a deep breath to calm herself, and to anyone else, she would have been trying to keep the grief in check. The interaction didn't go unnoticed, and I swore I saw my sister's hand glow bright red. LJ's eyes met mine, and I narrowed mine at her. She huffed out red smoke, and I swore there was the promise of death there. It was then I also realized that Uncle Mickey and Owen, who were on either side of her, had firm holds of her syth belt to keep her from moving.

"*We got her,*" Mom said, and I twitched my head in a nod.

Jess, however, turned to me, and I itched my temple, giving the impression I was just looking around. When my eyes met hers, she gave me a meaningful blink and turned back to the crowd.

"However, the Grand Duchess was more than that. Yes, she loved Ashridge with her every breath, but she was more than just your leader. She was a loyal friend and one of the best role models I could have ever asked for. As Grand Duchess, she taught me many things, including that the people of Ashridge are capable of so much strength and perseverance. They are hardy people who will fight for their way of life. For their families. For the betterment of their neighbors. They will not bow to tyranny, neglect, degradation of being's rights, or racism, nor will they tolerate bullies."

I fought the rise of my lips. Pride. There was so much pride for my kotě. She knew that this would set the stage for her rule over Ashridge. Crowned or not, she had to win the people over, but she was also sending a message, not just to anyone who thought this would be a weak transition, but specifically to the Grand Lord of Kaletta.

I saw her meet the Grand Lord's eyes and say, "I will rule Ashridge as my mother did. With the respect of her people. With love and strength. With honor and dignity. I will not cave to childish bullies, tactless threats, or boorish demands. I will do what is best not only for Ashridge, but also for my house."

Red crept up the Grand Lord's neck, just as fast as a smile crossed Jayden's face. Message received. The Grand Lord's hands balled into fists and released so suddenly, I saw his grey-blue power pulse over them. I looked across to one of the Vernadali nearest him and silently signaled for him to keep an eye on him. I had worked out hand signals with the on-staff Vernadali earlier today, and he instantly zeroed in on the Grand Lord, giving me a quick nod.

Jess turned to Sir and Lady Jilnore and bowed with her fist over her heart, saying, "Lady Amala Jilnore was my best friend. She died protecting her Grand Duchess, and I have no words for the loss you have suffered. She was loving, kind, fierce, and one of the most amazing beings I have ever known in my life. Nalsar and Ashridge have lost a treasure in her. To have had Amala in my life was the greatest gift. I will be a stronger being each and every day because of her love, kindness, and friendship. My love and respect will always be yours."

Sir and Lady Jilnore nodded and then fell to one knee, fists out. Jess turned to the crowd and said, "The Grand Duchess and Lady Amala Jilnore served Ashridge with love in their hearts. It is with—" She swallowed thickly, and I felt the grief in the words as she continued. "—my whole heart that I send them to the Five Angels."

A torch was handed to me, and I slowly strode toward Jess. When I reached her, she took it in her right hand but grabbed my other hand with her left. "Come with me," she mouthed, tears streaming down her face. So, I lifted my arm and guided her down the stairs. When we reached the base of the pyre, she took a shuddering breath before saying once again, "It is with my whole heart that I send you to the Five Angels. I love you, Mom. I love you, Amala."

With that, she set the torch to the pyre. We slowly stepped back as the flames spread. Once we had reached the top of the rise again, everyone in attendance sank to a knee and thumped the ground repeatedly in a steady rhythm that only fed the fire.

When the flames reached the Grand Duchess and Amala, I choked out a sob. Jess pulled her hands behind her back and gripped my hands tightly. It was the only physical comfort I could give her, so I whispered, "Good job, Kotĕ."

CHAPTER 35

AIDEN

THE STEADY THUMP OF those in attendance stopped forty minutes later, ensuring that the power coming from the citizens of Ashridge radiated toward the pyre to feed the flames enough to fully send them to the Angels. There was one noticeable difference: LJ. Her hands never stopped having a red haze to them. Her eyes had flicked to mine a few times, and I gave her a small nod, turning my attention back on Jess.

When everyone rose, it was the Grand Lord who left first. My eyes flicked to the Vernadali, and he was already shadowing him. I signaled for two more to follow, and they slipped off into the shadows. My gaze moved to my family, and each of them were looking for my command. I shook my head once, and they stood their ground.

I wrapped my Charge tighter around Jess and scanned everyone who moved toward the pyre to give their final respects before leaving. I had no doubt that there were dissenters in the crowd, many of whom probably couldn't wait for the marriage with Kaletta.

We stood there for two hours as their bodies burned and their souls were sent to the Five Angels. I had asked if she wanted to head back to her residence, and Jess said she would not leave the pyre until their bodies were ash. She stood tall and proud, watching them go. Sir and Lady Jilnore, Jayden, Ilris, Killy, and my family never moved from their spots as they watched the pyre burn. Tears were no longer constantly falling, but Jess let out a couple smaller sobs as the last of the general public left.

When it was only the family left standing there, she raised her hands and sent her power into the pyre, sending it crumbling to a pile of ash. When the last log fell and the flames winked out, the temperature instantly dropped, and everyone shivered. I flung my cloak around Jess' shoulders, and once I had it secured around her, she collapsed into my arms. The only thing out of her mouth was a whispered, "Your promise."

"I've got you, Jess," I whispered once I swung her up into my arms. I had taken no more than three steps before Auntie Clarice and Dad were on either side of us, Janreka at our backs.

She rolled into my chest as I carried her down the corridors to our residence, her fingers finding the rounded steel at my throat. Using my power, I opened the door and carried her in. I vaguely heard someone close the door behind me. "Give me a couple minutes to get her changed and settled into bed, then you have me for five minutes before I'm hers for the rest of the night. Auntie Clarice, you and Mom have control of Ashridge tonight."

I felt Jess nod her head in confirmation against my chest as I turned toward the bedroom and set her on the bed. She gripped onto my shirt, and I took a hold of her hands. "Jess, let's get you out of these clothes and into bed."

Something shifted in her into something more primal. I smirked before I pulled and held the claiming, and when I felt her caress down it, I knew this was the Irvian part of her. With her emotions so completely raw, she would only allow her mate to take care of her right now. Everything was too much.

I got a wet washcloth and wiped off the cosmetics and soot from the pyre from her face, arms, and chest. Slowly and carefully, I removed the crown and decoration, setting them on the pillow on the vanity. She watched every movement I made, and I felt an odd sort of primal satisfaction from undressing her and readying her for bed. This was what I was made to do.

It took a little longer than anticipated, but I finally got her settled into the comfort of the blankets and told her I would be back in a few minutes. Toeing off my boots and slipping into a pair of sleeping pants and a T-shirt before going back into the main room, I reached down and gave her a kiss on the top of the head.

"...make sure he stays there until the Grand Duchess wishes to speak to him," Dad was telling someone at the door.

Auntie Clarice and Janreka looked how I felt. "Reka, you have two options." Her head snapped up, and for a second, I thought she was going to try to fight me, but I said, "You can go back to your residence, take a sleeping draft to make yourself sleep, or you can take the guest room. I know you won't sleep much if you are worried about Jess."

She looked to Auntie Clarice who just said, "Your choice, baby girl."

"Aiden is here with her." She looked at me, and I could tell she wanted to stay but didn't want to intrude.

"Reka, just because I'm here doesn't mean you can't be. You are mourning your best friend. You loved Amala fiercely." I saw her shoulders sag slightly. "Now, your other best friend is ascending to the throne tomorrow, even if she doesn't know it yet."

"Tomorrow? Don't you think it's too soon?"

"Everyone who has to attend is here already. Why make them stick around longer than necessary? The rest is our fallout to sort though. I know there are trade deals you are trying to manage for Obsecuritan, and those can't be done if you are here for weeks on end. You need to take care of your people, too, Reka. Besides, I'm sure Mom and Dad are eager to get home as well." Dad just shrugged. "That reminds me. When did the twins and everyone else arrive? Not that Jess and I don't appreciate the support."

"Julian arranged for them to use a couple dragons for all of them to get here this afternoon after you arrived. Mickel has been up to his eyeballs in shit back in Nalrin, but nothing that affects Ashridge, so no need to worry. Logan and Amber specifically asked to see you before they leave, though. Maybe we can have a full family breakfast in the morning if you two are up for it."

I ran my hand through my hair. "I'll let you know in the morning, okay?" I flopped onto the couch, rubbed my hands over my face, and put my feet up on the oversized grey ottoman. "I'm assuming you are holding the Grand Lord hostage in his room until Jess wants to see him?"

Auntie Clarice walked up and handed me a glass of amber liquid in it, and I smiled. "Thank you, Auntie."

She rolled her eyes. "You need it after the week you've had."

Dad chuckled as I took a sip. "LJ will be staying right outside the door, and if he tries to take one step outside of it, she will probably incinerate him where he stands." Then he downed the drink that Auntie had given him.

"Tell her thank you for ensuring the pyre burned so hot and quick tonight. Jess would have stayed all night if that was what it took." I leaned my head on the back of the couch.

"You noticed, huh?"

"Dad, it's LJ. She never misses a chance to show off her elemental fire power." I snorted.

"Aiden."

"I'm not wrong, and don't try to come to her rescue in this case." I rolled my head to the side to look at him. Angels, I was so damn tired. "I really do appreciate it, so tell her thank you for me."

"Why hasn't she acted against Kaletta in retaliation for Amala's death?" Dad asked carefully.

"For the same reason she hasn't for her mom's. She doesn't have proof that he ordered it. Trust me, she wants him dead," I muttered.

The room was silent for a moment, and I could feel Jess unexpectedly calm in the other room. Maybe she had fallen asleep. I got up and went to check on her, and sure enough, she was out. Her breathing was even and she shivered slightly, so I pulled the blankets up tighter around her and tucked her in. Kissing her on the temple, I said, "I'll keep you warm, Kotě."

I shut the door quietly as I came back out. Reka was standing there almost bouncing on her toes in worry. "She's asleep. Reka, go get cleaned up and take the guest room. You don't get a choice anymore. Go. Shower and sleep."

Relief washed over her as she nodded. She went to the front door and let her Vernadali and other guards know she was going to stay here tonight, and when she passed me on the way back to the guest room, she gave me a quick kiss on the cheek. "You did good tonight, Aiden. I'm proud of you."

"We all are," Dad said, and my head snapped around. I didn't think my father had ever sounded prouder in his life.

"Seriously, Aiden," Auntie Clarice said. "You protected her tonight in every way. You did exactly what you should have done all night. She was always your first concern."

"She is always, and will forever be, my first concern. I've even told her that if she insists on making me a duke, which I loathe the idea of, by the way, I will always be a Vernadali first, her Vernadali. Now I'm also her mate, so she's doubly fucked. Not that I *can* be Duke. We have to find a way for me to marry her first," I said almost chuckling, but when I glanced at my dad, he had a contemplative look on his face. "What is it?"

"Did Jess tell you what she and I were talking about?"

"No. Care to enlighten me?"

"Nope," he said, shaking his head, trying to keep the smile from his face. "You gotta take that up with your mate."

"Mate?" Auntie Clarice said, looking between Dad and me.

"You can't tell me you didn't notice, Auntie." I smirked at her. I felt her power blow through the residence and couldn't help the chuckle that huffed out of me.

"OH, UNDERWORLD'S TITS!"

Dad and I blinked and then started laughing at her. "Way to take Mom's words right out of her mouth."

"Jess... Jess transformed."

"You seriously didn't notice? Underworld, Auntie, I'm surprised the dead didn't tell you. There were plenty there when it happened," I said, filling my glass with the rich amber liquid. I swirled it in my glass, letting the smell of wood smoke and cherries fill me. I didn't know what it was, but it was delicious.

"I didn't." Her voice was sad at the words.

"She's fine. Adjusting, but fine. I swear, for all the gossip that goes through this family, I would have thought everyone would know by now." I tipped back the drink and swallowed it in one gulp. I let the liquid burn down my throat and leaned my head back.

"Aiden, you are exhausted. You need to sleep," Dad said.

"I am, but first, the Grand Lord. What are we going to do about him? That speech she gave at the pyre tonight might as well have been a blunt declaration of *shove your marriage treaty up your ass*. He was livid."

"Jayden didn't seem upset. He looked proud of her." Auntie said, sitting in the large grey chair opposite the couch.

My head involuntarily turned in the direction where Jess lay. "I'm damn proud of her. She said it as a declaration to the people and to him. She straight threw the gauntlet in his face and said, 'Your move.'" I let out a heavy sigh. "We need a legal way to have Jayden, Ilris, and Killy in Ashridge. If they go back to Kaletta, we are signing their death warrants."

"And for more than just their siding with Jess tonight. You should have seen his face when he left and Jayden didn't follow him. There was a stare down for the ages there. Jayden drew a line tonight, and it wasn't with his father," Auntie Clarice said. My head jerked toward her, and I stared.

"Just how much do you know?"

"I'm the Gatekeeper to the Underworld; there's little I don't know. I know what the Grand Lord does to people with his preferences, Aiden. Jayden has done a wonderful job of hiding it. I'm sure that Jess and Janreka have both been part of that, but I'm not sure how the Grand Lord doesn't know. The Grand Lord doesn't hide his beliefs on the matter. He boasts about ensuring that only those who can procreate are together. He pushes the issue regularly in Nalrin. He fought your mom *hard* after the war. We've been trying to find a way to stop him, but Kaletta is so far from the capital, we would have to initiate martial law, and Julian won't do it. Not yet, at least. He's hoping to come to a diplomatic solution. Megan, too. Besides, Jayden and Janreka have been friends since before their Maltals. If you think I didn't know about Reka before she came to us about her preference for women, think again. Not that my Silnaree or I care, of course."

"She likes both men and women, not just women." I didn't know why I felt the need to make that distinction. I flopped onto the couch and watched as my dad paced the room.

"I know, Aiden. She clarified that. I also clarified with her that she should just find her heart match. Carrying on the line doesn't matter. If she doesn't have biological kids, Karlo might, and they will step in." When I lifted my head and met her gaze, her face was drawn.

"Auntie, I really don't think Reka would bind herself to someone just to carry on the line. Reka will bind herself to someone she loves and wants with every fiber in her being. She won't compromise."

She smiled softly at me. "I just want her to be happy."

"Dad, you are going to wear a hole in the carpet." Angels, my voice sounded tired even to my ears.

"I need to talk to Megan and Julian." Then he looked up at me and shook his head. "Aiden, you look like shit. When was the last time you got a good night's sleep?"

"Dad, I've been on the road since we talked via LightCall in Silentport. I've been charged up and worried sick about Jess. Do I really need to answer that for you?"

He smirked at me. "Get some sleep, Aiden."

"I need to stay awake for her. I promised her I would be there for her when she fell apart to help her keep going." My head was resting on the back of the couch again, and I could feel the exhaustion wearing on me.

"And you can't do that if you are dead on your feet." A mischievous smile crossed his face, and he stood up straight. "Do I have to order you?"

I let out a chuckle. "Gonna pull the Vernadali card, huh?"

"If it is the only way for my son to go to bed and sleep? Fuck yeah, I'll use it."

"I could go Empress on you, if you want," Auntie Clarice said beside me. I swung my eyes to her and stuck out my tongue.

"See, this. This right here is one of the biggest problems with being a Mathewson. In any other family, I would outrank everyone. Even being a Vernadali doesn't get me out of shit in this family. Not when your dad is Angels Blessed, your Popa is not only head of the continent, but also the damn dimension, oh, but if that isn't enough, the fucking Gatekeeper of the Underworld is your fucking aunt!" I couldn't keep the smile off my face as I said it, because while, yes, they were all royal pains in my ass, and while I often resented it, I loved them all dearly. I would do anything for them. They had certainly proven they would do anything for us as well.

"You love us," Auntie said.

"I do, and I appreciate that everyone came to support Jess today."

"The Grand Duchess was a dear friend, Aiden. You know Clarice, your mom, and I would be here." He sighed and ran his hand through his hair. "Your mom and I have done everything we can, but it's a mess. Angels, Jess has so much to do."

"Tomorrow. Let's deal with that tomorrow. Let's get Jess formally crowned, then she will work on that list." Auntie Clarice gave me a quick kiss on the top of the head.

"Goodnight, Dad. Goodnight, Auntie." They closed the door behind them, and I leaned my head back on the couch for just a moment, feeling a heavy weight settle over me, when Reka said, "Aiden, get up and go be with Jess. Curl up with her and get some sleep."

"I'm so tired, I don't think I can move," I said, smiling at her, and a moment later, I felt her power pull me from the couch and zap me on the butt. I yipped loudly and glared at her. "Thanks."

"Anytime." She studied me for a moment as I headed toward the bedroom. "What is it?"

"Thank you for what you said to Mom." I looked at her, not understanding what she meant. "About me not binding myself just so I can have heirs. That I'll only bind myself to someone because I love them." She was playing with her fingers. "You are right that ultimately it doesn't matter to me what is between their legs when I bind myself to them. I will only bind myself to someone if I love them wholly."

I leaned against the wall, knowing she just needed to get the words out. Her voice was low as she said, "But I would be lying if the thought hadn't crossed my mind that Mom and Dad would be disappointed in me for not having biological kids to carry on the line."

"Reka…"

"Don't, Aiden. I know they don't care. They wouldn't have dubbed me heir to the Gate if they did. You heard Mom tonight; she told you that she just wants me happy. I believe her. I know Dad does, too. So the issue isn't my parents. It's me."

"Do you have a new girlfriend you haven't told me about?" I cocked an eyebrow at her.

"No. No boyfriend, either." She huffed a laugh then looked at me saying, "No one of interest, either, so stop being an overprotective brother."

"Overprotective?" It was my turn to huff a laugh. "Reka, you could kick my ass any day. I feel sorry for whoever it is you end up with. They look at you wrong, and they will end up in the deepest parts of the Underworld."

"I'm not *that* bad." She smiled at me then, and I saw the tension leave her shoulders.

"If you say so." I pushed off the wall. "Now, both of us, bed."

Nodding, she went back to her room and said over her shoulder, "Goodnight, Aiden."

With a wave of my hand, the lights were out and I slid into Jess' bedroom.

When I pulled the blankets back, Jess' hand reached out for me, causing me to jump. "Hey, Kotě. I thought you were sleeping."

"I was, but your yip woke me up." There was a sleepy amusement to her voice that made me smile.

"Reka zapped my ass to get me to come to bed. Need anything?"

"Just you." She paused for a moment, as if contemplating something, but said, "Next to me, please."

"Your wish is my command," I whispered as I pulled her close and she wrapped her arms around me, resting her head on my chest. We lay like that for a moment, her fingers finding the rounded steel at my neck.

"Thank you for everything, Aiden."

"Sleep, Kotě. Sleep." I kissed the top of her head and fell into an exhausted sleep.

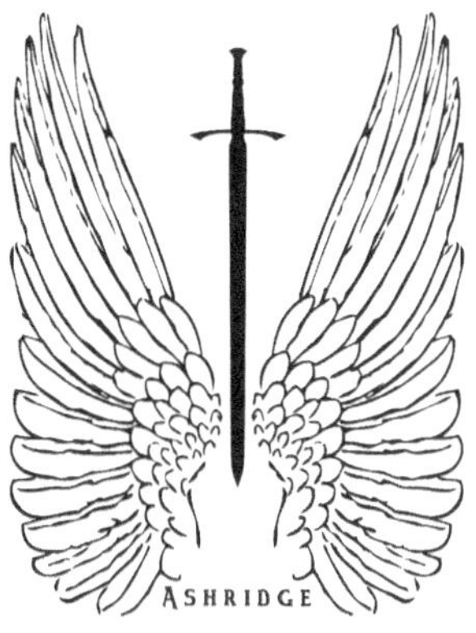

CHAPTER 36

JESSIKA

BREAKFAST WITH THE MATHEWSONS was just what I needed. It was just like it had been when we all went to Therth for Hailsim, a holiday just as the weather turned cold to allow the spirits out of the Underworld to dance for one night only. It was a time to celebrate family and to remind ourselves of what was really important.

After breakfast, Aiden warned me that they were planning the coronation for tonight, and I tried to get him to reschedule it, but I lost that fight. After a shower and about two hours of Janreka doing my hair, I was staring at a row of dresses and trying to choose which one of them I wanted to wear to my coronation.

The first was a sleeveless maroon and silver dress with a set of oversized skirts that required a full hoop skirt under it to ensure it lay right. It was heavily beaded in the bodice and had a matching sheer cape with intricate lace attachments that lay around my neck and shoulders. The second was a simple satin dark-blue and silver halter dress with a full skirt and clear gems around the belt at the waist. The third was a full-length black chiffon dress, with a wide V-neckline that extended off the shoulder wrapping loosely around my arms. Finally, there was a dark-purple floor-length satin dress with multiple layers of skirt that split up the left side almost to my hip. The only thing I could think of was tossing the skirt aside and letting Aiden take me against a wall in it.

"Well?" Janreka asked, looking at the dresses.

"Can't I wear a pantsuit or something? Dresses are so old and traditional."

"Jess, this is your coronation. I, at least, gave you modern ones instead of the ones from Mom's heritage closet."

"No on one and four." I wrinkled my nose, knowing she was right.

"I understand why you don't want to wear the first one. That hoop skirt would be annoying. You couldn't sit all day, but Mom wanted me to at least have it sitting here for consideration."

"Not to mention it's maroon, and I won't have any red tones of any sort in my coronation. That includes the Grand Lord. I want it ordered that all officials and guests are to wear black. Nothing traditional. I want all modern clothing. I want to see people coming in looking amazing. If I see someone wearing a stuffy old traditional dress, I will probably scream." I met her eyes, and she smirked, but I smiled devilishly. "And I want you in a fuckable little black dress."

Her eyes went wide, and then there was a flash of fear. "Mom will kill me because I know exactly what little black dress you are talking about. Let me guess, you want me to wear the lace up four-inch heels, too." I smiled at her, nodding. "And second, what are you doing?"

"It's all for the same reason. You have done so much here in Ashridge over the last week." Her face froze, and she said. "How..."

"Before breakfast this morning, Megan gave me the lowdown of everything that they had been doing. She said that you arrived two days after they did, and that you have been busting your ass doing whatever was needed."

"Okay, but what does that have to do with me wearing a skimpy black dress?" she asked, looking at me like I was crazy.

"I want you to feel amazing in whatever you wear today. It doesn't have to be that one, but I know how you feel deadly beautiful when you wear solid black. Not to mention the heads you turn with that particular ensemble. So, wear something that when you look in the mirror you want to fuck yourself because you look so damn good."

Once the shock wore off, she wrapped me in a tight hug and swung me around. "I love you, Jess."

"I know you do." There was a soft knock on the door, and I turned to say, "Enter."

It was Janreka's Vernadali. "Grand Duchess, Princess," she said, bowing with her fist over her chest.

"Yes, Natasha?"

"There are some final details the council wants answers on." Her eyes jumped between the dresses and then us. There was an amused tilt to her lips, and Janreka called her on it.

"You may speak your mind, Natasha. I've already told you if we are in private you can do so." I was amazed at how they were still trying to work out the bumps in their communication. Aiden and I ... I huffed a breath as I reached up to the necklace around my neck. Aiden and I were different.

"Grand Duchess, if I may be so bold," Vernadali Kapinov said.

"Of course."

"Don't go with the red one. The Grand Lord will take it as a sign you are on his side. I'm assuming by the speech you gave at the pyre that you are against the marriage contract and have no intention of going through with it, regardless of your relationship with Lord Jayden."

"Oh, she's good." I blinked and looked at Janreka. "You got a smart one there. Continue, Natasha."

"He has already stated the speech was an act of war, but he is just saying it's because you are in mourning and are young, so he isn't holding that against you. He believes you will see the error of your thoughts and come around." Then her eyes flicked back to the dresses and then back to me. "Go with the third one. It will be gloriously sexy on you. Not to mention, it will piss him off."

"Oh, Janreka, I really like your Vernadali," I said, never breaking eye contact with her. "She's smart and knows when to flatter someone."

"She and I are very like-minded," Janreka said, making Vernadali Kapinov blush incessantly.

"She's not wrong though on the dress choice. It's the one I was leaning toward. I don't want to look to the past, and while this gives nods to it in the chiffon, the style is much more forward than what we used to have. Shoulders and Maltals have never been on display, let alone on someone who has my shape." Janreka started to open her mouth, and I just looked at her and said, "Shut up. You know I don't need to hear it. I won't apologize for not being a small girl. The only one that my size matters to is me. Aiden worshiped me pretty thoroughly this morn—" I froze, and my eyes landed on Vernadali Kapinov.

Her eyes had just barely widened before Aiden was standing in the doorway. "Jess?"

I kept my eyes on Janreka's Vernadali. "Aiden, close the door."

"Yes, Grand Duchess." He presented every ounce of Vernadali.

"Natasha." Janreka's voice was commanding in a way I had rarely heard her use. When her Vernadali's eyes met hers, she continued, "Anything that comes from the Grand Duchess' mouth might as well come from mine. Is that clearly understood."

"Yes, Princess Janreka," she said, standing at attention.

"Swear it."

"I swear that anything that I hear while in the company of Princess Janreka and the Grand Duchess are considered binding and protected by the Vernadali."

"Anything that comes from me or the Mathewson family," I amended. "Is that clear?"

"Yes, Grand Duchess. With my life."

"Jess, please tell me what is going on?" Aiden said, and I felt his Charge wrap around me. "Why is she swearing Vernadali oaths to you and my family?"

"I fucked up, Aiden." I reached for his hand. His was instantly there, and he squeezed.

"I need more to go on than that."

I looked back at the very still Vernadali before me. Her eyes had focused on my necklace, they flicked to Aiden's, and then I saw as realization crossed her face. "May I speak, Grand Duchess?"

"You may."

"That is why you have no intention of marrying the Lord of Kaletta." Her eyes just barely flicked to Aiden again before she said, "You and Vernadali Aiden have a long history, don't you? This wasn't something that occurred just since his assignment by the Angels."

"As they say, it is complicated." Aiden let out a breath when he realized what had happened. Then he turned to me and gave me a questioning look, "How, exactly?"

"I may have forgotten she was in the room for a split second, because she does her job really well. I was talking to Janreka and may have, just maybe, mentioned how you thoroughly worshiped me this morning."

Heat sprang to those places he had enjoyed tasting, and I actually felt my nipples harden at the thought. There was a heat in his eyes that made me warm and tingly in all the right places. "Jess, you aren't helping."

There was a small chuckle, and I turned and said, "Vernadali Kapinov."

"Please, I am not thrilled with my surname, so call me Natasha."

"Vernadali Natasha, back to the matter at hand. You swear for the Matthewson family to be included in your protection?" I asked.

"If Princess Janreka wishes it. She is who I serve and protect."

"Princess Janreka is my sister in every right but blood," Aiden said. "Empress Clarice has been my aunt since birth. Therefore, for many reasons, I believe this oath would still fall under your oaths to Princess Janreka and that name scroll on your arm."

While my eyes never left hers, I saw her absently run a hand over it before standing straighter and saying, "Vernadali Aiden, you are an A2 rank, is that not correct?"

The three of us winced. Everyone hated that fact, CJ the most, but Aiden answered, "Yes, but I am not talking ranks here."

"While I personally stand by my oath to Princess Janreka, the Grand Duchess, and the Mathewson family, by virtue of the Angels rank, you outrank me, and therefore, you should order me to extend my oath to the Mathewson family. Princess Janreka would still be my first responsibility, but…"

"But you would be duty bound," I said, understanding it.

"But I am a Mathewson. It would be construed as personal preference."

"Not if I order you to do so," I said, crossing my arms and popping my hip out. The claiming pulled taut, his eyes lit, there was a single finger tapping on his cheek, and in one of the stupidest moves he ever had done, he took ahold of the heart at my neck, pulling me to him, and said against my jaw in that voice that had me melting, "Order it, Kotě." I felt the rumbling in my chest, and I had to suppress the purr that rose within me.

"Oh, fuck that is hot, and Jess, we are going to have to talk about this whole Irivain thing," Janreka said. "But, umm, we are still standing here."

Aiden's lips brushed mine before he whispered, "We have unfinished business, Kotě. Now order it."

"Yes, Aiden."

He stepped back, and I had to take a deep breath before I could speak. "Vernadali Aiden Mathewson, I, as your Angels sworn Charge, demand that you order Vernadali Natasha Kapinov to extend her oath to myself and the Mathewson family, by blood or otherwise, with her first responsibility being to Princess Janreka of the House of Heros."

"Did you have to say it so harshly?" He smirked and rubbed his chest. "That shit hurt."

I just rolled my eyes as he turned and repeated the oath, Natasha accepted it, and after Aiden nodded at her, she said, "So now that that is done with, can I say something else?"

I smiled knowingly at Aiden, and he narrowed his eyes at me with a small smile on his face. I turned back to her and nodded.

"What the fuck did I just watch, because while what Princess Janreka said is true, there is so much more going on."

"Short version?" She nodded. "Aiden and I dated a few years ago. Being who our parents are, we were able to keep it quiet and private. He left me, shattering my heart, by the way, and then the Angels decided to royally fuck us up by assigning him to me. Mom died, we made our way here. Lady Amala died, leaving just him and me alone. It sort of forced us to work some shit out. There are a lot of political hurdles, but Lord Jayden knows. He is very happy for us, but this cannot be leaked information. Understood?"

"Yes, Grand Duchess, but what of the marriage agreement?"

"I've been back for a day, Vernadali Natasha. There are a lot of things we are trying to work out. That is one of about ten thousand different issues to be sorted."

"Not to mention, a Vernadali can't marry their Charge," she muttered softly.

"Yeah, not to mention that detail." Aiden sighed heavily.

Janreka poked me, and I looked at her. There was a meaningful glare there, and I ignored it. "Don't ignore me,

Jess. Why didn't you tell me about this? Why didn't you tell me that was a problem?"

"Because I had to deal with my mother's assassination, Amala dying while protecting me, my transformation, coming home, trying to sort out how to handle the Jayden, Ilris, and Killy situation, while also having to figure out how to keep Ashridge together in one piece when I tell the Grand Lord to shove that marriage agreement up his ass." I let out a harsh breath. "Aiden is my mate, and sorting out when we can legally marry, while on the list, is a bit farther down. There are more pressing matters."

The squeal of excitement that came out of her had Natasha's syths in her hand and Charge through the room in a heartbeat. A glance from me and Aiden had her sheathing them.

"The claiming?" I nodded, and she wrapped me in her arms then pulled him in too. "Again, it's about fucking time."

"Simmer, Reka." Janreka just turned to Aiden and stuck her tongue out at him. "Now that we have the Grand Duchess' personal life locked back down, the Grand Duchess does need to actually get ready for the coronation."

"But—" Janreka started to say.

"He may be a pain in our ass, but he isn't wrong, Janreka." Wrapping my arm around her waist as I led her to the door, I reminded her, "Remember what I said about guest clothing requirements."

"Everyone wears black, no red, and that includes the Grand Lord," she repeated for me. When I raised an eyebrow, she continued, "And regardless of how much Mom tries to yell at me, I have to wear a little black dress."

"Well, preferably, because I'd fuck you in that dress." I heard Aiden clear his throat behind me, and it was my turn to stick my tongue out at him. He tapped two fingers on his cheek, and I wasn't sure just how much trouble I'd get into for that one. "But like I told you, you need to look in the mirror and know you look hot as the deepest depths of the Underworld."

"Yes, Grand Duchess," she mocked, and I pinched her ass on the way out the door.

Natasha laughed, and I shrugged. "She's my best friend. She just also happens to be his sister, so yeah, it's enough to make your head spin."

"See you in the main hall, Grand Duchess."

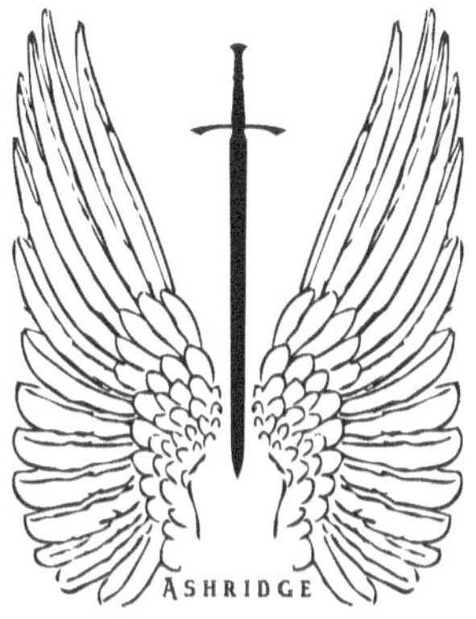

CHAPTER 37

JESSIKA

NO SOONER WERE THEY out of sight than Aiden pulled me fully back into the room, shut the door, and had me pressed against the wall. I felt the claiming go taut between us as he growled, and I didn't even try to suppress the purr this time.

"My kotě is testing me, isn't she?"

"I don't know what you are talking about, Aiden," I said as sweetly as I could.

"First, you let it slip about us, which could have very real ramifications, by the way." His voice was throaty and primal now. I pushed back against him, and while I almost had enough room to get out his hold, he tightened it, and I bit my lower lip. "Nothing to say, Kotě?"

"You fixed it. See? I knew I kept you around for something."

A throaty chuckle came from him, one that had me heating in all the right places. "Second, you stood there and told Reka you would fuck her. The image of you entangled with a woman, my kotě..." I felt his chest rattle against me, and I sent just a touch of my power into him, causing him to jump back. I hopped out of his grip, and the growl that went through him set off every instinct within me to run.

"Oh, you better run, Kotě." I took off down the hall to the bedroom, but when I felt him just steps behind me, I dashed around the chairs to the opposite wall. I made the mistake of looking behind me, and it cost me stumbling over one of the legs of the small table. Aiden caught me, and once again had me against a wall.

This time, however, his hands were under my robe, pushing against my hips. I pushed a bit of my power into him and sent it singing. His grip tightened on my waist as he softly bit down on my shoulder and growled. Instinctively, I wanted to submit to him, but I refused. This time, faking a second of submission, I rested my hand on his and zapped him before taking off at a dead run.

In the mirror on the wall, I saw him turn, head low, watching me through his eyebrows, and smirk. "Shit!" I heard him chuckle again.

A moment later, he had a hold of my robe, and I was twisting out of it and dodging under his arm, but I wasn't fast enough. Now naked, I was once again against the paneled wall. His mouth skimmed my jaw line, and that rumbling in his chest demanded submission. I didn't fake it this time when I melted against him. He could command it with a simple tap on his chin, but this was different. This was letting my beast side play. He knew just how to bring it out in me, and right now, all I needed was him.

"Aiden," I purred back to him. His teeth clamped on my shoulder, and I gave into him.

"My kotě." He pulled back and put his forehead to mine. "You are mine."

"I am yours." My eyes met his as I reached down, undid his belt, forced his pants down, and wrapped a leg around him.

The right side of his lip lifted as he said, "Hold on, Kotě. I'm not waiting to get you to the bed." Pushing me harder against the wall, he took all of my weight, like I was a feather, and slid into me in one full stroke.

His eyes never left mine as he slid slowly out, only to slam back in, roll against me, and repeat the motion. Angels, I loved this man. There was not one inch of him that didn't make me happy.

His nails dug into my ass, and I felt the pain turn to pleasure instantly. I knew I was close, and I closed my eyes, cherishing every inch of him. "Open your eyes, Kotě. I need to see you."

"I'm right here." I panted. "I'll always be right here, Aiden."

I ran my nails across his shoulders, and he shuddered, kissing me as he slammed into me, but stopped once he was fully seated again. Slow gentle rolling of his hips hit that spot inside and against my clit in all one motion, and I bit my lip, leaning my head back against the wall.

When he repeated it, one of the pictures near us fell to the floor, and another when he did it again. His eyes met mine playfully, and he repeated it, causing the last one to fall next to me, but I just smirked and said, "Are you going to just keep knocking pictures off the wall, or are you going to fuck me like I deserve?"

Wicked delight replaced the pure heat in his eyes. "Hold on, Kotě." He pulled me from the wall, and when we got back to the main room, he set me down, turned me, and pushed me over the arm of the couch, holding my arms to my sides so I landed face-first. "That is three times now that you have mouthed off."

The smack landed a second before I felt the pain on my left ass cheek. I smiled into the pillow as he rubbed it, and then he ran a finger down the center of me, flicking my clit, before he smacked the right cheek and repeated the motion. I moaned through the pain as he knelt before me and spread me wide. There was a light breath of air before he smacked my ass again.

"Aiden," I begged. I wanted to cum so badly.

"Kotě?" he teased as he spanked me again. I quivered under his touch as he rubbed both cheeks before spreading them.

"Please, Aiden."

"Cum for me, Kotě," he commanded with a chuckle as he blew lightly on my clit and smacked my ass again. That wave of pain sent a shock through me, and I came hard.

His face dove into me, licking and drinking up every drop. I was just coming down from the first one when his tongue flicked my clit twice before diving deep within me, sending me back over that cliff, but Aiden didn't stop tongue fucking me as I rode his face.

Pulling away, he braced me against the couch before he slammed into me. Fucking me hard, he leaned over, put his hand to my throat, and pulled me up.

"Aid—" My words were cut off as his grip tightened.

"Who do you belong to, Kotě?" he asked, each word emphasized with a thrust of his hips.

"You. Only you." I felt myself inching toward that cliff again. Only Aiden could do this to me. I reached around and grabbed his ass, digging my nails in and scratching deep.

His hiss was nothing but satisfaction to my ears. Pulling my head farther around, he kissed me but didn't let go of my throat. The kiss was deep, and I felt the claiming shine brighter within me. There was a strong vibrating tone to it, and he pulled back, gasping for air but never stopping his hips movements.

"You feel that?" He rolled against me, and I could do nothing but lean into him and moan my agreement. "Fuck, woman. You are going to be my undoing. I will die for you. I will protect you at all costs."

The claiming vibrated with more intensity, and Aiden's hips moved with more ferocity. "Fuck me, Aiden. Make me cum all over your cock."

There was nothing gentle now. He fucked me with everything he had, and moments later, I pulled on the claiming, which glowed bright as I screamed his name into the room and he moaned mine into my ear as he released into me.

I was in his lap on the couch a moment later and resting my head on his shoulder. We sat there for no more than a minute when there was a knock on the door and Vernadali Natasha was yelling, "Vernadali Aiden. I need to speak to you immediately."

"Nothing like good timing." He groaned, putting his head on the back of the couch. "Just a minute, Natasha!"

I huffed a laugh. "You know this won't be the last time this happens, right?"

"Yeah." He lifted me and carried me to the bed. "Stay here while I figure out what is so damn important." He kissed me softly.

"I do need to get cleaned up to get dressed for the—" I stopped at the growl that came from him. "I'll wait here for you."

As he walked out, I saw very distinct claw marks on his shoulders and ass. Looking down at my hands, I saw blood underneath my nails and smiled. I chuckled as I heard him slide his pants on, hiss slightly, and curse me under his breath before going to the door.

A couple minutes later, I heard a door shut. "Be right there, Jess."

He wandered into the small kitchen a couple doors down from the bedroom, and I heard him turn the faucet on before he was standing in the doorway. When he saw that I hadn't moved, wicked satisfaction crossed his lips as he said, "Good girl."

He spread his fingers into a V, and I opened myself to him. Slowly and carefully, he cleaned me up, but before he let me up, he kissed the area just above my clit, staring up at me and smiling. Crawling up my body, his gaze took in each and every soft curve of me, and he kissed each breast before he pulled me to him and just held me.

"Jess?" he said softly as I wrapped my arms around him.

"Hmmm?" My lips grazed that spot on his shoulder where I had claimed him as my mate, and I kissed it, causing a shudder to go through him.

"You know I meant every word I said when I was inside of you, right?"

I leaned back. "Aiden, where is this coming from?"

"You are my everything."

"And you are mine, Aiden," I said, kissing him gently, but I sighed. "But as much as I would prefer to just stay here in bed curled up with you all day, I do have a pretty important event I need to attend in less than an hour."

"You do," he said, but he refused to let me go for a long moment before kissing me once more. "I love you, Jessika."

"I love you too, Aiden."

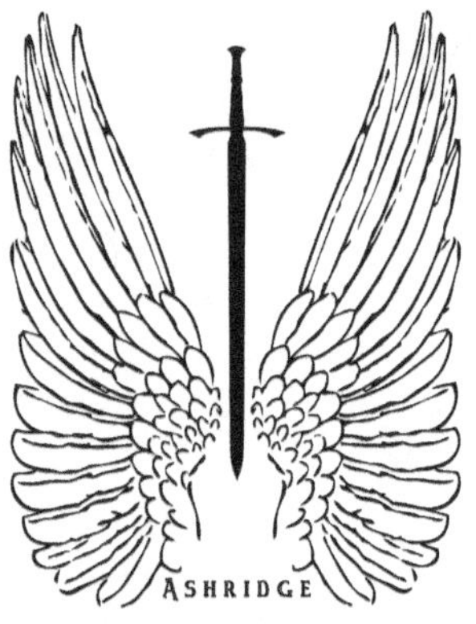

CHAPTER 38

JESSIKA

STANDING AT THE TOP of the stairs to the main hall was nerve-wracking. I only needed to stand there until they were ready for me. Instead, I paced and twirled the two-foot-long silver scepter that had been used for every coronation since the inception of Ashridge. I looked at its clear stone that looked like black pepper had been sprinkled throughout it. I had always admired the Peppered Diamonds of Ashridge. I had matching earrings on but refused to put on the necklace. It would have required me to remove Aiden's, and I couldn't do that. I wouldn't do that. I was going to be officially crowned the Grand Duchess of Ashridge, and I would do it with my symbol of dedication to Aiden around my neck. He hadn't taken his off, and I wouldn't be removing mine.

Sure, there were traditions that had to be met, and I would meet them where I felt comfortable, but I was Grand Duchess. I made the rules and laws of this territory, and I would not sacrifice myself or my values. There would be a balance. It would be hard, and I would certainly piss people off in the process, but while I agreed with much of what my mother had put in place, there were things we disagreed on. After the business with Kaletta was settled, I would make codicils to those declarations.

"Oh, Angels," I whispered just as Aiden opened the doors and I once again saw him in his Vernadali uniform. I swore I was never going to get used to it. *Breathe, Jessika. Breathe.*

Aiden bowed before me, his cape over his shoulder swinging forward like a shield in front of him. My eyes focused on the Vernadali crest, and when Aiden lifted his head to look at me, there was a small smile that took my breath away once again. Rising, he came and stood next to me. He scratched his temple, and I winked at him. He lifted his arm to shoulder height, bent at the elbow, and waited for me to take it.

It was time.

Since my father had already passed, other than Julian, he was the only one legally allowed to escort me down the aisle to the vicar that would be presiding over my coronation. There were over five hundred people crammed into the main hall, not including the Nalrin Guard, Ashridge Guard, and Vernadali that lined the halls. I half wondered if Empress Clarice's coronation had been the same, or CJ and Megan's wedding. Oh Angels, what if I trip? What if I fall? What if I forget the words?

I laid my arm on top of his, my breathing coming faster now in anticipation, fear, and worry. I felt like a pile of bricks lay across my chest and drums pounded in my ears. I knew that this day would come. I just didn't think it would be for another fifty years. Grief at losing my mother again washed through me, and I had to blink the tears away.

"Jess, calm down," Aiden said, pushing some of his calming power into me. It lightened the weight and lessened the pounding in my ears, but I wrapped my hand around his and squeezed it tight. There was a comforting tug on the claiming, and I knew he understood.

Without hardly moving my lips, I breathed, "Okay."

The music changed, and the anthem of Ashridge played as Aiden led me down the aisle. I held my head high, and I felt his fingers twitch beneath mine. I concentrated and tried to push comfort through the claiming, and he did the same.

We reached the front, where Aiden squeezed my fingers quickly before turning, bowing once more, and stepping to the side. I could still see him, and I saw Jayden out of the corner of my eye who moved to stand next to him—the two men who would forever be in my life. The two men who had the most to gain and lose by me being crowned today.

After a quick curtsey to the vicar, he nodded, and I sank to kneel on the small pillow at my feet. I took a little longer to adjust my skirts so I didn't sit on them, as well as to gather my wits. My heart was pounding out of my chest, and I wanted Aiden up here with me.

"You are strong, Jess. You will be one of the best Duchesses that Ashridge has ever had." Megan had pushed the message directly to me, and I smiled. Raising my head, I gave a quick nod as I met the vicar's bright blue eyes.

"Jessika Petra Valenti, are you or are you not the rightful heir to the crown of Ashridge?"

"I, Jessika Petra Valenti, am the rightful heir to the crown of Ashridge."

"Your consort will be?" the Vicar said, and my heart lurched. I took a deep breath and reminded myself that this was my territory. I made the rules. I reminded myself of every word in my preemptive pep talk before those doors opened.

I sent an amused calming feeling down the claiming, and I touched the heart at my throat as I met the vicar's eyes and said loud and strong, "I shall have no consort."

There was a collective gasp throughout the room. I turned my head slightly to where I knew that Jayden and Aiden were. I looked at both of them. Their heads were held high and each had matching smiles on their faces.

"I'm sorry, Grand Duchess?" the Vicar said again. "Ashridge has always crowned a married sovereign."

"And this time it will not. I am the sole and rightful blood heir to Ashridge. I will take the crown without a consort." I slowly took my eyes from Aiden's and turned to stare the vicar down. "The person who stands at my side on that throne will be there because I choose them and love them with my whole heart. I will not bind myself for the sake of old traditions."

The vicar looked to Head Julian and said, "Head Julian, do you agree to waive the requirement of marriage for the Grand Duchess to be crowned."

Seriously? They hadn't even thought of this possibility in preparing for my coronation? I turned to face Head Julian. The four-foot man stood, and the five long braids of his beard swayed and sparkled in the light. His eyes met mine, then he stared at the vicar for a long moment before he looked toward Aiden and Jayden who both nodded in unison.

Before Head Julian could speak, I stood and faced him, muttering a, "*Fuck this.*" I then said loudly, "I am the rightful blood heir of Ashridge. I am the Grand Duchess of Ashridge. There is no commandment, codicil, or declaration that states the Crown must be wed in Ashridge's ruling documents. Therefore, no assumptions will govern how I reign over my territory. I will not marry today. I will only marry and bind myself to the one who will carry my heart." My head was back and straight as his eyes met mine.

I would not cave on this. I would not be legally crowned if this was a breaking point. I stood there head high and unmoving. There was a twitch at the corner of his mouth before he said, "I concede to the wishes of the Grand Duchess. If she wishes to choose who stands at her side, she may. No marriage or binding is required for her to be crowned this day."

The room was so silent that you could hear the vicar's neck turn as he faced me again, and I met his gaze with a raised eyebrow.

"I repeat, I shall have no consort."

"Very well, Grand Duchess. Let us continue." He swallowed hard, and I didn't miss how his eyes flickered quickly to where I knew the Grand Lord was. I had to take a deep breath not to send my power flowing through the vicar standing before me. I narrowed my eyes at him as he looked at me again, and I swore shame and fear were mixed on his face.

"Jessika Petra Valenti," he continued after clearing his throat. "Do you wish to advance to Grand Duchess?"

"Yes."

"State your vows." I stood and turned to face the people of Ashridge.

"Here do I swear, by mouth, by light and dark, and by right of birth, to uphold the natural laws as gifted by the Five Angels.

I shall champion for change and safety within all of Ashridge.

I shall be loyal to the populace of the land and not the power within.

I shall listen to our estates and protect all the same.

I shall strike and spare, punish and reward in all matters,

In peace or war until the Underworld claims my soul and I depart these lands.

So say I, Jessica Petra Valenti, Grand Duchess of Ashridge."

I felt a wave of power hit me, and I forced myself to stand strong against it. I felt it settle into my very bones and warm me from head to toe.

"Please kneel," the vicar said from behind me.

I used my power to move the pillow for me to kneel on and adjusted my skirts as I knelt before the people of Ashridge.

"I present to you, Grand Duchess Jessika Petra Valenti." Tears filled my eyes, and I swallowed them. I felt the Ashridge crown sit upon my head and closed my eyes for the briefest moment as I saw my mom lying there in wait with it sitting on her head. I forced my eyes open and looked out toward the crowd who, as I rose, knelt to one knee, fists outstretched.

"Long live the Grand Duchess Jessika Petra Valenti!" Fists slammed onto the ground as they had at the pyre, and I felt their power flow and pool at my feet.

Lifting my head higher and squaring my shoulders, I waited a minute before saying, "I accept you, Ashridge." With those words, their power seeped into my bones.

As I looked out over my people, the only thought going through my head was, *"Heavy is the crown."*

CHAPTER 39

AIDEN

"Jess drew quite a line in the sand today," Popa Julian said as we sat in Jess' and my private quarters. Jess was getting changed, and Janreka was helping her get settled. She had drawn that line in the sand today. So, when she had asked for some time alone, I couldn't say no.

Leaning forward and resting my elbows on my knees as I clasped a drink in my hands tight, I looked over to Popa. His eyes met mine, and there was a small smile before I said, "Thank you for siding with her."

"She really put me on the spot, Aiden. Family aside, that can't happen again." He twirled one of the braids in his beard absently, and I knew he was making a point. It was the same point Jess had been trying to make. She needed to run Ashridge separate from the Mathewson name.

"I know, but someone could have reminded us of the assumption that she was to name her consort beforehand, so we could have avoided or prepared for it."

"That's true, but she told everyone today she would be ruling on her terms. Not the assumptions or beliefs of others," he said, chuckling. "It's going to be fun working with her."

"When do you and the family head back to Nalrin?"

"Karlo, Mickel, Logan, and the twins took the dragons back right afterwards. The twins will then head toward Kaletta to see if they can find out what they can find out." I rolled my eyes but smiled. "Megan and CJ will likely head back in the morning. They have Clarice's prowlers."

I turned to Uncle Alexei, who just walked in, and said, "When do you and Auntie leave?"

"In the morning. Erida said one of the supply trains along Silkar has been having trouble with bandits. We will teleport." He was smiling at Popa, and I tried to stifle the huff of a laugh that came out of me.

"You know I hate that you can circumvent dimensional lockdowns, right?" Now, the laugh at the look on Uncle Alexei's face, I couldn't hold back.

"Gatekeeper loopholes," Uncle Alexei said just as Auntie Clarice came in.

"What about loopholes?"

"The fact that you and Alexei here can still transport even though the dimension is locked down." There was no hardness in his voice now. This was obviously something that they had teased each other about repeatedly.

"Wait, if you can teleport, why couldn't you get Lemi?"

Uncle Alexei's face fell slightly, "It only works if you have the Underworld's darkness in your veins. So, we wouldn't be able to bring him with."

I nodded in understanding as Auntie Clarice smirked at Popa, flicked her eyes to me, and then said, "Not just me. Don't forget that because Janreka is my Suk'Natal, she can, too."

My eyes went wide. "What?"

All three of them laughed at me, and after looking at each of them, I headed back to the bar to get another drink. "I swear you are all trying to kill me prematurely, aren't you?"

I filled my glass and swallowed it in one drink. It hit all my senses at once and caused me to shake my head and let out a curse. I poured another, and when I turned to them, they were still snickering.

"I'm never going to be free of Janreka watching over my shoulder, am I? Angels. The shit I have learned since being assigned to Jess is astronomical."

"Aiden, the point is, if you and Jess need us, we can come help."

"If we call for help, you know our back is against the wall." I went to sit in the chair again and took a deep breath. "I've already told Mom and Dad this, but Jess doesn't want the Mathewson pull. She wants to do this on her own. She doesn't want help just because of me."

"But she is family. It's sort of what we are known for. You know, protecting our own and cleaning our own house?" Auntie Clarice said. "The Keller Wars? The incident with the twins in Maridel? We protect those we love and will endure the sacrifices that come with that."

Her eyes had darkened a shade at the mention of those losses. She had lost a brother and sister of sorts. Mom's aunt and uncle, actually. The twins were, ironically, named after the three of the family they lost in that war. They had told us amazing stories of Lindy, Jean, and Owen, and I wished I could have met them.

I shook my head to clear it and said, "I know. She knows that, too. I think after the last few days, she understands that we are there for her. She just needs to do this on her own. Ashridge is hers. She wants to run Ashridge on her own. It's important to her."

"We understand, Aiden, but the offer still stands. If you need anything, let us know." Uncle Alexei's eyes met mine, and there was a fierce determination in them.

"Shit is going to hit the fan, as your mom would say, so if you need troops, I'll send them. I will stand on those front lines and send that bastard to the Underworld myself." Auntie Clarice looked to Popa Julian and said, "As Head of Nalrin and the dimension, you sure you want to sit in on this discussion?"

His eyebrows shot to his hairline. "What haven't I been briefed on, Empress, that I should be?"

"Oh, don't you Empress me, Julian. This is a family discussion. I'm giving my nephew a heads-up of the shit show he is walking into."

"Then I'm overhearing what is being told to my grandson while I sit here enjoying a nice glass of bourbon." He leaned back in the chair, propping a leg up on the arm rest, smirking at us.

I just shook my head. "And you all wonder where Janreka, Karlo, the twins, and I got the sass." Popa just smiled at me as Mom and Dad walked in.

Dad walked straight over to the bar and poured a very heavy-handed drink, downed it, handed one to Mom, who downed hers and said, "More."

"Megs."

"More." She pushed the glass toward him, and he took it, immediately refilling it.

We all watched them as they took another shot and poured a third.

"Mom, Dad, umm... I really don't feel like carrying you to your rooms tonight."

Dad came and sat on the couch, and Mom proceeded to pace up and down the room. I pulled on the claiming, double-checking that Jess was alright, and when she tugged back, I let out a slow relieved sigh. I hadn't felt anything strange from her other than a determined fierceness and pride in herself, but I didn't know how far from her I would have to be not to get her feelings through the Vernadali bond. After Mom walked a few paths up and down, where I just watched her. "Mom, spill it."

"That woman of yours!" Her voice was stuck between admiration and frustration.

"I'm going to need you to elaborate on that, Mom."

"In the last two days, that woman has thrown dust in the Grand Lord's face and left him sputtering and fuming. He was pissed last night after the pyre, but after the coronation..." She sipped from her glass, and when she looked at me, there was a satisfaction in her eyes that almost scared me. "You should have seen him, Aiden. He cursed her name all the way back to his rooms."

"And that has you and Dad taking shots?"

"Angels, no. What has us taking shots is that we intercepted communication from the Grand Lord to his army at the ridge. He's sent for the rest of them."

Understanding flowed through me. "He thought he had Jess by the crown today. He thought she would wed Jayden at the coronation. That's why he didn't fight the coronation happening so quickly."

It was Dad who said, "Yes. He has been making demands here in Ashridge over the last week that Jayden and

Jess marry immediately upon her return to Ashridge. We denied the requests, but we didn't exactly have the authority. While her statements at the pyre last night were generalized, today she flat out denied marriage."

A primal protectiveness washed over me, and I practically bit his head off when I said, "She is mine, Dad. She won't marry anyone else."

"Everyone in this room knows that, Aiden." Auntie Clarice's voice rolled through the air with a touch of her power to bring down the tension. "Jess made sure you knew that during the coronation too. Were you not listening to her words?"

I had been, but I couldn't remember them now. It was Dad who repeated them, "The person who stands at my side on that throne will be there because I chose them and love them with my whole heart."

"She wanted you to know that it would only be you who stood by her side, and not as a consort, but as an equal. She stated twice there would be no consort to the Grand Duchess," Mom said, pressing the point. "Don't make your father or I whoop your butt. You are too old for that. So, pull yourself together."

Auntie Clarice sighed carefully before meeting my gaze. "That being said, Aiden, your mom and dad have been working through the contract, and while it states Kaletta will give agricultural and military support, it's not reaching the people."

I took another sip of the amber liquid in my glass. "The problem is that it is reaching Ashridge. It's accounted for, signed off, but then within a couple of days, it is destroyed by Kaletta soldiers. He is abiding by the terms of the agreement, but not the spirit of it."

"You know it's Kaletta soldiers destroying the shipments?" Popa Julian said.

"Yes. Amala and I caught a few of them in Silentport. They admitted they had orders. Jayden said he had spies in Silentport as well that reported that it was Kaletta cutting the pod markers for the crab pods off shore. Not to mention, when Jayden first got on the ship with us in Kaletta City, he said the Grand Lord wanted them married in six months. Obviously, you know how that went over." Then I reminded them of the one fact I couldn't shake. "Jayden sent us a Lark Messenger while we were in Shuset. He said that while he was at the ridge, that the soldiers boasted about Kaletta's assassination of the Grand Duchess."

Popa Julian, Uncle Alexei, and Auntie Clarice's eyes went wide, and when I looked back at my mom and dad, they said, "We have been looking into that. We haven't been able to find anything. Any Kaletta soldiers who we interrogated are mute on the point. There hasn't been a whisper of it."

"Why would Jayden lie about that though, Mom?"

"I'm not saying he would, Aiden. I honestly think that Jayden is on Jess' side. I think he would protect her to the death," she said. "I'm just saying that we haven't been able to get a whisper about it."

"Once it's proven, she will declare his head forfeit. She has already stated that if we get evidence against him, she will destroy him." I smirked and remembered the discussion with Jayden about it. "Jayden has also said that he would take his father's head if it were true."

"If Jess leaves anything left of him to dismember," Mom muttered, kicking back what was left in her glass.

I laughed out right at that. "Yeah, that's pretty much what I told Jayden, too."

"So, we know he is vying for the crown of Ashridge then," Mom muttered, staring into the bottom of her empty glass.

"Does he want the crown on his head? Or does he think he can control Jess through Jayden?" I asked, studying a spot on the carpet.

"The latter, I think."

"He has to know what a foolish thought that is. Especially after the pyre and today, right?" I ran my hands through my hair as I breathed, "Oh, my kotě."

"What did you just call Jess?" Auntie Clarice said.

I bit my lips shut, adjusted the rounded steel, and she raised her eyebrows at me. I knew I was turning probably twenty shades of red by now, and they giggled at me.

"Aiden?" Uncle Alexei asked, but his eyes narrowed as if he knew. When I shook my head again, he looked to Clarice and smiled broadly.

"Oh, now *that* is adorable," she said when she put it together. "Was that before or after the transformation?"

"Auntie," I said, drawing out the word. When she pressed, I said, "Is nothing sacred with you?"

"No. Not really," she said, waving her hand in the air. "Not when it can turn you those beautiful colors."

"Do you give the twins this kind of torture, or is it reserved just for me?" I refused to give in. "What else does the Grand Lord have planned?

"Deflection." Dad coughed and I glared at him.

"He did threaten that if the marriage didn't happen soon after your arrival, he may start withdrawing his aid," Mom said before looking at Dad. There was some communication between them, but she just said, "Something is brewing, Aiden. I don't know what, but something is coming."

"He won't do anything while the family is here." I breathed, realizing just how true it was. "He will wait until everyone has gone home and is firmly set elsewhere."

"We think so, too. He knows how much power is here. He isn't stupid. Okay, he is, but I don't think he understands just how much we have Jessika's best interest at heart. I don't think he realizes how much she is family."

Dad looked at me and said, "Do you want us to stay?"

"Yes. No. I don't know. It's really Jess' call, Dad."

"That isn't what I asked, Aiden. Do *you* want us to stay?" he said, making his point clear.

"Yes, because it would hold him off, but I don't know if he would see that as a threat or not. No, because you have already put off your own lives back in Nalrin to help Jess out here in Ashridge."

"Aiden, it's what I do. This one—" Mom pointed to Popa, who just chuckled. "—sends me in to fix things when shit hits the fan."

"I know, Mom."

"Hey! You have improved since the fiasco that was Bellstar." Popa smiled.

"Bellstar was a wretched hole that needed some serious morality cleansing!" Mom growled at him.

"Careful, Mom. If rumor is right, that is almost the same phrase that the Grand Lord is using about Ashridge."

Her head whipped around toward me, and the electricity hummed in the room.

"Shit! Sorry, Mom." I was instantly that eight-year-old kid who mouthed off one too many times. Dad was standing in front of me, and I hadn't even seen him move.

"Honey, Aiden is your son. You don't want to fry him like bacon," Dad said, holding his hands up between him and Mom. "You know what Aiden meant."

She stuck her finger toward me, that electricity wrapped tight around it but threatening to arc at me as she said, "Don't compare my statements to that piece of shit. You know Bellstar was a cesspool and needed new rulers. I just ensured that happened. It was also a very bad time in my life." Her eyes flicked to Dad and Auntie before saying, "And you two had a heavy hand in helping me remove their governor, if memory serves right."

"It does, and I sleep just fine knowing what I did all those years ago so, calm your shit, Megan," Auntie Clarice said in a tone I had rarely heard her use toward her.

"I meant what I said, Dad. I know that was not the right way to say it, but tell me I'm wrong." Mom's fingers twitched, and I yipped, rubbing my ass. "Okay, I can't blame you for doing that."

"Keep your 'tude in check, son." Mom readied her fingers to zap my ass again.

"Yes, ma'am." I rubbed the spot on my butt where she had zapped me and said, "I'm having flashbacks to when I was a kid."

"Well, when you are stupid, or say stupid things, you get your ass zapped," Mom said, calmer now.

"Back to the original question, though. I think you should head home, but talk to Jess. I'll update her on what you said tonight, and in the morning, if she agrees, you can head out," I said, still rubbing that spot on my butt. Electrical zaps stayed with you. I would take sparring with my dad over zaps from Mom any day.

Popa was staring at me and, after a minute, asked, "You are deferring to her?"

"Of course. I'm her Vernadali; it is my job to protect her. As her mate, those job descriptions are very similar. They may have different motivations, but they overlap. I want her happy and safe. That aside, this is her territory. She is the Grand Duchess. There is too much to wade through to bring up anything else. We need to ensure that Ashridge is secure, her people are safe and fed, and we kick this Grand Lord's ass to the Underworld." My eyes flicked to Auntie Clarice who smirked. "No, you can't have that privilege. That is Jess'. Not to mention that is a long line at the moment."

"Awww, you're no fun."

"It's been a long day, and I need to get back to her." My shoulders were starting to itch, and I didn't know if it was her or if I was the one anxious about getting back to her side.

"I think it's safe to say, most of us will leave in the morning," Popa said as I reached over to give him a hug. "All except for your parents, that is."

"We will head back in the morning, too," Dad said, surprising me.

"We will?" Mom sounded just as shocked as I felt.

"Megs, you and Aiden are right. There is no way the Grand Lord will tip his hand with us here. Strategically speaking, we have to leave." Dad kissed her temple.

"I don't like it," she said, crossing her arms. "Five days. It gives us time to talk to them and bring them fully up on everything that is going on, ensuring the council is working with Jess and not against her."

"Three."

"Fine. It's a good thing you are good in bed." She kissed his nose.

"GAHH! Mom!" I scoffed. "Angels, things I don't need to know about my parents."

They smirked at me and refilled their glasses, giving me a hug as I left to head to Jess. "Lock up behind you when you leave, please."

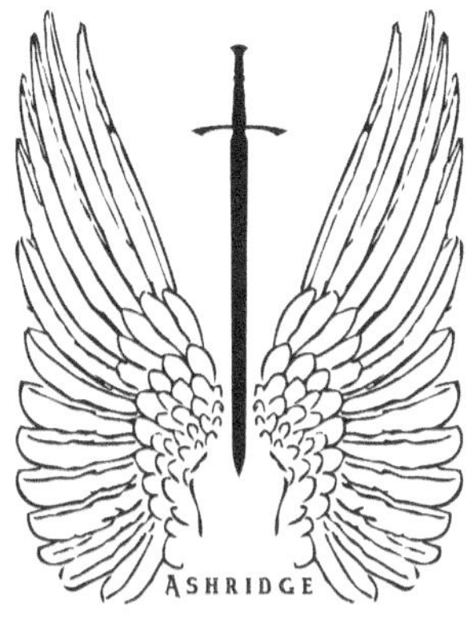

CHAPTER 40

JESSIKA

THE DAY AFTER THE coronation, everyone but Megan and CJ left. I was a little sad to see them go, but I knew I would see them again soon. With them all gone, it was time to speak to the Grand Lord, but it wasn't something I wanted to do on his terms.

I watched as Clarice, Alexei, Janreka, and Vernadali Natasha faded off in the blue-grey smoke taking them back to Therth. Janreka had told me she would be back immediately if I needed her help. When I asked how, since the continents were not allowing transport, Aiden had told me about the little loophole she had because she was Clarice's daughter. I laughed hysterically at the look on Head Julian's face. Aiden had told me how much it bothered him, but she was the Empress and Gatekeeper of the Underworld, so what were you going to do?

Now, I was standing in the courtyard and pondering just what to do about the Grand Lord. He had been begging for an audience, and I refused to do so where he would have any high ground.

"Aiden."

"Hum?"

"Summon the Grand Lord of Kaletta. Tell him that if he isn't in the main hall in five minutes, I will turn his armies stationed outside of Ashridge to goo."

"That's a bit harsh," Megan said. "I like it, but it is a bit harsh."

"He thinks I'm drawing lines in the sand and wants to talk to me. So, let's talk." I turned, strode for the main hall and to my quarters where I could change out of the jeans and T-shirt I had worn to tell everyone goodbye.

I looked at the royal dresses and wrinkled my nose. I hadn't grown any more accustomed to them, so opted to stay in my jeans but put a dress shirt on that openly displayed Aiden's necklace Just as Aiden walked in to let me know that the Grand Lord was indeed in the main hall awaiting to speak to me, I strapped on my syth belts and put my hair up in a neat ponytail.

He whistled appreciatively and looked me up and down. "I like this."

I smiled at him, and when I reached him, I gave him a quick kiss, opened his collar to his shirt, and brought my necklace out to the front where everyone could see it on him.

With a raised eyebrow, he said, "What do you have planned, Kotě?"

"Don't you trust me?"

He huffed a laugh and looked to the ceiling. "Angels, Jess. That is a no-win question."

I gave him another quick kiss and strode out of the room, leaving him to catch up.

"I hate it when you do that!"

"I know." I shrugged, and when I peeked around the corner, the Grand Lord was standing before the dais with two guards. He stood there in his bloodred tailored suit, picking at his nails, looking arrogant as all hell. His black hair, too thin goatee, and black eyes were too perfectly manicured for someone who should have been on the road for as long as he has claimed to be in his messages. I took a look around the corner and noted how his eyes kept flicking to my throne, and a twitch of his lips said all it needed to. To my surprise, Jayden, Ilris, and Killy were standing just to the other side of him.

"Did you ask for Jayden to come, too?"

"No." Aiden's eyebrows furrowed, and he looked a little worried. Megan and CJ were standing on the stairs just to the left of the dais.

I reached over and squeezed Aiden's hand. "Now or never." Striding out of the hall and right up to the dais, I stood at the throne that was now mine by right but still looked like it was Mom's. I took a deep breath and turned to sit. I couldn't overthink this.

By the time I looked up, all but the Grand Lord were bowing to me. He lifted an eyebrow and I narrowed my eyes at him. "You ask, no *demand* an audience with the Grand Duchess, Grand Lord, yet you do not offer her the respect of her station by bowing to her in her hall?"

"When that Grand Duchess ignores those requests for days, I'm not sure whether she deserves such respect."

"Be careful of your tongue, Grand Lord. She outranks you," Lady Megan stated without so much as lifting her head.

"It's okay, Lady Megan. Maybe he doesn't realize that the Grand Duchess, meaning me, has been preoccupied with having to light the pyre of not only her best friend, who his men killed, but also the previous Grand Duchess of Ashridge. Maybe he doesn't realize that even though I know *exactly* what he wants to discuss, that my messages to him earlier were not loud and clear enough. Maybe... the Grand Lord can't see past his own nose to realize I still have a territory to run." The red creeping up his neck was very satisfying. "I believe that is three times now you have turned that shade of red hearing the words coming out of my mouth."

Someone cleared their throat, and the Grand Lord's eyes went wide in realization.

"Now, are you going to bow before the Grand Duchess of Ashridge? Because if you do not, then this will be a very short conversation. I have many meetings that need to occur in the next few days, and I need to prepare for them."

Still red as the suit he wore, he bowed to one knee and punched his fist out. I made him stay there a beat longer than I normally would have, and then I said, "You may rise."

Once everyone was standing, I glanced at Jayden, and he was trying very hard not to snicker.

"Now, it is my assumption that you want to remind me of the marriage agreement between Ashridge and Kaletta. Am I right?"

"Yes, Jessika," he said, and I raised an eyebrow. He corrected himself through his clenched teeth, saying, "Yes, Grand Duchess."

"I am aware of it. I have also very openly stated that I will not have a consort. I will choose who sits in the throne next to me out of love and because I wish to be bound to someone for life. I will not do so out of a contract."

"Grand Duchess, it very clearly states that you will marry Lord Jayden Panahov."

"I am aware. We will renegotiate the contract. That is my proposal."

"On what grounds?" he sputtered.

"On the grounds that you have not provided for Ashridge in accordance with that contract. On the grounds that while you ensure that agricultural supplies arrive, are approved, and distributed, you also then send your Kaletta soldiers to destroy them before they can reach my people. On the grounds that the Kaletta soldiers plainly stated they were in Shuset for me, and I watched as your men slit *her* throat open." In an effort to keep any amount of civility to my tone, I said through my teeth, "You should be glad I don't hang you by your toenails in this hall until your head explodes."

His hands curled into tight fists, and I could see them turn white under the strain. He didn't deny it, and I almost called him on the rumors of him killing my mother, but he said, "Who do you think you are? You are a little girl trying to fit shoes that are too big for her. You dare speak to me with no proof as to the situation you are claiming?"

"Vernadali Aiden, please tell the Grand Lord what you found in Silentport with Lady Amala?" I tilted my head to the side and let a small smile cross my face. There was a small voice in the back of my head that said I shouldn't be showing all my cards yet, but I had had it.

Aiden was all Vernadali as he spoke loud and clear to the room. "While in Silentport, we found Kaletta soldiers destroying the food stores provided by Kaletta for the Ashridge people. Four of them actually. One of which claimed that you, personally, had cut his tongue out so he couldn't talk. Then while in Shuset, while resting for a night, Kaletta soldiers attacked the inn we were staying at. In that fight to capture, and do who knows what else to, the Grand Duchess, Lady Amala was killed by your soldiers as she did her duty to protect the Grand Duchess."

"You bitch!" Instantly, CJ and Aiden were standing in front of me, weapons drawn.

"A bitch I might be. No, right now I am certainly a bitch. You don't have to like me, Grand Lord. I am simply giving you the ability to fix a wrongdoing before we go on further. But in case you did not clearly understand my declaration at my coronation, while I care for Jayden very much, he will not become Duke of Ashridge."

"In accordance with the Ashridge–Kaletta contract, he—" I cut him off before he could go further.

"As I said, the contract will get renegotiated. If you do not agree to renegotiate the agreement, I will declare it null and void by decree and do whatever the fuck I want afterwards. Are we clear?" I leaned forward, rested my elbows on my knees, and let the room vibrate with just enough focus on his bones that it made his eyes widen.

"Yes, Grand Duchess. We can meet to renegotiate terms." There was a bite to his voice that I didn't appreciate, and I thought of Jayden.

"For now, as an act of good faith *on your part*, you will allow Lord Jayden Pavahov and his two guards, Ilris and Killy, to stay in Ashridge City permanently."

His eyes flicked to Jayden, and he studied him for a moment before saying, "Lord Jayden, do you agree to this?"

"Yes, Grand Lord," he said, but when he saw the look in his father's eye, he amended, "For now. I would like to see the terms of any newly agreed upon agreement between Ashridge and Kaletta before agreeing to a permanent stay."

"Agreed then." The Grand Lord huffed, and the look in his eye was almost lethal. This had not gone the way he wanted one bit.

"You are dismissed." I waved my hand and he stumbled back a few steps. I sat back tall and never once let my gaze move from him until he walked out that door. I acted as though I didn't give a care in the world, all the while my heart raced with all that I had just said and done.

Once the doors were shut, I looked at everyone, and there was nothing but shocked faces. I crumpled over, laying my hands in my face. "That could have gone so, so wrong. So much can still go so very wrong."

"But there is one thing for certain," Jayden said with amusement in his voice.

"What is that?" I mumbled, not willing to unbury my face from my hands.

"Jessika, look at me!" I felt Aiden's hand on my back and heard him whisper for me to look at Jayden.

When I did, I saw tears flowing down Jayden's cheeks, "Jessika, you stood up for us. There are dangers in that. He could use us as tools, and I will gladly accept that because he now knows where you stand, and you won't be pushed around."

"Jayden, if he uses you as a tool, it will be everything I can do not to kill him where he stands." There was so much lethal death in my tone that even Aiden's hand stilled at that.

"You mean that?"

"Oh, she means that," Aiden said beside me. "You don't even want to know what that felt like on my side."

OVER THE NEXT FEW days, we met with the Ashridge Council, where Megan and CJ helped in bringing us up to speed on everything that had been happening since I had left to go to the Curtails of the North.

We had smoothed things over, at least optically, with Kaletta, and the Grand Lord had taken to roaming the halls of Ashridge, under heavy guard. He often joined us for dinner in the dining hall and asked about what some of my future plans were. He was pleasant enough, but I knew he was feeling me out on his previous proposals.

Now, I was standing in yet another council meeting, trying to find out how to maintain some agricultural growth through the winter months as the temperature started to drop.

"The biggest issue right now is water for the fields around Ashridge. The storm that came through helped, but it won't sustain anything long term," I said, looking at the map in front of us.

"Jess..." Aiden drawled out my name and I looked at him. "Can I speak to you a second?"

When we reached a quiet corner, he moved his mouth close enough to my ear so that no one would hear. "Remember when Jayden said that he heard rumor of Kaletta soldiers in the Black Mountains."

My head snapped up, and Megan's voice was in my head. *"What? What is wrong?"*

I jerked my head toward her, and she made her way over. The council gave us a look, but they could screw off. Angels, I hated politics. Nothing had convinced me more than the last few days. Her eyebrows raised when she got to us, and I whispered, "Jayden mentioned there had been rumor of Kaletta soldiers in the Black Mountains. They could be re-routing the water sources away from Ashridge. We thought it was due to the lighter snowfall last year, but..."

"CJ and I were planning on leaving this afternoon. We will take the long way home, I think. Make a trip of it." She winked, and my eyes flicked to CJ, who rolled his eyes. I couldn't help but stifle a giggle.

I nodded and went back to the map. "Thank you, Lady Megan and Vernadali CJ, for assisting Ashridge in the last couple of weeks."

"Of course, Grand Duchess. It has been an honor to assist you in this transition. Please send word to Nalrin City if you need any assistance." Megan tried to ease some of the tension in the room with her words, but most of us were able to see through it. "I am sure that the council will be helpful in moving Ashridge forward."

I looked around the room and saw both my mothers' advisors and some of the ones that served as my tutors over the years.

"Council dismissed. We will reconvene tomorrow morning at 9:00 am."

"Yes, Grand Duchess," the room said in unison.

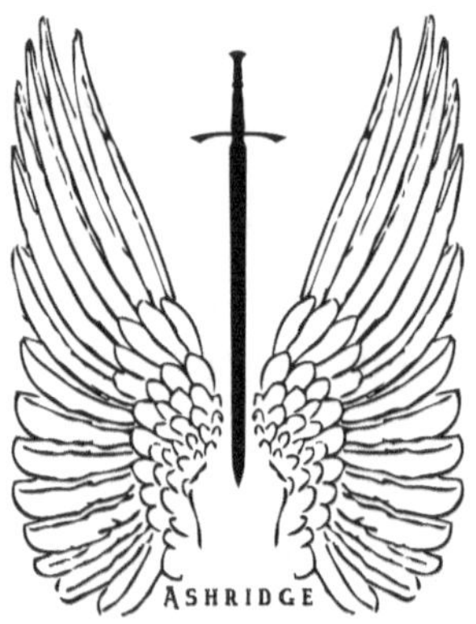

CHAPTER 41

JESSIKA

FOR TWO WEEKS, WE continued to meet with the Grand Lord every other morning, and the meeting we had the day before yesterday was not great. He kept pushing that I would marry Jayden, regardless of my stance on it. Jayden had even stepped forward and said that while he also cared for me, he didn't want to marry me.

It didn't seem to make much of a difference, but the Grand Lord would have to deal with it. It was why I wasn't looking forward to going to that meeting this morning.

"Jess, you gotta get up."

"I don't want to. I'm so tired of having to justify my position with everyone. Can't I just have a me day? Take a damn day off? Or at least a morning?" I pulled the blankets up over my head.

"No." His tone was final, and I pulled the blanket back just enough to glare at him.

"I wish your parents were still here. I'd send them in there and I could stay in bed!" I stuck my tongue out at him again, and he chuckled.

The blankets disappeared from on top of me, and I sat straight up. "Aiden!"

He was leaning against the door frame and chuckling. I didn't miss how his eyes roamed up and down my body, and I smirked, deciding to turn the tables on him.

I sat up and spread my legs wide, showing him I, indeed, had nothing on under my short nightgown. I leaned back enough that it pushed my breasts out, and when he growled from the door, I smiled at him. "Too bad you were being mean and stole the blankets."

One moment, he was at the door, and the next, he was leaning over me. The way my nightgown was sitting gave him quite an eye full. He took a hold of the heart at my neck, pulling me to him to kiss me. It was soft and gentle, and I smirked against his lips.

"Kotě," he said in warning as he fisted his hand in my hair.

"You said I was running late and needed to get up."

"Now you are going to be really late," he said, pushing me down onto the bed. As he did so, my nightgown slid up my hips. "Looks like I missed breakfast."

Slowly, he started kissing down my neck, and then my collarbone, to where that heart was. His other hand was palming me softly, with one single finger sliding up and down the center of me. Unbidden, a purr escaped my lips, and he chuckled.

BANG! BANG! BANG!

Aiden's Charge was wrapped around me tight, and he was strolling for the door, syths out in an instant. I had just gotten to the doorway to my bedroom when Aiden opened the front door to two guards, giving Aiden instructions.

"Jess, get dressed now!"

I turned and threw on a pair of pants, bra, and a shirt. "Aiden, get me a hair tie out of the bathroom so I can throw my hair up!" I shouted at him as I buckled my syths and walked toward the front door.

"What the Underworld is going on?" I demanded as we hurried down the hall.

"The rest of the Kaletta Army from the ridge showed up this morning."

"Aiden, you are not telling me everything. No lies. No half-truths." When he didn't answer me, I stopped in the hall and pulled him to face me. "Aiden, tell me."

"The Grand Lord is in the main hall with... hostages."

"What do you mean hostages?" I asked carefully as I stared back down the hall. "As in, he is holding hostages, or he is being held hostage?"

My mind was spinning, and I didn't know what to think right now. When I turned the corner and saw the sight before me, I saw purple. Everything went purple, and if it were not for Aiden's hand on my back, his syth in hand, I probably would have stormed him.

Kneeling with a guard behind each of them, swords crossed at their necks were Jayden, Killy and Ilris. Each of them had been beaten, and there was a very clear black eye forming on Jayden's face.

"Release them now," I said through gritted teeth, stepping around the corner and letting just the edge off of my power.

"No," the Grand Lord said. "This time you are going to listen to me, child."

"Why would I do that?" I was pushing my power back. All it wanted to do was to burst out in a wave.

"You will marry Jayden in a fortnight, or I will slit each of their throats."

My eyes met Ilris', and there was a small smile on his face that said he was ready to die to protect Ashridge, and my heart lurched. I saw Killy, who only raised his head slightly and mouthed, "It's an honor to serve."

When my eyes met Jayden's, he knew that I couldn't agree. There was a look shared between Aiden and Jayden then, and I froze. I looked at Aiden, and his eyes were sad.

I screamed through the claiming, "*You knew this was a possibility?! You talked to Jayden about this?*" He winced, and I knew he heard me. There was a quick nod.

"I'll repeat in case you didn't clearly understand me the first time," the Grand Lord said, and my eyes met each of theirs again. "Agree to marry Jayden in a fortnight, or I will kill all three of them."

I said nothing.

I couldn't say the word.

I couldn't agree.

I wouldn't let another territory use my friends as collateral. I focused on Jayden, and his lips moved, "*I love you, Ilris.*"

When I saw Ilris repeating the same phrase, "*I love you, Jade,*" it broke my heart. Killy met my gaze, smiled, and mouthed, "*Thank you, it's been an honor.*"

My hard stare met with the Grand Lord who was standing just behind them to the right, so he couldn't possibly know they were saying their goodbyes. My eyes filled with tears. I still couldn't bring the words to be voiced.

Aiden's Charge wrapped around me, and with a caressing tug on the claiming, I found the strength to say, "No. I have made it clear; I will not be bullied into decisions."

I never saw the command, but before I knew it, blood was in the air, splattering everything in its path. Screaming echoed in the hall, and then more blood sprayed as Kaletta guards crashed to the ground.

All I saw was Killy's head rolling toward my feet. When it stopped and hit the toe of my boot, everything went silent in my head. More blood sprayed into the air, and I felt it land on my face, but I just stared at Killy's vacant expression on his head as it sat at my feet.

Out of the corner of my eye, I saw an evil smile spread across the Grand Lord's face. "Keep stalling, Grand Duchess, and Jayden and Ilris will be next to die."

END OF BOOK 1
OF THE
ASHRIDGE DUOLOGY

The story continues with

Duchess' Throne: Book 2 of the Ashridge Duology

Books Also By Kimberly M. Ringer

The Ashstrike Sanctorum Series

The Astral's Bonded

The Exorci's Touch

The Five Angels Trilogy
The Five Angels
The Ash'bani

The Helena Crystal

A Five Angels Novel

Duchess' Crown

Duchess' Throne

Other Books

Ashes and Flame

Weekend with Rylie

Kimberly M. Ringer lives in Santa Cruz, California with her husband, little human (who isn't so little anymore), and two furballs, Wall-E (a Jack Russell mix) and Pippin (a Pomeranian Terrier mix). When she isn't writing, she is reading, playing with the dogs, playing video games or down at the beach. She's a bit geeky and nerdy, so sci-fi references and other things going on in the science world will often end up in her stories.

Contact Kimberly M. Ringer:
www.kimberlymringer.com
Instagram: @kimberlymringer
Facebook:
https://www.facebook.com/kimberlymringer

Sign up for my newsletter and receive freebies, coupon codes, and stay up to date on all things Kimberly M. Ringer and K.M. Ringer
Newsletter Signup

www.ingramcontent.com/pod-product-compliance
Lightning Source LLC
Chambersburg PA
CBHW061040190726
48286CB00006B/1541